BITTER LAK

BITTER LAKE

A Novel by

ANN HARLEMAN

SOUTHERN METHODIST UNIVERSITY PRESS

DALLAS

This novel is a work of fiction. Names, characters, places, and incidents are either the product of the author's imagination or are used fictitiously.

Requests for permission to reproduce material from this work should be sent to:
    Rights and Permissions
    Southern Methodist University Press
    PO Box 750415
    Dallas, TX 75275-0415

Excerpt from "Little Potato" by Malcolm Dalglish, copyright © 1985 by Tarquel Music now with Oolitic Music, used by permission.

Library of Congress Cataloging-in-Publication Data
Harleman, Ann, 1945–
    Bitter Lake : a novel / by Ann Harleman.
        p.   cm.
    ISBN 0-87074-404-6 (cloth). — ISBN 0-87074-405-4 (pbk.)
    PS3558.A624246B58 1996
    813'. 54—dc20   96-27939

Cover art by Lynn Watt
Design by Tom Dawson Graphic Design
Printed in the United States of America on acid-free paper

10   9   8   7   6   5   4   3   2   1

MAR 1 5 1997

Only Bruce

Human nature was originally one, and we
were a whole; and the desire and pursuit
of the whole is called love.

PLATO

ACKNOWLEDGMENTS

I would like to thank the following people: Don Berger, David Black, Rosellen Brown, Gail Donovan-Kesich, Connie DuBois, Shirley Enos, Barbara Feldman, Lev Fruchter, Freddie Jane Goff, Janice Gordon, Bill Henderson, Sarah Hobson, David Huddle, Francine Jackson and the staff of Ladd Observatory, Hester Kaplan, Greg Kesich, Margot Livesey, Jean McGarry, the Providence Area Writers Group (PAW), Harriet Ritvo, Mike Rosen, Bruce Rosenberg, Channa Taub, Janet Yanos, and John Yount. I thank especially Ilona Karmel, Kathryn Lang, and, most, Elizabeth Searle, godmother to this book.

I am grateful to the Rockefeller Foundation, the Rhode Island State Council on the Arts, and the Bread Loaf Writers Conference for their support, and to the Villa Serbelloni, the Huntington Library, and the Rochambeau Library for providing the ideal working atmosphere.

Parts of this novel, in a somewhat different form, have appeared in *Ploughshares*, the *New England Review*, the *Nebraska Review*, and the *Ohio Review*; Chapter 11 won the 1993 Judith Siegel Pearson Award.

ONE

1

JUDITH

Walking is really falling. Lift your foot, and in the instant before you set it down again, you're falling to earth—fighting the pull of gravity to stay upright. Gort told me that once.

By the end of Tuesday I figured I'd walked nine miles, a half-mile more than I'd walked on Monday, three miles further than the Tuesday before. I was learning how to keep ahead of my thoughts. My daughters would have one parent who was undistracted. And predictable: I got home at exactly 4:15, the time I used to get home before they fired me, came in the back way as usual, fighting the overgrown bridal wreath for the door handle.

Susie, lying on her stomach beneath the big bay window in the kitchen with her elbows on the *National Enquirer*, didn't look up. A parallelogram of sunlight fell across her head and shoulders. She was practicing Word Attack: her lips moved and stopped, moved and stopped, sounding out, swallowing each word in pieces.

"Hi, honeybug." Silence.

"Hi honey," I said again. "Hi honey hi Mommy how was your day fine how was—"

Susie squinted up at me. Her sty was worse, the skin under her left eye a tight, shiny half-moon of lavender. "Sharks have five sets of teeth," she told me. "At the *same time*." Her tongue pushed out her upper lip, exploring the double gap in her own teeth.

I put my purse on top of the refrigerator and shoved it way back; after the girls went to sleep I'd transfer the contents to the old leather suitcase under my bed. "When I was your age, I was reading *Snow White. Bambi*." This was a lie; at eight I had read, with horrified fascination, all of *Quo Vadis*. I could still see the engraving it fell open to whenever I picked it up, a naked, crinkle-haired woman martyr tied to a bull.

3

"*Snow White* is kinky," Susie said. "Jesus Christ."

"Susannah." I had to clamp my lower lip between my teeth to keep from laughing. "And what do you think 'kinky' means?"

"Weird and strange but you like it."

I bent down and held her face in both hands to get a closer look at her eye. She submitted for a second, then pulled away.

"Where's your sister? Isn't she back from Clesta's yet?"

"She's out front agreeing with the Action Man."

"With who?"

"The, I don't know. Pennsylvania Something Action. This old guy goes blah blah blah, and Lil goes, In general, I agree with you, and then the old guy talks some more. How do they have room for them, Mama?"

"What?"

"*Sharks.* How do they fit all those teeth in?"

"Lil didn't give this person any money, did she? Susie?" I lifted the lid of the green metal filing box on the counter and looked in. I must have had more than two singles on top of the coins.

Susie's head bent in sudden diligence over the newspaper; one hand twisted and untwisted the ponytail over her right ear. After Gort left this last time, she'd started stealing small amounts, never more than a dollar or two, from my purse, from the green box. What did she do with it? Gort and I had always, as he put it, lived against the grain (of America, he meant)—jobs that paid in freedom rather than in cash, a life not held hostage to *things*. He believed our family could live outside the net of materialism that had ensnared the rest of the country. He banned (unsuccessfully) Barbie dolls, Walt Disney, fast food restaurants. Until Lil's best friend Rhoda got her license last spring, neither of my daughters had ever been to a mall.

In the living room I took off my sandals and stood at the front window. The bare floorboards were smooth and cool. Balancing on first one leg, then the other, I rubbed the bottom of each foot. Between the dusty slats of the old-fashioned venetian blinds I could see Lil. Her back was toward me. Her bare legs above the heavy black leather combat boots were long, like her father's, and like him she had the neat, small Hutchins head. Her blonde braid swung back and forth. She was waving her arms

4

at a tired-looking middle-aged man who sat on the beige vinyl car seat that was propped against the fence. Even for our neighborhood, so close to the steel mill, it was an eyesore; Gort kept thinking he'd recycle it somehow. Late afternoon sun lit up the cobwebs that stretched between the seat back and the top of the fence boards.

I stood watching Lil—the strange, buffeting way she moved now, sort of banging the air with her body. She was tall for fourteen. I thought of how she'd been at three, at six, at nine. No one warns you about the losses. No one tells you you'll miss them, those earlier children. They disappear but are they still there, sealed one inside the next like those little wooden Russian dolls? Lil was closed to me now, like her father—I never knew what either of them was thinking. She shoved a hand into the back pocket of her khaki shorts and pulled out something which she thrust at the man on the car seat. The angle of her head said she knew (hoped?) I was watching. The man got up, slapping dust from his pants. I closed the blind and went back to the kitchen.

"Talking Dog Reveals: Astrology a Hoax!" Lil said when she came into the kitchen. Radiating good humor, she stepped over Susie and opened the green metal box and shoved a folded-up piece of paper inside. "There's your receipt, Mom." Gort gave to every cause, worthy or otherwise, that reached our front door. I was the one who insisted on receipts, to keep track of what we gave out—and never got back.

A job, I thought, I need to find a job. We couldn't go on the way we had for the past week and a half. Even though Gort would surely come home tonight—he'd never stayed away longer than two weeks in all these years of disappearing—we were down to less than ten dollars in the checking account. I'd lied to my daughters, pretended I was still working at Valley View Seniors Home. But I couldn't keep it up much longer. Lil was already asking pointed questions about how my day went, an odd little smile tugging at one corner of her mouth.

"Here, Princess. You can feed Spastica." Lil handed Susie the cat's blue china bowl, then took the plates piled with knives and forks out of my hands. Generous—because she expected her father home tonight.

"Thanks, hon," I said. She gave the little shrug that was her reply to most of what I said these days.

5

Sighing deeply, theatrically, Susie scooped Cat Chow from the twenty-five-pound bag in the broom closet. She set it down next to the water bowl, then opened the screen door and bawled, "Lustyka! Here-kitty! Here-kitty-kitty!"

Almost immediately the small ragged head appeared. The cat was old and seldom went farther than the bridal wreath bushes beside the back stoop. Suspiciously, she approached the bowl of food; grudgingly, she accepted it. When she first found us I'd thought for a long time and finally, remembering the Swedish I'd learned from my grandmother when I was little, I'd named her "joy." (The cat and I had both been pregnant at the time.) Lustyka hunched over the blue bowl like a miser counting money.

▼

Dinner was square hamburger patties (easier to put the whole package of ground meat in the frying pan, then cut it twice across with a knife) and frozen peas with pearl onions. My glasses were fogged from standing at the stove; I took them off and laid them on the Formica table. Everything blurred pleasantly.

"This is not a balanced meal," announced Susie, breaking a silence in which the only sound had been the dull chink of forks on plastic. It was as if the empty chair at the foot of the table—the empty place on which Lil had carefully bestowed plate and knife and fork when she set the table, and which she watched carefully now—imposed its silence on us. Silence, and waiting.

"See," Susie said, waving her fork at the refrigerator. On the door, held by a Smiley Face magnet, was the chart she'd colored at school, a careful circle divided into quarters labeled "Fruits and Vegetables!," "Meat!," "Milk!," "Bread and Cereal!"

A sigh slid out from between my lips. Nice Ms. Grundy, the counselor at Valley View, had made me promise not to sigh. Say what's on your mind instead, she'd urged. "It would *be* a balanced meal if you'd drink your milk," I said.

"There's ice cream for dessert," Lil told Susie. "If you finish all your cardboard and marbles."

6

"What flavor?"

"Cement."

"There's this lady who gave birth to a two-headed baby," Susie said loudly, looking from one to the other of us. "In Queens, New York."

"*You're* a two-headed baby," said Lil, "if you believe that stuff. Everybody knows those stories are made up. Mother—"

"Yeah, well, they're assholes."

"Susannah," I said; but part of me wanted to laugh.

"You let her get away with murder," Lil said to me. She sat rigid, twisting her napkin. Her eyes were on the empty place, not on Susie.

"She doesn't know what she's saying, honey." My voice assumed the flirty-apologetic sound it seemed to take on so often lately when I spoke to Lil.

"You just don't see, do you? You just don't want to see."

Here it comes, I thought. Always before, when Gort went away, Lil had been a comfort to me, almost motherly, filling the blank of Gort's absence. She and Susie loved these times, when they could watch cartoons on the wavery old black-and-white TV we'd inherited from Gort's mother, and eat meals like this one, with absolutely no soybeans involved. But this time, for the first time, it felt as if Lil had ranged herself against me—as if she were on the other side. But what other side was there? I said, "Lillian. Please. Let's have a nice family—"

"Nice family dinner. Nice family dinner." Lil's face was pale and her eyes were too shiny. I wanted to say, Don't make it harder than it already is. But lately a fight with me seemed to make things easier for Lil. So instead I said foolishly, "I know you miss—"

"*Daddy* would've made lentil stew," Lil said. "Or vegetarian chili. He'd never let us eat this crap."

I didn't point out that Lil hated lentil stew, which she'd once compared to rabbit shit.

Not looking at either of us, Susie began lining up pearl onions on her napkin. "These ones are *sunken*," she said.

Lil pushed back her chair and said in a cold voice, "You can't have a nice family dinner unless you're a nice family. I *hate* hamburgers! I hate"—she stood up—"peas! I hate—" An expression of bewilderment crossed her face. Then she coughed, threw her napkin at my ear, and ran

7

out of the kitchen. I could hear the thud of her combat boots as she took the stairs two at a time. What—who—had she been about to name as the object of her hate?

"This stuff tastes like Vicks Vap-O-Rub," Susie said. I'd thrown some dried rosemary onto the peas while they boiled. "*Now* can we have ice cream?"

▼

After dinner, watching the sunset from the window over the sink, I put away the dishes Susie had washed, though they were still wet. It was something Lil and I usually did together, Lil handing me the warm plates one by one after she'd dried them, me chinking them onto their piles in the cupboard. I was waiting for that one moment when the sky is no different from dawn. Today was the longest day of the year—the solstice, Gort would have reminded us if he'd been here. Leave the dishes, he'd have said, and taken us out to watch the sun go down and the stars appear in the violet sky. Made us feel what really mattered.

Lustyka ambled into the kitchen and took up her place beneath the birdcage that hung in the bay window. She sat looking up through the clear plastic bottom, occasionally turning her head to measure the distance from floor to windowsill to cage. The parakeets, one blue and one green, hunched on the topmost perch. A sign, scotch-taped to the bars by Susie and decorated with a border of yellow flowers, said "Mary + Jim." I thought, I'm just barely hanging onto my family, just hanging around the bodies in which my daughters were last seen. They could slip right away from me. Them, too.

The flat disc of the sun dropped behind the house in back of ours like a coin into a slot. The sky burned red-orange and lavender and sour green, the colors inside the blast furnace at the mill. Gort had taken me there years ago, when he first started working for Bethlehem Steel. Sixteen years since I'd moved to this small sooty city in the middle of Pennsylvania, and I still hadn't gotten used to the briefness of its sunsets, swallowed first by the city, then by the valley that surrounded it. The weather report had been wrong. There'd be a storm: I could smell it. Putting the last wet dish onto the stack, closing the cupboard doors, I thought of sunsets back home in Orient, Iowa. How the last leisurely light would cross the pasture to the creek, burn for a long, long moment on the water, and be gone.

▼

In the high room under the eaves, I lay down in the dark wrapped in Gort's old sweats. The pants covered my feet like a child's sleepers, and the elastic waistband came up almost to my breasts. My hipbones jutted up to meet my palms; when I lay on my back like this, the flesh fell away and I was as thin as when we first married. I freed the empty sleeves of the sweatshirt and pulled them tight around me. The soft, unwashed cotton held Gort's smell, a smell like bread.

Where was he? Usually he'd come home in time for dinner—never later than the girls' bedtime. He'd tuck them in and read to them and they would see that he was back.

I'd opened the window to the humid night, and the air vibrated with the odor of lilacs. Late-blooming Chinese lilacs that Gort had planted when Lil was born: their fragrance was strongest when they were dying into leaves. It made me feel breathless and hot, and I thought of how Gort had liked to make love when I was in bed with a cold. Inside the humid cave of my breathing, we both felt feverish—irresponsible, floating. Then, slow and luxuriant, gates would slide open one after another and close smoothly behind us. That was always where we met—that place where our bodies could speak for us. Where there were no words, and no words were needed.

A flake of plaster detached itself from the ceiling and settled softly on my forehead. When I tried to brush it away, it clung to my sweaty palm. The smell of lilacs reached for me like an undertow.

▼

The sound of birds on the roof wakes me, the click of their feet across the shingles like my mother's treadle sewing machine, surprisingly loud. There's a heavy, sweet smell. I lift my head from the damp crook of my arm. Everywhere there are lilacs. By my cheek, in the triangle between my breasts and belly and

9

my pulled-up legs, along my naked back. I roll over. A broken-off branch jabs my spine. Sitting up, I wrap my arms around my legs. My own flesh comforts me, the creamy feel of my breasts brushing my bare knees. There are lilacs heaped on the tangled army blankets at the foot of the bed, lilacs arranged in a row along each side. Like being in your coffin. Gort is at a funeral right now: he's paying for his last year of engineering school by working as a freelance pall-bearer. The breeze through the open window carries the late afternoon voices of children.

He appears in the doorway then. Catholic funerals last longer—two hours this time—though they don't pay extra. He didn't mean to shout at me, before. The lilacs are to say he's sorry.

I take him in my arms in his scratchy black jacket among the crumbled blossoms. The smell of crushed flowers is all around us, sweet as ether. We laugh, listening to the noise on the roof. Gort says, "Birds in galoshes."

▼

Wind rattled the leaves of the oak outside the open window. A breeze stirred through the room. I sat up and pulled the sweatshirt off over my head. Sounds came from Lil's room next-door, the squawk of drawers being yanked open.

I always knew, when he began to get lighter and lighter, his body so light on top of me, as if his bones were hollow like the bones of birds—I knew then that he was about to go away again. When I could hardly feel him at all, no more than a breath in my ear, till sex stopped altogether, and we lost our way of talking. I'd know then that things were getting too much for him again. Me and the girls, his Aunt Clesta, his loony boss at Bethlehem Steel whose job depended on the ideas Gort came up with— too many people wanting him. He'd move into the unfinished half of the attic where he kept his telescopes, taking his sleeping bag and the black marbled copybooks he used for his journal. Gradually he would become a person who left no trace. No dent in the cushions where he'd sat; no bits and pieces (a penciled list, a crossword puzzle, a book of poetry turned face down) on the table by his chair. I'd watch him then, not knowing what I was warding off, only that somehow my watching might keep him safe. Finally he would leave. His college roommate Jerome's trailer up near

Scranton, or Bitter Lake, or camping in the Alleghenies—we never knew where for sure. Somewhere in the hills of Pennsylvania, which he loved. I'd be so tired then, from watching, that I'd let him go with something like relief. After a week or two—never more than two—when he felt whole again, ready for us, for life in the valley, he'd come back.

Until now.

Through the walls I could hear the sound of drawers shutting briskly, one after another. What was Lil doing?

I'd learned to live with Gort as he was. It wasn't the life I'd planned for myself, growing up in Orient, Iowa. And yet, in a way, it was. I'd vowed, the way all of us vow, that I would not be like my mother. Shuttling between worlds, as if she lived in a dream and every now and then real life made itself visible, floating by just out of her grasp, in the corner of her eye. *Stay in one world*, I'd told myself. In a way, it was Gort who'd taught me how. There was a poem he used to recite—a love poem. He'd said it so often that I knew it by heart.

> If they be two, they are two so
> As stiff twin compasses are two;
> Thy soul, the fixed foot, makes no show
> To move, but doth if the other do
>
> And though it in the center sit,
> Yet, when the other far doth roam,
> It leans, and hearkens after it,
> And grows erect as that comes home.
>
> Such wilt thou be to me, who must
> Like the other foot obliquely run:
> Thy firmness draws my circle just,
> And makes me end where I began.

He *would* come back—I was where his circle ended. I had to believe that; if I didn't believe that, I'd have nothing. Till then I would stay in one world, this world, with my children.

There was a crash of thunder, then another. I got up to close the window. Outside, the sky gathered light into itself like a vast in-drawn breath, paused, then flung it back. I heard Lil's door open, wheezing on its hinges, heard the glass knob bang into the wall. As I got out of bed to go after her, the rain started. It came in blundering gusts and racketed down the shingles into the roof gutters like acorns from the oak tree in October, loud as the clatter of Lil's combat boots going down the stairs.

2

L I L

Chinky nailed me in the foyer, at the door to my Great-Aunt Clesta's part of the house, gargling threats. He was this butt-ugly black Chinese chow with reddish pop-eyes, supposedly a watchdog.

"Hey, bullshit," I told him.

He followed while Doc hauled my duffel bag up the long winding stairs. I carried the telescope myself, and the big green book of star charts. On the landing, where the kitchen was, we stopped. Doc's black face was shiny with sweat. His tongue flicked out to moisten his lips, like a minnow flashing back and forth. He threw his head back and bawled, "C. H.! She's here!" and we went up the last little half-flight of stairs.

Clesta hugged me. She was still in her nightgown—lavender silk with billowy sleeves—and she smelled like Yardley's Lavender. "Lilly," she said. "Lilly-Lil. My. You're bigger." She didn't sound surprised to see me, even though it was six-thirty in the morning. Mom must've called last night to ask if I was there.

"I'm the same height I was last week," I said. "Five-eight and three-quarters."

Behind me, Doc said to Clesta, "She'll never be a beauty. Not like you were." He fingered the skinny gray fringe of beard around the edge of his jaw, and sighed. "Well, time flies, is what it is. You get old, every fifteen minutes it's time for breakfast." He went back down the steps to the kitchen.

In the living room, morning sun squirted between the closed drapes. The two grandfather clocks, Big Gramp and Little Gramp, ticked unevenly, like two old men's voices going *tsk*, *tsk*. I was tired. I'd spent the night at Rhoda's—her room had its own door to the backyard, so Mrs. Vilardi wouldn't've had to know anything about it, except of course that my mother called there, too.

13

Clesta's place was the two upper floors of the house she'd inherited from her mean dead husband—I thought of him as the MDH—who'd died way before I was born. He'd been wicked rich, according to Gramma Maude—his family's name, Oberdorf, was on whole buildings at the college on the other side of town—but Clesta didn't seem to have much money. She rented out the first floor of the house, and ever since I could remember, she'd lived on the top two with Doc. People thought he was a servant, because he was black and did all the cooking; I wasn't sure what he was, exactly, but I knew he was way more than that. I loved Clesta's because it was so full of stuff, so different from our house. I could enjoy it (except for the food, which nobody could've enjoyed) without feeling like I was betraying Daddy, because he loved Clesta, too. Family photographs covered every tabletop, some of them a hundred years old, with dim, round-eyed faces. Chair legs carved in the shape of curved animal paws; blue-and-white tiles around the fireplace that showed all different Bible scenes; even the knives and forks at dinner (I'd have to watch Clesta for when to use what) would have handles that twisted into lilies. The navy blue velvet drapes and all the MDH's dark wood furniture made the room feel cool even in summer. When I was little I used to lay my tongue against the knobs on the wooden ladder-back chairs; they tasted dark and bitter.

Clesta lowered herself onto the brocade sofa and patted the seat beside her. "So, Lilly-Lil. Tell me."

I knew better than to complain to Clesta about Daddy not coming back—she wouldn't stand for anybody ragging on her beloved Gordon. So I just told her about the end of school and finally making the swim team—my father couldn't swim a stroke, he'd be wicked proud of me when he finally came back—and Rhoda's new hunter green Camaro. Clesta's head quivered from side to side in little half-circles as she listened. When she laughed, her eyes got shiny like old china; there was lavender in the creases around them. She didn't ask why I'd come or how long I planned to stay. She never hassled me.

"You'll have a good time this visit. Where's my snivvy?" She stuck one hand down between the seat cushions and brought up a crumpled Kleenex. "You can play with your cousin Daniel. He'll be here on the bus from Philadelphia, tomorrow noon. You can cheer him up." She blew her nose and stuck the Kleenex back between the sofa cushions.

Daniel was going to be here?

"Play?" I said. "Give me a break, Clesta. What's the matter with Daniel?"

"Car accident. Lost all but the big toe, on his left foot." She made a fist, then stuck out her thumb. "Now they're saying he'll always limp. Not badly, mind. But he thinks it's the end of the world, naturally. Young folks! You'll be good for him—he's a gingerly person, needs spicing up. All the time you spent in that body cast when you were little. You can tell him how everything heals, in the end. Seven, were you? That time you broke both legs, up at the lake? Poor child."

"I don't remember," I lied.

Daniel living here definitely stuffed my plan. I'd counted on being the only Young Folks at 110 Wesley Street and having Clesta to myself. Plus watching color TV, which my dad wouldn't allow in the house, and reading Clesta's books on sex. But those weren't the main thing—the main thing was to figure out where my father was and get him to come back. Clesta hadn't spoken to Mom since the day of my parents' wedding; she said she didn't approve of cousins marrying, but I knew it was because she blamed my mother for hypnotizing my father with sex and turning him into an engineer with a family to support. I mean, she loved him as if he were her son instead of just her nephew.

I needed Clesta. So I said, "Okay. I'll cheer him up." Thinking, Daniel won't want to hang out with me any more than I want to hang out with him.

"On the other hand—" said Clesta. Then she shook her head. "Open the drapes, will you, Lil?"

I pulled the gold rope with its little tassel and steered the heavy velvet past a bunch of photographs on the windowsill. A dead beetle lay next to them, shiny green-purple like an eggplant. Below me was Doc's garden, all overgrown and wild, bordered by a high stucco wall. It had all this old-fashioned stuff in it—a sundial, wisteria, a grape arbor—and I'd always thought of it as the Secret Garden. "On the other hand, what?" I said.

"Oh. Nothing." Clesta's face had this funny look, as if she were listening to something I couldn't hear. Then she smiled. "On the other hand, there was a glove. Child—come have breakfast."

She had to use both hands to push off from the sofa. Chinky stalked over (chows' back legs don't have any knees) and butted her, and she scratched his woolly head. "A-chink, a-chink, a-chow!" she murmured. He gazed at her out of small red eyes.

▼

Recovering from dinner (roast pork with prunes; orange jello salad that tasted like children's aspirin), I lay on my stomach in front of the fireplace on a rug patterned with liver-colored roses. Doc and Clesta were in the kitchen doing the dishes. I had the copy of *The Hite Report on Male Sexuality* that I'd found in the linen closet under a pile of purple towels. For some reason I hadn't felt like reading what I'd brought with me, *Watchers of the Skies* or *The Collapsing Universe*. I felt in my shorts pocket for the photograph, an old one I'd taken out of a red plastic frame that I kept on my bureau. Dad and me, when I was about four, with me in the crook of his arm. The book he'd been reading to me, *Greek Myths*, was face-down on his knee. Light from a window behind us made a white blur all around his head. We both were laughing.

I slid the photograph between the pages of the book and lay without moving. In the lamplight I could just barely make out the blue-and-white tiles around the fireplace: Jonah sticking out of the whale's mouth; Noah beside the Ark with a row of animal heads hanging over its side; Moses parting the ocean into two neat scrolls. In a blue the color of ball-point pen, the figures looked like the ones I used to draw myself when I was eight or nine, scratchy and clunky-looking, with arms and legs like logs. I liked to read the Bible—the Old Testament—then draw the figures, nude if that fit the story at all. I was always frustrated by the men's crotches because I wasn't sure what went there. I *still* wasn't.

My finger traced two figures on the cold tile. Running, bodies curved like question marks, heads turned back toward what they'd left behind. Eve's arms were crossed in this coy way over her breasts and she held an apple in one hand. Behind her Adam, his chest smooth and narrow like

16

my father's, had a fig leaf curled across the fork where his legs split off from his body. On their faces, which were turned back to where they'd been, there was this terrible sadness.

▼

I laid my stuff out on the bureau scarf: blue-green eye shadow; lipstick; Mom's Skin Perfecting Cream. Then I pulled Bear and Bella Squirrel from the bottom of the duffel bag and propped them on either side of my pillow. I put on my black cotton nightshirt with ON THE BOARDWALK IN ATLANTIC CITY across the front. I lay down in the green glow of the night-light and began to dream my way into the painting that hung by the bed, the way I always did when I stayed at Clesta's. A girl stood at the beginning of a road that stretched into mist and leafless trees. She wore this long, bunchy blue dress and a white cap. Across her shoulders she balanced a rod with ropes on each end holding buckets that hung down below her waist. She held each rope just above its bucket, and her eyes looked off down the road.

I'd learned not to try to understand my father. Not trying was the one thing I could give him that he wanted. He wasn't like other people's fathers—like Mr. Vilardi, who sat around the house watching the Phillies in his sleeveless undershirt and called me Curlytop—and I was grateful he wasn't. But now I wondered, where did his silences come from? Were they like a bad mood, or more like a dream about sad things? *Waking life is a dream controlled*—Clesta liked to quote that. *Waking life.*

I put up one hand to touch the edge of the painted girl's dress. Her whole body seemed to be leaning toward something, but stiff—as if she couldn't go there, only wait. She sort of vibrated with waiting.

This time he hadn't come back when he always did. He'd never stayed away longer than two weeks before. This time, for the first time, it felt wrong to stand back, like the girl holding onto her buckets. Like my mother, who always let him go. I thought of how he'd been before he left, suddenly full of energy after he'd acted strange and slow all winter and hid out in the attic a lot. None of that energy was for me. He didn't seem to see me, no matter what I did. The way it was the summer before I turned seven, right before Mom made him stop taking me to Bitter Lake.

17

▼

That June a new baby appears. Daddy says, "Fishing, Lilly!" and we get in the blue Dodge and go. We leave the womenfolk (there are two now) behind.

At sunset the frogs make a sound like rubber bands. I'm standing on a thick, alligator-skinned limb halfway up a big cedar that grows straight out over the lake. Unlike my father, I know how to swim. Naked, except for the puffy plastic water wings I don't really need anymore, I look down through cedar fronds. The sun makes a shining path across the water. I hold onto a branch near my head and watch for the flicker of sunfish where the water darkens.

A blue jay lands at the end of the limb. Its beak opens, I can see the black tongue inside. I laugh; the bird flies off.

"Daddy. Hey, Dad!" I look back to where my father's orange life-jacket, glowing in the sunset, moves between the green canvas tent and the fire with its thin flag of smoke. "Daddy, look! Watch this!" He looks up then. His face is full of light.

I jump.

▼

The room was wicked hot, but I was shaking under the sheets. I pushed myself out of bed and stumbled out into the dark hall.

Clesta lay propped on half-a-dozen pillows with Chinky beside her, watching Johnny Carson. She never went to sleep before three in the morning—something to do with the MDH. She only slept on real silk sheets, with colors like the hearts of flowers: blue-violet, ivory, rose. The room smelled like mint and oranges.

"Lilly-Lil," she said, and moved some pillows over against the other side of the padded headboard for me. I settled into the cool, slippery silk, then felt something sharp. From under my butt I pulled out a large, bent tube of Bengay. Peter Pain ran across the front with little horizontal speed streaks behind him. I lay back on the pillows exactly parallel to Clesta. There was a little pile of orange peels on the sheet between us.

"I can't sleep," I said.

Clesta flicked the remote control and Johnny Carson became a mouth soundlessly moving. "Journey-proud."

18

"What?"

"Journey-proud. That's what my mother—your great-grandmother—used to call it. When we couldn't sleep the night before a trip, because we were too wrought up."

"I only came across town. Besides, I already made the trip."

Chinky raised his head, and I reached across Clesta to pat him. He curled his lip.

"It's the heat," said Clesta. "Makes him morose."

"There's always some reason to be sad." I sifted the pile of orange peels through my fingers. Behind Johnny Carson's head the word DISAPPEARED replaced HOLLYWOOD, big white letters spread out across a green hill.

Clesta sighed. Her wide, flat breasts rose and fell under her night-gown. "Your father's . . . not at ease with life. The greater your gifts, the more people demand of you. The more ways you can disappoint them. Now, how early did he know to turn to Nature, I wonder? I remember the very first time he ever ran off. Hitchhiked to Canada all by himself. He couldn't have been more than twelve. Gone six weeks, and all he would say was how he'd seen a great horned owl close enough to spit. I thought then, young Gordon is just one of the naturally solitary."

He can't manage without us, not really. Without me. I threw an orange peel at Chinky, who growled.

Clesta picked up a picture from the night table and handed it to me. "His father was the same—my brother Bob. Look. Even when he was a boy, you could see it."

In a long, narrow frame was a series of three pictures in which a boy sat on his mother's lap. The boy had fair hair and large, dark eyes. First he was crying, one round tear on his cheek like a blister; then laughing; then twisting around to touch his mother's face. She looked the same in every picture, no smile, high, scratchy lace collar and pearl earrings. That was before the Hutchinses lost all their money. Rags to rags in four generations.

We had this weird family tree, because of my parents being cousins. Old Bob, the one Clesta always wanted to tell stories about (my father's father), and Gramma Maude (my mother's mother) were Clesta's brother and sister. So my grandfather was also my great-uncle, and my grand-mother was my great-aunt. Rhoda said her mother said that was why we

19

were all so strange. Daniel's father, the Philanderer, was my father's brother, which made Daniel and me cousins twice (I *think*).

My grandfather died when my father was fourteen; Dad never mentioned him. He killed himself—that was what Doc said—but nobody in the family ever talked about that. They just said, died.

Clesta put the picture back on the night table, next to a photograph of Captain Sam Hutchins in his Civil War uniform.

I grabbed my chance. "What happened to him?"

"People like them—Bob and your father—they don't look at things the way we do."

"But what *happened?*"

"Oh, Lilly. Ask your grandmother. Maude was his favorite sister, not me."

"I never *see* Gramma Maude. Tell me a story." My heart started going hard and slow. "Tell me about Dad."

"Such a sensitive child. I believe he thought Bob was always there somehow after he . . . died. Invisible. Watching to see how your father measured up. Because it all fell on Gort then—James had already gone wild, and your grandmother Eulalie just sat in that hot little house all day reading books on how to raise him. God rest her soul." Her eyes came back to me. "Now, Lilly. I'm tired."

"*Please*, Clesta?"

"Journey-proud," she said again. "Now, *I've* never liked to travel. Even when I was younger, and not afraid of dying in some strange bed and somebody having to come and fetch me home, all that trouble and expense." She squinted at me. "Did I ever say that poem for you?"

"Just one story? I miss him." I let my voice sound pitiful.

She pulled herself straighter against her pillows.

" 'Here I am where I longed to be.

Home is the sailor, home from the sea,

And the hunter home from the hill.'

Now who was it wrote that? Anyway, it's carved on his tombstone. Good, isn't it?"

We were a family of quoters. My father quoted poetry; Doc quoted the Bible; Clesta quoted everything.

"It's lame," I said, giving up. Relief came sneaking over me, like slid- ing into a hot bath. Maybe Clesta was right not to worry—she'd known my father a lot longer than I had.

We watched Johnny Carson interview some bald-headed fashion designer. The flickering light from the television clung to the edge of Clesta's profile, her hooked nose and wild eyebrows. "Fashion!" she said. "Those fairies in New York City that don't want women to look like women." She sniffled. "Fashion is spinach!"

My arms and legs, my whole body felt loose and warm. I kissed her dry, soft cheek and slid off the bed.

"Now, before you go, where's my snivvy?"

I reached across and fished it out and handed it to her. She started thumbing the remote control until she got to the horror movie.

In my room, I pulled the rough cotton sheet up over my face. I made my hand a fig leaf, moving it across the soft new hair. The feeling piled up, then let go. Afterwards my belly ached, a slow, sweet ache. I fell asleep.

▼

I stayed at Clesta's almost a week. At first all Daniel wanted to do was fish. Rhoda's parents shipped her off to her grandmother in Idaho for the summer after Mrs. Vilardi found birth control pills in her sock drawer, so I didn't have anybody to hang out with. Clear nights I kept for my tele- scope; in the daytime I checked out Clesta's place for clues about my father. There were so many places to look—the storeroom, Clesta's room, her walnut secretary with the secret drawers, Doc's closet. But I had to give *some* time to old lamestain Daniel, or Clesta would've thought I was blowing her off. At least I didn't have to babysit Susie while my mother went walking all over the city pretending to look for work. As if she could fool me.

At sunrise I'd slip past the closed door where Clesta slept with a chair propped underneath the doorknob and feel my way downstairs along the wide mahogany banister. Daniel'd be waiting for me outside the door to his room, on the kitchen landing across from Doc's, his hair sticking up in slept-on shocks and his eyes puffed from sleep. He'd stand there holding the two rods, his old one and his new one—a seven-foot graphite with a Shakespeare reel, a bribe from my uncle—straight up in one hand.

We'd slide the heavy door open and go out into the sun, coming up red at the end of the alley. Daniel was wicked tall for his age, even taller than me, and narrow all over. When he walked, he sort of wagged each foot at the ankle. It made a little flapping motion, as if his jeans had ruffles at the bottom. On his left arm, just below the sleeve of his T-shirt, was this blistery scar like a coughdrop, pink and shiny, where something'd gone wrong with his smallpox vaccination when he was a baby.

We never caught anything. The first morning, Daniel popped out his spool and changed his line to six-pound test. But after the second day, he didn't bother. I made him bait both our hooks—Daddy always did it for me, I couldn't stand to stick my hand into the can of coffee grounds and feel around for the humid, shifty bodies. My father doubled the worm up to pierce it quicker, then cast as soon as he could. But Daniel threaded the hook slowly through the worm's light-colored collar while the brass spoon swung above it and flashed in the sun. (I'd told him to use a bobber, not a spoon, with worms; but he wouldn't listen.) Then he'd stand there watching it curl and uncurl, hopelessly.

Afterward he'd hand me his old fiber-glass rod and we'd cast out into the Lehigh River. I could do a snap cast, like cracking a whip. It'd been years, almost half my life, since my father'd taken me to the lake; but my arm remembered. Daniel and I leaned on the wall of the bridge with our butts to Lancaster Avenue. The cement was cold and rough under my bare arms. All the trucks rocking past made the bridge vibrate and swing. In my stomach I could feel the long drop down.

"My folks aren't gonna make it," Daniel said on our third morning. "They mailed me separate postcards."

The real reason they'd sent Daniel to stay with Clesta was sex. Three adolescent boys in the house, Doc said, was three too many. So they parceled them out—my Uncle James's three sons by three different mothers—to relatives, and went on a two-week package to Puerto Vallarta. To work on the marriage, Doc said; it sounded nasty and boring to me, like two people trying to fix a broken-down car.

Our voices went out over the water into the moist air. The nice thing was we could talk without looking at each other. I lowered the tip of my rod until I felt the spoon swing at the end of the line. I said, "Maybe you'd be better off with just your dad. He'd have to pay attention to you then."

"My dad has this girlfriend, Lois, he'd just be with *her* all the time. Does your mom have guys stay over? Doc said Uncle Gort split, like, weeks ago."

"Two weeks and four days." The sun, coming up behind Bethlehem Steel on the other side of the river, hurt my eyes. Next time I went home I'd look for my father's fishing hat with the shady brim. When I'd searched the garage I'd seen that his spinning tackle and tackle bag were gone, but not his boot-foot waders, so he hadn't gone where there were streams.

I didn't want to talk about my father, or about what I planned to do— not till I decided whether Daniel could be trusted. With a stupid, ordinary father like Uncle James, would he be able to understand about my dad? I concentrated on my retrieve. What most people don't realize is, you have to go slow: reel in, let it sit, reel in, let it sit.

For some reason—maybe just because he was the son of the Philanderer, as Clesta called my Uncle James—Daniel couldn't let it go. "Doesn't she at least have a boyfriend—"

"In Zaïre," I said, real loud, "know what they do? They eat termites live. Just pluck them right out of the air when they fly by."

"Gross," he said, in this fascinated voice.

"First they pull off the wings. Then they—"

My rod dipped. Praise God! as Doc would say. I don't know why they call it a nibble, it's more a hand grabbing yours. The pull went right up through my arms, as if my wrist was about to snap. Then my thumb found the catch. I released it, and the line traveled away from me fast. I could hear it sing in the guides.

"Set the hook!" Daniel yelled.

I yanked the rod up hard. The line went slack. I'd forgotten to close the bail.

"Must've just snagged on something," said Daniel, who hadn't noticed about the bail. "Doesn't your mom at least go on dates? I bet she at least does that."

23

"In China," I said (I was starting to get really steamed), "they eat live monkeys' brains—"

"Cut it out, Lil. People who do stuff like that aren't even human," he said. *I'm it; you're shit.* He had this preachy side to him—sanctimonious, was Clesta's word; *she* thought he'd outgrow it. He started reeling in. "I'm hungry. There aren't any fish in this dumb river, anyway."

My heart flopped in my chest. "There *are*," I said, too loud. "There *are* fish in there." I looked down into the blurry brown water. Maybe not pickerel or bluegill—but there *could* be carp. They can live in any kind of water, even polluted. Suddenly it felt as if we were dangerously high up, as if there were things my body knew—like the things it remembered— that I didn't. I yanked my rod up and reeled in, fast. The wormless hook swung wildly back and forth until it got tangled in the line. *Lighten up,* I could hear Rhoda say. I mean, what did I care whether we caught any fish or not? Probably Doc would refuse to cook them anyway, or else he'd stew them up with raspberries and turnips.

Daniel stood his rod against the cement wall and started untangling my line. He looked at me sideways. "What would it feel like to be a fish?" he said. "No arms and legs. No clothes. Awesome! Just moving through the water with nothing."

He had sex on the brain as much as my Uncle James ever did. I turned my back to him and the river. From the lunch sack I took a chicken sandwich and an orange and a paper towel folded into a square. By the time we were halfway through, the sandwiches were gritty. Afterwards the orange was as good as water, sliding along the roof of my mouth.

We always left by nine-thirty; Clesta liked to see us at the breakfast table even though we never ate anything. At the Moravian cemetery the sidewalk narrowed and we had to walk single file. I dropped behind. Daniel walked with his head down, running the butt of his fishing rod along the iron fence with a dull clanging sound. *Could* he be trusted? He was gingerly, all right—he'd been no help at all with the fish. And I didn't like the stupid way he'd talked about my mother. But he *was* persistent. That was a quality that could be useful. I watched him walking ahead of me. The pale no-color hair dovetailed into a point at the nape of his neck, like my father's. The scruff, Clesta called it—*I'll take you by the scruff of the neck*—but it was tender and pink.

24

3

JUDITH

On the left-hand side of the sheet of graph paper I printed WOULD LIKE TO DO; on the right-hand side, COULD DO. I drew a vertical line in red crayon to separate the two sides. On the left were: Jazz Musician, Baby Nurse, Puppeteer (??); the right side was blank. Setting my cereal bowl on top of last night's dirty dinner plate, I put my elbows on the kitchen table and leaned my chin on my palms. Nine in the morning and already ninety degrees. I pushed my uncombed, unwashed hair out of my eyes.

Now that I'd told my daughters the truth about losing my job at Valley View, I felt—not lighter, or less alone, as I'd thought I would—but as if I'd delivered myself into their hands. Especially Lil's. I could see she thought I was falling apart, and that made me fall apart faster. Still, maybe it was better. I was a terrible liar, mostly out of laziness—it's so much easier to keep your story straight if you tell the truth—and Gort would have seen through me right away once he came back.

"Baton Twirler," said Susie. She upended a box of Cheerios over the big yellow mixing bowl at her place and thumped its bottom. "Circus Shark Trainer. Mom! We're outta milk."

"Get real," Lil said. "Animal Keeper, maybe. God knows she's had plenty of practice with you." She was sitting on the counter next to the sink, bare legs dangling down. Morning sunlight picked out the silver of the drawer handle below her black hightops, the pale gold stubble on her shins. I could feel her watching me, as if she were trying to decide something. Yesterday afternoon she came back from Clesta's. I didn't tell her how I'd missed her, missed the back-beat of her stereo through the floorboards, as if the house's heart had stopped. It was the first time she'd gone off without saying anything; I wanted to tell her how it made me feel ashamed to have to call people up and ask where my own daughter was. She believed that adults were impervious, that only the hopelessly incapable among us had such feelings; she had no right to the safeness of that.

But I was afraid that if I guilt-tripped her (as she would say), she'd go away again. So now I didn't say anything, just tried to be calm and welcoming, the way I did with Gort. I'd had sixteen years of practice. No, fifteen, I thought sadly. The first year everything had been all right—had been wonderful, which was what I meant by "all right" back then, nineteen and newly pregnant and Gort's love like a pearly sheen all over my skin.

Susie, scrabbling through the Cheerios with both hands, said, "Deliver Newspapers. Veterinarium. Jockey."

"Soda jerk. Mailman. Butcherbakercandlestickmaker," said Lil in a bored voice. One leg jigged rapidly up and down, thumping against the wooden cabinet.

"Got it!" Susie said. She tore open a paper packet and extracted a blue plastic bubble-wand.

"Finish your juice first." I unwrapped a butterscotch-frosted Twinkie.

Lil said, "Don't eat that!"

"Why not?"

"It has *beef fat* in it."

I bit into it. Lil said, "Not to mention that it expired five days ago. Don't you read labels?"

"It tastes okay," I lied.

"God. What am I going to do with you. You don't even want to know simple facts, do you? Not if they're inconvenient. Simple facts that could save your life."

I looked back down at my list and drew an arrow from "Baby Nurse" into the right-hand column. A lot of the residents at Valley View did wear diapers. The heel of my hand left a sweat-print on the light-green paper. I turned it over. On the back was a scribbled diagram that started out as several intersecting triangles with labeled points, then gradually became a witch in a tricorn hat. The witch's nose was labeled "B." Underneath was a list—

> Measure up kitch window
> Lumberyard
> J.

—and then one of Gort's palindromes: ABLE WAS I ERE I SAW ELBA. He was always scribbling on something—brain-jogging, he called it—the black marbled copybooks were kept hidden away, but he left loose pieces of paper everywhere. I'd gotten this from the string drawer. He could have done it years ago. The lists I'd been finding the last several months—among the hammock cushions, under his placemat—seemed to have more and more items that didn't belong. *Jerusalem artichokes. Go to Chile? Original Sin.*

"The soap. Come on, Lil. *Gimme* it."

Lil held the plastic bottle out of Susie's reach. She leaned over, making her wait, and turned on the faucet and drank from her cupped hands. At the sound of water the parakeets started chirping.

"Goddammit, Lil."

Lil handed Susie the bottle. "Little baby bubble blower."

Susie squirted a green stream of Liquid Joy onto Lil's hightops. Lil swiped at her. She leaped sideways and ran with her three-quarter-time horse's gait into the living room, where I could hear her whinnying over the maddened chirping of the birds.

Upstairs, I stood in the middle of my bedroom shaking. I wanted to strangle my daughters for making this time even harder than it had to be; and at the same time I felt such pity for them that my stomach ached with it. I hadn't changed the sheets since Gort left; I'll do that, I thought, it will calm me down. I made my own bed first, yanked the fraying sheet tight, shook out the two green army blankets, pounded the pillows. *Qui fidelis est in parvis*, Mrs. Muschlitz taught us in sophomore Latin: He who faithful is in small things, so will be in large. I banged my knee on the bedpost on my way out. My upper arms and thighs always seemed to have one or two bruises, green-and-purple like irises. Nice Ms. Grundy said I did it to punish myself. For what? I'd asked her; and she'd said, Ah, now that's the question, isn't it?

Susie's sheets and blanket were flung all over the bed, along with her baby dolls, each one stripped naked and tied to the back of a stuffed rabbit or dog. I kicked the toys into a corner. *Solomon Grundy, Born on Monday*, went through my head as I stood there. *Christened on Tuesday, Married on Wednesday.* But instead of changing the bed, I slumped down onto the floor among the tortured, dusty dolls.

Something on Thursday, Worse on Friday. I had an appointment with Ms. Grundy at Valley View at eleven; she was counseling me for free until I found a new job—my non-income slid me all the way down her sliding scale. I knew I wouldn't go today. I hated being forced to sit in a chair and open my mouth and consider things for an hour every Wednesday, like taking your soul to the dentist. Ms. Grundy asking questions I couldn't answer, like why hadn't I called the police about Gort, and didn't I mind the way he took his freedom while I was stuck with old people's diapers and raising the girls. Didn't I know this was the eighties, that women didn't have to tiptoe around the edges of their men's lives anymore? "Your world is so *small*, Judith." Ms. Grundy was too worried about my so-called lack of friends. Too interested in my girlhood in Orient, in how I'd watched my friends and my friends' mothers, learned to do what normal girls, normal women did. Was I planning to spend my whole life in impersonation, Ms. Grundy wanted to know. How could I explain to her, how could anyone understand what Gort was really like, who didn't know him? *He's magic*, I could say—but the thought of her skeptical pale-red eyebrows stopped me.

I couldn't call Ms. Grundy to cancel—the phone had been shut off on Friday. I owed the phone company $75.22, but it might as well have been five times as much. Any such amount had moved beyond my reach in the moment when old Mr. Yerkes grabbed a handful of my left buttock for the last time, and I delivered his lunch of creamed chipped beef and pureed peas upside-down on his stomach. His eyes gazed at me with reproachful lust, milky all around the iris so that they looked not brown but blue. The sweet shitty smell of his unchanged diaper. My job; my whole life. I wanted to kill him. I believe you can feed yourself, I'd said, and smoothed down my blue cotton skirt and walked out into the corridor where Nurse Julian, with the cheery heartlessness of bosses, fired me.

I pulled myself up off Susie's floor. Ms. Grundy would never in a million years understand the comfort of being disconnected—like my father turning off his hearing aid when people said things he didn't want to hear. Once you know something, he'd say, you can't unknow it. There are all kinds of techniques that teach you how to remember; but you can't learn how to forget.

> Died on Saturday,
> Buried on Sunday
> And that was the end
> Of Solomon Grundy

Lil's one window had its roller shade pulled down to the sill, and the room was filled with orange light. The stolen WRONG WAY sign on the wall glowed an evil red. The floor was covered with books, star charts, and musty discarded clothes. I picked up the starplotter just before I would have stepped on it. The lucite was foggy and yellow, and the mysterious, carefully inked symbols that looked like a magician's spell had faded. Lil and Gort had made it together when she was four, when he began to introduce her to the magic that lies beneath the ordinary world, the hidden everyday magic of stars and tides and microscopic creatures.

At the foot of the bed, tucking the clean bottom sheet tight, I felt something under the mattress. Something hard and lumpy. I pushed further, between the mattress and the muslin-covered springs. There was a sudden sharp pain in my finger, as if something had bitten me; but I kept hold and pulled it out.

The carved silver handle was heavy and cool in my palm. The steel blade, not freckled with rust anymore, shone in the orange light. There was blood on it. Turning it over in my hands, I saw blood bright along the side of my ring finger. I tested the cold edge of the blade with my thumb. It sank instantly into the soft pad of flesh, sharper than it had ever been when it lay rusting in the kitchen drawer.

My hand shook. How long had Lil been sleeping with the big knife pressed between her mattress and the springs? I stood at the foot of the bed, my mind running over alternatives. She'd felt nervous without Gort in the house and taken this for protection. She'd been listening to Clesta's stories and taken it for a keepsake—the hundred-year-old handle with its engraved initial rubbed to an unreadable flourish; the wide blade forged fifty years ago by Gort's father at the mill. I thought, If I say anything it will make things worse. The way it does with Gort. I wiped the blade on my skirt, then lifted the mattress and laid the knife on the springs. The mattress dropped down with a soft thud, and a puff of dust flew up on either side.

In the living room Susie zigzagged in and out of a shaft of sunlight, a trail of iridescent bubbles floating behind her. There were little sparks as they burst one by one. Lil was slumped on the wooden park bench (Gort hated furniture with stuffing), one elbow propped on the curly iron arm. Waiting.

"You hurt yourself?" She eyed the rust-colored splotch on my blue-and-white dress.

I pretended not to hear. It frightened me how much I wanted to hit her. I was so angry, Lil made it so clear that only her father's return interested her, that I didn't trust myself to say more than, "Stick around, okay? Keep an eye on your sister. You do dishes, please," I said to Susie. "And put all that cereal back in the box."

"Why doesn't Lil have to do dishes?" Susie stopped galloping and threw herself face-down into the rope hammock in the corner. "It's not fair," she wheezed into the dusty red and blue pillows. She made two syllables out of it: fay-uhr.

"*Life* isn't fair," I said. "I'm preparing you for life."

"Yeah, well, that's bullshit. I didn't ask to be born."

"You did. You knocked on every womb in Heaven. Knocking and knocking, until I finally let you in."

"That's where you made your mistake," said Lil. She got up and snapped on Gort's mother's old black-and-white TV (one of Gort's reluctant concessions to modern life). Large grinning turtles cavorted across the screen.

Susie flopped over onto her back. She pulled the various fringed and embroidered pillows over her head and shoulders and stomach. "Fuck you," came muffled by corduroy and striped satin. There was a juicy sneeze. "I'm dead."

▼

On Heckewelder Street I nearly crashed into a man with a baby-carrier strapped to his back. I slowed down and walked behind him. Perhaps the baby (who was maybe ten or eleven months) would turn around, scanning the way babies do. I was breathless from walking so fast, almost running, as if I could outrun it all: unhappy daughters and messy house and no money and the waiting. The baby distracted me. I would have had more children—six babies, a dozen—if I could have talked Gort into it. This baby's hair, dark with sweat, stuck to its head like the painted hair of an antique doll. I got ready to slide my spectacles down my nose and look out over them: babies like that. We passed the 5 & 10 and Eddie's Touchless Car Wash. The baby didn't turn around. I could feel the sweat collecting on the backs of my knees, between my breasts. Finally I got tired of the slow, shuffling pace. When I passed, the baby was smiling tenderly into its father's clavicle.

This morning I really *was* on my way to look for a job. Lacey, my next-door neighbor and best friend, had fixed me up through her husband. Paul was an electrician who did a lot of renovation work. The job was some kind of carpenter's helper. All you have to do is go there, Lacey'd said when I protested. It's just over the bridge—you can walk there, Judith. (Lacey knew I hadn't driven in years.) Just let the guy get a look at you. He owes Paul a favor.

A look at me? A big-boned woman with frizzy brown hair, in a plaid cotton sundress and spectacles. Not glasses—perfectly round discs of glass held together by metal across the nose and hooking behind the ears. A woman nobody paid any attention to. A woman in early middle age who didn't know a hammer from a hacksaw. It would have to be some favor.

On Broad Street, stretched out on the low cement wall in front of Irving Trust, was the man I thought of as Thomas. Always, even in summer, he wore many clothes: boots, heavy jeans, a padded, vaguely military jacket. I sat down a few yards away in the patchy shade of a pin oak. I thought, If only I could stay here all morning—not try to cross the bridge, not have to meet the measuring look of Paul's friend. A crow the size of a Pomeranian, with slick blue-ink feathers, paced the sidewalk in front of me. Thomas lay on his back in the sun, his eyes closed. He reminded me of Gort—the way Gort had been this past winter—long, narrow face, pale eyelids that seemed like not enough protection for the eyes beneath. Was this who Gort would have been without us, Lil and Susie and me?

▼

Without his glasses, Gort's face looks nude; you can see how one eye turns slightly inward. He's sitting on the bare wood floor in the unfinished half of the attic, next to his rumpled sleeping bag, with his legs stretched out in front of him. By his feet is an empty white porcelain pot. The skylight above his head holds a

31

dim winter sun, a few maverick snowflakes. In the corner his telescopes point at the floor.

It's Sunday morning, I can hear the bells, but I don't go to Mass anymore. (How long now? Must be two years.) I sit on my heels beside the chamber pot, holding Lustyka in my arms for warmth. Gort starts to speak, falls silent, starts again. He doesn't look at me, but at the bare feet protruding from his blue pajamas.

I'm afraid to hear. All these years, and he's never wanted to tell me what he was feeling, no matter how much I longed to hear. Now I don't want to anymore. I know it's something better left unsaid. "Hush," I say. "Hush, it's all right," and move over to him. He smells like milk gone bad. I pull his head down into my lap. Pliable as a rag doll, he lies with his head next to the cat's rump, his legs and buttocks still sitting.

Lustyka, rumbling softly, starts to wash herself. The pink triangle of tongue makes its way slowly along her haunches and into Gort's thick, pale hair. I look up at the skylight and wish I were out there. We sit like that, with the bells' slow tolling and snow zigzagging in the cold sun and the cat's tongue rummaging tenderly through Gort's hair, while my own eyes slowly close.

▼

A leaf spiraled down from the pin oak and lay on my knees like a cupped hand. I shook my head hard and pinched the flesh of my upper arm. Last winter—I remembered the constant feeling of holding my breath, as if, if I let it go, *he* would go, would dissolve or disappear. Other times, the feeling of wanting to shake him, make him talk to me. It had been a relief to see him packing, finally. The going away and coming back renewed—that was the way Gort was. Once Lil, when she was three or so, had gotten into the ant traps I kept on the top shelf of the linen closet; when I caught hold of her—shouting "*Why* can't you be good?"—she'd sobbed, "I couldn't, so I didn't, so I couldn't-didn't." Oh, I'd thought then: that's Gort. Whatever it is we all want from him—talk to us, let us know him, *hold* him—it feels as if, if he did it, he would die. He can't, so he doesn't.

Thomas slept on, one cheek turned to the ledge. I imagined laying my face against the cement, warm and rough and smelling of sun. Across the street two policemen leaning against the S & D Delicatessen shouted at a third. "Bucky! Hey—Short Ass!" He turned and waved, then disappeared into the post office. *One world at a time.* I picked the pin oak leaf off my lap. Deep green, with scalloped edges that looked as though they'd been bitten off: a find. A sign. I opened my denim bag and slid the green, supple leaf into the zipper pocket between a locust leaf and a brown moth with outstretched papery wings. I saved only the perfect things, the ones that were completely intact. I got up and started walking toward the river.

Twenty minutes later I stood with my feet on the bronze plaque that marked the middle of the Lancaster Street bridge, the way I did every day, unable to make myself go beyond it. Raised letters arranged in a semicircle said "A.D. 1936." I had no idea what stopped me every day in the same spot. It was as if the blank windows of Bethlehem Steel where it rose steeply to my left were a hundred warning eyes. One of those windows was Gort's; if he'd been here, he might have glanced up from his computer screen and seen me and felt—what? Hunted; or cherished. It would depend on his never-foreseeable mood. The house where Paul's friend was working was on the other side of the river; I'd been ashamed to tell Lacey that that put it out of my reach. She knew I didn't drive, but she didn't know that, for almost a year now, I'd been unable to make myself walk across the bridge.

The noise of traffic passing sounded remote, as if the wind were sweeping it into the water. The river was light-and-dark like taffeta. I was standing, frozen, looking down through the scrolled iron railing, when a woman walked past me headed for the other side of the river. First I didn't see her, then I did. A white cotton shirt, a man's shirt, curved high on her shoulders over a slight hump, and her abundant, dry hair was gray streaked with white. She moved slowly away from me, braiding her hair as she walked. Her hands curved and straightened, curved and straightened: take from the left, flip across, take from the right. The fingers were long and bony and shiny-knuckled. Suddenly I couldn't bear to lose sight of those hands. I began to walk behind her. The woman walked faster. The long fingers flashed: in, out. We pounded along the iron walkway, and I breathed in hot dust and cinders and the sour, carbolic smell of the river. Then we were on the other side.

We turned onto the Boulevard, past the Tilghman Building, the main library, Hess's department store. The sun pouring down evenly on everything gave the street a bleached, moon-rubble blankness. Here and there businessmen walked in pairs toward lunch, insulated by their spacesuits of blazer, shirt, striped silk tie. We turned west, away from the river. The woman's white shirt showed two gray wings of sweat. The hands stopped, pulled a rubber band off one wrist: twist, tuck, snap, and under.

We angled right, then right again, along a series of wide, curving streets where I'd never been before, beneath huge, old chestnut trees. Here and there one of the big Victorian houses had new paint in Necco-wafer colors and a brass-bright lawn. Two young girls, squinting against the glare, pushed peach-faced babies in strollers. The woman plunged into traffic against the light. When she turned her head, I saw that her right eye was covered with a black eyepatch. She cut in front of a garbage truck and turned down a side street. When I reached it, she was gone. The noon sun shone straight down through the arches of the chestnut trees; nothing moved. I breathed in the smell of fresh, hot tar. The street sign said "Schoener Place"—the street where Paul's friend was.

From further down the street came a steady scraping and the stutter of some kind of machinery. I walked toward it. My short-sleeved dress was bunched wetly under my arms. I stopped in front of a high wooden fence. Its wide boards were weathered, blue-painted. Not cobalt, not turquoise, not indigo—some unnamed, undiscovered color. I stood in the sun with my thighs stuck together under my skirt and my eyes on the blue-painted boards. I knew without looking that this was the house.

"Help you, lady? You lost or something?"

Halfway along the fence, which stretched from the sidewalk into the backyard, a middle-aged man stood at the side of the house in a sleeve-less undershirt and jeans. He shaded his eyes with a trowel. The sun lit his bald head and flashed off the metal blade.

I said, "No. No—not really."

"You look awful hot. Like a drink of water?"

A drink of water was suddenly the thing I wanted most in the world. I started up the brick path between overgrown andromeda and laurel. Near the porch were two ceramic flamingos weathered to pale orange, one of them headless, with a bony leg alertly raised. The house, a dirty yellow—the only eyesore on the street—had elaborate weathered-wood trim around every window, at the eaves and along the rim of the porch, like battered lace.

"I hate this stuff," the man said. He shoved his trowel under the upper edge of the yellow siding and pulled. There was a dull screech. He tore off a large piece and threw it into the bushes. "Am I right? Aluminum." He spat contemptuously into the lush weeds along the foundation.

In the side yard a younger man was scraping blue paint off the fence boards. The balding man shouted, "Hey, Irish! Bring me a cuppa water," and the young man threw a metal tool into the grass and went behind the house. He returned with a styrofoam cup, handed it to the older man without a word, then went back to his scraping. His bare back was reddish brown and shiny with sweat. A ponytail of dark-blonde hair curled damply on his neck.

The balding man crouched down in front of a large square hole in the brick foundation. Beside him was a pile of bricks and a wheelbarrow full of wet gray mortar. I sipped the cool water and watched him load his trowel with mortar, butter a brick, bottom and ends, set it on the topmost layer of bricks, then pick up another one and do the same thing all over again. "Brick," he said. "Brick and stone. Build just about anything out of stone."

"Shit!" shouted the man called Eli. He scuffed at a pile of blue paint-shavings. Both men, hot as it was, wore heavy dome-toed shoes the color of mildew. My bare toes in their rubber-soled sandals curled under in sympathy. With quick, almost violent motions Eli unbuckled a leather apron with bulging pockets and threw it, clanking, into the weeds. He stomped towards us. "Why the hell can't she just replace the goddamned fence."

"Excuse the boy, ma'am," the older man said, looking up at me. He picked up a hammer and knocked old mortar off the end of a brick. "Same reason she wants all these basement windows filled in. Place's got to look authentic. Re-stored. Cedar ought to never been painted in the first place."

Up close Eli had an oddly familiar, cheesy smell. He looked no more than twenty-five, but he was somehow disturbing. I stood there rolling the empty Styrofoam cup between my palms. Smiling, Eli reached for it. His bright, white teeth were all of a size, like Chiclets; there was a gap between the two front ones. I recognized the smell then, stronger, on his fingers: it was semen. I pulled my hand away and took a step closer to the house. The balding man ran the sharp end of his trowel between the bricks, deepening the lines of wet mortar.

I said, "Turn the boards around."

"What?"

"Turn the boards around."

He said, "Hey," and put down his trowel. "We could, at that. Irish, them boards painted on the other side?"

"How should I know?"

"They're not," I said. I'd seen the other side of the fence as I approached the house. I took a breath. "Paul sent me, Paul Danyluk. About a job?"

The balding man looked up at me. His face, burned the rose color of the bricks, was inscribed with a pattern of pale lines across his forehead, around his eyes, like the stitching on a quilt. His eyes moved slowly downward from my sweat-streaked hair to my rubber-soled sandals. Finally he said, "Danyluk, huh? Well, we need *somebody*. Am I right, Irish? We could try you out, see how it goes. It'd be an apprentice, say, and just generally help out. Say, six-sixty-five an hour. That's a lot more than minimum."

A dollar more than Valley View had paid me. "Okay. No. I don't know." Backing away, I tripped on a loose brick and banged into the corner of the house.

The balding man stood up. "You can start tomorrow. I'm Bob Johansson. Hop, to my friends and enemies." He stuck out a large hand and without thinking I took it. His calluses scratched my palm. "Irish here is Eli Byrne." Eli put out his hand, but I was already backing away.

"What's your name?" Hop raised his voice. I was halfway down the path. The suggestion of a breeze cooled the wet back of my dress.

"Judith," I called back. "Judith Hutchins."

"We start work at eight," he shouted, and vanished inside the house.

At the bottom of the path I put my hand on the fence, sticky with beetle tracks, its paint flaking in the noon sun. It had lost its blinding blueness. The breeze lifted, carrying the smell of fresh-sawn wood. I turned and began to walk back the way I had come.

▼

"Your kids went out someplace."

I paused with my key raised. I hardly ever made it past Lacey in daylight—maybe one time out of five.

"About an hour ago." Lacey stood on her front steps in full sun, which made a burning bush out of her light-red hair. In the scuffed yard, nominally separated from ours by a sagging wire fence, her three-year-old, Joey, sat on an anthill watching the ants crawl over his bare legs.

Lacey stepped clumsily over a low spot in the fence. She was seven months pregnant, exactly. I knew, because she'd asked me to be her labor coach; we'd gone to the first Lamaze session together the Wednesday before. (Paul, who fainted at the sight of blood, had failed the test of Joey's birth; so he was out.) Lacey came and stood beside me on the porch. Her bright skin was speckled all over—arms, neck, bosom—like a leopard frog. When she was eleven she'd read on the back of a comic book that iodine would cure freckles and she'd put some on every one; it had taken weeks for all the flamingo-colored splotches to fade.

I patted her pink-checked belly. "Hi, Baby."

"So. You get the job?"

"Don't you think you ought to pull Joey off of there?"

"Moles' balls. What for? Black ants don't bite. It's only the red ones bite. Did you get the job or not? Paul'll be pissed if you didn't. The guy owes him."

I said, "I guess so. I guess I did."

"Well, jeez, Judith, which is it? Did you or didn't you?"

"I did."

Lacey beamed. "Hey, that's great! You are now leaving the ranks of the unemployed, honey."

Black specks traveled purposefully, rapidly, over Joey's mushroom-colored skin, swarming up his ankles, along his calves, over his knees to his thighs. Watching them, I felt my own skin prickle. Joey's head, with its fizzy light-brown hair, was bowed over his knees. He growled soft syllables of encouragement.

"They probably have germs, or something," I said.

"Honey. The whole morning he was hollering. His yelling could peel paint, you know?" I did know. "He's happy, then I leave him be." Lacey pushed her hands deep into the pockets of the pink-checked apron she wore over a pair of Paul's khaki shorts. The cotton pulled tight, rubbed to pink-and-gray across her belly. Every time I saw her I thought how truly strange it was, to have another body *inside* yours; it just didn't seem plausible, and I'd done it twice.

In companionable silence we watched Lustyka pick her way towards us across the patchwork of small yards. Seeing Lacey, she hunkered down in the skunk cabbage and morning glories that grew along the trampled wire fence. I never discouraged them because I liked the white sparks among the green; Lacey, because it didn't occur to her.

"Deloy deloy deloy," Joey sang to the ants. "Oy deloy deloy."

Lacey put her palms flat against either side of her back. "Peacock piss, am I beat. Time to start the roast for supper. Grocery shopping tonight, okay? I want to leave about eight."

I thought about pushing a wire cart up and down the aisles with Lacey, looking into the bins of cabbages and potatoes, smelling the cantaloupes for ripeness. Looking and touching and not talking. No need for impersonation, the way it always seemed to be with other women, at PTA meetings or the Friends of the Library. Lacey understood without explanations; after I'd been with her I always felt happy for a while. But I shook my head. We had enough canned stuff and TV dinners to get by until I started getting paid again. When she saw my empty cart Lacey would try to give me money, and I didn't want that. I said, "Thank Paul for me, okay?"

"Well, okay. You need anything, honey, you come over. Company. Anything."

She trundled back across the two yards. I watched her scoop up Joey and go into the house, where, I knew, she wouldn't be putting any roast in any oven. Lacey often lied, unless you could get her to say "I." As in *I'm making a roast for supper*, which she hadn't said. The screen door banged behind her, and I could her hear her saying, "Paul? Where are you going? *Paul*."

There was mail in the mailbox; I could see it through the three little holes over the American eagle. I was surprised; usually Lil got to it first. Both of us looking for the same thing. Then I saw there was a perfect, shining spider web stretched across the black metal lid. Lil, thinking of what her father would have wanted, must have decided not to disturb it. It seemed to fasten at one end to the metal catch, and at the other, to the wooden siding above where the mailbox hung. The filaments were as fine as baby hair. They trembled in some current of air too light for me to feel. The spider, dark and not very big, swung near the center of the web where it was densest.

Lacey's voice rose. "—*hear* me?"

I put my keys in my mouth. With one hand I raised the lid of the mailbox, carefully, inch by slow inch; even so, the whole web shivered. With the other hand I dipped inside and pulled out the clutch of bills and supermarket circulars. Nothing from Gort. Why had I thought there might be? He never wrote us when he went AWOL; but then he'd never stayed away this long before. I let the lid down gently. The web was still whole and perfect.

4

L I L

Once my mother started her dumb carpenter's job, I finally got a chance to make some money. Mom suddenly started parceling out the chores she used to do herself. The dishes and the dusting and Lustyka were Susie's; Susie was mine. I saved as much of what my mother paid me—three dollars an hour, seventy-five cents below the going rate—as I could. I made her pay me every day. On days when Susie was the Second-Grader from Hell I got some comfort from counting the bills rolled up inside the little wooden doll that my Uncle James and one of my ex-aunts brought back from Leningrad. My money fit exactly inside the largest one, if I took the two inner ones out; I dropped the change down the middle of the rolled-up bills, then screwed the top back on. The painted eyes looked so innocent.

By now my father'd been gone three and a half weeks—longer than he'd ever stayed away before. Last time—last January, right after Christmas—he'd only been gone five days. He must've really missed us, even if he didn't say so. Definitely, it was time for action.

My mother had less time to notice every little thing I did; but that wasn't what pissed me off. She was different. She didn't seem to need me anymore. Her face had this expression like she was thinking about something more interesting than us. She went around talking about two-by-two furring, mortise and tenon joints, orbital sanders, blah blah blah, until I said, Oh, *please*. She'd always been like that, trying to blend in, sticking close to the walls as if that way no one would notice her. At the Aquarium on Sundays, just my father and me, he used to read the descriptions on the walls out loud. "'For their chief means of defense, other reptiles may rely on deception, and through camouflage or mimicry appear to be something they are not.' Why, Lilly," he said, "that's your mother." Okay, when I was a little kid I didn't mind how she was.

40

Now it pissed me off. It was dishonest—worse, even—it was cowardly, to hide from the truth. To only see what you want to see.

Her second week on the job, Mom set it up with the dweebs she worked for so that we could go over to the house one evening and see what she was doing. I said I had a date. I liked to use the word *date* for when Daniel and I did something together—a word I'd never use to him. I liked to see my mother stop what she was doing, while the vein down the center of her forehead started pulsing. Her face would have the same expression as the housewife in "Chemical Boobytraps," one of the many movies Mr. Burson showed us in Chem 1. Some hands put a jar of hydrochloric acid into a refrigerator; the Modern Housewife comes into the kitchen and BOOM! the refrigerator door flies off and hits her in the chest. I didn't know why I wanted to make my mother look like that. Afterwards I'd feel really nasty; but I kept on doing it.

I took advantage of Mom and Susie being gone to finish searching my mother's bedroom. I was beginning to think that the so-called grown-ups in my family had screwed up—*were* screwed up—that it was all up to me now. I saw that I'd have to put together some kind of strategy, like they say on the TV news. But before I could make plans to go and get Dad, I needed a better idea where he was. I mean, he could've been *any-where*. He used to talk about Ladakh and the snow leopards; about this mountain in Peru where they have this big telescope and you can see the part of the sky that you can't see from here.

After my mother and Susie left, I hauled out the old leather suitcase under Mom's bed. It was small and square, the kind of case you put make-up in. When I lifted the lid, there was a bunch of dead things. And they say *I'm* weird. Leaves and dried-out moths and dead beetles—even a grasshopper. In the mirror inside the lid I saw my own face, with an expression that was butt-ugly and eyes as green as my mother's. I slammed the case shut.

I checked out the toes of her shoes, under her mattress, her drawers. She didn't even have any old love letters. There was nothing except a note that said, → *Clesta's fix furnace. Back @ 6*, which'd slipped under the butcher-paper lining in her underwear drawer. I took that.

▼

41

"*Originally a friendly animal, the sea otter is now suspicious and distrustful of man. It never comes ashore even to breed.*"

Daddy has to bend down to read the plastic-coated plaque beside the observation window. He's all mine today, Sunday. Mommy thinks he took me to eleven o'clock Mass, but we're bunking church. I listen, pretending to be the only daughter of a widower, his sole support and comfort. I breathe in the sharp smell of chlorine, the odor of salt and mildew. At five I'm already tall enough that the bottom of the window reaches to my knees. I can see all I want of the cloudy green water, the bright-colored sea anemones like fingers grabbing, the sea otters.

"'*A fur-bearing marine animal of the genus Enhydra—*' What do you know, they belong to the weasel family."

My red quilted jacket is too warm. I pull my arms out of the sleeves and leave the hood on my head so the coat trails down my back like a cape. I lean against the pocked cement ledge. On the other side of the glass, sea otters wheel and glide, on their backs, their bellies, their backs. They have stubby whiskers around their mouths, and their wet fur sticks up in reddish brown spikes.

"'*It is believed that the animal mates for life.*'"

I watch one especially. It's just about my size. It swoops close to the glass, then hovers in the water, watching me. I can see its shiny, smooth nose, like licorice. I imagine the ears hidden deep under its fur.

I stop listening to Daddy's schoolroom voice. I start to run. Holding my jacket out at each side like wings, I do figure eights and twirls. The sea otter moves with me. I go close to the glass; it does, too. I move away; it pulls back. All the way down the long, echoing corridor, I see my red reflection and, next to it, the sea otter's identically looping shape. Then Daddy comes up beside me, and he's running, too. The damp cement walls bounce the sound of our laughter back to us.

When we get home, Mommy's lying on the living room sofa in the late afternoon dusk. On the table by her head is a poinsettia with big shiny leaves; the red flowers jump when my father turns on the lamp. She turns onto her side with her back along the sofa's back and one hand under her cheek. Sleep smooths out her face. She is snoring lightly. Daddy lifts the lid of the pine bench and takes out the yellow afghan knitted like a shawl, in little sunbursts. Moving slowly, he unfolds it. Its edge settles lightly into the bony hollow below her neck, and she sighs.

In the kitchen after supper, I stand on a wooden stool to reach the sink. Mommy and I pretend that I get the dishes as clean as she would. Holding a dish towel, she moves close beside me and says, in a low voice, "Was he with you the whole time?"

▼

When Mom and Susie got back, Susie came into my room full of how great it was, how she got to run the circular saw, how nails were named after pennies, eight-penny, ten-penny, blah blah blah. I gave her the sign Daniel'd taught me, thumb and finger in a circle, for Asshole (Size Small); but of course she didn't get it. I got ripped all over again. Maybe my mother could fool her dweeb boss and fool Susie; but she couldn't fool me. I knew she was just hiding again. *Other reptiles may rely on deception.* I put the cap on my telescope and set it in the corner. Then I got into bed with my clothes on and pulled the sheet up over my head. When the door closed behind Susie, I turned my face to the bitter-lemon smell of my sweaty hair on the pillow.

I'll find out where you are. I'll find you.

▼

It was the third of July. My mother had the day off from work, so I had the day off from Susie. There was nothing to do—Daniel was in Philadelphia for a checkup with the specialist (Bone Man, Clesta called him, and I pictured a skeleton in a white coat and stethoscope). That always used to be what I loved about Clesta's. That feeling of time slowing down. But now I used every spare minute to search for clues. In Clesta's linen cupboard, flipping through the soft, stacked towels for something to read, I caught this flash of black-and-white, and my stomach jumped. But it was only the dustjacket for *The Hite Report*. I looked through all the stuff in the cupboard then, breathing in Yardley's Lavender and the sweet smell of starch; but there was no speckled copybook filled with dark, curly writing and little drawings. Dweeb, I said to myself. Why would there be?

I went downstairs to the Secret Garden, to think. In the crisscross shade of the grape arbor it was warm, then cool, then warm. Coughing— I always coughed on the first drag—I sent a burst of smoke up into the leaves. When I leaned back against the wall, the warm stone bit into my shoulder blades and spikes of ivy caught in my hair, which I'd skewered up into a bun with a pencil stuck through to hold it. The noise of far-off fireworks came over the garden wall like the sound of popcorn popping. I riffled the pages of *The Hite Report* until I found the photograph of Daddy and the piece of graph paper I'd taken from the kitchen table the week before. Carefully I unfolded it. Mom's list of jobs took up most of the back. On the front was my dad's drawing of the witch-in-the-hat and his beautiful curly printing. *Measure up kitch window, lumberyard, J. ABLE WAS I ERE I SAW ELBA.* From my shorts pocket I pulled the note about Clesta's furnace. These three things were all I had of him. For now. In my mind I called them The Documents. I laid them side by side on the gravel and picked up the knife. Old Bob's knife. I kept it shined and sharp. It showed how tough we were—me, my father, his father, who'd forged the blade himself, at the mill. How brave. I let my thumb rest on the cool, blue edge, and shut my eyes.

▼

In Chef Chan's Restaurant where we go on Fridays, a big stone gargoyle guards the cash register, smooth and shiny and black. Its head is studded with spikes, its mouth stretched in a wide snarl. It's the exact height of a four-year-old girl.

"Look, Lilly!" Daddy runs his palm over the black teeth like a row of arrowheads inside the curled-down lip. "They're sharp. Like real teeth. Feel."

My mother says, "Gort. She's too little."

My hand is shaking but it fits inside the gleaming stone snarl. Daddy's smile leaves my mother beyond its edge, in darkness. "Hey—that's my girl!"

▼

I spit on my thumb and rubbed it over the carved handle scroll by scroll. Careful how I touched the blade, I breathed on it, then wiped it across

44

my shorts. I thought, I won't give up or out, no matter how bad it looks. Dad had left my mother—who wouldn't leave such a coward! But he needed me. I knew he did. I wouldn't let her or anybody else talk me out of finding him. Able was I.

I slid the Documents back inside the book and wrapped the knife in its towel and squashed Doc's pack of Camels into my shorts pocket till I could sneak it back into his left church shoe.

▼

The tiled kitchen floor was dusty and cool under my bare feet. At the kitchen table Clesta, in a lavender muumuu printed with magenta roses, or maybe cabbages, rattled a street map. Doc stood at the sink chopping. On the counter next to him there was this shiny brass box with some kind of fancy carving all over it.

"Vine over to Lancaster, then down York," Clesta said to his back. "A Breast Man! Like something out of the Early Christian Martyrs. Just hacks them off all day long."

Doc said, loud, "Why, here she is, praise God!" He looked over his shoulder at me, then quick picked up the brass box and shut it in the cupboard. "How come you not totin' no book?"

I said, "Clesta? Where are you going?"

"Leave your great-aunt in peace," Doc said. "You forgot about the viaduck," he told Clesta. "C. H., why won't you let me drive you? Gonna be awful hard to figure out a way to Acton Medical. Why, that's clear across town."

When she drove, Clesta didn't like to turn left. She had her own special routes to and from places where she went a lot. The A&P; the hairdresser; Our Lady of Perpetual Help, where she sometimes went to Mass now even on weekdays, in a real dress and a hat.

"Where are you going?"

"Oh, just to the doctor, child. 'Tisn't serious." She didn't look at me.

"Plus," said Doc. The minnow-tongue flickered. "I worry that ugly old car'll break down. It was a dog, it'd be dead by now."

"Laurence's Buick is a handsome, solid machine," Clesta told him. "Your taste is all in your mouth. Up University to the First Presbyterian, then over. These days it's safer riding than walking. 'Tisn't a case of Walk and Don't Walk, it's Risk and Don't Risk, the way people drive these days."

She made a note with a stub of yellow pencil. I couldn't wait for them to give me an opening—I'd wait forever. I went and leaned on Clesta's shoulder. I actually snuggled. "Clesta. Daddy's been gone almost six weeks." I stretched it a little—really, it was four. "Don't you wonder where he is?"

The day before, I'd called the police. Despite what my mother likes to think, you can't just sit around with a hand over your eyes, hoping. The guy I talked to was useless, a real dweeb. When he finally got what I was saying—I had to take the handkerchief off the mouthpiece—he claimed they couldn't do anything unless somebody came down to the station in person and filed a report. I was over eighteen, wasn't I? I'd hung up on him. Obviously I needed a grown-up to front for me. My mom was out—in the first place, I didn't want her help, and in the second place, she'd just say to wait till he was ready. That left Clesta; but I'd have to ease her into it. I made my voice gentle. "Don't you think we should try and get hold of him? Just, you know, make sure he's okay?"

Clesta's pencil stopped. She looked up. Her eyes turned navy blue, the way they did when she was really ripped. The map skated across the table.

Then Doc was behind me, grabbing my arm. "Lord bless us and save us! You ain't got the sense God gave a gander!"

Clesta's head was wavering in those little half-circles. "Child! Why don't you move back here where Doc and I can look after you properly?"

"I'm not a child," I said.

Different-shaped jars of colored water lined the windowsill behind Doc, red and blue and green, like sourballs. I stared at them hard, willing the tears to stay in my eyes and not ooze out. I never cry. In Chem 1 we did the chemical composition of tears: mucoproteins, sodium chloride, sodium bicarbonate, lysozymes, plus some other stuff I forget. Tears have as much salt as blood plasma; you need that stuff in your body.

"And furthermore," I told Clesta, "you might be interested to know that people who wear purple a lot have a royalty complex. Illusions of grandeur." I'd read about this in Rhoda's mother's *Psychology Today*. I rubbed my arm. White stripes stood out against my tan.

Gently Doc pulled the pencil out of Clesta's fist. "Drink your tea now."

He gave me a mean look. His black face got shiny purple like an eggplant when he was mad. But he didn't dare say anything in front of Clesta. He went back to the sink.

Clesta said in a weak voice, "When's dinner? What's taking you so long?"

"Soon's I get this here together. Shape of a cat," Doc said. His fingers patted at the mound of raw chopped liver on the cutting board, but he was looking at Clesta. "This parsley here's for whiskers."

Clesta stood up, leaning on the back of her chair. "Topiary chopped liver. Well, Michelangelo, I'll leave you to it." She licked her index fingers and smoothed down her eyebrows. "And you stay out of trouble. Let us have no more frumpus," she said to me, and turned and billowed slowly out the door.

Doc called after her, "C. H.! You never finished your perfume tea."

A machine-gun rattle of fireworks came through the open window. I picked a crescent of onion off the cutting board and sucked on it. "I don't think Clesta ought to talk to you that way," I said to Doc in this respectful, sort of placating voice. Maybe *he'd* call Missing Persons for me.

He stepped up close and gave me a look mean enough to bend turkey skewers. "Lillian, you listen here. Leave your great-aunt alone. You don't fool me with your tell-me-a-story, not one iota. Your great-aunt's been sent trials you ain't even dreamed of. That sombitch husband— That husband of hers. After she had her breakdown, he used to come with a picnic hamper in his hand and sign her out of the asylum on Sunday afternoons and take her into the woods and rape—" His tongue flickered.

"I know what rape is," I said. I wasn't interested in stories about the MDH. I'd already heard from Gramma Maude how Clesta'd only married him to restore the family fortune, and how he'd died, thank God, a few years later, blah blah blah. "What's in the box?"

"Box?"

"The one with the designs on it. On the counter, before."

"Box? Box? You surely want to know a lot of things don't concern you." Doc leaned closer, and I could see he was about to tell the real truth about something, the way he always did when he wanted to scare me. "Well, you can stop worrying your great-aunt about her brother. Your

47

grandpa took a aluminum ladder out into a thunderstorm one afternoon, and the good Lord saw fit to strike him down with lightning. Nineteen-and-seventy-three, that was—no, seventy-four. In the fields over by Hellertown, where he and your daddy used to go lookin, for arrowheads."

I leaned away from Doc, who was breathing funny, as if he was about to have a hissy. Outside, the fireworks were getting louder. A rocket fell with a long, shivery, downward sound.

Doc said, "He'd no earthly reason to be there that day, and no use a-tall for a ladder. Draw your *own* conclusions."

So *that* was how. I did the math in my head. In 1974 my father would have been fourteen—the same age I was now. I tried to imagine how it would feel to have your father do that. It made me queasy to even think about it. I leaned further back, and my elbow sank into the pile of chicken liver. It felt disgusting, slimy and slippery, like worms. I grabbed the washrag off the faucet and scrubbed my arm.

Doc'd been watching my face. Now he pointed his knife at me. Chef from Hell. "The Good Book says, Look not upon the wine when it is red. Now you know, Miss Nosey Parker. You can leave your great-aunt in peace. She has got *enough* burdens to bear."

Bullshit.

I turned my back on him and left. What most people don't realize is how little anybody else cares what you do. I wasn't interested in Doc's secrets. I had secrets of my own.

▼

Daniel had my dad's tilted way of moving; he had the same thick, ginger-ale hair. It turned to colors in sunlight, the way my father's and mine did, like a bleached-out rainbow. Daniel looked so familiar, I felt as if I knew him like I knew myself. As if he were the brother I should've had. Or *been.*

My aunt and uncle had sent Daniel to Clesta's for what was supposed to be a couple of weeks, claiming he needed to get out of Philly and breathe fresh Pennsylvania mountain air. Then they just forgot him. My Uncle James was like that—not a mindful person, Clesta said; and my aunt wasn't Daniel's mother. She was James's fourth wife, or maybe his fifth—we'd all lost track. Clesta was happy about it; she liked having Daniel there and didn't care if James never asked for him back. So when I told him, finally, how this was longer than my father'd ever been gone before, how my mother was just letting him stay gone, Daniel got it right away.

Of course his first idea was that my dad was with a girlfriend. Just because *his* dad was a scuzz, I told him, didn't mean everybody's was. He got pretty ripped over that and didn't speak to me for a couple of days. Finally I had to apologize—bow down to his weird, wussy code of honor. After that, though, we were partners. Co-conspirators, like they say on the news. He checked out Clesta's place while I finished searching ours.

I found Daddy's old khaki fishing hat, not in the garage but in his place in the attic, inside a folded-up army blanket. All the flies were okay, not bent or anything, the flies Old Bob'd tied. I loved their names. Ambrose Bucktail Streamer; Golden Furnace Streamer; Bubble Pup (yellow and flossy with black wings—good for smallmouth); Gray Ghost; Lefty's Deceiver.

I wore the hat at night, with Daniel, after he got a job bussing lunch tables at one of those restaurants with a fake-Irish name and we couldn't go fishing anymore. In the evenings we went to his new friend Tim's to play Nintendo, or to the movies. Mostly we went for walks. We'd go across Broad Street to the Moravian cemetery (squeezing between the iron palings) and sit on the cool grass smoking and talking. In the quiet night we could hear the crickets; the traffic sounds were far-off, like the sound Gramma Maude's bees made inside the hive. When we ran out of conversation and cigarettes, we'd experiment for a while with tongue-kissing and touching, looking over each other's shoulder into the dark. I thought it'd be good practice for the real thing later. We never laughed at each other, not when I belched in the middle the first time we kissed open-mouth, or when Daniel pinched his finger in his own zipper, or when I started coughing and bit his tongue. We didn't go all the way. The Honorable Daniel wouldn't let us. Each time, we stopped short, but less short than the time before.

My mother'd always thought she knew what was going on with me; and up to now, she'd always been right. For some reason I couldn't stand to think that anymore. She was getting strange herself—she'd suddenly started wearing lipstick, old ones in these wussy colors like candy pink and tangerine—but she expected me to just stay the same old Reliable Lil. She seemed to worry even less about where I was than she did about where my father was. It was part of her way of hiding from things: don't ask questions, then you won't know, and what you don't know, you can't worry about. Like that saying of Clesta's: *What the eye doesn't see, the heart doesn't grieve for*. I'd stand at the front door wearing an Acid House T-shirt, and Mom'd smile and say, Have a nice time. She probably thought it was some new kind of Smiley Face, only neon green. Dad would've noticed—*What's that on your shirt, Lilly?*—would've seen its shivery freaked-out eyes. Maybe not this past year; but before that, before he got so quiet.

Daniel touched me so lightly. Gingerly—Clesta's word. Daniel touched me so gingerly that I learned not to flinch. He kept his sneakers on the whole time.

5

JUDITH

The men were putting in steel girders to shore up the sagging second floor. They had to start each one from outside the house, through a hole in the wall. I stood and watched an orange-painted beam threading in under the floor joists, like a giant knitting needle picking up dropped stiches. Then I buckled on the heavy leather apron Hop had given me. The pockets held wrenches and a hammer, a retracting metal tape measure, and two sizes of pliers, one needle-nosed. When I moved they clanked and knocked against my hipbones. The weight steadied me.

This morning I was supposed to weather-strip the doors. It was mid-July; in the three weeks I'd been working at the house on Schoener Place, I'd progressed from jobs like ripping up mildewed indoor-outdoor carpeting to real, if elementary, carpentry. The first week I was sore. I had to take hot baths every night, and Susie rubbed my legs with witch hazel and talked about growing pains. Then I started to get stronger, especially my arms, and now I hardly ached at all. I got the big mahogany front door off its hinges. Morning sun filled the doorway. I unrolled the aluminum J-strip and cut a rabbet the same width along the top of the wooden door-frame and down the latch side. ("It's a male-female thing," Hop had said the day before when he showed me how to do it, "you dig a channel, slot the stripping into it.") The warm, dark wood smelled like lemons. The silvery J-strip flashed in the sun. I got the power screwdriver out of the tool-box and started putting in the flathead screws. I was almost finished when Hop came up behind me.

"You measure that?"

"No."

He pulled out his tape measure and stretched it across the J-strip, then across the rabbet. I held the door steady against my thigh, remembering that this job was temporary, the word *tryout* loud in my head.

"Some eye. You're a lucky lady." He snapped the tape measure shut. "Next time, measure."

Eli came in from the kitchen carrying a short-handled shovel. "I put all the shit in the dumpster. The stuff that was in the fireplace. But I'm tellin' you, things're getting out of hand. Could even be one of those poultry ghosts."

"Poltergeist," I said.

Eli shot me a look. His eyes were as shiny as marbles. Whenever we worked in the same room, I'd feel those eyes on me, bright brown, what I called to myself the Burning Gaze. For some reason they made me think of Mrs. Muschlitz: about three-quarters of the way through Caesar's *Gallic Wars* she'd called me in after school and said, Switch to French. You'll never be a real Latin scholar—too much sex drive. Eli's eyes made me aware of how frizzy my hair got when I sweated, how baggy the seat of my jeans was because of the weight I'd lost—thoughts I hadn't had in years. Thoughts I didn't know what to do with.

"Naw, it's some sorta animal. Raccoon, maybe," Hop said. "What I can't figure out is how it gets in and outta here. We got everything sealed up tight—no loose boards under the porch, cellar windows all bricked in."

"There was stuff moved around in the kitchen when I came in this morning. Hammer and stuff knocked onto the floor." Eli went into the living room. "I mean, I look in the dumpster," his voice floated back to us, "I think I'm gonna see dead body parts in there on top of the old kitchen casings."

The radio came on. Dolly Parton sang wistfully about islands. Eli shouted, "Oh, Dolly!" The volume shot up.

Hop put one hand on the door. His fingers were skinned; they always were. "Fabric stripping just don't hold up. This here'll last a lifetime."

I looked at him. He said, "Anyways, a door lifetime."

Dolly Parton switched to wings and white doves. Hop moved his palm along the edge of the door. He said, "I knew a man once, was in love with wood. Somebody'd hire him to build a deck, say. They'd agree on so much for materials, so much for labor. Armijo'd build it fancier—bigger, more benches and planter boxes—and when he got money that was supposed to be for his labor, he'd go to the lumberyard and buy more wood. Cypress, redwood, clear cedar. He never had any money to live on. Let his house go, then his furnished room, his phone. Ended up living in his pickup."

This was the longest speech I'd ever heard from Hop. I murmured, "That's a shame."

"No, it wasn't. See, that was his passion. He lived his passion. White-collar folks don't understand. They got no compensation what it's like, no compensation whatever. You're workin' with something alive." Hop stroked the shining dark-red wood. "Am I right? I ever have a house of my own, I'm gonna build it all outta wood."

In the living room Eli yelled, "Don't she sound Irish? Straight up, now. She *could* be Irish."

▼

I'd taken the job because we were broke, the way I'd taken the job at Valley View two years earlier, the way the women I'd known growing up in Orient took jobs—to help out. A year and a half of Cedar Rapids Community College hadn't left me with a wide range of choices—not that it had mattered, until now, since Gort's and my life was so aggressively simple. We were out of step with the times, but I liked it that way. It felt safe. There were no malls in Orient, Iowa, even by the time I left at nineteen to marry Gort; the life I'd known before him had been the life—not bleak, but certainly spare—that my parents still lived. I wasn't suited for modern life, as I once tried to tell Ms. Grundy, who'd raised one skeptical eyebrow.

The job with Hop had seemed, at first, like one more stop-gap job, a job I'd have taken even if Gort were here, worthless except as a means of keeping our life together intact. But as the days went by, there were more and more things I liked about working at the house on Schoener Place. The chalky plaster dust that caught in your throat, like clapping erasers after school. The paper bags of big sixteen-penny nails, like sacks of little bones until you heard the clink. The feel of hammering—not pounding at all, more like urging, like rocking a cradle or pushing a swing: learn the object's rhythm, then match it. When you did, each nail seemed to give off light.

In school the only one of those springtime standardized tests I'd ever done well on was Spatial Relations. Good with her hands, my teachers said—the praise reserved for children who were likable but slow. (On the rare occasions when he got irritated with me, Gort would say, *You learn everything through your body.* But it was, I knew, the very thing he'd loved about me at first.) In the house on Schoener Place that was fine. Words weren't worth much there: Hop couldn't tell me what he wanted, only show me; I never saw him pick up a pencil except to mark the place for a nail to go in or a saw to start. And there was something strange: I never dropped things, broke things, bumped into things, on Schoener Place. At first I thought it must be just a new kind of impersonation. But no, the inside had an outside now; you could see Judith any Monday through Friday, pounding and sawing and sanding.

Little by little our life began to take on a pattern different from the one it had had. I went out every morning so early that other people on the streets walked quickly with closed faces, so early that Thomas slept on his wall without moving. When I crossed the bridge—it was easy now—the brown water held a trail of mist slowly erasing itself, like the wake of a single boat. I missed Gort then. But I was used to missing him, even when he was there. Not only me—it was that way with everyone who loved him. You never got enough of him, he was always out of reach, somehow. And how it made you want him, that out-of-reach part—*yearn* for him. Or maybe the yearning itself was what you loved?

By mid-July Gort had been gone five weeks. The longest he'd ever stayed away before was two. I would have worried more if I hadn't begun to be angry. He hadn't left enough money for this long an absence. Usually his boss, Arthur, another natural yearner, would have called before now to see if we needed anything (to see, really, whether Gort was back). Arthur didn't call; but it didn't matter. We were managing. Coming home on Friday afternoon, I'd stop at Kentucky Fried Chicken on my way down Broad Street. Hop paid us in cash, counting out bills as soft as quilting squares into my hand. About six o'clock Lacey would come by, stepping carefully over the layers of mail on the front porch (the spider web had gotten so big that the mailman refused to use the box), in her graying chenille bathrobe with Joey half-asleep under one arm. We'd sit on the living room floor with Lil and Susie eating watermelon pickle and sugary fried chicken (which Gort had never allowed in the house) from a red-and-white-striped box, and double-chocolate brownies that Lacey, boldly meeting Lil's eye, claimed were homemade.

In spite of the long, hard work days and having to deal with the girls alone, I felt free and light. As if Gort had breathed up all the air and occupied all the space, and now it was there, it was ours. It scared me that I could be so happy without Gort; I took refuge in anger. I told myself what I told Lil and Susie: that he'd be home soon. He'd step through the screen door at dinnertime as if he'd just come back from a weekend camping trip, expecting us to be waiting, in suspended animation. Well, we weren't. It was beautiful and comforting, this pattern that our life had taken on all on its own, and I let myself enjoy it the way you do something that you know will end. Every Friday, when I asked the henna-haired girl behind the counter for twelve pieces of chicken, she'd say, It's cheaper if you buy a dozen.

▼

After lunch Hop had me start removing the Roman shades on the second floor. This seemed like a comedown, and I was slow and sulky. As I dug a crowbar into the rust-clogged spaces between the brackets and the shades, I could hear the insistent, cheerful rhythm of the men's hammers from the kitchen below. The dust-brocaded shades were as heavy as rugs. In the master bedroom I grasped the thick, yellowed cloth and it crumbled away in my hand, sifted down onto the parquet floor like ashes. I sneezed. The room was dark, like Lil's room, and just as dirty. I began to worry about her, and then to worry about how I hadn't been worrying enough about her. My best time for worrying used to be in bed at night; but these days, after a long day of physical work, I fell at once into a deep, bland, dreamless sleep, the kind of sleep that comes at the end of illness.

Lil wouldn't talk about Gort, although I tried. She wouldn't say she missed him, or was mad at him for staying away. She seemed more interested in trying to upset me. First her clothes got peculiar—tight and shiny, shades of black (which I'd formerly thought was a single color), like Rhoda Vilardi's; I didn't say anything. Then she cut her hair off on one

55

side and greased it into stiff little half-inch-long spikes. Her soft, fierce mouth and the spikes and her chains gave her a kind of barbaric beauty. But I thought of the knife; when I checked, it was still under Lil's mattress. Maybe, I thought, it's just part of the outfit. Rhoda had been sent home from school in March for carrying a switchblade in her purse. Then this morning Lil had come down to breakfast in Gort's fishing hat, shapeless khaki stuck all over with flies his father tied, iridescent orange and yellow and bronze. She sat down at Gort's place. Oh, she knew me. In the shadow of the hat brim I saw she'd shaved off her eyebrows.

Yanking at the heavy cloth, my nostrils full of fine, peppery dust, I thought: I should do something. Try to talk to her—again—tell her again how taking care of Susie is a real contribution, even though she hates it. I leaped back, coughing, as the last shade hit the floor. I thought of Rhoda, nails and safety pins in her pierced ears and a necklace of bullet-casings around her neck. Once I'd seen her herd a spider all the way across the kitchen and out the back door rather than step on it. It was the tenderest kids, I told myself, who dressed like armadillos. And anyway, Rhoda was in Idaho. Lil seemed to have drafted James's middle boy as her replacement, a nice boy schooled by Jesuits and very shy, and her cousin. But then Gort and I were cousins. And by the time we married—at nineteen, both of us, far too young—we'd been having sex for almost three years.

I kicked the shades into one big, hairy pile. Standing on the little stepladder, I started unscrewing brackets and prying them loose from the blistered window frames. I did not want to think about how happy those three years had been, how deeply I had felt Gort's contentment. I went back to worrying about Lil. Babies were easy, they fastened onto your flesh with their little fish-mouths, and you felt such pleasure, till you almost asked, who was feeding who. But fourteen—didn't they need space between you and them, like the extra bit of fabric set into a garment at the seam, for ease?

I was picturing my mother hunched over her old treadle sewing machine and thinking the word *gusset*, when the sound started. A sort of unearthly wailing, muffled but terrible. I jumped off the ladder and ran downstairs.

In the kitchen Hop and Eli stood looking at the sheetrock they'd put up that morning. The anguished noises seemed to be coming from behind it. "Gotta get it off," Hop shouted. "Thing'll die in there!" They worked fast, tearing at the seams on either side with crowbars—they hadn't taped or mudded yet—and yanking the drywall off the studs. Nails popped out into the room like sparks.

The yowling stopped. Something shot through the opening and landed in the far corner where the stove had been. Landing, it looked like a cat in a cartoon—skidding on all fours, back arched, fur standing on end. Its body alternated orange and white like a poorly pieced quilt, with a dirty white ruff. It huddled angrily beneath the capped-off gas pipes. When I took a step foward, it ran past Eli out the back door and into the yard.

Hop stood wiping his shining head with his handkerchief. He hawked and spat into the plaster dust.

"Break," he said in disgust.

When I went out into the backyard Eli was standing by the garage. He stood with his back to the house, and his buttocks in faded, paint-stained overalls were neat and round, like two grapefruits in a sack. Watching him from the doorstep, I thought how nowadays the main feeling young men called up in me was fear. The narrow hips; the narrowed eyes; the haughty invitation—all used to beckon once, with their edge of danger, even though (or because) I'd never been with anyone but Gort.

Eli wheeled, still zipping, then saw it was me and relaxed. His thick plastic safety goggles were pushed up on his head like a World War I fighter pilot. He grinned. The little dark gap between his front teeth reminded me of how, in grade school, we used to paste a square of black duct tape over one tooth, wait our chance, then smile.

"Hey, Jude," he said.

"It's *Judith*." Those bright-brown eyes had been watching me all day; I put a hand to the bare back of my neck. My hair was scraped into two bunches with rubber bands, one above each ear, the style my mother used to call "swamps."

"It's a good old song," he said, unperturbed.

Old. "You should watch out," I told him. "There's a lot of poison ivy in those weeds." Hating how maternal I sounded, I coughed. I could still taste plaster dust.

Eli pulled a pack of Marlboros out of his overall pocket and tapped one out. "Come over here and talk to me. How come you never talk to me?"

57

He sat down on the lowest limb of the sycamore. Wincing, he pulled a hammer out of his back pocket and hung it in the cleft of a branch higher up. Near his head the wooden swing hung by its one rope. He thumped it, and it moved back and forth like a slow pendulum. Without actually deciding to, I found myself sitting down on the ground next to him. The earth was scuffed bald from generations of swingers' feet.

Eli rubbed his thumb over the filter end of his cigarette and dropped little sequins of ash on the ground by my ankles. "Hop won't like it if he sees you smoking," I said.

"Saint Hop." Eli's voice shifted up an octave into a mimicking whine. "A workman's life ain't nothin' but compromise. White-collar folks, they just don't *know*." The swing had slowed to a stop. He reached out and hit it.

"Hop's been really good to me. As far as I can see, he treats you pretty well, too."

"You been here, what, three weeks? Listen, Miss Apple-a-Day. He gets back a lot more than he gives. Like it says in the Bible—cast your bread upon the waters."

"What do you mean?"

He ground out his cigarette under one heavy workboot. "Check this out. He gets two smart, hard-working, and, in your case, grateful workers for the price of one. Have a Nice Day."

"But—he pays more than minimum wage."

"He pays us right around half what first-year union carpenters make."

"But we *aren't* union."

"Fuckin' right. Minute I get my little blue card, I'm outta here. I'm history." This time he gave the swing a good whack. It missed my ear by an inch.

"Hey," I said. But Eli was sucking his palm, his eyes screwed up in pain.

"What's the matter?"

"Sliver."

My mother used to say, Leave a sliver alone and it'll travel through your veins to your heart. "Here," I said.

He stuck out his hand. The fingernails were dirt-scalloped and there were bits of sawdust caught in the bright hair on his forearm.

I stood up to get a better grip. I clamped Eli's fingers in one hand and pushed at his palm with my thumb. His dark-blonde hair was right under my chin. I pushed my glasses up. The sliver was a big one, long and wedge-shaped, with the thick end embedded in the fleshy pad of the thumb. I put my two thumbnails together and pinched hard. Eli shouted "Ow!" into my ear, the sliver bounced out, and I said, "Done."

He kept hold of my wrist. His finger and thumb made a bracelet around the bone.

"Done," I said. "It's *gone.*"

His look was like some kind of weight on me. My stomach tugged the way it did in elevators, and I knew what he was going to do before he did it.

With his free hand he pulled my face towards him, bunching my chin between his fingers. His breath smelled like grass clippings from the cigarette. Into my cheek he said softly, "Wouldn't you like to sleep with me? Straight up—wouldn't you?"

"I'm *married,*" I said. I tried to pull away; his grip tightened just enough to hold me. He gave me a skeptical, amused look.

Inside the house Hop called out. Eli let go of my chin and reached up to unhook the hammer. "You're kind of like this place, you know?" He waited for me to ask how; but I turned and started walking back to the house. *Amused*—this boy. When we were out from under the sycamore Eli threw the hammer up over his head. It tumbled over and over like a cheerleader's baton.

"You're both under construction," he said. He caught the hammer— those rabbit-quick reflexes were good for something—threw it up again, then turned and caught it behind his back. Twirling the hammer in one hand, he went inside the house without looking back.

▼

Married.

The Sunday after the wedding we go with Gort's brother, my cousin James, to Tilghman Park. We're tired—we both work, Gort is still in school— and we throw ourselves down in the grass and sleep. In midafternoon, when we

wake up, James is sitting with his back against a chestnut tree reading *Future Shock*. Gort gets up. He has special balsawood pins, red and yellow, that he ordered from a catalog; juggling improves your concentration. The side of his face is marked with red crisscross lines from the grass. So far he can only manage three pins. James and I watch them float up, over and over, yellow and red against the blue August sky. They seem like part of the sky, part of the park. Lyre-necked geese shuffle through the mud along the shallow river; bees spill out of flower sockets; children run toward Frisbees, their voices chiming across the grass.

I think, I will never be happier than I am right now.

A small plane appears overhead, a skywriter, and begins to loop a slow, shining trail of white across the blue sky. Gort stops juggling to look. We all look. The plane glints like a darning needle, back and forth across the blue sky. We watch until it flies away. The word is NOTHING.

Gort keeps on looking up into the silence and the light, as if an answer might be found there. His face, its grass-printed cheek turned toward me, makes me think of the word "luminous." He is like something shining—beautiful, cryptic, out of reach—like the skywriter's slowly vanishing trail. I remember what he's told me, about how the stars are spinning all the time. How the universe is filled with dark matter, like a special kind of gravity, that surrounds the stars and holds them in place. Watching Gort's—my husband's—face, I feel my own heaviness. Steady, comforting, invisible—like dark matter. The luminous matter of the stars is what we see; but the dark matter is all that keeps them from spiraling off into nothing.

▼

Eli was nothing like Gort.

At four o'clock we quit for the day. It had been a long, hot afternoon—the crowbar kept squirting out of my sweaty grasp; the raw patch on my hand grew larger—but I'd hung on. I'd stuck with Latin, too, even though Mrs. Muschlitz was right, I wasn't very good at it. At ten to four Eli and I started putting lids on paint cans and glue cans, rounded up hammers and pliers and screwdrivers, collected lunch rubbish in a green plastic garbage bag. Hop pulled a puffy blue golfer's cap over his bald spot and said goodnight.

I was right behind him, picking at my workshirt where it stuck to my shoulder blades. A Bekins van rumbled heavily past. Down the street a child's voice sang, "Me! Hey—*me!*" When I looked back from the bottom of the path, Eli was still standing in the doorway. His face was in shadow. But the way he stood—the ready angle of his arms, the hips pushed out, the feet set firmly on either end of the threshold—made me think of Lil. I could still see her, at the age of two or so, when we'd been ignoring her all one summer morning: at last she came striding on fat bare feet into the middle of the Sunday papers and stood as Eli was standing now, hands set fiercely on her nonexistent hips, and shouted, "I want— I want— *somesin.* I want somesin!"

Eli came halfway down the steps and stopped, looking at me. He didn't say anything: just those eyes. Sunlight on his bare burnished shoulders made me shiver. I forced myself to turn and walk away.

Maybe, I thought, maybe it's me. Maybe I'm the one who wants— *something.*

TWO

6

JUDITH

It was two days after the cat was walled up that I found Mildred.

That day I stayed on after Hop and Eli left. I'd been tiling the kitchen counters all day; when four o'clock came, there was only about three square feet of backsplash to go. I liked to hang around after the guys had gone, wander alone through the house in the mellow late-day light looking at what I'd made: *my* baseboard; *my* weather-stripping; *my* counters.

I loved the glowing colors of the tiles, blue and scarlet and olive (they were Mexican tiles; apparently the owner's passion for authenticity stopped at kitchens). I liked setting them into the mastic one by one, exactly a knife-blade apart, liked especially going around the edges of things—the moment when each tile would either break where I'd scored it or wind up in the discard pile. At first my discard pile was pretty big; now, there were hardly any.

After I'd pressed the last tile into the wall, I ran the spirit level over the whole section. The bubble stayed right in the center of the tube. Hop would be pleased (he would check, I knew): one more job that he could safely turn over to me. One step closer to getting off probation. I scraped my trowel off and rinsed it clean along with the rubber float. While I scrubbed my hands with a nail-brush and Lava soap, I looked out the window over the sink. The low sun's rays caught in the elbows of the sycamore. A single bird sang one trill over and over, like the bell on a bicycle. I was tired, the good kind of tired that sings in your muscles. I dried my hands on the old undershirt we kept by the sink. The girls were at Lacey's for dinner; I'd go up to the third floor and watch the sun set.

In the second-floor hall I put one hand on what looked like a section of mahogany paneling and pushed. The panel slid sideways into the wall beside it, revealing a doorway ("pocket door," Hop had said when he gave me a tour on my first day), and I went up a steep flight of stairs to the attic that spanned the whole house. The four sides met in a peak overhead ("hip roof," Hop had said); there were big skylight windows set into the rafters on every side. They opened onto chestnut trees with shiny dark midsummer leaves that swung and glittered, filling the attic with green-tinted light. But the weird thing was, the room was full of dummies— life-size mannequins and parts of mannequins. The man who'd sold the place to Mrs. vande Zaag had been a supplier.

I sat down at the top of the stairs. The wrenches in my leather apron clanked. Around me, arms and legs sticking out this way and that caught the light, smooth and nude like peeled willow branches; it was like sitting in some kind of strange and magical forest. Under the eaves a male mannequin lay face up, in a sort of clearing, with a disembodied hand laid across its crotch. A female hand: the fingers were tipped with red nail polish.

In the shadows under the eaves, one of the dummies moved.

I sat dead still. My heart was up in my windpipe.

A voice said, "You're a sensible person. In my heart, I know."

It was a full, unhesitating voice. A woman's voice, and instantly I stopped being afraid. I stood up. Out of the triangle of shadow, around the corner of the table, came the woman with the eyepatch—the woman who'd led me across the Lancaster Street bridge that first day. Her white shirt glowed in the green light.

We met under the peak of the roof, in a narrow space between dummies. "I'll do-si-do with you," she said. We traded places. She was so short I could look down and see the zigzag of scalp where she parted her stripey hair.

"Please," she said, "do sit down," in a voice that suggested afternoon tea.

I said, "Are you—Mrs. vande Zaag?"

She had a laugh like climbing a creaky ladder. "Child. I am a squatter."

"You *live* here?"

"For the moment." She fished a man's pocket watch out of the neck of her shirt and held it out at arm's length, squinting. There was a scattering of little dark moles at the base of her neck, like seeds. She saw me looking and put a hand to her throat.

I said, "My name's Judith."

She stuck out her hand, and I grasped the long fingers briefly. "I'm Sunshine."

"*Sunshine?*"

"Well, okay. Mildred. Mildred P. Rust."

I asked how long she'd been there, and she said six weeks. The same length of time that Gort had been gone. She put the watch back inside her shirt. "I had my eye on the place well before that, though. Knew I'd be needing a bolt-hole. When Charley Rust starts tying you to your chair, you know it's time to leave. Leave him, leave the trailer. In your heart, you know."

She picked up a loose arm that was lying on the floor and stroked it. I could hear the late-day sounds of the birds and the voices of children playing in the street below. I sat there with my arms around my knees while the light slowly reeled in and the shadows thickened around the pale limbs of the dummies, thinking of questions I wanted to ask. What did she mean, tied her to her chair? What had happened to her eye? But the silence held a warning, like moments with my mother when I was little, the two of us sitting on the back stoop after dinner, tracking the pale-green cabbage moths that eased out of the spicebushes at dusk. I'd sit with my arms around my knees, careful not to move, so that Mama would keep on sitting, too.

On the floor beside me was a dead wasp. It looked perfect, wings standing out from its body like organdy. I was trying to figure out a way to harvest it unobtrusively, maybe slide it into one of my apron pockets, when the woman suddenly turned and made a sideways lunge. When she turned around again, there was the patchy orange cat that had almost gotten walled up alive, spitting and twisting. She got a hammerlock on it and turned it on its back. With one hand she pried open its jaws and began pulling out shreds of something white while the animal heaved and crackled. When she finally let go, the cat shot off into the eaves and disappeared behind a pile of pale arms and legs. The woman rolled the gooey shreds into a ball and threw it after him.

"Depraved appetite," she said. "Kleenex, paper napkins, toilet paper. Can't take your eyes off him for a minute." She seized an ankle in each hand. "I'm sorry you have to go."

"Listen—Mildred," I said. "We'll be on the second floor next week. As soon as the kitchen cabinets are in."

She swiveled on her bottom so that her back was toward me. The white cotton cloth of her shirt pulled tight across the top of her spine where it curved in what my mother called a dowager's hump.

I stood up. I didn't want to leave. I thought, I'll come back; I'll come up here and sit with her again like this. There was no reason I could see for Hop to know about her. Not, anyway, from me.

As if I'd spoken out loud, Mildred said, without turning, "Thank you. You're a kind person. It was a Christmas tree needle, if you want to know. Come again, and I'll tell you the story."

I left her sitting in the green dusk in the lotus position. I was halfway across the bridge and the western sky had turned the fizzy deep rose of cherry soda before I figured out what Christmas had to do with it.

▼

I didn't exactly decide to go to Eli's that Friday—I just went.

It was cold for the middle of July, and raining, a dense, slow rain. I'd never been unfaithful to Gort—never slept with *anyone* other than him—and I didn't think he'd ever been unfaithful to me. I knew how hard it was for him to be close to anyone; he couldn't have managed with anyone but me. I was family; and I was willing to pay the price in silence. In my case, yearning—hope, really—and the memory of past times had kept me constant. Even on this day, at first, that was true. I kept thinking of that day in the park right after we got married, of Gort trying to juggle. My mind held so firm to the picture of the red and yellow pins floating up and the white letters looping across the blue sky, that I didn't notice the rain until I'd gone half a block. I had to go back for my umbrella. Eli had told me the address of his rooming house—he'd left work early that day for reasons he didn't explain—and I walked the seven blocks from Schoener Place along streets that narrowed and grew shabbier. It didn't feel—not then—as if I were walking *toward* anything. More as if someone had handed me a list of my life, and this was the next thing on it. I hadn't stopped being certain that Gort would come back, the way he always did. But that was one world; this was another. On Immig Avenue the skinny frame houses rose steeply from the sidewalk, and the narrow street slanted steeply downhill; the whole effect, in the dark, wet afternoon, was like being dropped down a well. Slowly I climbed the wooden steps of number 324. One of the splintering double doors stood open. I went in, up two flights of dark, rubber-coated stairs, till I found the door with the EXIT sign nailed to it.

Eli swung it open before I could knock and pulled me inside and said, "Hey, Jude." Then he had both arms around me; and then, since the room was mostly full of bed, we were on the bed. We didn't speak.

His skin, from the waist down, was white. He looked as if he came apart at the waist: dark reddish brown chest and arms above, frog-pale legs below. He took his socks off last, standing on one foot then the other. I looked away from his short, stiff penis and turned my back. Wishing I could have come at night, when it was dark, I pulled my white cotton sweater over my head. I stood up and slid off my new tight jeans, and my underpants, with their washed-out elastic, came off with them. My pubic hair was flattened from the tight denim.

On top of the jumbled sheets and thin scrubby blanket we swiveled to face each other. Eli put out his hands and unhooked my glasses and laid them, very gently, on the table behind him without turning around. Everything blurred. Eli stroked the rough skin of my elbows. He fingered a purple-and-green bruise on my thigh. He whispered something I couldn't hear, or maybe it was just a catch in his breathing. Then he began to trace the flat little whorls of hair, one by one. I thought of warning him I might be rusted shut, from lack of use. I hadn't noticed before how big his hands were. One by one by one.

Afterwards he slept instantly, lying on his stomach with his face turned toward me and one white leg across my belly. Now and then a faint snore ruffled his lips. It felt good to be alongside another body again. The weight across my stomach held me down, like the lead blanket they give you for X-rays at the dentist's. Heavy and safe.

In the blue, rainy light the room was cluttered and bare at the same time. Without my glasses I could make out newspapers piled on the floor, clothes draped over the painted metal radiators, a single ladder-back chair.

On the far wall was a fireplace with one-by-fours nailed across the opening in an X. Some brick-and-board bookshelves stood on one side of it; on the other side was a door.

The leg moved, was withdrawn. Eli turned over and looked at me, his eyes slowly clearing. He propped his head on one hand, and smiled. Chiclets. Against the dust-rimmed curlicues of the dark wooden headboard, his hair looked soft and light. His bright-brown eyes seemed lighter too, and larger, the irises not brown but a tarnished almost-yellow, as if they were lined with rusty foil. He put his hands on my breasts where they hung on my ribcage like triangular flaps, from nursing. The nipples tightened, and he said, "Berries. No, beetles."

"Lil used to call them pincheons," I said. "My daughter. When she was little. I couldn't figure out what she meant. Finally I said, Show me, and she pulled up my shirt, and then I remembered. How when she was a baby she could be kind of rough and I'd always tell her, No pinching. I'd always—"

"Judith."

This time he made me keep my eyes open. He made me look at him, at us, the whole time. This time, I wasn't rusted shut.

Afterwards I lay with my head on Eli's thigh, at the crease where the hair began. His skin smelled the way your hands do when you're peeling potatoes. I remembered a dream I used to have over and over the summer I was fifteen. The summer my father and mother first sent me East to stay with Clesta, and Gort and I fell in love. In the dream I'm standing at the top of Clesta's long, curving staircase. I put my hand on the mahogany banister, and I begin to float down endless stairs. I sweep along, flight after flight, without my feet touching. Faster, faster—until finally I'm flying, connected only by the tips of my fingers skimming the smooth shining wood.

The ticking in my pelvis slowed. When I lifted my head, there on the pale flesh of Eli's thigh was a perfectly printed ear. Eli stirred but didn't wake. I pulled one of the blankets around my shoulders and got out of bed. The floor was cold. I couldn't see my sneakers. When I looked under the bed, there was such a welter of shoes there that I gave up and padded across the room barefoot.

The books, mostly paperbacks, were piled every which way on the pine boards next to the fireplace, everything from *David Copperfield*—an old high school text with doodling on the page edges in lead pencil that came off on my fingers—to *Marathon Man*. No clear clues to Eli's character, but he must have read a lot: there was no TV in sight. The bottom shelves held a set of the *Encyclopedia Americana*; POD–RAC lay open face-up. *Poltergeist*, I read, *a ghost that manifests itself by noises and rappings.* So he'd looked it up—I was surprised, and realized I liked being surprised by Eli.

The door by the fireplace led into a kitchen. It was a narrow alley with cupboards, sink, and stove all on one side; at the other end, a gray window shone with rain. The walls and cupboards were painted the shiny orange-yellow of schoolbuses. Underneath the window was a cardtable and two black metal chairs. I sat down in a chair wedged tight against one yellow wall and leaned my elbows on the skittery table. Its vinyl top held a ketchup bottle and three cans of scouring powder. One by one, I picked the cans up and shook them. They were all empty. I felt happy the way a child is happy, without asking why.

The window beside me reflected a woman in a red-and-blue-striped blanket like a shawl, with lips curving upward and rain-dark eyes. I leaned closer and looked down. Without my glasses, the yard below was a blur of white-starred wild blackberry bushes and weeds. A high board fence lined with rubbish cans separated it from a parking lot. On the windowsill was a small blue bowl full of what looked like polished pebbles, shiny black and dark gray. I put my fingers into the bowl. The stones were smooth and cool. They all had the same triangular shape; some were blunt, some surprisingly sharp. Falling between my fingers and clacking into the bowl, they reminded me of my mother's button-box, an old round Buttermints can, green with gold lettering. Every shape and size and color of button was there: small white ones off my father's shirts, rhinestones with silver shanks, cloth-covered ones that matched some long-ago dress. I'd plunge my hands into them, cool and clattering.

Eli came into the kitchen so softly I didn't know he was there until he picked up the other chair. He turned it around and sat on it astride, in his narrow bright-blue underpants. There was something like relief in the almost-yellow eyes as they rested on me. Relief that I was still here? He leaned his chin on his forearms along the back of the chair. "Hey, Miss Smiley Face. You like my sharks' teeth?"

"Your what? Oh." I took my hand out of the bowl.

"They belonged to my mother. Only thing of hers I have. She grew up on the Gulf Coast of Florida."

"Is she dead?"

"Nah. She ran off with somebody when I was a baby. My grand-mother raised me—she adopted me. Pop wanted it good and legal so my mother couldn't get near me. So, like, I'm my own father's brother."

Floodlights went on in the parking lot outside. Through the dirty lace curtains they threw a dim pattern of blossoms over Eli's bare shoulders and the side of his face. He looked at me with some kind of expectation. The old riddle ran through my head: *Brothers and sisters have I none / But this man's father is my father's son.*

This was somehow closer than sex, this conversation—closer than I'd bargained for. I looked away. A black ant crawled slowly along the windowsill. I picked up the blue bowl and held it in my hands. "Susie would love these," I said.

Eli felt my withdrawal, because he said in a loud voice, "Pretty fucked, huh, Smiley Face. I can handle it. Women don't stick? Hey, nobody does." One bare leg, pale and covered with fine blonde hairs, jigged up and down. "So, you want some wine or something?"

"No, thanks. Lil— My daughter only promised to babysit till eight."

I crossed the thin cotton blanket over my chest and leaned against the wall. The sharks' teeth fell through my fingers and clicked lightly into the bowl, cool and sharp as ice chips, one by one.

▼

At the corner of Church and Fogel, in front of Stefko Drugs, someone handed me a leaflet. My fingers closed around it automatically. The leaflet-giver, a girl in fatigue pants with a red umbrella, danced across the street toward a group of people getting off a bus.

I stood waiting for the light to change with the rain falling in my face (I'd forgotten my umbrella at Eli's) and my arms wrapped around my body, hugging my surprise that I could want something, and have it, and then be free to leave. Two black kids in windbreakers, laughing and punching each other in the arm, waited next to me. At my feet a rainbow of oil fanned out over the blackly shining pavement. There was the smell of exhaust mixed with wet tree-bark and cinders. I looked down at the damp, shrimp-colored paper in my hand. The front said, in large purple letters, "BEWARE of Religious Fanatics Handing Out PAMPHLETS"; underneath was a boy in a T-shirt that had "Fanatic" inside a red circle with a bar across it. I smiled down at the oily rainbow. I was happy.

When I got home, Lil had moved out. This time she'd gone for good. Her jeans and T-shirts, her telescope—everything was gone. I stood in the middle of her unnaturally clean room, stunned and terrified. Part of me was already thinking that this was my punishment for sleeping with Eli. Something made me feel under her mattress for the knife that I hadn't let myself think of in weeks. There was nothing but the dusty, blue-striped box springs.

7

L I L

Daniel was the one who found the envelope. Life is wicked unfair! It was a Thursday, the third Thursday in July; my father'd been gone for forty-five days. We were hanging out on my front porch the way we usually did afternoons after Daniel got off work. Our house was just about halfway between Brannigan's Restaurant and Clesta's.

Susie was trying to get Daniel to hear her catechism. I think she realized it appealed to his weird, wussy moral code. She picked up a book that was lying face-down under the rhododendrons and handed it to him. Then she got down on her knees and bent over and laid her forearms on the grass. She pushed down hard with her toes and stood on her head. Her hair spread over the grass in thin, greasy strings. She was wearing the same plaid shorts she always wore, and no top. Her nipples were the same color as the tanned skin on her bony chest.

"What are you *doing?*" I said.

"It makes the blood rush to your brain. Go on, Daniel. Ask me the first three pages."

Daniel opened the book, which was covered with a grimy brown jacket cut from a grocery bag. He looked at the flyleaf. "Whose book is this?"

"How should I know," Susie said. "I can't read cursive. Mine got lost, so I took that one. Ask me the first question of the first page. 'Who made you?'"

"Who wants to know?"

"Come on. Act right, Daniel."

They started in. Daniel could be Mr. Tender-Hearted with Susie; but me—the person he'd promised, a *solemn vow*, to help—he didn't do shit for. Even though he knew I was counting on finding some kind of clue. I'd given up on Missing Persons—there was no grown-up I could get to front for me, and anyhow I'd realized how he'd hate for strangers to come after him.

I skated one bare foot through the topmost layer of mail on the porch floor, not really hoping—I'd already been through it three times that day. I went and sat down on the top step and listened to Susie babble. My mother was such a hypocrite. I mean, she hadn't been to Mass herself in years, but she made Susie waste three mornings a week at Our Lady of Perpetual Help. The main thing *I'd* gotten out of catechism class was how holy and evil things came in sets. I mean, the Ten Commandments, the Seven Deadly Sins (PEWLAGS is how you remember those: Pride Envy Wrath Lust Avarice Gluttony Sloth), the Four Cardinal Virtues (I used to picture big red birds with halos). Having all those sets to concentrate on is wicked handy for *some* people; it lets them not see what they don't want to see. I'd quit going to church (Fallen Away, Clesta said, Lapsed) when I was nine. After that I spent Sunday mornings reading the *Star-Ledger* with my father, who was an agnostic but wanted us, Susie and me, to make up our own minds.

But the stuff was like some drug as far as the Honorable Daniel was concerned. He was Congregationalist, the same as most of the Hutchinses, and hadn't been exposed to sets and incantations and martyrs and other colorful stuff. "—to judge the living and the dead," he repeated after Susie in a dazed, solemn voice.

I said, "Hey. Want to play Slap Jack?" He acted like he didn't hear me. Cracked out on catechism, he laid the stolen book face down on the car seat and leaned back against the rain-streaked vinyl. Then he sat up again quick, as if someone'd pinched him on the butt.

"When you die, they fold your hands like this." Susie, lying on her back in the limp grass, laced her fingers together on her bare chest. She closed her eyes and pointed her toes. "Dead people have goose bumps all over."

Daniel wasn't listening. He'd shoved his hand down between the beige vinyl back and the seat and was feeling around.

"We need something to drink," Susie said.

She got up off the grass and went inside. Daniel kept on poking around in the car seat with his arm shoved in up to the elbow; finally he pulled out a thick manila envelope. My heart started going so hard I could feel it.

"What's that?" I said. I got up off the grass and went over and reached for it. Daniel jerked it away.

"Come on, Daniel. Give me that."

The wooden gate scraped open. My mother came into the yard. She was wearing the old green shirt that made her look like a Girl Scout troop-leader, but she had on new jeans that fit tight, and her hair was curled at the ends, the way she'd started doing. Before she got her dumb carpenter's job, she always used to pull it back in a braid, or two lame bunches, one behind each ear. Now, the way it brushed her shoulders gave me a queasy feeling. She had on her New Look, so out of it that she didn't see us at first, and she was wearing *orange* lipstick.

Daniel pushed the envelope into the front of his army jacket and zipped it shut.

"There's no more Gatorade." Susie came out of the house with her arms around a carton of milk and a glass bowl of blood-colored pears. She set them down on the cement walk at the bottom of the porch steps. I stared at Daniel, squinting to let him know I was steamed; but he wouldn't look at me.

"Hello, uh. Dan," my mother said. Then, to Susie, "Honeybug. Don't you think you should put a shirt on?"

Susie sat down next to Daniel and handed him a pear. She said, "Shirts are for girls."

"You are a girl," my mother said.

Behind her back, I got Daniel's eye. I made an "O" with both hands, for Really Big Asshole.

Daniel said he had to go, ma'am, and before I could figure out a way to stop him, he was down the walk and through the gate. Susie stood watching me, whistling through her teeth like a teakettle. My mother said, "Now, why did he run off like that? Have you girls been teasing him? Is he shy?"

Try light-fingered; try promise-breaking sleaze.

I watched Daniel walk down the street toward Heckewelder, flapping his ankles, and thought, I'll get it somehow; I'll make him give it to me. I stuck out one foot and pushed the milk carton. It fell over at my mother's feet, with the large red letters that said "Vrouw's (Rhymes with Cows)" facing up. At almost the same instant, the sun came out. My mother's glasses flashed in the sunlight—long, short, short—like a signal in Morse code. She stood still and looked at me, surprised, while milk seeped into the dry yellow grass. I brushed past her and went inside to start packing. I'd have to move back to Clesta's. Because I knew— I *knew*—that envelope was my father's.

▼

We met and stepped back, met and stepped back. The pull was like a fish on your line. At first all I could see of Susie was her dirty fingers with the nails bitten into scallops. On the next pass, her knees showed at the bottom. The sheet folded smaller and smaller between us until all of her was there. Her forehead, where her bangs stuck up with sweat, was all clenched from concentrating. I dropped the sheet into the wicker basket. We started on the next one.

"The rain it raineth on the just," Clesta'd said in her quoting voice half-an-hour before, floating through the living room with a teacup in her hand. Eleven o'clock on a Tuesday morning, and she was still in her nightgown and what she called (smoothing its peach satin folds along her hips) her *peignoir*. Pain Wear, she said. Susie, who'd come over after breakfast and just hung around, was watching a rerun of the Preakness with Doc while the Electrolux hummed all by itself in a corner. "Somebody ought to bring in the wash," Clesta'd said, her voice downshifting to normal, and looked at me.

In the Secret Garden the air felt heavy. When I unsnapped the wooden clothespins, the silk sheets slithered onto me. They smelled like grass. Susie and I worked in silence. I was thinking about the yellow envelope—the reason I was living at Clesta's now. I'd searched all the likely places in the first two days after I'd moved back in. The storeroom off the kitchen; Daniel's drawers (full of dirty underwear that smelled); the secret drawers in the cherrywood secretary where Clesta kept important papers. When I'd asked Daniel for it he'd said, What envelope. When I kept after him he got his holy look (*I'm it; you're shit*) and said it was sealed and he hadn't opened it, it wasn't addressed to him, and he didn't think I should either. He wouldn't tell me what he'd done with it. I was ripped—but I knew I could break him sooner or later. I had my strategy. Plan A was find it myself; Plan B, argue Daniel into it. If those didn't work, and it looked like they wouldn't, there was Plan C. Starting tonight, in the Moravian cemetery. Plan C for cemetery.

"Peacock piss!" Susie said, on the fourth sheet. "This is so fennamin."

"What is?"

"Folding *laundry*. A person could go bored to death." Third pass, and her face showed. She moved a wad of bubblegum from side to side in her mouth. "Wait, it's all whomper-jawed."

I pried the sheet loose from her fingers and backed up and unfolded it. Then we started on the pillowcases, and when those were all folded in thirds and thirds again, we took the basket inside. Clesta liked the sheets to go right off the line onto the beds; she said it was the next best thing to sleeping in a state of nature. *Silk* sheets? But if there's one thing you can't expect from adults, it's logic.

We made my bed last. I took the bottom, where the knife was. I showed Susie how to miter corners, and she smoothed and tucked, concentrating so hard that she forgot to chew. I could tell she'd come over to Clesta's because she thought she had something to tell me—she'd had this slightly swollen look all morning.

When we got done I swung my legs up and leaned back against the wooden headboard. Kitchen sounds started coming up from downstairs; Doc liked to bang pots and pans for a while first, like some kind of fanfare. Susie wandered around the room, picking things up and putting them down again, babbling shark facts. Such as, more people are hit by lightning than get bitten by sharks. Good thing I'd moved the Documents and my money doll to the top shelf of the closet. Not that $57.28 was enough to get me to any of the places on my list. And what if I picked the wrong one, and he wasn't there? I'd have to come back and start saving all over again, and without any babysitting money now that I'd moved out. The yellow envelope could have a letter from my father saying where he'd gone—a bus ticket, even a plane ticket—it'd looked fat enough.

The rain had started, little drops that ticked on the window like Clesta's clocks. A mosquito whined in my ear. Susie flipped through

Sweeper in the Sky: The Life of Maria Mitchell, then started picking over the stuff in my blue padded jewelry box. She took out a twisted glass bracelet and shoved it up her arm.

"Hey," I said. "You could break that." Mom'd brought it back for me from a trip to Orient, to see Grampa Eugene in the hospital, when I was eight. She'd hugged me first, not Susie who was two then and disgustingly cute yelling *Mama! Mama!* Not even Dad. Me—she'd missed me the most.

"Flamingo shit."

Since I'd moved out, our next-door neighbor'd been keeping an eye on Susie while my mother was at work. Mom trusted Lacey not to judge us because she lied all the time herself; but I'd seen her watching me, adding up the pluses and minuses. It's the most self-righteous people who tell the most lies. Look at Daniel. How would he know the envelope wasn't mine if he'd never looked inside? When I'd searched his room I'd found two copies of *Hustler* under his mattress. He was virtuous when it suited him, when it gave him a chance to watch people twitch, the same way he baited hooks when we fished. Well, no good talking to men, anyway; they never really listen. There were, as I knew from watching my mother with my father all these years, better ways to get their attention. I can't believe she thought I didn't know what went on during those Sunday afternoon naps they took together.

Susie was eyeing my telescope. "Don't even think about it," I said.

She kept her back to me, but I could see her take a deep breath. The Big Moment was here. "Doc says you and Daniel are both abandoned. He says, small wonder." She craned her neck to look up at the gunmetal crucifix over the dresser. "Kinky! You're gonna hate it if Clesta makes you go to Catholic school. You'll have to grow your eyebrows back."

"What are you talking about?" It was true that my Uncle James hadn't called or written; Clesta'd put on a dress with a waist and right-angled the Buick across town to enroll Daniel at Most Precious Blood. But my mother—

"The nuns make you say Please and Thank You to everything that moves. You have to give your own money to the Missions, to buy babies from pagans. Sit up straight. Fold your hands. Blah blah blah. Nuns suck."

"You don't know what you're talking about." I kept my voice steady.

"Mom says maybe you're gonna live here for good."

"Dumbface." My voice came out louder than I meant. "For the *summer*, maybe. It depends how I feel." I nailed the mosquito. It left a rusty pear-shaped stain on Clesta's lilac-printed wallpaper. My own blood, probably.

"Big whoop." Susie blew a bubble that looked as if it was going to be successful, then popped.

I got off the bed and went over and pulled the glass bracelet off her arm. I held it up to the window. In the rain-spotted light the metal strands in the center looked rusted. I thought of my mother's lipstick, of how she stayed out past dinner. My mother was—used to be—the most forgettable-looking person I knew, walking around the edges of a room in her mouse-colored clothes; but when she took off her glasses, her eyes were like Susie's, the color of mold on cheese. Then she'd rub the bridge of her nose and put her glasses back on, and you'd immediately forget. Not anymore. Now she was suddenly this *noticeable person*, with long hair and new black clothes—leggings, even. I hated that, my own mother's legs like that.

I dropped the bracelet on the floor next to the radiator. The wooden bottoms of my sandals stomped down hard.

Susie yelled, "Don't! Don't!" She was pulling at the greasy web of gum across her nose and chin. Her voice had that gulpy sound that meant she was about to cry.

"Go home," I told her. "You're acting like a kid."

"I *am* a kid!" She was steamed now, her face red and shiny under the gum. "What do you su*spect*?"

When she ran out of the room there was a funny-cornered bulge in the back pocket of her shorts—an old fake-silver bangle I'd never liked much. Dinner smells came up from the kitchen, roasting fat and something else that smelled like wet washrags. My feet kept on going all by themselves. They kept on stomping until there was nothing but glittering crumbs.

▼

Rhoda's last letter'd gone on and on about how sex could make you just totally lose it. So far the closest I'd come to sex—*real* sex, not the kind of fooling around I did with Daniel—was putting condoms on bananas in health class. But it crossed my mind that if our night-time sessions got good and heavy Daniel might get confused enough to give me what I wanted.

At supper Clesta told some long story about my grandfather, Old Bob, when he was little. How he was everybody's favorite and she and Gramma Maude could never compete with him so they competed *for* him instead, blah blah blah. I licked off my soup spoon and looked at my reflection in the silver bowl, my face pulled back from big fleshy lips like a camel's. I tried to imagine Clesta and Gramma Maude as little girls, but I couldn't. When Clesta stopped for breath, I tried to get her onto my father; but she said, You don't really know a person until you know them from both sides, their parents and their children. What about people who don't have any children, I said—*I* certainly wasn't going to—but she gave me her dark-blue look and went back to Old Bob. I stopped listening and concentrated on hiding as much eggplant souffle as possible under my potato skins. I'd gone vegetarian, to defend myself; but Doc was right behind me.

After supper I checked myself out in the long mahogany-framed mirror in Clesta's bathroom. There was my body from the knees up, in my zebra-striped bikini underpants and an old bra of Rhoda's with a lot of hooks-and-eyes. Extra Support, it was called—wasted on me. The flesh-colored cups hung down like flaps of tired-out skin. I twisted around to get the back view. Being too tall at least meant I had long legs. Just below the backs of my knees, the mirror ended. The curlicued mahogany baseboard ran right around the room, carved in this design like clenched feet. The whole place was more like a chapel than a bathroom.

Maybe I should shave my legs? I opened the carved wooden door of the medicine chest; but there was no razor. Just Bengay and iodine and Pepto-Bismol and a lot of prescription bottles with yellowed labels you couldn't read anymore. I opened a dark-blue glass jar of zinc ointment and smelled it. Instantly I saw my father on the beach at Bitter Lake, with his white-coated nose flashing in the sun. My stomach jerked. I couldn't afford to think about him now—I needed to keep my head clear for what I had to do. I stuck the cap back on and closed the door. When I'd redone my bangs, the clippers'd gotten too close; from the front, with the rest pulled back, I looked like a skin chick. I took out my ponytail and my hair fell down on my shoulders. The light from the stained-glass window behind me turned it blue. I pulled on an old cotton shirt of my father's and buttoned it all the way up. That looked kind of lame, so I undid the top two buttons the way Rhoda would. Then I thought about walking down Broad Street with Daniel, and I buttoned it again.

"Praise God!" Doc said when I came into the kitchen. He cleared his throat with a soft pigeon sound. "Thought you was in the *bath*tub again." The fancy brass box was on the counter beside him. He threw his dish towel over it. Right now, if he only knew, I couldn't've cared less what he was up to.

Clesta turned from the sink to look at the two of us, Daniel and me, standing in the doorway in identical buttoned-up white men's shirts. She knew something was going down.

Doc said, "Stay in there too long, your flesh shrivels up. Tips of your fingers get like walnuts." He held up one pink palm.

"You have her back by eleven," Clesta said to Daniel, as if he were my date. Actually he was going to Tim's to watch *The Terminator* on his VCR; I'd insisted on walking him there.

Clesta suddenly lost interest in us. She turned back to Doc. "It's time," she said. "Doc, it's *time*."

I thought she meant, time for Daniel and me to leave. But she was staring at the brass box.

We left in plenty of time to stop by the Moravian cemetery. Moonlight made puddles of milk on the gravel paths and the small flat gravestones shone like Clesta's Limoges dessert plates in the dark grass. I led Daniel to our favorite spot, under the stone angel. Its long, flat grave-stone made a good place to lie down. The grass was full of chiggers.

We unbuttoned our shirts and pulled off our jeans. Then we lay down side by side on the cool marble with our legs tangled together and kissed for a while. That was the part I liked best—the stuff with tongues. We'd gotten pretty good at it. Breathing hard through my nose, I could smell the grass, which must've been mowed that day. I had to fight not to sneeze.

Lightly—gingerly—Daniel squeezed my breasts.

"Go ahead," I whispered. He hesitated. "Go *on*," I said.

Daniel's hands moved across my shoulders and around to my back, then paused. He struggled with the hooks-and-eyes on Rhoda's bra while I stroked the coughdrop blister of his vaccination scar. Rhoda said always breathe into guys' ears, it makes them crazy; but I felt bogus doing that.

When Daniel got the last hook undone and put his hands where the cups had been, I said, real soft into his left ear, "Daniel."

"Huh."

"Give me the envelope."

"Huh," he grunted. "What."

He was breathing fast and loud. I lay back on the cool, smooth marble and he climbed on top of me. I could feel his penis through both our underpants, pushing down on my crotch like a fist. This was the part I didn't like.

Daniel started bumping up and down. In the sky behind his head, thin clouds slid by. I squinted and the moon blurred like the bowl of one of Clesta's consomme spoons. Daniel's nose hit my collarbone.

I said, "The envelope. The one you found in my yard."

"What. Enve—lope." His pelvis banged mine, bone against bone. His breathing went faster, louder. *Huh ahuh ahuh*—the sound the joggers make, running by you on the Boulevard. He sounded almost ready. But something weird was happening. My stomach felt fizzy—not my stomach, but lower down. I tipped my head back. The angel spread her white wings against the dark-blue sky.

Suddenly Daniel held himself up off me with his arms.

"Go on," I said into his ear.

"I gotta—stop," he panted. But his pelvis kept on going. I arched my back to catch it—not me, my back arched itself. Like fishing—something my body knew that I didn't. Something our *two* bodies, rocking up and down, back and forth, knew. It felt scary, as if the gravestone was the top of a wicked tall building, and rocking too far would take us over the edge.

I pressed both palms against the cool marble and wiggled myself free and sat up. Daniel's round butt in the white underpants kept on going up and down as if I were still under him. I didn't want to see it. Rhoda's bra hung from one arm; I turned my back and started untangling it in the dark. The night noises came back from wherever they'd been—the swish of traffic out on Broad Street, the ringing of the crickets. Daniel grunted and flopped down onto the gravestone. He just lay there. Little bugs spurted up from the grass around my bare feet. I couldn't see them but I felt them.

I was pissed at Daniel for holding back; but I was relieved, too. Coward, I said to myself. Wouldn't a person do whatever she could, whatever she had to, to find her own father? Lamestain! I wadded Rhoda's bra up and threw it into the dark. By the time I got my shirt buttoned, Daniel was standing on one foot on the marble slab, pulling on his jeans.

▼

I couldn't've been gone as long as it seemed, because when I let myself in and went up the stairs, Doc was still in the kitchen. I'd been going to get the whetstone on my way past and work on the knife; but I could hear him moving around. I stopped on the dark landing outside the kitchen door.

Doc stood at the sink with his back to me. He was wearing saggy blue-striped pajamas, and the curlicued brass box was on the counter beside him with its lid open. Only the light over the drainboard was on. I couldn't see what he was doing. Maybe it was the warm-milk-with-cinnamon routine he and Clesta went through when her insomnia got really bad? But the smell wasn't like that—more like burned toast.

I stood and watched. Doc's elbows kept moving. His hands were busy doing something in the sink, on the drainboard, inside the brass box, back in the sink. Finally he tucked the box under his arm and reached up and pulled the chain. The light went out. I backed down the steps and waited in the curve of the banister until the voice of the Late Night Preacher started coming through his closed door.

"He's a mind regulator. He's a heart fixer. God from Zion." The words oozed out like drops of cod-liver oil. The volume went up louder. "God made a *heaven*. And God made a *earth*."

The deep, shivery voice followed me into the kitchen. All there was was a few charred scraps of paper in the metal sieve at the bottom of the sink, and two wooden matches.

"Uh-huh, man *never* has knowed. As much as God."

The paper was blue and had a funny feel—tough—like skin. I thought I saw something in the ashes, thin and glittering, like a needle; but when I pulled up the sieve it disappeared down the drain. There was only paper and a lot of ashes. That was all.

8

JUDITH

Rain. It seemed to rain every time I went to Eli's; and that was strange, because it was the driest July in decades. There was a fire-watch on the mountain, where the trees were all brittle and the creek beds dry.

All the lipsticks I'd ever owned I kept in the bottom of the bathroom cupboard. They stood in rows like toy soldiers, next to some old baby shoes so small they fit in my palm, scuffed, with gray laces that looked sucked-on. Before I went to work I'd reach in with my eyes shut, and whichever lipstick I touched first, that was the one. Strike Me Pink, Desert Blossom, Fire and Ice. I'd stroke it on until the bathroom mirror gave me back a frizzy-haired, serious woman whose mouth didn't belong to her. I'd put the tube in my pocket; and if I went to Immig Avenue that day I didn't bring it home again. I set it on the glass shelf in Eli's little medicine cabinet.

It was always Eli's; never the high bed under the eaves.

Once Clesta, talking about her terrible dead husband, said, He had me in thrall. She said that, thrall. It sounded like something large and soft, thrown over you, comfortingly warm until you tried to struggle out of its folds. Laurence had one arched eyebrow; after he died, Clesta went to see, over and over, the movie in which an Italian waiter with an identical eyebrow turned for an instant, arched, and was gone. She said the word "passion" meant suffering, as in The Passion of Christ.

It wasn't like that with Eli. Between him and me it was simple hands and hair and skin. He held still for me—that was my power over him. All his—not violence, exactly, but almost violence—became a kind of suppressed vibration all over his body, like a shudder running just under the skin. For me. I loved his thighs, which were large for his height and muscular—round and hard, like a hog's back. I loved the way the pale hair grew on his red-brown chest and his white stomach, my tongue tracing it

86

from where it started under the flat, dark-rose nipples, grew in from the sides, dovetailed neatly down his belly until it stopped at his thick, stubby penis.

Times when everything worked, I lost myself, was whirled down into the pleasure of it, into my body—oh, when it worked! At the Allentown zoo there was a white peacock, lush and cold, its whiteness holding colors captive like water under ice, until it spread the gleaming fan of its tail. When it worked, our lovemaking was like that. Each time, Eli would cease to be Eli; I would cease to be at all. Each time, it was the way it used to be, long ago, with Gort. *You learn everything through your body.*

The other women, past and maybe present, all had children. Not Eli's, but could have been. "Just a roll of the dice," he said, showing that he didn't know the first thing about parenthood. He liked me to talk about the girls. What's, uh, Lee up to? How much was Suzanne's take last week? He liked a house with children sleeping, their milky smell, the sound of their breathing. Sometimes when he talked like that, two vertical lines would appear between his eyebrows and for a moment he'd look much older than the twenty-four or -five I assumed he was. He'd sound older, too, and I'd find myself feeling under the bed for my shoes, wanting to leave. Eli would tease me about having had my way with him ("Don't you know it's rude to eat and run?"); but then I'd catch him looking at me with that expression he had, the old Burning Gaze converted into a look of *waiting*, like the first time, in the schoolbus-yellow kitchen, when he'd told me about his mother. Afterwards it always frightened me that I'd felt in some way closer to Eli than I'd ever been to Gort. Gort had talked to me about the stars, the nesting habits of the barred owl, the cold, pure beauties of topology; but never about his mother or his father or his father's death. Eli's other women protected me then. I didn't think about them, or (sometimes) even really believe in them; but their existence must have reached me, because after that first time, I made Eli use a condom.

I liked it best when we didn't talk. When Eli fell asleep immediately after and lay with some part of himself on top of me, or his whole body sometimes. That lead-blanket safety, after the small neon flash of fear when he entered me. I never thought of Gort then. Eli was a world apart from Gort, and I was a different person there. While Eli slept, I lay there happy and thoughtless. Learning the wallpaper, squinting to make out its rosaries of once-pink flowers that came in five dim, reassuring patterns. I lay and waited for the pleasant ache of sex to fade, while the rainy, blurred blue light slowly left the room.

I was careful not to let myself fall asleep—because what if I dreamed, then, of Gort? The two worlds would have come together. So I never slept, with Eli. I could have said exactly where each pattern started to repeat.

▼

Later, going home, I'd feel as if I were entering someone else's house, my feet echoing across the empty floors. I'd sit down on the back stoop by the bridal wreath awhile before going to face the girls; that was when I'd think of Gort. I'd remember the early days, wonderful days, when Gort and sex and love and my own body were like newly discovered planets, dim and beckoning.

The year after I started high school my mother began sending me to Clesta's for the summer. It was just after my Uncle Bob's suicide, and I felt at the time that it was somehow connected with that; years later I understood that those years were the time of my mother's deepest withdrawal. In those long summers we became the stand-ins, Gort and I, for Clesta's dead brother, and for the children she'd never had, as well. We were brother and sister, Gort and I, to Clesta's way of thinking.

But not to ours. Gort and James had moved with their mother to a little house on Saucon Street that my uncle's insurance paid for, with just enough left over to let my Aunt Eulalie spend her days inside it reading books on how to mourn. In the long summer evenings Gort and I would wait for her to fall asleep, then take his dead father's car. Gort didn't like it, but I made him; I was discovering my power to make him do things— things he would never have done with anyone but me. It was marvelous, wild, exhilarating. As if there were other, secret rooms to him, and I was the only door. The only thing Gort wouldn't—couldn't—do was talk to me. I didn't know what he felt about anything that really mattered. About us, or about his father's death. Did Gort see him in dreams, as I did—my Uncle Bob—running into the green light of a summer storm, the flash like a giant light bulb exploding, the body afterwards, charcoal bones, eyes like cinders?

There was a dead-end street near the train tracks that was always empty after dark. Gort would roll the windows up and lock all the doors. The Dodge, almost new then, had a front seat that was an unbroken expanse of slick, sliding sky-blue leather; the pleasure we gave and received there made everything else unimportant. We had no idea that everyone didn't have what we had. We didn't know what we had. How is it that what exists so purely and completely in our bodies has to be named before it can be known?

Once we were going at it pretty heavy, when another car suddenly appeared on the deserted street. Keeping its lights on, it began a series of maneuvers—backing up a few yards, stopping with a jerk, going forward; whenever it stopped, a white arm would come out of the window. Then the lights would go off and on, off and on. While we watched, this happened several times, growing more sinister with each repetition. I could feel Gort trembling when he stretched across me to check the door on my side.

Then I realized. "It's a driving lesson," I said. But Gort had already started the car and shoved the gear shift into first. After that we went to the river instead, where girls stood twined around their boyfriends, motionless as ivy, against the iron railing—a maple, a couple, a maple, another couple—in the warm summer dark.

Because we didn't know what we had, we didn't think to protect it. Gort had been my cousin before he was my friend; my friend before he was my lover. Gort had been my family, always. We didn't need to talk, the silence of families held us. Perhaps we could not have broken it even if we'd wanted to. There was never any decision—the one real decision every girl comes to—never that jumping-off moment when you ask: Let him come close? Gort saved me, so I thought, from that.

▼

I made up my mind to go to Clesta's—to try and make Lil come home. It was the last Monday in July. Lil had been at Clesta's for more than a week; Gort had been away a month and a half. I'd stayed in one world. Gone to Schoener Place; bought groceries and wheeled them up the hill in our stolen wire cart; paid the phone bill; gone with Lacey on Wednesdays to Lamaze class, where we both took breathing lessons. That had always been my role: I was supposed to be the one who stayed. *Yet when the other far doth roam, / It leans, and hearkens after it.* But, more and more, there was relief in Gort's absence, and a kind of rest. The longer he was gone, the more the yearning for him—the longing that had always been there, even when he stood right in front of me—the more the yearning eased. It scared me to think about that. Lil and Gort gone, Susie and me staying—our family divided in fact the way it must have always been divided underneath, like a fault line opening. How could I not have seen it before? Gort always with Lil, taking her to the zoo, the Observatory, camping at Bitter Lake, just the two of them.

When I got to Clesta's, the heavy outer door was unlocked; in my sneakers I went quietly up the carpeted stairs. Dread made me stop for several minutes on the kitchen landing.

I hadn't been to 110 Wesley in a long time. It had never been easy to go there, once Gort and I were married, not even at family gatherings: the not speaking, Clesta's three-cornered strategies for communicating with me, Tinker to Evers to Chance, Gort used to call it. It got so he would just go over there alone, or with Lil. In the last few years, as Gort went there less and less, 110 Wesley gradually became Lil's place.

Now, standing outside the kitchen door with one hand on the cool mahogany banister, I wondered if Lil even needed me. Maybe it was better to watch and wait, let her have her head, the way I'd always done with her father. Who was I to say what either of them needed? But I was here now; I would try. I walked up the short set of steps to the dining room.

They were all still at breakfast, all except Daniel. Doc sat across from Lil taking one of the quizzes in *Redbook* (Is Your Skin Too Oily? How Good a Friend Are You?). The Racing Form was spread out next to him. At the head of the table, Clesta, always a slow starter, sat in her peignoir staring down into her boiled egg. Lil was reading a book covered in the dustjacket of *War and Peace*, way too big for it.

I coughed and rattled my lunchbox. They all jumped. Doc half rose from his chair. Clesta looked at Doc. Lil's face went through a fast slide show of expressions—surprise, dismay, fear. I realized she was afraid that I'd somehow persuade her to come home; that meant there was a chance that I could. She looked down at her egg. Her freshly clipped hair looked like a band of Velcro above her forehead.

Doc cleared his throat. There was a mumbled set of good morning's—Lil's had to be frowned out of her by Doc—and then he said, "Sit down now, do. I'll fix you a egg."

I used to hate everything about those eggs: the smell; the way mine had of suddenly caving in, so that its insides leapt out and slopped all over my saucer.

While Doc was in the kitchen, we sat in silence, the two egg-contemplators and I. Everything was still the way it had been when I came every July on the Greyhound bus from Cedar Rapids. Uncle Laurence's furniture darkened the room and imposed a kind of hush, like church. The big oval dining table with its smooth, reflecting surface; the sideboard displaying two squat blue-and-white china jars the size of a two-year-old child. (Gort hated those jars; when he was little, Doc used to threaten to shut him up in one.) Lyre-backed chairs stood around the sides of the room, as if many more guests were expected. The walls were hung with dark, shiny paintings of dead birds and saints. ("Well, Judie," my mother had said when I'd told her I was going to become a Catholic like Clesta, "none so zealous as the convert.") I let my eyes rest on the photograph of Michelangelo's Pieta.

Lil said, staring hard at my mouth, "You're wasting your time coming here."

"Eat now, Lilly-Lil," Clesta told her. "You hardly eat a thing. You'll get sick, and then where'll you be?"

Doc set a plate down at the place where I stood. "C. H. is right. They's a good many strands of the flu goin' around." He sat down and shook out the Racing Form.

"Eggs are really little coffins," Lil said. Then, still looking at my mouth, "I'm not going back."

I sat down next to Doc and rubbed the lipstick off my mouth with the back of my hand. Did I want this cold, stern daughter back? I tried to arrange my face to look as if I did. *Qui fidelis est in parvis.*

"Lil." Why was it always so hard now to find the right words, with her? "Why don't we go down and sit in the garden. I just want to talk to you. Don't you think you owe me that much?"

Doc said, "Hey! Untangle Me is runnin' at Aqueduck again. By Entanglement out of Solicitor . . . odds 5 to 2? Who do they think they're foolin'?"

Lil said, "I have nothing to say to you. Nothing whatever."

The ticking of the grandfather clocks in the next room dropped into the sudden quiet. I knew I had to be very careful, had to say the one right thing, or Lil would close up. She pulled Doc's *Redbook* across the table and sat frowning into it, chewing on the end of her braid, as if she'd forgotten me; but a softness at the corners of her mouth, where yellow bits of egg yolk clung, said she was waiting. Waiting for the one right thing. Doc pulled a red pen out of his shirt pocket and started marking up the Racing Form, his eyes flicking back and forth between Lil and me, making sure we meant Clesta no harm. Clesta studied her egg. I studied the stone figures of the Pieta: the weight of his long body across her knees, holding her down; the bony arm dangling. When I was little I'd thought the two figures were man and wife.

Suddenly Gort seemed truly gone. In this room where I hadn't been for so long—where I hadn't been without him—he was freshly absent. The yearning came back with such force that I had to hold onto the edge of the table.

Doc reached around behind him for the large brass-handled tray on the sideboard, old pages from *Godey's Ladies' Book* under glass, and started loading dishes on top of the bustles and pompadours and twirly lace parasols. When he'd finished he elbowed through the swinging door into the kitchen, where we could hear him singing over the noise of the faucet.

> I and Satan had a race, Halleloo, Halleloo
> I and Satan had a race, Hallelujah

Clesta sighed, a long breath outward, and her shoulders in the lavender silk relaxed. One by one she picked up the pills lined up on her linen placemat, put them into her mouth, closed her eyes, and gave a violent shake backward. Then she took a swallow of tomato juice. Each time her head went back, her throat looked naked and vulnerable, as if someone held a knife there. The long cords of muscle stretched, quivering, into the hollows of her collarbone. Yet there was something predatory in the quick backward snap of her head. What kind of bird is it that steals other birds' young and raises them as its own? I understood suddenly how Clesta had taken Gort, after his father died; how she'd tried to take me, that summer when I was fifteen. *Wouldn't you like to come and live here?* (showing me the lovely room with an extra bed for girlfriends to stay over, a television set). *Keep an old lady company?* And my mother had agreed, had sent me summer after summer, until Clesta found out about me and Gort.

Clesta saw me watching and said irritably, to Lil, "Old people take pills. That's what they do. Just like young folks take cod-liver oil."

What young folks did was hold the glass dropper over the bathroom sink every morning and put three careful, molasses-colored drops into the drain. If I could catch Lil's eye, she'd know what I was thinking—we'd both be thinking the same thing—and we'd laugh, like we used to. I watched her squeeze her eyes shut and suck the last of her egg off the spoon in one swallow. Then she opened her eyes and smiled at Clesta, and Clesta smiled back.

It isn't any use, I thought. Lil would never come home now, and I didn't have it in me to force her. I thought, There's nothing I can do. Yet somehow I couldn't make myself leave.

Lil pushed back her chair and stood up. "I'll be in my room," she said sweetly to Clesta. "Just yell if you need me."

Doc paused in the doorway with two bulging garbage bags. "Back in a minute, C. H."

"Hey," from my suddenly soft-voiced daughter, "I can do that."

They started down the stairs, each holding a green plastic sack by the neck. Doc was singing to himself in a low voice. *Satan mount de iron gray, Halleloo, Halleloo.* Chinky and I trailed along behind.

In the little vestibule Doc took the second green sack from Lil and went outside. Lil turned, but she didn't start up the stairs. She stood waiting, her back in its blue cotton shirt tense, expectant. Her eyes were green and glittery. I realized it had been months —five? six?—since I had seen her cry.

"Lil," I said, "come home, honeybug. We miss you." The blue back waited. "We'll go"—the blue shoulderblades tensed—"away somewhere, the three of us, go to Atlantic City—" Not right, the back said, and I knew what it wanted me to say—that we'd go and look for him—but I couldn't say it. I tried again. "Lil, I know you miss—"

"*You* don't, though." She turned around. Her eyes had gone blank and shuttered, like her father's. She was looking at my mouth again. "You don't miss him. One less thing to worry about. Well, now I'm gone, too. I'm staying here."

Out in the little courtyard Doc's voice rose in song and garbage cans clanged. Chinky backed into the boot cupboard beneath the stairs.

Lil looked so much like her father, standing there with her arms folded across her chest and one shoulder hunched forward. My heart squeezed up and made a fist. My whole body wanted to get out of there, out into the air, into the muggy summer morning. When I tried one last time, my "Lil, honey" came out sounding like I didn't much care.

She looked me up and down, once, slowly. A little contemptuous smile tugged at the corners of her mouth. She said, "You'll be late for *work.*"

My palm tingled with the urge to slap her. In the courtyard Doc sang,

Satan mount de iron gray, Halleloo, Halleloo
Jesus mount de milk-white horse, Hallelujah

Lil turned her back. Closing the inner door behind her, she banged it so hard it bounced off the jamb and stayed open. I could see her crouch down to pull Chinky out of the boot cupboard. "Coward," she said softly. "Coward."

▼

Lil stands holding the coffee can. Her red parka is bright in the snowy cold; her hair shines. She is four, or maybe five.

She found the bird lying next to the morning paper. A chickadee, tarnished and gray with cold, the kind of bird you never find in gutters. The kind of bird that goes somewhere else to die. In the warm kitchen, we laid it out on the linoleum, noted its clenched feet, its cracked beak, the dull shell of its eye. Lil wrapped it in an old undershirt. She fed it, prodding the lifeless head with a spoonful of oatmeal, of milk. She crouched down with her behind in the air and her cheek on the floor by its head, and she sang to it.

A, B, C, D, E, F, G
H, I, J, K, L, Elemento, P

It was hours before I could persuade her that the bird was dead. Finally she let me cut a brown paper shroud from a grocery bag.

Now she looks at me fiercely across the yellow plastic lid of the coffee can. Her eyes say it is my fault. Underneath the cinders and old frozen snow, the ground is hard; it rings against my shovel. My fault my fault my most grievous fault. *The cold air is like iodine in our mouths.*

No, she says afterwards. Her hair crackles with electricity when I put my hand to it. She will not help me put out birdseed for the other birds. She will have no other birds.

▼

I turned onto Broad Street thinking of Lil, ten years into the past, and tripped on a big maple root that had cracked the sidewalk in front of Irving Trust. My knee hit the pavement. When I pulled myself up, Thomas's eyes, small and close, looked straight into mine. He crouched on the cement ledge in layers of dim sweaters tied at the waist with rope, poised as if he were about to jump. Pin oak leaves clung to the front of the topmost sweater. I changed my mind about sitting down for a second and walked on.

Hop and Eli were working on the upstairs bathrooms. The fixtures—toilets, sinks, bathtubs, everything—had had to be removed while we redid the floors with fake turn-of-the-century tile, a pattern of interlocking pieces shaped like chicken thighbones. Now the floors had been grouted and sealed and the fixtures had to be put back.

"You're late," Hop said when he saw me. "You finish this, and Irish can help me with the tub." He handed me a big lump of wax shaped like a collar. "You can't lift the toilet, give a holler."

"Wait a minute," I said. But he was already clumping rapidly down the hall. Guessing, I set the collar around the top of the hole and pushed and pulled at the gummy yellow wax until it seemed to fit. The feel of it made me think of honeycomb from my mother's hives. I walked the toilet across the floor and heaved it up onto the collar. It was something to do that took my whole body. I stopped thinking about Lil and Clesta and just did what I was doing. I got two Stillson wrenches out of the toolbox and was lying on my back with my face under the tank, trying to tighten the union, when Hop and Eli came back with the old claw-footed porcelain tub. They let it down outside the door with a thud. I squirmed to sit up, banging my head on a corner of the toilet tank.

Eli slapped the side of the tub. "Hey, Jude. How do you like this baby?" The two men stood leaning against the doorframe.

Eli's way of dealing, on the job, with the fact that we were lovers was not to deal with it at all. He acted the same as before; the only thing that might have given him away was that the Burning Gaze had died down to a smolder. Sometimes when I felt him looking at me I'd stand still for a second, savoring the amazing joyous novelty of being the one who is wanted. It was as if there were two completely separate Eli's. There was the Eli (Irish) I knew at work; there was the Eli I lay beside in the dim blue room on Immig Avenue. The two were as different as sun and rain. And why not? Weren't there two of me—Judith of the blue room, and the Judith I was everywhere else?

Eli kicked the side of the tub with his heavy workboot. "Reminds me of this house I took a tour of in Philly once. Real old place, a museum. Real ugly. Everything was curly or had feet or noses or something. The door knocker was this hyena head."

"Let's go," said Hop.

I pulled my legs in and sat with my arms around my knees while they trundled the tub into place. They had to tip it to get it under the china handles that said Hot and Cold in blue script; its porcelain paws scraped the new pea-green-and-salmon floor. I thought of Clesta's little chapel of a bathroom.

"It's ugly," I said. "And there's no shower."

Hop sat down on the curled-under edge of the tub. He'd started a beard—to make up for his bald head, he said—and the lower half of his face looked as if it had been dipped in sugar. "Looks're never the whole story." He looked sideways at me. "Take Irish, here. Old as he is, he gets himself up to look like a juvenile delinquent. But the women're all over him like a herd of locusts. Am I right?" He turned toward Eli where he stood leaning against the wall and pulling on the lobe of one fleshy ear. "Tell me, am I right?"

Eli said, "This town is nothin' like Philly, though."

In the afternoon I countersank nails in the upstairs hallway while the men worked on the wiring in the master bedroom. A smell like burning leaves filtered out into the hot, airless hall. The head of the nail-set was as broad as the face of my hammer; I couldn't have missed if I were blind. It was just clank, clank, clank. It left my mind too free, and what I thought about was Lil's face when I came into Clesta's dining room. What I thought about was the way Gort's absence had become suddenly, briefly, real; and whether, even if I wanted to make him stay a ghost, I *could*. Untangle Me. My hammer bounced a little every time it hit, as if the nails were punching back. I couldn't find a rhythm that fit.

In the bedroom they turned on the Phillies. Eli said baseball was too fucking slow; Hop said it was a contest of skill, a real man's game, and if he hadn't bet so much on it he'd have had himself a house long since. He said your baseball man was a real philosopher. "Lookit Sparky Andersen. What's was is Was; what's *is* is Is. Hey, the three greatest Americans of all time were Abraham Lincoln, Woodrow Wilson, and Sparky."

I kept going, inching my way along with a miserable clank, clank. Eli came out on his way to the bathroom and stood watching. Finally he said, "Wait till Mr. Wonder Bread finds out you used galvanized nails."

▼

That afternoon I stayed late, to make up the time I'd lost that morning—something I'd never bothered with at Valley View. I did it now whenever something happened, like Susie making a fuss about being left with Lacey, to make me late. I didn't want to lose this job.

Whenever I stayed late, I'd wander around the house awhile, looking at my work, then go up to the diamond-shaped room at the top of the house. Sometimes Mildred was there; sometimes there was no sign of her. The roof windows were always open onto the chestnut trees, a mass of floating green. Some days we sat and watched rain collect on the slanting panes and drip off the rim into the leaves; mostly the low late-day sun filled the room with green-spangled light, as now.

Today Mildred sat in front of an open window with her back to me. Her body was like a bell: head bent, arms tucked in at the sides, the small hump rising at the top of her back. Over the white shirt she wore a sagging sweater knitted from yarn that changed color every few inches—a kind of yarn I hadn't seen since my mother's long-gone knitting days. Its blue-yellow-red-green stood out starkly among the shadowed clay and ivory limbs of the mannequins. She heard me and turned. Her eyepatch, which I always forgot about, gave me a twinge of surprise.

"Judith," she said. "Why, yes, Judith," as if I were the latest in a long stream of callers.

I sat down beside her on the paint-spattered floor. She smelled the way Gort did when he'd been off camping for a while, a smell like boiled cabbage, and the beautiful striped hair was greasy.

I held out a crumpled brown paper bag. I'd taken to bringing food whenever I came up here—bologna sandwiches, granola bars, a peach, a thermos of red wine.

She opened the bag. "You brought me a real glass," she said, and smiled. She pulled her watch out of the neck of her sweater, consulted it, then dropped it back down. The paper bag she folded carefully in thirds.

Nothing had been said about poltergeists for a couple of weeks. Maybe the men had gotten used to finding rubbish or worse here and there; maybe they'd decided it was just an occasional visitor from the streets south of Schoener. Whenever I tried to suggest to Mildred that her time there was shrinking, she evaded me. She had a method that wasn't changing the subject so much as never lighting on one in the first place. Conversation with her was a kind of patchwork in motion. I'd tell her bits and pieces of my life, past and present, and she'd tell me bits and pieces of hers. Sometimes one seemed to be an answer to the other.

Last time, I'd told her about Eli—why, I didn't know and didn't ask myself—and now she said, "I saw that boy of yours yesterday. Out back peeing on the garage."

"Mildred! You shouldn't even be in the house while they're here. Are you crazy?"

"Charley Rust used to talk to me about sex, about his *needs*. I'd tell him to go hang it on a clothesline."

It had taken me a while to piece together Mildred's story. At first I thought it was her husband, Charley Rust, who'd tied her to a chair; but it turned out he was dead. Her son, Charley Junior, was a guide on the buses to Atlantic City, the ones the gambling casinos ran. He was divorced, three kids, no money, which (as Mildred put it) was why he'd had to kidnap her and force her to babysit. Though he wore a stomach supporter, he never got any tips, because people were out of money by the time they got on the bus to go home.

Mildred peeled back the wrapper from a granola bar and bit into it. "Charley Rust used to say, Better a dinner of herbs where love is, than a stalled ox and hatred therewith."

"Verbs? What've verbs got to do with it?"

"*Herbs*. A dinner of herbs. It means, better to have the food be not-so-hot and the company you eat with be who you want. Dinner of herbs. Where love is. It's too—silver. Charley Rust likes that kind of thing, too. Stuff like *All my life long* and *Not a day goes by*. He'll put a record on the old record-player that belonged to my mother, the kind like a big black morning glory that you have to wind with a crank. He'll play those old records over and over. *Just a gigolo—Everywhere I go*. Sad, gaudy songs." She put the last piece of granola bar into her mouth and started sucking the sticky crumbs off her fingers one by one. One shiny seed clung to the skin at the base of her throat, like a new addition to the little constellation of moles there. "And all the time he had a mistress. In my heart, I knew. A woman practically the same age as me. Why doesn't *she* mind my grandkids?"

"Couldn't you have called the police? Or Social Services? There's such a thing as elder abuse."

"She drove a big green car, carpeted all over."

Before I left I ought to try one more time. "Mildred. We've already started on the second floor. The first floor'll only take another week or so—two at the most. They talked about working on the siding while the weather holds, but it might not." Mrs. vande Zaag insisted that Hop finish the whole inside first, then do the outside, except for the foundation work which he and Eli had done before I got there.

99

"First-off, after he passed on," said Mildred, ignoring me, "I went to live with my married daughter. Charley Junior phoned all the time, threatened his sister. I moved in with my school friend in Delaware. Charley Junior sent flowers FTD. You know what men *really* want?" She stretched out one arm and slapped the pale buttock of a reclining dummy. "You make believe you're a sweet-smelling do-nothing who sits on a cushion all day. All the while, unbeknownst, you're toting groceries and scrubbing toilets. The Donkey Princess. Scraping and scrubbing out of sight somewhere, where they don't have to know. Then come the flowers, la-dee-dah."

While she talked, the light receded down the large room; bit by bit it left the cheeks, necks, limbs of the dummies, as if it were slowly being peeled away. After-dinner sounds came through the open windows: the growl of lawn mowers, the high, sharp voices of children.

Mildred used her teeth on the cellophane around a box of raisins. "Your ex, was he the kind always buys American cars?"

Suddenly I wanted to say his name to this person who didn't know a thing about him. "Gort doesn't buy *any* cars," I said. "We've had the same car ever since we got married. Before, even. It used to be his mother's."

"How come you split up, then?"

"We *haven't* split up. He left for a while, like a vacation—sort of. He went away two months ago and he hasn't come back."

Mildred clicked her tongue. Her one eye shone with sadness. I could see she thought I'd been left in the usual way, lost him to someone with a bigger car.

"Some raisins?" She rattled the box at me.

I shook my head and got up to leave.

"Oh, if he knew I'd told," she said happily. "Oh, he'd gnaw his knuckles."

9

JUDITH

July was nearly over. There were whole days now when my new life felt as if it had always been my life. As if Gort were one of those all-American disappeared fathers who divorce their children along with their wives and go off somewhere, fathers-in-theory, their biological job done. As if Lil were a daughter away at boarding school, too absorbed in her own unfolding life to phone home. All the time, some part of me knew that it was fragile, this world I'd constructed, this one world—a bubble inside a bubble, like diagrams of the fourth dimension in the books Gort read.

Lil had resigned as babysitter on the day she moved out. While I worked, Susie spent the days at Lacey's or stayed in our house watching soap operas while Lacey kept an eye out across the two yards. Catechism class kept her busy in the afternoons; she'd cut so many after-school sessions during the year that the nuns, who were always harder on public school kids, hadn't let her make her First Communion with the rest of the second grade in May. The further away I slipped from the Church myself, the more important it seemed to give the girls a chance to believe. Lacey didn't mind babysitting as long as I replaced what Susie took, which I did every payday, wondering why Lacey didn't just hide her purse. I didn't ask her. She was touchy all the time now, with the testiness of late pregnancy (nine months of premenstrual tension, was how Lydia Kobayashi, the Lamaze instructor, put it); she'd stand on her porch holding the top of her stomach and abusing Paul, who was somewhere inside. "Oh," she shouted one evening, really furious, "I'll just fucking *outlive* you!"

After the first week Susie'd started going around with wads of cotton in her ears. "Joey yells," she said. "He yells all the time. And he's smeary."

"Shhh," I said. "Lacey'll hear you." We were standing on the front porch.

"I tell him, You are the snot-nose of the world. Hey—this looks like the cheese on a Domino's pizza." She poked the spider web that draped the mailbox. By now it had swallowed the head of the tin eagle and nearly covered the flag in one outstretched claw.

"Don't, Suze. Leave it alone."

"In Egypt they pull the brains of mummies out through their noses. *Ancient* Egypt. Mom—how do you flirt?"

The low sun came through the broken lattice and fell in ragged diamonds across the porch floor. I scuffed through the mail with one foot, pushing at supermarket fliers and white-sale ads. "I don't know," I said. "I never really did any flirting. I think you smile a lot and blink and look interested."

"Lacey says it's like starting a avalanche. She says only nignoramuses think they can play with fire and get off stocked free."

"Lacey likes to hear herself talk."

"*Is* Lil a nignoramus?"

"She's just talking, Suze. Come on—time for dinner."

"You don't tell me *anything*. Jesus H. Christ."

"Susannah!"

"Peacock piss." She flicked the spider web.

"Leave that *alone*. Go inside and wash up. And put a shirt on."

Susie pushed the cotton back into her ears and squinted up at me. With her chin thrust out, her eyes green and glittery, she looked suddenly like Lil. *All right*, I'd thought the week before, after I'd gone to Clesta's, *if that's how she wants it*. I'd remembered the knife: Lil could take care of herself. I would stay here and hold onto what was left.

"Go on," I said, more gently. "We can have the Hungry Man fried chicken ones. You can set things up in front of the TV."

She took her hands off her hips and went inside. I heard the TV come on, loud—Susie liked to compensate for the uncertain picture— and then the lilting, grisly voice of her favorite newscaster.

As I was nudging the shaky silver trays into the oven, the phone rang. It had been shut off for so long that I wasn't used to it anymore. My heart leaped as if an alarm had gone off.

It was Gort's boss at Bethlehem Steel.

"Judith? Good evening. I hope I'm not calling at an inopportune moment?" That was the kind of language Arthur used, courtly, hopelessly old-fashioned, like Arthur himself. The company had to keep him on because he was a relative. He loved Gort, and so they kept Gort on, too. Of course it helped that, in exchange for a fragile and limited freedom, Gort worked cheap. He'd never worked for anyone else.

I reassured Arthur; and he began his stately progress through the usual polite questions—my health, the children's (he remembered their names), the weather. I held the receiver a little away from my ear; it always seemed strange, talking to someone I couldn't see. The disembodied voices made me feel cut loose, unanchored. He'd tried to call a few weeks earlier, Arthur said, his voice oddly apologetic; but the phone had been (he hesitated) nonfunctional.

"—then, you see, Judith, difficulties arose. The production people were in a quandary. I hated to bother Gort when he was busy, er, busy with his own projects—" and he launched into a long, technical description in which the word "hydraulic" was the only one I recognized. On the wall by the phone Susie had taped drawings of Cat Houses—two-storey houses with upper windows for eyes, triangular ears instead of chimneys, whiskers around the front door. I ran my finger around and around the crimson nose of a yellow Cat House while Arthur talked on. In recent years lithium or something like that had made him calmer but less interesting—ironed him smooth. When we first married he used to call Gort in the middle of the night with incomprehensible stories of attack and pursuit. Because he was the one Arthur turned to, the only one who could save him from his terror, Gort never had the heart to cut him short. I thought of our first night in this house: Gort standing naked at the telephone in the dark kitchen—I'd forgotten to have the electricity turned on—while I held up the cue cards I'd made for these occasions, pointing my flashlight at each one. *More in Morning! Goodbye. Someone at Door! Goodbye.* Gort patiently shifted the phone to his other ear and leaned against a carton. I could see the movement of his thin ribs; his penis in its shadowed nest of hair trembled lightly. I shined the flashlight on my last card. *Fire! Goodbye.*

Then I heard what Arthur was saying, heard it very clearly. They'd fired Gort. Fired him weeks ago, almost two months ago.

"—and I wanted you to know, Judith, how very sorry I am. My influence is sadly diminished, I fear. I shall find retirement something of a relief. You'll tell me, won't you?"

"What, Arthur? I'm sorry—tell you what?"

"Whatever assistance I can render, I should be happy— I shall miss him greatly. And now I must say goodbye."

"Wait!" But the low, courtly voice was gone.

While I was standing there with my hand on it, the phone rang again.

My mother's "Judie?" had its usual peremptory sound, like a doorbell. "How come we never hear from you anymore?" Her voice sounded far-off, farther off than Iowa, as if she'd already started thinking about something else by the time I picked up the phone.

"Hello, Mama. Hi, Dad." The line had that velvety plumpness that means an extension is open somewhere. My father had to be on the upstairs phone; but he didn't answer. He wasn't one to give himself away.

"How's Susie? Lil? Gordon?" my mother demanded.

"Fine—fine." One out of three, anyway.

Susie came into the kitchen. She pulled a piece of paper and a pencil stub out of the string drawer and began carefully printing, leaning on the kitchen counter.

My mother was sewing or darning something as she talked. Her voice clicked on and off, like a bad connection, when she licked the end of the thread or bit it off. I pictured her shiny-knuckled grip on the needle, the tiny stitches so fine they won prizes. My father listened in silence while my mother and I had the same conversation we always had, brief because of her conviction that long distance should be reserved for tragedy. The farm was falling apart; the tenants didn't care, renters never do; my father's health was worse.

"Uh-huh," I said. "Uh-huh."

Susie handed me the piece of paper and left. It said, SEE WHAT HAPENS WHEN U PAY PHONE CO. There was a Mr. Yuk face at the bottom. Out in the living room the TV went up. *At least FOUR people are DEAD and over one hundred INjured as a gunman raged through Winston Alabama today.*

"Scriabin," said my mother. "I'm working on Scriabin now. Chopin got to seeming too tinkly."

All the time I was growing up, my mother had held a grudge against music because it had trapped her into farm life (and not even a real farm—tenants worked our place while Dad sold Travelers Life & Casualty all over the tri-state area). My father had first seen her playing a Bechstein grand in the window of Geiser's Music Store, in a blue taffeta dress; he used to say he'd picked his wife out of a shop window. They married. A dozen years went by before she touched a piano again.

Sources CLOSE to the President say he had FULL KNOWLEDGE of Foster's acTIVities.

"Judie, I don't believe you've heard a word I've said." My mother's voice was thin and cold: an Iowa morning in winter, on the way down to the schoolbus. Air that glittered like ice-coated wire fencing; my eyes would water and my eyelashes would freeze. They'd snap off, *ping, ping,* in the deep cold.

"Sorry," I said. "So, how's Dad?" Realizing too late that probably we'd already been over that.

"Judie," my mother said. "He had a *heart* attack. Put Gordon on."

"He's not home."

"Not home? It's dinnertime there."

"He's—away."

"What? What's that? Cough if you have to."

"He's on a business trip." My head ached from too many disembodied voices. I was angry at Gort for making me lie, all these lies. But I kept my voice firm and bland. My mother had been known to read my mind, when she was tuned in.

"Your Aunt Eulalie died because she wouldn't cough. Choked to death on a sliver of lamb bone in the Lehigh Club dining room. Wasn't he on a business trip the last time we called? How come he has to travel so much all of a sudden? Don't you miss him? You—and the girls?" *Ping, ping.*

"It's more money," I lied, inspired.

My mother sighed loudly in agreement. "Nowadays, you break a five-dollar bill at the grocery store, it's gone. Loaf of bread, carton of milk, gone. Why, this last time your father was in the hospital, they sent us a bill for fourteen hundred dollars. For a twenty-minute *procedure.* Do you imagine Medicare will pay that?"

Time to take a look at the WEATHER. Gale-force WINDS with possibility of tornadoes —

"So. Are you coming or not, Judie? He won't last forever."

There was a click on the other end of the phone. The connection thinned out to just my mother and me. Guiltily (this was my father's second heart attack), I said, "I'll come for a couple of days. As soon as I can get a Friday off. Maybe next week." As I spoke I felt a sudden unexpected longing for the farm: the smell of grain, like sunburned skin; the chill, pink sunrise. In that light, I thought, I'd be able to see clearly.

After we hung up, I went into the living room. Susie's bare brown back, where she sat on the floor in front of the TV, was suddenly so dear to me; I wanted to get down on the green rug beside her and put my face against it. Instead I said, "When I was little, know what I thought? My grandmother came to Iowa for a visit, and when I was told she was my mother's mother, I burst into tears, I was so mad. Till then I'd thought that all the time I was growing up, my mother was growing *down*. Until finally I'd be the mother and she'd be the child; and then we'd start all over again in the opposite direction. Like a seesaw."

"Uh-huh," Susie said. Her eyes never left the screen: the news had been replaced by the nightly *MASH* rerun, which she loved the way other children love the Muppets.

"How about studying your catechism? Don't you have a test tomorrow?"

"I know it already. Why-did-God-make-you-God-made-me-to-know-Him-to-love-Him-to-serve-Him-in-this-world-and-to-be-happy-with-Him-forever-after-in-Heaven." She settled back down on her stomach.

I took my headache out onto the front porch, where I could hear Lacey's stereo playing the Beach Boys. The sun had nearly set; rosy light struck the Chinese lilac and lit up the spiny brown skeletons of blossoms I hadn't picked. I took deep breaths of the mild evening air. Lightly, with the tip of my finger, I touched a strand here and there along the outer edge of the spider web. Gort told me once that a spider's filament is spun from water. No matter where I touched it, the whole web shivered—a balance as precarious and powerful as a family.

I was angry and frightened. I fought the urge to tear it down, pull the whole thing off and throw the gummy mess into the peonies. How could Gort not have told me? "Projects of his own," Arthur had said. Maybe

Gort had said he was going to start his own business. They'd fired him and he hadn't even told me. Hadn't trusted me enough to tell me. But the thing that frightened me most was that I wasn't really surprised. Arthur's call, like my mother's, had told me something that in my heart, as Mildred would say, I already knew. Knew, and didn't want to know. How long could I go on holding our new life together, against such incursions?

An earwig fell into the web from somewhere. Instantly the spider appeared, dark and shiny as shoe polish, with long jointed legs like fingers. The earwig broke loose and started thrashing toward the edge of the web. I watched the spider throw a lasso of sticky, clay-colored filament. I watched the earwig struggle, swaddled tighter and tighter, until it was a creamy bundle, and the head snapped off in the spider's jaws.

▼

Eli lay on his back, not touching me, one hand curving gently around his slack penis. I lay beside him with my legs as straight as his, looking up into the soft blue blur of the room. I hadn't figured out a way to tell him I wouldn't be around for four days. Looking sideways, I studied his hairline. At ear and temple, the start of the hair was quiet, gradual, as soft and pale as the hair on his belly. The beard on his smooth full cheek surprised my hand as if a peach had sprouted bristles. He opened his eyes and said, "This is how we'd lie."

"What?" I said.

"On our tombstone."

Rolling up on one elbow, he held my breasts and studied the veins, leaned closer and smelled them. He ran a fingernail tenderly along the edge of my shoulder; then he was on top of me, and there was the anticipation of pleasure, like the flicker of a small bright fish, and then I lost myself. "Do you like this," he said in a hoarse whisper, coming into me from behind, settling his body on top of mine until we lay perfectly aligned. "Do you like this," face-to-face with my legs propped on his shoulders. "Do you like this," running his wet thumb slowly along the vein in my forehead while I came. Rain slid down the windows. When he fell back onto the sheets, we both slept.

In my dream I came into a white-swathed room, a room with doors and walls and windows all draped in my mother's bee-veiling like huge drifts of cobweb, white and luminous. In the middle of the room stood Gort. He was wearing his red plaid shirt with all the pockets and his old khaki pants that had one knee torn. He didn't speak. He turned around, and sticking out of each hip-pocket was a stalk of lilac. They burned, a deep vibrating blue-violet, in the white room.

My own snoring woke me. I eased out of bed without waking Eli and padded naked into the little bathroom. In the mirror over the sink, my face looked tarnished, or maybe it was the rain-pocked light from the one small window. When I turned my head, my shoulder smelled like Eli, my skin the same as his if I closed my eyes. He said I looked better with my clothes off than on; and I knew, despite what the cold glass of the mirror showed me, I knew that for him it was true.

I opened the medicine cabinet to make the mirror go away. The hinges squawked. There was the row of my lipsticks, eleven of them counting today's Strike Me Pink. The side of a box of Tampax (not mine; but not new, either) said A MESSAGE FROM THE MAKERS OF TAMPAX TAMPONS.

Eli called out to get dressed, we'd go out back and pick blackberries. I sat on the toilet. My body felt good all over, newly discovered, as if each cell had been separately warmed and burnished. My urine made a joyful noise on the porcelain. It was the first week of August, Eli shouted over the rush of water; they wouldn't wait much longer. He'd gotten it into his head that he had to have a berry pie; nothing I said could discourage him.

"All right," I said finally. I closed the medicine cabinet and came out of the bathroom. "You need a jacket, though. It's cool out, and really wet."

I hooked my spectacles over my ears and stepped into my new soft cotton underpants, then started putting on the rest of my clothes, retrieving T-shirt and sweater and long flowered skirt from where I'd thrown them earlier. My pelvis was still ticking. *A message from the makers of the female body.* Eli pulled on a dingy olive green cardigan, catching his shirt-cuff in his fingertips the way a child does before he thrust each arm into its sleeve. One shoulder of the sweater was torn; the blue of his workshirt showed through. "I had this great bomber jacket, black nubuck, but it blew away."

"Blew away?"

"In the hurricane last spring. I'm going out the door, see, tryin' to get it on, and the wind whips it right out of my hand. Three seconds, it's down the block and around the corner. Even if I'd still had the Harley, I couldn't've caught up with it."

In the narrow yard there was a smell of soot and wet leaves, and the iron light of late day. The rain had stopped. Eli set a tin scrub-bucket down in the lush weeds by the fence, where blackberry bushes as tall as I was filled the gaps between boards. The berries were big and not quite ripe; their segments were shiny and hard, like the backs of black ants. They dropped into the bucket with little thumps until we'd covered the bottom; then they made no sound at all. We squatted in the weeds, plunging our arms into the wet, splashy leaves. Rainwater darkened Eli's little tail of hair. It clung to the back of his neck like a question mark.

"Aren't you gonna ask what happened to my bike?" he said after a while.

I hadn't been. It seemed wiser—prudent, Mildred would have said— not to learn too much about Eli's life when he wasn't with me. There were things like the Tampax box; and other things, more sinister— several hundred-dollar bills tucked inside his copy of A Separate Peace; a green-and-yellow cardboard box that said "Remington .38 Special, 158-grain lead (+P)" in the bathroom wastebasket. Better not to know, I told myself, and did not ask.

He was looking at me, the almost-yellow eyes held that waiting look. "Okay," I said finally. "What happened to your motorcycle?"

"Somebody splashed it, last November. Whole shed where I kept it burned down."

I watched my hands moving in and out of the dark-green leaves. Thorns stung my wet skin.

"Things got kind of gnarly there for a while. I was playing cards with people I shouldn't've. Owed the wrong people money."

I thought of those rabbit-quick reflexes, that shudder running just under his skin. I bent my head and picked faster.

"I wasn't dealing," Eli said quickly, "if that's what you think. Those scum are the *lowest*."

I was silent. It hadn't even occurred to me to think that. After a second Eli started picking again, too.

"You know, Jude, you have to take a risk once in a while. It's weird—you're the most unadventurous person I know, but you're with me. And you don't know anything about me. You don't even know how old I am." He waited, but I didn't ask. "Thirty-one," he said. "Three hundred and seventy-five months."

Only three years younger than me.

A small boy appeared from around the corner of the triple-decker. He wore a dirty yellow oilcloth slicker and seemed to be pulling something on a string.

"Aren't you even curious? I want to know everything about you. And Lee and Suzanne. How come we never go to your place? I want to meet them. I know where you live."

Why was he going on like this? Maybe it was the pie we were preparing for, its promise of domesticity.

The little boy came closer and stood watching us. He couldn't have been more than four. At the end of his string was a turtle. Big—maybe two fists across—and muddy, it hunkered in the weeds like a round, too-perfect rock.

"Nice turtle," Eli said.

"Tortoise," the boy corrected.

Our hands dipped in and out of the wet leaves, quick as knives. The boy flapped his slicker and watched us. "You guys berry-pickin'?"

"Berrying," I corrected.

I put a berry in my mouth. It was bitter on the outside, and sooty, but sweet when I bit down. I held one out to the boy, who shook his head suspiciously. Hauling on the reluctant tortoise, he began walking slowly away.

We picked faster, in silence. The wet leaves sent sprays of water over us finer than rain. I thought of a day when Lil was the size of the boy in the yellow slicker, and Gort and I took her to the zoo in Allentown. We stood watching the elephants bathe. They lifted their trunks and shining sprays of water uncurled into the air. One sank down on its huge haunches and another embraced it heavily from behind. Around them the others kept on sending water into the air, a cloud of fine glittering spray, like needles of light. When I turned from watching their clumsy tender entanglement, Gort's eyes were on my face. They said for him what he couldn't tell me in words. Those eyes said, I love you like the elephants love.

Eli had stopped picking. He reached out and wiped the corner of my mouth with his sweater sleeve. The wet wool smelled like smoke, from his cigarettes.

"Mud," he said. His face wore the expression that Gort's had that day with the elephants, tender and fierce, a look of ownership.

That was when I realized what I had done. This was the first time I'd slept, at Eli's; the first time I'd thought about Gort when I was with him. I hadn't stayed in one world.

I flinched away from Eli's hand. I straightened up and started back across the wet grass.

▼

I made the pie anyway. I told myself that, after all, arrangements had been made—Susie at Clesta's for the night, bribed with a promise of Green Hulk comics. But the truth was that I didn't want to leave. I didn't want to go back to the house that now, worse than feeling like the house of strangers, might feel like my own—a world, a life, continuous with this one. I wanted to sit on and on in the yellow kitchen eating tough, salty pie and drinking wine and watching Eli rub his rain-wet hair on a dish towel. Even though it had become a betrayal.

A damp breeze came through the half-open window. Dinnertime sounds came with it—the clang of pots and pans, barking babies, someone's clarinet playing the first line of "Strike Up the Band" over and over.

Eli said, "So—what about Friday. Hop'll be in Hellertown all afternoon. You want to come over?"

"I can't," I said.

The shiny look of expectancy settled on his face. His head tilted toward the window, into the draining summer light. He waited. Finally I said, "I have to go to Iowa. To see my folks."

"Iowa?" The shine faded. "You never tell me anything."

"I don't *have* to tell you anything."

Eli set his elbows on the sticky green vinyl tabletop and leaned

111

toward me. He leaned with his whole body—I could see the muscles rise in his upper arms—as if across the table there were a huge and powerful magnet, a flesh-magnet: me. "Let me come with you."

"What?"

"We can borrow Pop's van. We can camp. I've always wanted to see the West." He threw me his jack-o'-lantern grin.

"Eli," I said. "I'm *married*. My parents think of "—I stumbled over the name—"him as their son."

"So it's time for a reality check."

The clarinet began struggling with the refrain. *Strike up the— Strike up—*

"Jude," Eli said. Very slow; very patient. His hands gripped his bare brown shoulders. The knuckles stood out white, a warning. "The guy's been gone, what? Two months? Time for a reality check, Jude. For all you know, he's got somebody else."

Why was I so sure that he didn't? After all, here I was, with somebody else. Suddenly I knew what it was Gort longed for. Had always longed for. Not our combined magic, that third we made between us; but the opposite. Order, distance, solitude—the other side of silence. A pearl in the brain.

I looked out the window, past the blue bowl of sharks' teeth and the damp red dish towel piled beside it on the sill. What I felt was exhilaration. A gift of energy, a power not mine but offered to me— like skating fast across the waxy, dark-filled ice of Nonesuch Pond in March. It was new to me, this feeling. Gort never fought; his eyes would go blank and shuttered and he'd leave the room before anything might be said that could not be rescinded. *You can't take back the spoken word*, Clesta used to say.

"Goddammit, Jude—" Eli's voice was loud now, and not at all patient. "You're so goddamn"—he searched for a word—"*resigned*. Don't you know you have to *demand* things? Otherwise nothing goes down. Life isn't gonna hand you stuff like some kind of smiley-faced Santa Claus."

I kept on looking out the window; I thought, this is our first one. *Lovers' quarrel*: the words frightened me. In the middle of the pane was a dimple like a tear. I looked down through the black crisscross grating of the fire escape, no stairs to the ground, just a landing dropping off to nowhere, the high stutter of the clarinet like someone far off calling my name.

Eli's hand grabbed my chin. He jerked my head around to face him. "You're with *me* now! Goddammit, Jude!" He was shouting but his voice was hoarse and desperate, and the hand around my jaw trembled. "Goddammit, when am I gonna be real to you?"

For the first time, then, I felt my power. All that I knew about yearning gathered and turned itself inside-out in a sort of dense, soft explosion, and I was on the other side. Couldn't Eli see what was happening to me? But he kept on holding, shakily, onto my chin. I thought of how Gort went away and came back, away and back. I said quietly, "I'll be back Tuesday."

I knew how to lead us away from the dangerous edge of talk. I got up and went into the other room. I took off my clothes and left them on the floor where they fell.

Afterwards I was careful not to fall asleep. While Eli smoked silently, sulkily, I sewed up the rip in his sweater. He didn't have any green thread. I sat up in bed, naked except for my glasses, and wove coarse black cotton thread in and out through the damp smoky-smelling wool with stitches as fine as Mama's. Invisible mending.

1 0

L I L

Life seemed like the holy cards Clesta used for bookmarks—the kind with that funny plastic coating. Tilt the card one way, and Jesus is watching you out of mousy brown eyes; tilt it the other way, the eyes close, God is dead.

I'd been at Clesta's almost two weeks and I still hadn't found out where Daniel had hidden the envelope. Some co-conspirator *he'd* turned out to be. I'd confided in him—*trusted* him—and he wouldn't do the one thing I asked, all on account of (he claimed) his stupid moral code. Rhoda thought he'd really douched me over. Dump him, she'd said when she called the night before (collect, from a booth, because her grandfather'd put some kind of lock on their phone); but I couldn't. Not yet. I'd given up on saving enough money for the bus. If I just knew where Dad was, and if he wasn't in Chile or someplace like that, I could take the Dodge and go look for him. Right before he went away, he'd driven it to the service station on Heckewelder for a tune-up and shocks and new tires—practically the last thing he did. Did he think my mother would suddenly start using it? Driving was one more thing Mom was afraid of; so naturally she pretended the car didn't exist. Her expired driver's license was in the bottom of her jewelry box under a lot of old red and blue pop-it beads. I'd taken it, just in case. I'd bought a map of Pennsylvania at Lu-Art Copy; but I couldn't make a real plan until I'd found the envelope.

Then I had my revelation. I was in the storeroom off the kitchen when it came to me. It was my place—the place I went when I needed to be alone. That afternoon I'd gone there because of Doc, who'd been guilt-tripping me, as usual. Some guy in a three-piece suit'd come to see Clesta. Looking through the crack between the parlor door and the jamb, I could see Chinky stretched out between them with his head laid lightly, watchfully, on his paws. Clesta leaned her chin on one hand, pleating the skin of her cheek. She had on a navy blue dress and her gold earrings in the

114

shape of elephants' heads. The man shook out some papers and started reading in a drizzly voice like a minister's. I'd never trust a man who parts his hair in the middle. What he read was a lot of weird questions. *Do you know the extent of your estate? Are you of sound mind and mental powers?* (Clesta hesitated a second on that one.) *Do you know the natural objects of your bounty and affection?*

"If it isn't Miss Nosey Parker." Doc'd snuck up behind me on his rubber soles. "Come away from there and let your great-aunt lay out her will in peace. Sufficient unto the day is the evil thereof." Then, more to himself than to me, "She *got* to do it every two-three years, way things change in this family." When I didn't move away right off, he said, "You go do your parkering somewheres else."

The hot, dry, breathless air of the storeroom was like being wrapped in blankets. Dust swam around in the light from the dirty skylights. Most of the floor was thick green glass—a skylight into the garage below—fenced off with a railing. I went along the wooden walkway to the back corner where the trunks were. Lay out her will, I thought; her *will?* I sat down on the floor and leaned against a black domed trunk that smelled like mildew. I'd already searched them all. The steamer trunk was full of evening gowns and feathered hats and fabric for dresses that never got made. The other trunks had dishes and glassware and stuff like that. Wineglasses and vases with C O H cut into them, Clesta Hutchins Oberdorf, the O twice as big as the other two letters, as if the MDH'd been twice as tall as anybody else. Everything was gritty from years of dust seeping in under the lids. There hadn't been any yellow envelope.

Lay out her will. Laid out. In my whole life I'd only ever seen one dead body. When I was six I'd hidden under the black skirt of my Grandmother Eulalie's casket at Kemerer's Funeral Home—after I'd snuck downstairs from the room where my mother'd left me with a bunch of stupid coloring books. The word *wake* sounded grown-up and glamorous and I didn't want to miss out. "Handsomer in death than she ever was in life," I'd heard Gramma Maude say to Clesta. "Look at those *cheeks*."

I never cry. To distract myself I reached up and unsnapped the catch of the steamer trunk. Dresses came tumbling out—taffeta and sugary net and silk printed all over with peacock feathers like staring eyes. Everything had this stale, ghost smell. "Get a grip," I said out loud, the way

Rhoda would've. Clesta wouldn't die. She *couldn't* die. She was the only family I had left that I could count on.

I'd brought my mail with me—I always came to the storeroom to read it. I was ripping open a letter from Rhoda when my revelation came: *Put things back where they belong.* That was it! Daniel had put the envelope back where he'd found it. Just what his wussy kindergarten *code* would say to do.

I skimmed Rhoda's letter without really seeing it. She'd broken three ribs slam-dancing at the only club in Boise—stage-diving, I bet, like I'd seen her do at Club Baby Head—and now she was stuck in Idaho until school started. It was so unfair. I mean, Rhoda used *dental floss.* (I never told my mother that, naturally; she'd've been reassured.) Across the top of the paper Rhoda'd printed in red, BOISE SUCKS IT REALLY SUCKS IT REALLY REALLY SUCKS BIG TIME.

I folded the letter and stuck it in the envelope. My fingers shook, I was so excited. The question was, how was I going to get hold of the envelope without my mother or Susie or Lacey seeing? I wet my fingertips and smoothed my eyebrows the way Clesta did. *Calmly, calmly. Let us have no frumpus.* They were growing in fast—it was like running my fingers along two toothbrushes.

I opened the other letter that'd come that day. It was from my mother. She was leaving on Thursday to go see my grandparents in Orient, Grampa was sick but don't worry, back Monday.

Tilt life one way; tilt it the other. Here was my chance. What Clesta called the Long Arm of Coincidence. I'd go tonight. I wouldn't have to keep on kissing up to the Honorable Daniel. Or even kissing him. Put things back where they belong? That envelope belonged to *me.*

▼

"I'll tell you a story," Clesta announced after supper. Something'd put her in a reminiscent mood just when I needed to split. Doc was out in the kitchen scrubbing pots—Clesta always ate too slow for him—and Daniel'd gone to Philly for the Bone Man that morning, so it was just Clesta and me. She pushed away her untouched Pistachio-Prune Surprise.

116

"The Lehigh Valley, as your German ancestor with his small-eyed peasant shrewdness foresaw in the spring of 1741, grows a lot of things. Corn, tobacco, barley, apples; pasture for horses and dairy cattle; scratching space for God's own amount of hogs and hens. But the main thing it grows is steel. That, Sebastian Dussinger didn't foresee. He saw the bright Pennsylvania sky narrowing down like a funnel, and the ribbon of river where South Mountain meets the valley floor. He never imagined the mill, eating up land to the north and east. Nor the snuff-colored smoke filling the valley."

There go the clocks. Eight-thirty.

"In the steel mills the blast furnaces are the first and last thing. Six of them in a row, Lilly-Lil, in a room the size of an airplane hangar. Feeding time, which is about every twenty minutes, a stoker shovels in coal on a long wooden-handled shovel. Inside the furnace, light explodes. The stoker looks as if he's shoveling fire.

"That's my brother, Bob. Your grandfather."

Old Bob. I should've known.

"The *heat*, child. Inferno doesn't begin to cover it. When the fire is feeding, and you see the heart of it—apple green, cobalt, rose—the heat puckers the skin on your face like crepe paper.

"The strange thing—inside all that fiery heat there's water. Those men are wet all day long. *In the sweat of thy face shalt thou eat bread.* Under the heavy green cotton pants, the shirt with your name sewn inside the collar, your body runs with sweat. Handkerchief tied around your head under your hard-hat, and the sweat rolls into your eyes anyhow. Only dry place is the inside of your mouth."

Sneakers; flashlight; knife. What else?

"The roar of those furnaces crowds your ears and scours the inside of your head. The men hardly speak at all. Costs too much. *Them that say don't know, and them that know don't say.* Whatever your job—puddler, scarfer, teemer—there's danger in it. You keep the beam of your attention narrow, and steady; you concentrate on the slap of a handle into your palm, the heave of a shovel. You think steel, Lilly. *Are* steel.

"Child. Be patient.

"End of the day, your grandfather shoves his card into the slot until he feels the click, like teeth snapping shut, then puts it in the metal pocket with his name on it. There's a shower outdoors so those who want to can wash—strip and stand barefoot on the cold cement while the water streams over their chests and bellies in the tracks laid down by their own sweat—but most don't. The married men put on the plaid wool shirts and jeans they wore that morning, roll their workclothes into bundles to take home. The unmarried men like Bob just hang their hard-hats at the back of their lockers and go. Moving slower than they have all day, getting up a face for the outside. Learning to talk again.

"'Seen Roger's new DeSoto?'

"'Hell, yeah. He sure got the rough end of the pineapple.'"

The rough— Oh.

"The way out is through a long corridor. Halfway down there's a display case with a glass front, five or six feet long. Inside, two long shelves of skulls. Some are human; most are the skulls of apes. The company's founder had a son, an amateur archaeologist, he disappeared off the coast of New Guinea around the turn of the century.

"Don't interrupt.

"The skulls he found are set out on the shelves, not in any pattern like smallest-to-largest, but in groups that seem somehow natural. Child, the devilish designer of the case lined the back with mirrors. As you file past, between the skulls, your own face looks back at you."

Not a pretty sight.

"No matter how often they've walked down that corridor, Lilly-Lil, none of the men can manage to keep their heads turned away the whole time. Your grandfather dreads this moment more than any other in the day. I don't suppose he ever in his life heard the phrase *memento mori*— wouldn't have known what it meant if he had. But looking into that case he knows those skulls have something to say to him."

Shit. Where'd I put my house key?

"Outside, the air feels like a woman's palm on their burning brains. Their steel-capped boots clump on the blacktop. Gaslights throw splotches of yellow light. Their voices hit the air loud, but they can't tell that yet. The older the man, the longer it takes. The Good Providers— the ones who get blind drunk every night of the week but show up at the mill the next morning—look out toward the iron bridge downriver from the mill. Thinking: House'll need a new roof come spring. Thinking:

Biscuits and gravy, meatloaf, beer. Coins click in their pockets. Someone starts to whistle.

> Life would be cheerier on Lake Superior
> How would Peking do?
> I'm gonna corner ya in California—
> Any old place with you."

And they say OUR songs are weird.

"Out of the yard, past the slag heaps, your grandfather turns north. To his right is the mountainside tattooed with logging scars. To his left, across frozen fields like wrinkled blankets, he can see lights tapping on one by one. On the road home he keeps pace with a low-lying moon. He bathes in the blessed silence, Lilly, falling through the air like moisture. He whistles.

> I'd go to hell for ya, or Philadelphia—
> Any old place with you

His breath floats in front of his face. Mama was dead by then, he was coming home to just Maude and me.

"I know, Lilly. Just wait, now.

"Well, the mills of the gods grind slowly, but they grind exceeding small. Ten-twelve years of this, with time out for the war, and your grandfather goes back to school. Maude and I had both married by then, he didn't have us to support. He got the message, you might say, of the display case in the corridor. Nights, he sits in his workclothes at a too-small desk. He holds onto a yellow No. 3 pencil and he listens. Oh, Lilly. That takes five more years. By the time he marries the jittery, big-eyed woman who stood at the front of his last classroom, he's a middle-aged man. She gives him James, a disappointment from the day he draws breath. Bob sets his hopes on his second-born.

"That's your father."

Finally.

▼

Chinky tailed me to the bottom of the alley, his nasty black tongue hanging out from the heat. One by one the streetlamps popped on in the muggy

119

dusk. Little bursts of insect noise came from the bushes. It would've only been a medium night for the telescope—starry but not really clear—but it was great for my purposes.

It was a relief to be doing something. I'd been a coward last week, in the graveyard with Daniel—really skeeved out; now was my chance to redeem myself, show my mettle, as Clesta would say. The Hutchins mettle. My arms swung smoothly, confidently, as I walked. My sneakers didn't make a sound on the brick pavement.

A gusty, damp wind was blowing straight down our street as if it were a tunnel, swirling grit and crumpled paper around. Nobody else was on the street. The houses and trees looked somehow not familiar, as if I'd been away a long time. The recycling bin on the corner seemed like it was in the wrong place. Passing Lacey's, I could hear Paul's voice, then hers, ragging on him like she always did. Our house was dark.

In the yard I went straight to the car seat. Without turning on my flashlight, I shoved my hand into the crack between the back and the seat. I felt back and forth, but there was nothing. *Dweeb.* It *had* to be there. I started at one end and shoved my hand along every inch, pushing as deep as I could, all along the crack. Nothing. I couldn't believe it. I sat down on the sticky vinyl. Next-door Lacey's voice got louder.

"—or not? Paul? I asked you a *question.*"

The house, then. Maybe Daniel'd gone inside—maybe bribed Susie with an offer to hear her catechism—and hidden it in there.

I felt my way along the porch steps. The door was open. Just a crack—I didn't notice until my key touched the lock. The door swung inward by itself with a low groaning sound like Chinky in his sleep.

I froze, one hand still holding out the key, and listened. The silence had this fullness to it. No sound; but someone was there. I grabbed for my jacket pockets; but there was nothing in them except my father's flashlight. "Shit," I said out loud; then clapped a hand over my mouth. I'd forgotten the knife.

I looked around the porch. In the dingy light from the streetlamps I could see piles of mail, a rusty lawn chair folded up, Susie's rubber rainboots, an old metal washboard. Moving real slow and quiet, I edged across the porch and picked up the washboard. I stepped through the door sideways so it wouldn't open wider and make more noise. I held the washboard up over my head. My arm was trembling, and I willed it to stay still. The Long Arm of Coincidence popped into my mind. I felt a giggle welling up, like gas.

Slowly I moved forward, into the dark hall. In a way I didn't believe there was anybody there, didn't believe there was danger. It felt like a game, lifting one foot in front of the other and feeling for the floor, the way you do in Blind Man's Buff. But my heart was bumping, like a fist banging on my breastbone from the inside.

Somewhere ahead of me I heard something. *Jude*, it sounded like. Or maybe, *You?*

I whispered, "Daddy?"

Then I saw it. A shape, dark on dark. Too short to be him. My arm stiffened and swung all by itself. Then it exploded. I heard a crack, like a tree limb snapping. There was this bright far-off pain, then it zoomed in close, first hot, then icy cold. The floor buckled. I went down.

When I opened my eyes a man's face hung in the air over me, wavery as if it were underwater. He was babbling something. *Lee? You Lee?* I lifted the washboard to hit him again. But when I looked at my arm, it was still stretched out on the floor.

Then it was light, it was morning, I was late for school. A shadow between me and the window. Why was Lacey here? "Lil? Don't move. Don't try to get up."

But I had to get up, I was late. Only there was this pain, it kept getting bigger, like a cold wave spreading. It was all through my chest now, the way it felt when I breast-stroked underwater too long. The sun was all around, and I was falling but not falling, like a Ferris wheel. I could smell Lacey's bathrobe—dried milk and bacon grease. I tried to push myself up—time to get out of bed—but my left arm seemed to be moving farther and farther away. The Long Arm, I thought, and heard a silly giggle from somewhere. And then it got dark.

THREE

11

JUDITH

I pushed my cheek at my mother's, kissing air as she nipped me wetly on the earlobe. No arms: she didn't like to be touched. Two pairs of glasses clicked. When I stepped back, we stood for a moment facing each other: two women the same height, with the same broad shoulders, short waists, large hands.

"How was the trip?" my mother said. "Are you tired, Judie? You're so thin! How about a cup of tea and some Lorna Doones?"

My mind passed quickly over the plane trip my parents had paid for—the missed connection in Cedar Rapids, the Greyhound bus with its smell of oranges and mutter of restless babies; the drought-scoured August fields and hopelessly hopeful For Sale signs. "I'm fine," I said. "Really, Mother."

In the parlor Winnie, my mother's ancient springer spaniel, struggled to her feet with a surge of her old enthusiasm. I sat down on the sofa, tugging at the skirt of my blue sundress, which seemed to have suddenly grown shorter. I held out my hand. The dog's muzzle pushed at the air next to it.

"She can't see so well anymore," said my mother.

"Can't see so well?" My father's felt slippers slapped the wood floor between rugs, and he made a sound as he walked into the room, a low tuneless hum. Or was it just breathing? "Can't see so well? Hello, Judie." He hovered in front of his chair, then slowly lowered himself into it. "Dog's blind as a barn owl at noon."

The dog circled crookedly next to his chair before it folded down onto the rug, one leg at a time. My father was thinner than he'd been two years ago, his pants gathered into clumsy pleats by his belt like the old men at Valley View, the ones who still got dressed every day. My mother, by contrast, filled her homemade brown knit pantsuit to its limits. In her

125

ears she wore her Swedish mother-in-law's garnet-and-pearl earrings, in honor of my visit. The weekend stretched ahead like the endless fields out the bus window. Despite the second heart attack, my father didn't look sick to me, only old. I should have known. *Urgent, emergency*—words my mother had always used to mean, *I want.* And I? I'd wanted a reason to come here; but what had I hoped to find? These people—these two old people—could not give me what I needed. Whatever that was.

"Your father's been after me to have her put to sleep." My mother pulled off her white Red Cross sandals and wiggled toes that even in this heat were encased in peanut-colored nylon. "But I won't. I just won't."

"Mmm," I said, softly noncommittal.

"What?" said my father. "What?"

"Judie agrees with me," my Swedish mother said. Then, in a low voice to me, "His hearing's worse."

"Blind. Deaf. Knotted up with arthritis," said my father. "Animal's useless, Maude. Don't even bark anymore."

"Well, Eugene, there are plenty of *people* walking around with all those problems, and then some." She clicked her teeth together as if she were biting off thread. My Swedish grandmother used to click her teeth against what she considered undue emotion; I couldn't remember my mother doing it before now. She turned to me. "I wish you'd brought the girls, Judie. It's been almost three years since we saw them last."

"It would've been awfully expensive. Besides, they're pretty busy this summer. Susie has catechism class"—my father snorted at this, but said nothing—"and Lil's helping Clesta." It sounded like a perfectly normal family, and I hadn't lied at all—like real estate ads that tell the literal truth but lead you to imagine something else. I was clicking the clasp on my purse open and shut; when it yawned I could see two or three leaves, no longer green, and the papery, torn wing of a moth. I hadn't used it in weeks, not since I started wearing clothes with pockets; it felt as if the things inside had been put there by somebody else.

In this room that had not changed since I left high school, I was a daughter. Eli had no place here, nor Gort. Even the girls receded, became once-removed: a daughter's daughters. The air in the room, close and damp and still, smelled of the same disinfectant it always had, like sugared pine needles. The half-stripped woodwork, a project abandoned forever with the arrival of my mother's grand piano, was streaked with milky residue. Wooden shelves held the same accumulation of Reader's Digest Condensed Books and, on the top shelf, my father's photograph albums from the war, the ones I was never allowed to look at because of the naked men on beaches. The slippery green sofa where I sat was the one my dates (few and far between) used to shift their haunches on while they waited for me to come downstairs. The chair where my father sat was the one he'd always had, blood-colored vinyl with a footrest attached, so that when you pulled a lever your feet shot up level with your chin.

"Well," said my mother, and pushed herself off the sofa. In her stocking feet, with the dog following, she padded across the parlor into the next room. There was a rustle, a cough, some squeaking. Scarlatti poured through the narrow doorway. Music has charms to soothe the savage breast, Cicero said. (A lot of people think it's *beast*, Mrs. Muschlitz told us; you can see they're wrong.) Not my father's breast. He reached up to his ear. His fingers fiddled with it urgently until finally, with a sigh, he leaned his head back against a square of yellow felt with TRAVELERS' LIFE & CASUALTY embroidered across the top in blue. A mildly blissful look came over his face. He was shut away inside his silence just as my mother was shut away inside her music. Two separate—separated—worlds.

In the dining room my mother shifted into a melody that made me think of clowns with ping-pong-ball noses. Naked music, she'd have called it: no underbrush, no place to hide a hesitation. I could hear my mother approach and back off and approach again, until she got the shape right. Gradually the music smoothed out, as if it had begun to move forward on its own, carrying my mother with it.

▼

My hand was on the picket gate, my feet on the dry corded dirt of the path. Bees tugged at the hollyhocks. In the fields across the road the corn stood stunted and brown, obscenely preserved, like shrunken heads. I felt the way I used to years ago, returning home from summer visits to Clesta—awkward and alien. I looked down at the tin mailbox and its blurred lettering ("The Hall's," with the misplaced apostrophe that had caused me so much adolescent anguish), then back at the deep, shadowed porch on its four ugly pilings of river rock. At an upstairs window a white curtain wagged. Too far to see who. I turned and started up the path that led behind the house, along the foundation of the old storehouse. My shoes struck with a sound like cleats on the hard, ribbed ground. The cold-frames by the barn had broken panes. The plants inside, which shouldn't have been there past May, were small and brown and stiff, as if they'd been bronzed, like outgrown baby shoes, right where they stood. At the corner was a mound of dirt with a shovel stuck in it. I put my hand in the iron triangle of its handle and pulled. It might as well have been sunk in cement.

Past the barn, I stepped up onto a large, flat tree stump. Blue morning glories sprawled over it, and there was clover growing in its crevices, the first thing I'd come across that was unequivocally green. In front of me a cloud of gnats hung in the air like the flocking on a hat veil. The fields beyond, cordoned off by Meriwether's Cold-Weather Wire, were pasture. Maybe the neighbor who rented it had brought his cows in early? No; there they were, in the next field over. They reclined, as still as boulders, or stood leaning their heads against each other's flanks. The light breeze carried the smell of cow dung. I took off my glasses and wiped the sweat from my face with one bare arm.

Overhead a single bird flew, low and purposeful, and dived into a clump of scrub oak. Deliberately, I jumped off the stump and plunged into the cloud of gnats. They vanished as completely and mysteriously as they had when I was a child.

▼

Four-year-old Judith squats beside her mother. They've been to the creek (crick, Mama calls it) to pick watercress, crouching carefully on the wet rocks. The cold creek water stung when it sucked her fingers, and she could see all the way down into it. Now they're working in the vegetable garden. Mama is pulling up deer-tongue and red fescue, tender and bright as parsley. Her hands dredging the dirt are broad-backed and long, with shiny knuckles. Judith is too young to tell the tiny shoots apart, too young to know what to take and what to leave. She is salting slugs.

She crouches in the tall grass at the edge of the garden, where new Bibb lettuces dot the sandy soil like small, bright shells. Her corduroy shorts—not warm enough for June, but Mama never notices things like that—leave her legs bare. Queen Anne's lace, coarse and full of chiggers, brushes her knees. In a semicircle around the clearing, as far as she can see, are trees. Her mother has taught her to call them by their names. She shades her eyes with one hand while the other wags the saltshaker. White and black and scarlet oak, sugar maple, swamp maple, walnut, birch, elm. The hot, clear morning sun comes slanting between the trees. Sassafras, dogwood, redbud; butternut, hickory, hawthorn. So many different colors of green. Who would think there could be so many of a thing?

"This afternoon we can finish what we don't get done," Mama says. "Tommy, feel how warm it is out."

Judith watches the light jingling in the leaves. Mama often talks to this Tommy. He is a little boy, but bigger than Judith, because he can read. Judith thinks that when she's older she'll be able to see him too.

"Mama. Look." Her mother's back, in a white cotton undershirt that belongs to Judith's father, flashes in the sun. "Mama, look how many." It can take a while to get her attention. Sometimes Judith thinks that when Mama can see Tommy, she can't see her, Judith.

Finally her mother turns around. But when Judith parts the deep, soft grass to show her, the slug bodies have melted into the ground. They're the same color as the moist earth where the grass springs out, only they glisten more, like spit. She can hardly find any of them. Nevertheless Mama smiles at her, a smile like the sun pouring straight down.

Rising, her mother slaps her knees and haunches, and the dirt leaps off in clumps. She stretches. Her fingers dig into the deep blue sky. "Time to see about lunch."

They leave the warm, rain-washed mud, the prickling grass, the dry click of Japanese beetles. In the drying mud of the path, hoofprints like shallow cups hold water blue with sky. Mama stops to wipe Judith's face on a plaid shirt-sleeve dangling from her waist; then they start up the hill. Between them they swing the big basket of weeds and pulled-up dirt back and forth, a handle each. The *top of the saltshaker is wet where it has come nose-to-nose with slugs. Judith puts her own nose against the cool china, but it only smells like salt.*

▼

By the time I turned back, the sun had gone, leaving behind a chalky green sky. I walked slowly. I'd come back to Orient thinking that here, somehow, I'd see more clearly: that was what I'd said to Eli. But it seemed as if the past was all I could see, the time between then and now a hole into which I might possibly fall. I walked carefully back to the house, watching the summer sky hold onto that mineral light.

▼

"Have some more potatoes," I said, holding out the white bowl with a single blue flower on the side. More potatoes, more cold pot-roast, more snap-beans. More anything.

"You are being ridiculous, Eugene. You know that?" My mother's voice was a shade too loud, just enough to remind my father of his handicap.

Stupid to feel like this; I wasn't a child anymore. But how I hated it—then and now and all the years in between—the clang of voices and of wills, that could only end in greater distance. I planked the bowl down on the wooden table and looked around the room, counting up signs of renewal. A new flesh-colored refrigerator that spit ice through a hole in its side; on the floor in front of the sink, a bright patch of new linoleum in the same pattern of vague yellow-and-gray swirls—my mother must have saved the extra all this time. But there were rosettes of ancient dirt where the baseboard had been pulled loose to accommodate it, and the room held the same vaguely medicinal smells of Spic and Span and rosemary. What would Eli have made of all this? I pushed the thought down—my mother had a way, when she chose, of picking up what was in your mind—but not before it occurred to me that Eli would have approved of her. *She* certainly knew how to demand things.

"—up on a ladder, Eugene," my mother was saying. "Too late now. Leave it for Zachary." Zachary was the current tenant. My mother turned to me. "Your father thinks he's going to clean out the roof gutters."

I studied the cross-grain of the pinkish gray meat on my plate. So far my mother hadn't asked about Gurt, except for the quick obligatory How-is-he; I didn't want to draw her fire.

"Maude, you are an interfering old woman." My father's eyes shifted to me. "Judie, your mother is an interfering old woman."

"Eugene. You know I'm right. You aren't up to these kind of chores anymore." And to me, "You know what your father did this past winter?" She waited for an answer. Reluctantly, I shook my head. "He killed my bees."

"Judie, that's a crock. They died of old age."

"They were in the barn. You know, Judie, it's empty now we've let the cows go. And in November, what does your father do but shut the whole barn up tight. So they'd stay over the winter, he said. When the cold came, they couldn't get out. They died in there. Just froze to death."

"Old age, pure and simple." But my father's voice had a defeated sound. Beneath one eye, the tarnished skin showed the shiny track of what could be (my father?) a tear.

After the dinner dishes had been stacked on the drainboard, the ice cream served and allowed to melt ("Berries've all gone by," my mother said sadly), my father and I sat on at the kitchen table. My father pulled up a metal tray on rickety folding legs, stacked with the week's accumulation of the Orient Gazette. He unfolded each section, thrust it aside if it was news; if it was advertisements, he scanned it carefully, page by page. When he saw a coupon he wanted, his breathing deepened and he snipped it out with a pair of nail scissors. Soon his placemat held a little pile of scalloped newpaper pieces. The two of us sat in silence, like the times when I was little, and dinnertime came and went (I'd put a dish of scrambled eggs at each place, and toast with the burned part scraped away), and bedtime came and went, and finally just before midnight there would be a phone call. I'm at the Twi-Liter Motor Inn, my mother's voice would say, I'll be home in the morning.

Now my mother, who no longer traveled further than the piano, reappeared with Winnie swaddled in a yellow towel. "I thought now would be a good time to give her a bath. While it's still hot," she said, as if the weather gave any sign of breaking. "Here. Dry her, Judie, would you?" She handed the dog to me. I hastily uncrossed my legs to make a lap.

"How's this sound?" asked my father without looking up. "Mauna Loa macadamia nuts, three-and-a-half ounces, a dollar fifty-nine."

I should have refused this task, I'd almost certainly do it wrong. I moved the towel gently over the trembling dog. My father hadn't been able to eat nuts for years.

"You'll never get her dry that way," said my mother, from the sink. "Rub harder."

"Was it Kraft Lite salad dressing we got for eighty-seven cents at the A & P?"

My mother shuffled dishes into the sink. Angrily, my father repeated, "Was it Kraft Lite?"

"Make her lie down," my mother said. I pushed unsuccessfully at Winnie's damp haunches. Finally I folded the thin legs under the heaving stomach. Wet, her sparse fur was even sparser; I could see a wart in the center of her head.

"Chrissake, Maude." My father got up, brushing clippings onto the floor. The phone on the wall next to the refrigerator began to ring. He bent down and pulled the plug out of the jack, then went slowly, haltingly, out of the room. In the doorway he tripped on the rag rug. Righting himself with a hand on the mission-oak bureau, he squinted fiercely down at the empty floor. "Damn dog."

My mother took a small medicine bottle from the windowsill and stood beside me. I could hear the far-off plaintive ringing of the upstairs extension. "Hold her now. I'll put in her eyedrops."

I laid my arm across the dog's back and cupped the two front paws, so small and light that I thought, Milkweed pods. My mother seized the muzzle in one hand and touched the dropper to each silver eye in turn.

"Oh, girl." She clicked her teeth. "Oh, girl. You make me sad."

▼

That night I couldn't sleep. Stars, hot and blinking in the muggy dark, crowded the window by my narrow bed, my girl's bed, their presence like a noise that would not stop. Finally I got up, pulled on underpants and an old sleeveless shirt, and went downstairs, the way I used to do when it was desire, and not stars, that woke me.

In the dim light my mother's Bechstein loomed, blue-black. It stood in the center of the room where the dining table used to be. ("Damn piano," my father would say every evening when we sat down to dinner in the kitchen, an invocation, the way other fathers said grace.) The only other object in the room, standing in the far corner with its handle propped against the wall, was an axe. On top of the piano, on a crocheted doily that needed washing, were a small lead bust of Beethoven and two photographs in black dimestore frames. One was a group portrait with handwriting across the bottom: "July 4th, 1917, Swedish Ladies Band of Margie, Minnesota"; in the center, cradling her trumpet and sitting so straight that her little flat hat looked like a saucer on her head, was my father's mother. The other was a snapshot of Gort and me on our wedding day, taken by his mother, my Aunt Eulalie, just before we started down the aisle. I picked it up and held it to the light.

▼

All eyes are on them—the couple at the top of the aisle, waiting for the organist to find her sheet music. Cousins should not marry: *the eyes moving speculatively over the bride's satin-covered stomach hold visions of babies with missing limbs, or too many. Her father has declined to give the bride away. No one will give her; she will give herself.*

The groom is pale in the formal black cutaway he uses for work as a freelance pallbearer; his damp, no-color hair is combed sternly back. The bride wears the yellowed satin gown in which her favorite aunt—who is not among the wedding guests, who will never speak to her again—married a man she has luckily outlived. The bride, too, is pale, except for the bright lipsticked slash of her mouth, the deepest red she could find in Walgreen's, brighter and deeper than blood.

The groom smiles, his smile a lifeline, a rope pulling her toward him, toward the life they will make together. The organ sounds its first long, interrogatory note.

▼

I lifted the cover from the keyboard, pinching my fingers rather than let the shiny wood bang. I propped open the top, like a huge wing, and started picking out a tune. Softly: it was after midnight.

133

Many a tear has to fall (pause, pause)
But it's all (pause, pause)
In the game

Music has charms. I'd been fifteen, sixteen, seventeen, quick and shiny as the spring trout in Bitter Lake; my father could hardly bear to be in the same room with me; I spent hours in the dark attic, sitting on top of an old chest of drawers, looking out into the night sky. In the summers we'd danced, Gort and I, to out-of-date songs with lyrics that cracked your heart. We'd made love. Made it.

Suddenly there was such pain, as if the axe in the corner had come down on my breastbone. The tiny hairs along Gort's cheek; the shine of his breath coming toward me in the dark; the sudden force of his tongue, like a muscle. *Just let go,* I'd whisper. So open—I could see into him then, see everything. My fingers traced the round rayed scar on his shoulder.

I looked up, and the great dark wing of the piano seemed to expand and grow darker, like a shadow falling over me. I had to slump over on the piano bench to hold the pain.

I shut my eyes and waited. He'd spent more and more time where I couldn't follow. The telescope, the roof, the observatory on the mountain. Always going higher. Escaping, as if my body laid some claim on him. One night last February I'd gone toward him where he sat naked on the bed pulling off his socks and looking out the open window into the night sky. The lamp threw my shadow across him. He started, and one arm went up to shield his face.

Even my shadow was too heavy.

When I got up from the piano bench I wasn't the same person as when I'd sat down. It hadn't been more than five minutes; but I was changed. I saw, finally and for the first time, how far we'd gone from each other. Before, I had only known how to be steady, how to be the one who waited. *Thy firmness draws my circle just, / And makes me end where I began.* When he came back—if, if he came back—could I tell him what I knew now, that things would have to be different, that *I* was different? That I could not live to be his grounding, anymore. I stood with one hand clenched around the edge of the piano lid and pushed my palm against the shiny dark wood.

Then he'll kiss your lips
And caress your waiting fingertips
And your heart

I stroked the smooth, cool keys. *And your heart— your heart—* But I couldn't find the right key to finish the tune.

▼

"*What* were you trying to play, down there?" asked my mother. Legs straight out in front of her, she was sitting on the bare boards of the attic floor, surrounded by old *National Geographics* and letters tied into bundles with string. She wore brown men's socks rolled down at the ankles, and her shins were scribbled with blue veins. On the floor beside her a Coleman lantern glowed; the electricity didn't reach up here. I sat down on the top step of the narrow staircase and breathed in the attic smell. In summer the smell was hot musty dust, as now; in winter it was cold musty dust.

I shook my head.

"I wonder why you've never learned to pick out a tune. All you need to do is hear how far it is between notes. The *intervals*."

"You just guess at the distance, and jump?"

"We're not talking about tightropes, Judie. It's not a high-wire act." My mother sighed and shifted her buttocks. "You must take after your father, after all."

"What's the axe doing in the dining room?" I said.

My mother looked at me, and I thought, She knows. She guessed, and that's why she hasn't asked where he is.

But she only said, "Oh, your father took a notion to break up the piano. In March, I think it was. Of course, he didn't have the strength to even *lift* an axe that high. I told him he could just take it back to the barn himself." She clicked her teeth.

Except for the square of splintery boards where we sat, the floor joists, like the rafters, were exposed, with silvery insulation packed between them all the way into the eaves. In summer I'd played up here for hours most days; usually I'd played Orphanage. Under the eaves all of my dolls

135

had lain in neat institutional rows. I remembered the hard pink flesh of their eternally reaching arms, their identical expressions of aggrieved surprise. Every day the ritual was the same. I'd undress each one, slosh it around in a yellow plastic tub of water, then dress it again, pushing the stiff little splay-fingered hands into flannel sleeves, and lay it in its silver bed between the floor joists.

"Mama. What did you do with all those dolls I had?" I said. Maybe Susie would want them.

"Dolls?"

"You remember, Mama. I had my whole collection up here. There must've been a dozen or more."

My mother smoothed the glossy pages of the magazine on her lap: coolies in pointed hats, an insincere sunrise behind curlicued rooftops. "I always wanted to go to China. Wanted to for years. But do you think he'd take me?"

The pale-spotted hands moving back and forth across the shiny pages reminded me of darning lessons—my mother's hands pulling the sock heel tight over the smooth wooden egg, her needle glinting in and out. Darns that, later, even with your heel wedged into too-small winter boots, you couldn't feel, the stitches were so fine.

One hand moved to a bundle of letters tied with a broad blue ribbon. "Oftentimes the well one is the one who dies first. You hear how the husband has a heart attack, prostate, this, that, and the other. Then, all of a sudden, the wife goes."

She leaned back against the brick chimney that went all the way down through the center of the house. Her elbow nudged the Coleman lantern. In the trembling orange light her face was like a very old child's. For a moment I saw the little girl trapped inside, a child the old woman had swallowed, a child that I, reaching in deep and pulling it out through the slack mouth, might save.

Mama.

As if I'd asked a question, my mother said abruptly, almost in a whisper, "Life is too short to do what you ought. Do what you *want*." She leaned forward and touched my hair.

Was this what I had come for? I held myself still under her touch, so rare I couldn't remember the last time I'd felt it. Downstairs the phone began to ring, thin, insistent. Neither of us moved. I thought how you could shut yourself in, or shut everything else out: how my mother and I were not so different after all.

My eyes followed hers to the dormer window with its square of starry sky. I sat still and let her hand rest in my hair. Far away, I heard my father's feet stumbling on the stairs, his voice calling, "Judie? Judie! It's long-distance!"

"I don't remember any dolls," said my mother softly, and clicked her teeth.

12

JUDITH

I followed the EMERGENCY signs with their stark black arrows through corridor after pale-green corridor, a long, zigzag tunnel of smells familiar from my days at Valley View: the smell of bleach, disinfectant sweet as cola syrup, the nutlike smell of vomit. The cement floor sucked at the rubber bottoms of my sandals. Now and then a discreet, summoning bell sounded overhead, like the bells in department stores. People brushed past in green hospital cotton; the flat fluorescent light canceled their faces.

In Emergency Doc and Lacey and Susie were standing at the desk. Doc was lecturing the impassive, middle-aged receptionist; Lacey leaned against the other end of the black Formica counter, the sash of her bathrobe trailing on the floor, eyes nearly closed.

Susie ran to me and wrapped her arms around my waist. When she caught sight of me Lacey straightened up.

"Christ's suspenders!" she shouted across the little lobby. "About time you got here."

Doc, who had stopped wrangling with the receptionist, regarded Lacey coldly. She glared back. He stalked over to me.

"I got to get back to C. H.," he said. "Now you're here, they can go ahead with fixin' Lil." He threw a look in Lacey's direction, then patted my arm. As he walked off I could hear him muttering, "Straight is the gate. And narrow the way."

Lacey offered to take Susie home with her, but Susie tightened her arms and dug her chin into my breastbone. Lacey said to me, "I'll stay if you really need me. I'm just frazzled. These last three hours with old Coals-of-Fire have about done me in." I shook my head. She knew something was fishy; but I could see her decide that now was not the time. She hugged me, sideways, reaching around Susie and her own stomach, tied her robe shut, and left.

Doc had already filled out a form and given the hospital Clesta's credit card. I hadn't even thought to call Bethlehem Steel's personnel office, but of course we probably didn't have health insurance anymore. Lacey, claiming to be Lil's aunt ("So, when is your sister's baby due?" the receptionist asked chattily, shuffling Lil's papers and fastening them with a yellow paper clip), had done the rest of the paper work. There was nothing for me to do. The receptionist pointed. Lil had been put in a little examining room down the hall to wait for me.

A single lamp shone on the pale hair spread over the white cotton sheet. At the bottom of the high wheeled stretcher Lil's bare feet stuck out; the soles were dirty. She lay with her eyes shut and one arm across her stomach. Between wrist and elbow the arm curved in a shallow S.

"Judas Priest," Susie muttered, and let go of my hand. We went and stood on either side of the high metal stretcher.

It was the first time I'd seen my daughter in two weeks. I went up to the stretcher. Lil was breathing in quick little sips. Her face was terribly pale; with her damp bangs pushed back, her high forehead looked naked. It shone in the light. She sighed, coughed; the cough turned into a sob. Her eyes flickered open. "Mom," she said softly. "Oh."

I put my palm across the high, shining forehead.

"Mom. The back of my stomach hurts."

Her forehead felt hot. I gripped the cold, shining chrome of the stretcher. "Honeybug. They'll be here in a minute. They'll fix it."

Susie gripped the crossbar of the stretcher with both hands and looked longingly toward the door.

Lil's arm jerked, and she said, "Oh." Up close the flesh was soft and white and doughy, like flesh immersed in water for too long. Even now, though, she didn't—wouldn't—cry. There was a green cotton blanket folded across her knees. I shook it out and laid it over her.

Suddenly the room was bright, full of the same cold light as the corridor. A burly, curly-haired man in a dark suit came in, moving fast. Crisply he invoked my name, his name, then snapped on the lighted X-ray screen. Lil's bones jumped into view, stark and lavender, with cloudy dark-blue fissures.

"This is no greenstick fracture," Burly Curly announced. "Look here— and here—" His fingers tapped the dark parts one after another. His mustache wagged over a lower lip which was very full and red, and which he kept wetting with his tongue as he bumped out words. The gentler ones—*radius, humerus*—had a sound like waltzing. I studied the little silver clamp that held my daughter's bones to the box of light. I could almost hear the bone crack, like a light snapping on. Lil's arm glowed with a holy, radioactive radiance.

"Mom," Susie's voice said. "*Mom.*"

I was swaying, knees trembling, legs gone as soft as Lil's arm. Strange: *broken* sounded like something hard, and *fracture*; but there was the arm, limp and noodly. Someone shoved a molded plastic chair under me. Susie tried to push my head between my knees. "To get more blood in," she said.

The doctor hurled himself out of the room and they wheeled Lil away. There was a form in my lap. *Mercy Hospital . . . transfusion . . . event of such a . . . release and indemnify . . .* I thought of Lacey's sister's child, HIV-positive from blood they gave him when they took out his appendix. If only Gort were here, I thought, for the first time in weeks, forgetting how he fell apart when anything happened to the children. Who am I to make this decision? Susie pushed at my elbow, turned the pen right side up in my fingers. I shook my head No, then Yes. I forged Lil's mother's signature.

At midnight Susie and I sat on a musty couch in the third-floor waiting room. Twenty-four hours since Lacey had phoned my parents' house; twelve hours ago I'd still been in Orient, waiting at the Greyhound station for the bus to Cedar Rapids. On the wall across from us was a large painting of Jesus in a surgical-looking white gown surrounded by children of various sizes and colors. *Suffer little children to come unto me.* All those hours Lil had lain there, dozing then jerking awake with pain, because Mercy wouldn't show her any mercy until they'd been released and indemnified.

I grabbed Susie's hand and pulled her out into the corridor. Double doors at the far end, where a few stretchers waited, led to the operating rooms. I started walking toward them. There was a baby crying somewhere, an insistent, angry sound. A stretcher wheeled past with its attendants walking sideways like crabs on squawking rubber soles; one of them punched a button on the wall and the doors opened. Yawning, a fist over her mouth, Susie watched it disappear.

On the first stretcher we came to was a child. As we walked past she stirred—asleep, drugged, maybe dreaming. Her head was nearly bald, with a few tufts of fine, colorless hair on the shiny skull. I could see the green veins underneath the skin.

"Ow. *Mom.*" Susie crooked one shoulder and pulled away from my hand in her hair, my fingers twined in it and rubbing over and over along one sticky, healthy strand. Somewhere up ahead the baby kept on crying. A head lifted from the next stretcher. It had white, wiry hair and dark eyes with purple bruises under them; there was a strip of surgical tape across the nose. "You're not my son!" it said in an accusing whisper, and went back down.

The baby's crying pulled at me, I felt it at the bottom of my stomach. Like nursing: the tug at your nipple that goes all the way down to your soles. I'd forgotten that feeling. The surprise of it, that first time with Lil—the child who, I'd thought when I found out I was carrying her, was the end of life as I knew it. And hadn't that turned out to be the truth? But not the way I'd thought.

They came for the old man. The double doors swung open and he was wheeled inside, crying, "Where'm I goin'? I need a bag, for my teeth. Where's my son?" I couldn't bear the sound of the baby any longer. I took Susie's hand and walked toward it, stumbling with tiredness.

Down a smaller corridor, in a room by itself, we found a tiny infant, three or four weeks old. It was dark-skinned, like a thin little monkey, and its high-sided metal crib was like a cage. It lay on its stomach with its behind in the air, moving small starfish hands across the wrinkled sheet. The room had the sweet, warm-urine smell of Mr. Yerkes at Valley View.

I reached through the bars and began to move my palm slowly, evenly, against the baby's back. It was hot and damp through the hospital flannel. There was a pacifier lying on the sheet. I reached in through the bars with my other hand and picked it up, stroking the damp little back in calm, automatic circles. I brushed the pacifier across the baby's mouth. The crying dimmed, shortened to sobbing, stopped. The tiny mouth closed around the orange rubber knob.

"*Moth*-er," Susie said—the melody of exasperation, high-low, like a doorbell. "Keep. Out," she read from a black-bordered sign taped to the doorframe. "Medical. Person—personal. Only. Mom—a person could *die* from touching that kid. Come on, let's go back. It could be a Pagan Baby. I think it is. Come *on*."

141

"It stopped crying," I said.

A few minutes after we got back to the main corridor, the heavy double doors parted and a stretcher came through, wheels complaining on the cement floor. Lil was propped on one elbow, eyes shut, coughing. Her left arm lay across her stomach. Under the ceiling lights the cast was bright, bright white. Bent at a shallow angle, it ran from her knuckles all the way to her armpit.

We followed the stretcher down a side corridor. The nurse handed me a kidney-shaped metal basin and crackled into the room opposite.

Standing on her good side, I held the basin under Lil's chin. With the other hand I bunched up her damp hair, crimped with sweat, and held it back. She retched, over and over, a dry, tearing sound. "Can't get it *up*. Can't." The slender neck bent over the basin, the shuddering shoulders, looked too frail for the stark white weight of the cast. Above the wing-shaped violet birthmark, a little pulse in her neck jumped. She smelled like cloves from the anesthetic.

Finally she spit some greenish mucus into the basin. I let go of her hair and put my palm flat against her back to help her lean over it. The white cotton johnny, untied at the nape, fell forward. It slipped down her arm, revealing the smooth, pale skin of her back and side, the ribs moving in and out, the curve of her breast with its soft, rosy nipple. I had forgotten how beautiful her body was—it had been years since she'd allowed me to see it.

Susie had backed up to the wall and was standing with her little plaid behind tight against it. She said, "A person could get really sick in this place."

Lil stopped shaking. I felt her lean suddenly, heavily, against my hand. Slowly I let her down, inch by inch, until she was lying flat. I drew the cotton johnny up over her chest, her shoulder, and tucked the thin tie, like a shoelace, under her neck. Her eyes were closed. A silver strand of spittle stretched from the corner of her mouth into her hair. My fingers trailed over the bright, unscarred surface of the cast, cold and damp like stones lifted from the creek. I put my hand on her cheek with its stripe of fever-red.

There was nothing to say, but for once it didn't matter. She didn't need words from me—just this. Her forehead lifted toward me the way it did when she was small, coming to meet my palm. Her lips moved without sound.

Mama.

When we came out of the hospital the sky was beginning to lighten. A macadam path stretched ahead of us, then a numb expanse of parking lot, then blue-violet blankness out over the valley. The crickets had long since stopped: funny how you never notice the exact moment when they go silent. I stumbled, and my head brushed a white pine outside the Emergency entrance, loosening a shower of dry, sharp needles. Susie picked up a clod of dirt from beside the path and flung it at the pale horizon, then stretched her arms out wide. Skidding on the thin layer of pine needles, she began to run.

I stood under the tree until the last needles flickered down, like a dry weeping. It was then that I thought of the body cast when Lil was six, the broken legs, the fall into the lake. This wasn't the first break; that had happened long ago.

▼

They kept Lil at Mercy because the break was complicated and needed watching. When she woke up and found out she was in the children's ward, she was really mad. But things seemed to go well, or at least better, between her and me. I sat on the narrow bed, clear of the cast which was slung from an elaborate arrangement of pulleys, and refrained from asking questions; she let me brush her unwashed hair with an old nylon stocking pulled over the bristles.

My daughter was someone with secrets now. She'd gotten upset when I picked up her jeans jacket to take it home for washing—pulled herself up in bed, yanked her cast off the pulleys, shouted at me to leave it alone. When I handed it to her, she thrust her good hand into the pockets, and her face cleared. I'd found my mother's old washboard in the pile of folded clothes that the nurse brought up from Emergency. She wouldn't say why she had it—wouldn't even say how she'd broken her arm, at first. Her face got that closed look like her father's. Finally she mumbled something about a ladder and losing her key.

I let her keep her secrets. When she comes home, I thought, we'll talk about it then. I was happier than I'd been in months. It was the way it had been when Lil was in the body cast. Gort had stayed home, unspeaking, unable to get out of bed, so devastated that we thought he'd have to be hospitalized, too. I'd been all alone then, the only one Lil had. Her eyes following me as I moved about the bright yellow-painted Children's Ward, that frightened question flickering in them: Is this how the world is? At six she'd been too young to frame the question; now she was too proud to ask. But she needed me. No words. Just my hands moving gently through her hair or setting a cup of apple juice on her tray; my body in the straight-backed chair beside the bed while she dozed. I watched her then—her face smoothed out in sleep, eyelids trembling with some dream beneath the half-grown-in eyebrows—and it seemed as if I had my daughter back.

▼

One secret I couldn't let Lil keep, because I knew—better than she did—what it was. The day before, Sunday, Eli had called me at home and asked me out to dinner. He had something to tell me, he said, something important. He settled for lunch.

I got to Brannigan's exactly at noon. When I saw that Eli wasn't there yet, my stomach uncurled a little, and I sat down in the tiny foyer as far away from the lacquered hostess and her podium as I could get.

"Do you have a reservation?" Her voice was like tapioca, vowels you could sink a spoon into. Her eyes, under false eyelashes like little awnings, traveled over me from the ankles up.

"Byrne," I said, hoping Eli had thought to make one. The silver-tipped finger moving down the list must have found us, because she left me alone. I was sweating, in my blue flowered sundress, the nervous kind of sweat that you can smell on yourself. I had something of my own to say to Eli, if I could make myself say it. When I'd gotten home from the hospital at dawn on Saturday, Lacey had been waiting for me. She hadn't wanted to say anything before, while I was so upset, but there was something. A man had come and banged on her door Thursday night and told her to go over to my house—a man with big white teeth and a tail of dark-blond hair, who'd taken off down the street, running, as soon as he'd seen she understood. I hadn't been this angry in years—not since Gort had telephoned from the hospital in Scranton to say that Lil had dived into the lake. My anger terrified me.

I crossed my legs and leaned back. The rose-pink plush gave out a soft obscene sigh. It was Lil's fourth day in the hospital. At Mercy that morning I'd just missed Clesta, who'd left some funereal-looking mauve gladioli and a pile of old *Redbooks*. My arms were full of items the nurse had read off over the phone: flop-eared brown rabbit; toothbrush; *Sweet Valley High*, numbers 3, 7, 27. Daniel came in as I was leaving. He had something for Lil, he said, holding his hands behind his back. When he brought it out—an entire box of Twix bars, her favorite—I saw disappointment on her face, then anger. She wasn't easy to please, my daughter.

At 12:19 Eli came through the brass-trimmed doors wearing a wide, pale tie and a wide smile. He said, "Hey, Jude."

"Hi," I said. It came out a whispery croak. Eli's smile dwindled and he took a step toward me; but the hostess intervened. "*This* way," she fluted.

We followed, Eli first, then me. His little ponytail was undone, the dark-blonde hair tucked inside his shirt collar. At a table by the long greenhouse window, we stopped. Eli pulled out my chair and I sat, bumping my head on a pot of devil's ivy.

Eli sat down across from me. He looked around the room. "I like restaurants with atmosphere. There's this place, in Philly? You walk in, the whole floor is glass, with fish swimming around underneath."

Most of the tables had pairs of businessmen talking in the hushed tones of undertakers, or pairs of women with starched hair and beige dresses. The waiters and waitresses, even the busboys, wore green satin shirts with a shamrock embroidered in silver on the back. One of the busboys looked familiar. I realized it was Daniel and lifted my hand, but he disappeared through the swinging doors into the kitchen.

Eli leaned toward me. His face had that waiting look, but different, more urgent and yet hesitant at the same time. I took off my glasses and laid them on the green linen tablecloth. Without them, the room softened into a verdant blur. As Cicero said, or maybe it was Caesar, the world wants to be deceived.

"Hey," Eli said. "You look kind of burnt. What's going down?"

I took a breath. "You tell me," I said.

He tried to look as though he hadn't heard me. "What about, uh, Lee? How's she doing?"

"Lil."

"Well, she okay? Hop said she broke, uh, her leg or something."

"She's going to be"—I paused, watching his face—"fine." His gaze broke. He reached for the fat fake-leather menu like a family album and disappeared behind it.

A green-shirted waiter appeared at my side. Young, with dark hair he had to keep tossing out of his eyes, and busy elbows. After he'd recited the specials, Eli ordered pasta (spaghetti, he called it). I ordered quiche. What else do you order in a place like that?

When he'd collected our menus and gone, Eli said, "How come you left on Thursday? I thought you weren't gonna leave till Friday morning."

"How come all these questions? How do *you* know when I left?"

"I don't know—I guess Hop must've said something."

I couldn't remember telling Hop. So Eli must have come to the house that night, Thursday night, to try and get me to take him with me. Suddenly I felt tired. I hadn't slept, really slept, all weekend. I didn't want to think about Eli and his claims; my mind was full of Lil, full of possibility. She hadn't said she'd come home with me when Dr. Hurly Burly released her, but I was sure she would.

A couple with a small boy were being seated at the table next to us. Eli turned his head to watch. The man had on what Lil and Rhoda would have called a Full Cleveland—polyester suit, white belt, white shoes. The woman's yellow hair was pulled back in a high ponytail so tight it looked painful. As soon as she sat down she dipped her finger into her water glass and started pasting back little wispy hairs that had escaped. Every few minutes either the man or the woman said to the little boy, "Urric. Sit still. Urric." Eric. They must have been from Philadelphia.

Our food came. My quiche lay on a spray of silver-green lettuce like a curly fan. Eli made conversation—the Phillies, Hop, the right way to tape and mud—winding his linguine around his fork and talking between mouthfuls; but I could feel his foot jigging up and down under the table.

146

The sun fell through the long glass window at my elbow and glinted off our ranks of unused silverware. I was going to have to get angry with Eli—that is, I *was* angry, but I was going to have to show it—and it scared me. Not because it was Eli; because Gort and I never fought. I massaged my whole-wheat roll into a pile of golden crumbs. The yellow-haired woman next to us pulled a lipstick out of her purse. The top had a little mirror on the end that she looked into while she bullied her mouth into a deeper shade of terra-cotta. Eli's eyes flicked sideways. The woman began to comb her eyelashes with a tiny gold-toothed comb. I thought, How can he even be interested? Lil would have said that the female half of the species is struggling to evolve *past* that.

"You're not eating," Eli said.

"My stomach hurts," I said, and found that it was true. Part of me must really have hoped that he'd own up, come clean, even have some kind of explanation. That we could somehow go on from there. He'd gone to get Lacey, after all: it wasn't really hit-and-run.

At the next table the little boy listened intently to our waiter's litany. He had large black eyes and was the shuddery kind of child that belongs to parents who only have one. When his turn came, he ordered a butter-pecan sundae. "Butter-pecan, butter-pecan," he sang. "Urric," said the woman. The man said, "Bring him the chicken crepes and potatoes Anna."

Eli's fork clattered onto his plate. "This is no good."

I looked at him. One foot boyishly tapping, one knee jigging up and down: I could feel the table pulsing.

"I'm no good at this kind of stuff. Jude—*talk* to me."

"I *am* talking to you."

"You know what I mean. Be real with me. Let *me* be real—"

"Eli." I took a breath. "What were you doing at my house on Thursday night?"

"Your house? What do you mean *?*"

"You know what I mean. You were there. You—" My mouth was dry; I needed water, but my hands were shaking so hard I couldn't lift the glass. "You broke Lil's arm." My voice was suddenly loud. I shouted, "You broke my daughter's arm, goddamn you!"

Eli was pale. He looked ashamed, surprised, admiring (*You have to*

147

learn how to demand things) all at once. The blonde woman and her husband were staring at us, their son forgotten.

"I'm—look, I'm sorry," Eli said. He looked miserable. Over Lil? Or because the words were so obviously hard for him to say? "I wanted to see you, that's all. Shit, Jude. I'm fuckin' *in love* with you."

"You hurt my daughter."

Eli pulled a pack of cigarettes out of his shirt pocket, tapped one out, lit it. His large hands trembled slightly, almost invisibly. He leaned forward.

"I can't sleep with other women anymore," he said miserably. "I don't even want to." I saw on his face the yearning I knew so well myself. "I'm thirty-one years old. I don't want to live like some kid. Sneaking around. Home before dark."

Forgetting that he was the one who was in the wrong, I put out my hand to soothe him, the way I would with Susie. He pulled away.

"You don't know anything about me. You got problems? Let me help you. You act like I'm just a body. Some kind of a carrier for your husband's ghost, some kind of a, a dybbuk. Surprised? See under Poltergeist. I can read."

So that was what he thought. That afterwards while he slept, his rose-brown cheek turned to the pillow, I was with Gort, as if a door I kept shut slid open for half an hour. I couldn't tell him that the opposite was true. I thought of his fingers wiping the mud from my cheek, my needle dipping in and out of his sweater. I couldn't tell him that he'd been too real.

Eli ground out his cigarette in a puddle of clam sauce and leaned across the table. He grasped my wrist exactly where the pulse flicked, and his eyes, so near I could see the yellow flecks in their brown, held an expression close to fear. His hand tightened as if to hold me down. "*Jude.*"

I pulled my hand away, worming it out of his grip. Sweat that slicked my palm.

Eli pushed back his chair. Standing up, he reached into his shirt pocket and held up a small square of blue cardboard. "Union," he said.

I didn't know what he meant at first. The word resounded in my ears like a caption for our held hands, a label for what he wanted from me. What I couldn't give him.

"I'm in," he said impatiently. "I passed the exam for master builder. I'm Union. Today's my last day with Saint Hop." He put the card in his shirt pocket and stood there looking down at me. His big hands hung from his arms like mittens. He said, "You know where I live."

He walked quickly away, a blue blur receding down an alley of green. I picked up my glasses and hooked the ends over my ears. At the next table our waiter set down three plates in front of the occupants. The little boy's held a cloudbank of pale ice cream. I should have felt proud— I'd done it, stood up to Eli, stood up for my daughter. I settled my glasses more firmly on the bridge of my nose, but Eli's back, turning the corner under an arch of palm trees, was still blurred.

13

LIL

Once I got home from the hospital I knew what I had to do. Home being Clesta's. My mother'd gotten up close to me at Mercy, when my defenses were down—she didn't rag on me about what was I doing at the house at night, and I appreciated that—but I knew better than to go home with her. It would've weakened me, my sense of purpose—my *resolve*, as Clesta would say. So I went back to Clesta's. Not because of the guy who'd decked me—not because I was afraid. If I'd just remembered the knife I'd've gotten him first; a few more seconds and I would've gotten him anyway, with the washboard. There was something funny about him, something bogus. In the five and a half days I was stuck at Mercy I'd had plenty of time to think. It crossed my mind that he might've had something to do with my mother, might've *known* her. But that was crazy. How would she have gotten mixed up with gangsters when she was afraid to even cross the Lancaster Avenue bridge?

I spent my day out of the hospital just lying there, watching the girl in the painting, the girl in the bunchy blue dress. I was still kind of wasted from the anesthetic, or maybe it was the pills they gave me to take at home. I kept drifting off. Then Doc would start banging pots and pans in the kitchen downstairs, and I'd come to. The cast felt burning hot on the inside, but when I touched the plaster it was cold. *Think*, I told myself, *think, lamestain*, and clenched my left hand into a fist so the pain shot up my arm and woke me. *The envelope.* I lay there with my arm across my stomach like this big cement log, and tried to figure out how to do what I had to do.

The only place where Daniel and I could go at night, where we could get away from other people and chiggers, was the Old Observatory. Nobody used it anymore since they'd built the new one. It faced out over the valley, on the edge of campus, out of sight of everything else. Also, it had a little romance to it, which I thought might be a good thing, in the circumstances. I'd always loved the place. When I was little it used to make me think of Sleeping Beauty's castle, all those big dark pines and spruces and wild overgrown shrubbery. You couldn't see the entrance unless you knew where it was—only the big copper dome sticking up out of the trees. My father'd given me my own key when I turned ten. I don't know where he got his. We started going there on clear nights when I was five, as soon as I could use a telescope.

▼

First we look for Venus—It's the easiest. Then Ursa Major. Daddy's hands shine in the dark. His voice shivers, reciting the constellations like a witch's spell.

Daddy, I say, I don't see it. Ursa Magic.

Major, says my father. Say it right, Lilly.

Ursa Major.

Look—it's easy, he says. In summer the handle of the Big Dipper points straight down. Just go from one star to the next, like your Dot-to-Dots.

Daddy's flashlight is red, not yellow, so our eyes will stay used to the dark. He points it at the chart for June. I can't read yet, not really. To use a star chart, you don't have to; you just need to find north. The letter N was the first one I learned.

I go back to the telescope. My father's arm around me holds me steady on the ladder. I know I can never fall. At home I practiced winking for hours in front of the hall mirror, first one eye then the other, winking and winking until my eyes watered. But now they keep shutting both at once. Finally I find Ursa Major.

Next, Libra. Everything looks different from when we sat with the big round charts on the living room floor. (Imagine the sky is a big bowl upside-down, my father said, and your head goes up into the middle of it, like a hat. The biggest dots were the brightest stars. Blue was hottest, then:

green
white
yellow
orange
red

It felt wrong that red was the coolest.)

151

The last thing we look for is the Little Dipper. I'm having more and more trouble winking.

Imagine the telescope is your eye, Lilly. A magic eye.

I try again. I can't find it, I say.

Daddy cocks the telescope. I know where west is. I still can't find the Little Dipper. But my father has his sad voice now.

So I say, I see it. Daddy, I see it!

And he hugs me tight, tight. Hey—that's my girl.

▼

The hard part was getting past Clesta's room where she lay in bed with one hand in Chinky's knotted fur. On her TV the ten o'clock weatherman bounced his pointer on the map to show a storm coming across the country, like Miss Kaplan explaining Sherman's March. I inched sideways along the mahogany paneling, the way they did in Clesta's old private-eye movies, careful not to bump it with my cast. Then downstairs, past Doc's closed door next to the kitchen. Luckily, he had the Late Night Preacher turned up good and loud. "Son of Man!" The voice prickled the hairs on the back of my neck. "Go out in that valley. And preach to those—dry bones."

Not much chance I'd be heard over that. I ran down the stairs, pursued by the rolling, hungering voice. "Son of Man"—the deadbolt slid back and I eased through the half-open door—"Can these—bones— LIVE?"

Daniel was waiting for me in the courtyard. The night was cool for August; a clean cool breeze, almost like fall, blew on my scalp where the bangs used to be. Daniel had on his skanky old army jacket, and I wished I'd brought a sweater. No pockets. I had to let Daniel put my flashlight— my father's old one—in his. The stupid cast made everything harder.

In the day and a half since I'd left the hospital, I'd worked out my plan. *Strategy*—the word had a sly, scratchy sound, like my dad's plastic mesh fishing net. First, the place—romantic, dark, and bugless. Second, don't mention the envelope (last time, in the cemetery, that might've been what kept Daniel from getting confused enough). Third, be a Hutchins. I'd skeeved out, basically, last time. Not now.

"Why go all the way to the Observatory?" Daniel asked as we turned off Broad Street onto Spangenberg.

I was sure he knew what I had in mind; but I played along. "Because it's such a clear night. Clearest one in three weeks. Look."

The sky was navy blue, moonless, thick with stars. They seemed to spin without moving, like when you hold your breath a second longer than you really can. Daniel tripped on a brick and went back to watching the sidewalk.

"I didn't mean, why tonight," he said. "I meant, why not just use your own telescope? The one in your room?"

"*Because*," I said patiently, "mine is just a six-inch. The one in the Old Observatory is ancient, but it's twelve inches."

I wasn't scared, but I did feel sort of wired. I'd thrown away the pills Doc'd set by my place at lunch and dinner. It bothered me that Daniel and I were walking out of sync. No matter how I tried to let my legs glide along by themselves until they kind of sneaked up on his rhythm, the way I used to with Dad, I couldn't make us match.

"Or why use a telescope at all? Why not just stand on a hill and use your eyes?"

"When it comes to the stars, what most people don't realize is, the human eye is just about worthless." Quoting my father, I start to chill out a little. "In fact, the whole human body is a bad design. Any half-decent engineer could've done better." We passed under a streetlight, and I could see from the look on his face that Daniel wasn't listening. "Now, here's *my* idea," I said loudly. "Solar discs. Just a flat, round shape—no arms and legs and things hanging out. No broken bones."

He looked up. "Yeah, but how would you walk?" he said, and I saw Clesta's fist with the thumb stuck out. I felt sorry for Daniel then, and sorry I wasn't with him because I wanted to be.

"Roll," I said. "You'd just roll along on your edge, like a wheel. And all your energy would come from the sun, you wouldn't need to eat or piss."

"What about sex?"

He *would* ask that. He was almost as big a hypocrite as my mother— half of him didn't know what the other half was up to. I stopped feeling sorry for him.

"Two of you would just sort of clap together," I said. "Like magnets.

When you pulled apart, there'd be another little disc in between you. All ready to roll."

"Sounds like an Oreo cookie."

We'd almost walked past the turn-off. I grabbed his arm. "This way."

I pulled him up the cinder path through a bunch of rhododendrons sticky with spider webs, and juniper bushes that stung my bare ankles. We went up the steps to the big wooden door. I lifted the chain off over my head and felt for the key and coaxed it into the lock. It was two years since my father'd brought me here—it was before he started to look sad all the time, walking around with one shoulder hunched like someone trying to hide a hole in his sweater—but my hand remembered. Turn to the left, push.

Inside, Daniel pulled his flashlight out of his jacket pocket and snapped it on.

"All the way back," I said. I followed him across the vestibule, down two steps, along the narrow corridor with huge dark windows on both sides. "Birds try to fly right through here," I said. "All day long you hear this thump, thump." I'd never been here in daylight, but the bushes outside were full of dead birds.

We came to the spiral staircase. Daniel fumbled in his pockets and handed me my flashlight, the special red one. I held it in my left hand—I still wasn't used to the weight of the cast but I could use the hand for small things—and felt along the scabby iron railing with my right. I went first. The iron steps squawked under my hightops and the frame shook, tugging up from the floor. Daniel put a hand on my back. He'd been acting weird since I'd come home from the hospital—*solicitous*—as if I'd suddenly become fragile.

At the top we came out into a small round room with no windows. Hot, from the heat of the day sealed in. There was the stale, library smell I remembered—crumbling paper and flour-paste and dust. Swiveling my flashlight around, I showed Daniel the round walls, the dark copper dome over our heads. Hot, cottony air filled my throat. We were inside a bell of heat, like lightning bugs in a jar.

"Where's the light switch?" Daniel said in this take-over voice that turned into a squeak at the end.

"No. Someone'll see."

154

Now that we were here I almost wished we weren't. I hadn't been in this room for so long. It felt wrong to be here with Daniel. We walked slowly around the room with our flashlights. There were a lot of old curling astronomical charts taped to the curved walls: Leo, Orion, Cassiopeia. "There's Ursa, the Bear," Daniel said. The one constellation *everybody* knows. Next came a framed engraving of a guy. "Nicholas Copernicus," I told Daniel, and put my flashlight up closer. His hair, almost shoulder-length, bushed out over his ears like my mother's high school graduation picture. Next to him was a chart that measured off the universe in light years: the sun was a tiny dot, and the earth wasn't there at all.

Stacked on the floor were boxes and boxes of books, as if someone had been up here moving things around. I didn't really think it was *him*; but I knelt down to look. Virgo, the Observatory cat, started and blinked as my flashlight beam moved across her, then put her head back down on *The Crime of Galileo*.

"Lil," Daniel said. "Show me how it works." His light shone on the telescope, which anyone would've had to admit was huge.

First I went over to the wall and grabbed the thick braided rope and pulled. There was a loud grinding noise above our heads. We both looked up. The dome split; the two halves started pulling away from each other. We could see the sky.

I laid my flashlight on the table next to Daniel's, one red, one yellow. They shone out from the edge. The metal barrel of the telescope felt cold. My hand wouldn't reach around it, or both hands, even—it was the size of a cannon, probably. I showed Daniel the two ship's wheels you turn to set the direction and angle of the telescope. This is the pier here's the focus here's how you change the refraction.

"How come you know all this?"

"My dad taught me."

"Was—I mean, *is* Uncle Gort an astronomer?"

"No, but he wanted to be. Astronomer, or biologist—just, you know, study things. The natural world. We used to—" My voice sounded strange and quavery. I said, louder, "You think *this* one is big. The one at Kitt Peak is a hundred and twenty-eight inches. You sit *inside* it. Even then, you don't see the whole sky. There's a whole quarter of the sky you can't see from the Northern Hemisphere. You have to go to Chile. Cerro Tololo." I rolled the "r" so hard that little bits of spit sprayed Daniel's cheek.

"We could stop off and visit *my* dad," he said. "In Puerto Vallarta." Like he thought we could trade Runaway Parent stories.

I put my eye to the eyepiece. At first all I saw was a dark-blue blur. Daniel's yellow flashlight hurt our night vision but for some reason I didn't want to ask him to turn it off. I felt for the corrugated ring further along the barrel and swiveled it back and forth until the stars burst clear.

Every time, no matter how often I did it, it was always the same. It was like falling—like falling *up*. The darkness unfolding and opening; the stars spinning toward me. I let it pull me out further and further. All I wanted was to be out there, out of myself, out of my body.

"Lil? Lil—you okay?"

Slowly I pulled my eye away. I leaned against the pier and lifted my damp hair off the back of my neck and flapped it up and down. "Here," I mumbled to Daniel. "You look."

But Daniel came around behind me and took my hair in both hands. I felt him pulling—left, right, left again. He was braiding my hair. It felt creepy. I grabbed onto the cool, solid barrel of the telescope. *Strategy*, I reminded myself. In the darkness I could hear Daniel breathing through his mouth the way Susie did when she was practicing Word Attack. When he came to the end, his fingers kept on going, down my back and under the edge of my T-shirt and across my ribs to my breasts. I made my shoulders relax. *This time it's going to work.* I turned around. We stood there kissing. It was hard to keep my balance—Daniel kept leaning into me, so that I rocked back on my heels.

My T-shirt I just left on—pulling it over the cast was too complicated. We peeled off our jeans inside-out. When it came to our underpants, Daniel hesitated. I took mine off, then pulled at the stiff elastic of his. Finally he rolled them down and kicked them off.

It pointed straight up, a little larger than a man's thumb. It *looked* like a thumb. The back of my neck prickled. "Isn't it supposed to be bigger?" I said. I kept my voice level.

Daniel reached for my hand. I took a step back, breathing slow and deep. He said, "Lil? Are you afraid?"

Afraid. Whose daughter did he think I was? I reached out my good hand and he pulled it toward him.

It felt gristly, nosing my palm; but the skin was like warm velvet. His balls felt strange. What had I expected? Hard, maybe, and covered with short stiff hairs, like sycamore burrs. But they were soft and pouchy.

We lay down on the wooden floor. There was something I'd never felt before, this humming, like my body had little pockets of humming all over it. It scared me but I didn't want it to stop. Daniel's bare back was smooth and warm, like fruit that's been left in the sun. I thought of my mother's flavor-of-the-week lipstick, of how she'd started staying at work way past dinnertime. *What the eye doesn't see.* I put my right hand on Daniel's butt. His hands went all over my body like a little kid feeling for the right puzzle piece. The cast kept getting in between us. I stuck my left arm straight out on the floor and Daniel got on top of me.

The breathing started—*huh ahuh ahuh*—that sound that runners make. I could feel the sweat between our two stomachs, and his penis pressing into my crotch. The humming got deeper, wider, as if all the little pockets were spreading and melting into each other. We were both bumping up and down now. Our sweaty stomachs quacked whenever they pulled apart. Daniel's hand pushed at my legs.

Rhoda'd said it would hurt; but it didn't. Not then. More like at the doctor's, when he pushes the wooden spatula into your mouth and presses your tongue down. Say *ah*; and you do. And then it felt different. It felt completely weird, not something but some*one*. Someone *inside*.

It stopped being Daniel. Bucking. Bumpy. Little hisses in the dark over my face, into the side of my neck. It stopped being someone I knew. My braid felt like a string of bones under my back. I was there in the hot, breathless dark with nobody I'd ever met. Looking up at the two tracks of light, one red one yellow, above our bodies, I tried to remember the constellations, *Andromeda, Antlia, Apus.* My cast banged on the wooden floor. I felt pinned down all over, like when I'd had the body cast. The sound of the breathing pounded on and on. *Caelum, Camelopardalis, Cancer.* Someone's wet face buried in my shoulder. Someone's nose knocking on my collarbone. I turned my cheek to the cool, dusty floor.

Cygnus. Cygnus. Cygnus.

Afterwards I couldn't speak. Daniel slid off me and I inched away, bumped over the bare floor on my bare butt until I was by myself. My eye-lashes were gummed together; I had to blink hard to get my eyes open. I took a deep breath all the way down past my lungs into my belly. That was when it hurt. The pain was the center of me, like a hard hot bone. It felt like it had been there always.

When I sat up, my T-shirt was bunched up under my arms. With my right hand I pulled it down, first one side, then the other. I patted around in the dark until I found my jeans. I wiped my thighs with them, rubbing hard; then I turned them right side out and sat up and put them on. They stuck to my skin. I found the canvas sling and struggled with the buckle. Everything smelled like library paste.

I heard Daniel stand up, zip, pad barefoot across the room, one foot hitting the floor heavier than the other. There was a thud. The red flash-light rolled toward me across the wooden floor, winked, and went out.

Slowly I stood up. My hair had unraveled—there wasn't any rubber band to hold it.

Daniel was standing at the telescope with his eye to the eyepiece. He let out a sigh and turned around. "Lil?"

I still couldn't talk.

"Lil? You okay?"

Okay?

Daniel laid his hand on the barrel of the telescope.

"It's like—it's like the river," he said. The word "river" came out a squeak. "There's *everything* in it."

More than anything, I didn't want him to know how I felt. I didn't want him to take any more of me. "Bust *this*," I said when I could trust my voice. "It's over us, not under us. If it was a river, it'd be upside-down."

I could feel him look at me. The yellow light from the flashlight on the table cut between us and made a knothole of light on the opposite wall. He said, "Lil. Listen—"

I pushed past him and got busy closing up. It took longer with one arm. For a second Daniel just stood there. Then he came over and picked up his flashlight and followed my hands with the light, trying to be help-ful. He kept on trying to talk to me. Finally I said, "Look. If it hadn't been now, it would've just been later. You wanted to do it; so we did it. So what?"

By the time I finished saying it, it felt true. There was a kind of clearing in my head, with room enough for what I was saying, and nothing else.

Daniel put his hand over mine. I pulled my hand away. The flashlight beam crossed my face for a second, like a slap; then I turned my back and started yanking at the braided rope. The dome over our heads began to close with a loud, retching sound.

Daniel sat down on the floor to put on his hightops. I held the flashlight so he could tie them, and I did not let it shake. It was my one and only chance to see his foot—I already knew I was *never* going to do this again—so I looked. I could take something of his. The part with the four stubs was like a seashell, curved and fluted; the big toe looked like an afterthought. He tried to hunch over so I couldn't see. My stomach jumped, but I made myself keep looking. When he was done I gave him back the flashlight and went over and picked up mine from where it had fallen. The lens was cracked right across; I couldn't get it to go on. Across campus the clock in Oberdorf Tower started to chime. I stood holding the broken flashlight and counting. Nine. Ten. Eleven. It felt much later.

"Let's jet," I said.

We started down the twisting iron stair. Daniel went first because he had the light.

▼

In Clesta's bathroom I pulled the chain on the tulip-glass light over the toilet and washed. I washed my body, clumsily, holding the washrag and soap in the same hand. I washed my T-shirt and jeans in the sink—my underpants were back in the Observatory. In my jeans pocket the lump of cheese I'd forgotten to give Virgo melted and stuck to the flannel lining. I washed and washed. But I couldn't get rid of the smell. The skin of my shoulders smelled when I bent my head. I couldn't get the smell of *boy* off me.

I sat up in the wicker rocker in Clesta's guest room until it was almost light. The white cap of the girl in the painting got whiter and whiter; the leafless trees were like black skeleton-fingers grasping for her while she

159

stood stupidly within reach. I didn't want to know what I knew now; I wished, as much as I'd ever wished for anything, that I could give it back. *The envelope*, I said to myself, over and over; *the envelope*. I didn't know if Daniel was going to give it to me or not; for the first time, I didn't care. For the first time in a long time, I wanted my mother. I couldn't, wouldn't give in. I sat in my dark room in the dark without rocking and looked out the window, watching the stars shrink and fade.

The earth; then the sun; then the Milky Way. Go in the other direction. North America; Pennsylvania; the Lehigh Valley; 110 Wesley; me. A dot on a dot on a dot. Can these bones live?

He took away the sky from me. Now when I looked at it, I'd remember, I wouldn't be able not to, I'd remember how it felt.

14

JUDITH

When the doorbell rang, it gave me a jolt like an alarm clock. Hardly anybody used it, even strangers—it hung by a single frayed wire. It was noon; Susie had gone over to Clesta's to watch Saturday morning cartoons in color. Alone in the house, I was jumpy, my stomach skittering the way it used to do before a Latin test: I couldn't get used to the idea that Lil had gone to Clesta's when Mercy released her two days before. I'd been so sure she'd come home. On my way from the kitchen to the living room I thought, Maybe it's her, Doc bringing her back, with her things.

On the porch was a young black woman in a hot-looking navy blue uniform. *Lil*, I thought, and the quivering in my stomach turned into thudding, *Lil and Rhoda. Trouble.* Then I remembered Rhoda was out west somewhere.

"Mrs. Hutchins?" The woman stepped up close to the dusty screen. Her hair was braided and pinned up on her head, and she wore glasses with clear plastic frames. When she smiled there was a gap between her front teeth like Eli's. "Mrs. Gordon Hutchins?"

I admitted it.

"I'm Officer Bassette." She held her ID up to the screen. "I'd like to talk to you for a few minutes. Can I come in?"

"Oh—oh, sure, yes." I held the door open and Officer Bassette stepped carefully off the mat into the living room. It was a gloomy day, hot and sticky and sunless; but I didn't turn on the lamp. "What is it?" I said. "What's the matter?"

I could hear her breathing. She sat down, abruptly, on the park bench by the front window. Drops of sweat trembled on her forehead and along the part in her hair. I thought, This is going to be bad. To stop her saying what she'd come to say, I asked, "Would you like a glass of water?" and she nodded gratefully.

161

When I came back from the kitchen she seemed to have gotten hold of herself. I handed her the water and sat down on a canvas chair across from her. Ice cubes clicked against the side of the glass, Susie's Mickey Mouse glass, with a festive sound.

"I'm sorry," Officer Bassette said after a second, breathless from drinking so fast. "You got to understand, Mrs.—Mrs. Hutchins—this is my first time." She drank again, then set the empty glass down on the floor between her navy blue oxfords. Her shoelaces were tied in double knots, and the crease in her trousers was so sharp they stuck out in two pouts above her blue-stockinged ankles. I heard her take a breath. Her feet were large for her height, like Susie's. I kept looking at her feet.

"We, uh, we have reason to believe—" she stopped; then it all came out in a rush. "I'm sorry to tell you this ma'am but your husband's body was found this morning about three A.M. The Towanda police called us a hour ago." Papers rattled. "Ten-forty-three A.M. Ma'am?"

I felt flooded with cold, as if someone had flushed ice water through me. A cold almost like relief. This was it, the worst thing; it had come, finally, and I could see its shape, tight and knotted like Officer Bassette's blue shoelaces. I thought, in that second after she spoke, *Now he's safe.*

Then I felt myself shuddering all over, and then Officer Bassette was kneeling beside me and her arm in the hot, scratchy serge gripped my shoulders. "Breathe," she said, "breathe deep, now." I smelled freshly ironed cloth and the faint, smoky odor of her sweat.

She handed me a Kleenex folded in four like a greeting card, and waited. I suppose they train them to do that—to wait. The backs of my hands were wet. Waiting seemed like a good idea, so I did, too. I wasn't thinking—there were things in my mind but they were anonymous, invisible, like a familiar landscape in dense fog—but I wasn't listening, either. When Officer Bassette came to the end of what she was telling me, she had to say it all over again. How the body (*the body*) was found upstate by two vacationing fishermen out from Philly, Vernon Brooks and Eric Ciraco, who called the Towanda police; how the Bradford County Department of Health sent out their agent, George N. Freitas (I stored all these names carefully, they were real and specific, not like the Body); how the Body was sent to Scranton, where the assistant M.E. ("M.E.?" "Medical Examiner—that's, like, used to be the Coroner, like on TV?"), Dr. Maxine Cheng, made her inspection to determine the manner of death.

"That's the whole total picture." Officer Bassette had gone back to her place on the park bench. She lowered the papers she'd been reading from—the M.E.'s report, faxed from Scranton—and looked at me, scared and young and earnest in her coronet of braids like a black version of a Mennonite farm girl. "So now, what we need, for a positive ID we need to know some physical characteristic of the deceased. You see what I'm sayin'? Birthmark, scar—that kinda thing. Tattoo?"

The Deceased.

"Ma'am?"

"Can—I see him?" I said. The words seemed to fall from somewhere far away, one by one, like stones.

"Ma'am, the M.E. doesn't encourage next-of-kin to view the body. It's not necessary, you see what I'm sayin'? Certain cases, what they do, they'll show you photos, but. In this particular—"

"I need to see him." There was Gort, my husband; and there was the Body. How could I make them come together, otherwise?

"Ma'am. The thing is, is that—" She put out her hands and patted the air between us, as if comforting a child. On her left hand was a wedding ring, shiny new gold, and I understood her fear.

"What is it?" I almost said, *hon.*

"The thing is, a drowning incident, the, well, the body—deteriorates. The longer it's been in the water, the harder it is to . . . to . . ."

It was then that I understood. I thought of Gort's father, my uncle Bob: the one gesture of perfection available to anyone. Perfect, complete, irreversible refusal. I leaned into the wall and shut my eyes.

"Mrs. Hutchins?"

"How long?"

Officer Bassette looked down at the papers in her hand. "About eight weeks. Near as they can tell. I'm sorry, Mrs. Hutchins, I'm really really sorry."

Eight weeks—around the solstice, then. "You said, drowned."

"It's right here. See, with Manner of Death, there's four possible ways"—she was talking faster, but it seemed to calm her, talking about procedures—"Homicide, Accident, Suicide, Natural. And Undetermined, but that's usually a polydrug kinda thing, where there's so many different substances in the body that the M.E. can't tell which one, you know, did it. You see what I'm sayin', there was no drugs or evidence of foul play with—your husband. No, no note or anything. So the M.E. ruled, Accident."

Maxine Cheng, that was her name.

"A small round scar like the sun, the way a child would draw the sun," I said. And in that moment the Body became Gort.

"Excuse me?"

"To identify him. My husband. Right below his"—I had to pause for a second to turn Gort's naked back to me, feel the scar under my fingers— "left shoulderblade. About the size of a dime. With little rays all around it, from the stitches."

Officer Bassette had pulled out a green ballpoint pen and was filling out a form on her lap. "Funeral parlor?" she said gently. When I didn't answer, she added that the state of Pennsylvania would transport the Body from Scranton (not the boat or the tent and things, they'd been left where they were). "No monies are involved."

"Kemerer's Funeral Home," I said finally. Gort's mother, my Aunt Eulalie, had been buried from there eight years ago; it was the only one I knew. Officer Bassette wrote that down, too. I watched her large, round, girl's handwriting embroider, upside-down, the empty places on the form until nothing was left. When she'd finished, she thanked me and got up to go. Without thinking, I held out the damp, crumbly Kleenex, and she took it.

As I pushed open the screen door, someone's house alarm went off. Over its distant, high-pitched sobbing, Officer Bassette said, "Good luck," and shook my hand. While we were inside, the sun had come out. Officer Bassette looked out over the yard into the bright sky, and I could feel her relief at being *out here*. She said, "The weather vasculates so much lately." Then, slipping her hand out of mine, "Goodbye, Mrs. Hutchins. You have a—" Her teeth with that little gap clamped down on her lower lip. *Nice day*.

After the police car had gone, Lustyka appeared from beneath the shiny dark-green leaves of the rhododendron bushes, lashing her tail. I went down the steps. She let me pick her up and I stood holding her thin body with the ribs like bars beneath the warm fur, while the distant alarm shimmered on and on. The sun shone through the lattice as if nothing had happened, flashing off the glossy optimistic circulars spread over the porch floor, blue and yellow and red, so that they hit my eyes with bright little slaps.

▼

Afterwards everything went so fast. The funeral home, the lawyer (Clesta sent over her Mr. Archimbeault, who looked through Gort's desk in the attic and found a will, an insurance policy, all that), the cemetery. I suppose people thought—I would have thought, if it had been someone else—that I was numb, frozen. It wasn't that. I felt in motion, felt I had to *stay* in motion. Like the burned-out stars Gort had told me about, orbiting frantically for hours (*are* there hours, in space?) before they finally yield. I thought of Gort's body, traveling: Bitter Lake to Towanda to Scranton to home. I kept moving, too, one thing after another, practical matters.

The first thing I did after Officer Bassette left was go to Kemerer's Funeral Home. I decided not to tell Lil and Susie, or Clesta, or anyone, until the police said it was definite—until the body came from Scranton the following morning and the physical identification was made. There was that small hope, that they were wrong, that somehow, despite the driver's license and the Triple A card (Gort didn't believe in credit cards), the body was just that—a body. Foul play: a stolen wallet. The rest of me, the part that *knew*, went to Kemerer's. From somewhere, somehow, I knew there had to be a funeral, for the girls. I'd have had the casket open, if I could, so they could see him, could know with their own eyes.

On the large wrought-iron sign beside the brick walk you could see where *& SONS* had been removed and *Jr.* added. The yew and juniper all around the huge old house had been trimmed so relentlessly that they looked like the green-painted cones and spheres that come with the villages for electric trains. The marble steps leading up to the massive carved wooden door were just steep enough to remind you how small you were.

Inside, drapes were drawn everywhere, all the light was artificial, eternal, like a shopping mall. It could have been any time of day, any day of the year. Everything, even the walls, seemed to be dark shiny wood, like my grade school back in Orient. It *smelled* like school—raisins and PineSol and carnauba wax, and some complex smell underneath that said, *generations*. A red-haired girl in a black jumpsuit asked me to wait— "He's making an arrangement right now"—and led me in past a door that said "Clergy Only" and sat me down on a sofa. By my elbow a table held a stack of round black lace chapel caps, like pancakes, and black silk yarmulkes folded in half. After a few minutes a heavy mahogany door opened and a young woman emerged, almost as pregnant as Lacey; a three- or four-year-old boy in denim shorts and a Donald Duck cap with a yellow bill dragged at her hand. She stood still and watched as the red-haired girl led me past, looking like someone without a destination. In the gap where a button was unfastened on her bright pink shirt, the top of her belly was dark and shiny.

Sitting down in a chair across from Otto Kemerer (Jr.), I felt as if I'd been called to the principal's office. Everything in the room was low and calm and muted—the timeless, calculated light, the serious browns and maroons of the room, Mr. Kemerer's steady, practiced voice—as if to say that, here, entropy did not exist. As if to baffle grief. A fan swiveling in the corner threw pillows of air at me.

I was tired from walking in the afternoon heat—Lacey would have driven me, but then I would have had to tell her, and I couldn't, not until I'd told Lil and Susie (as it was, I'd been lucky that Lacey wasn't home during the half-hour the police car stood outside the house). I leaned into the chair's motherly padded back while Mr. Kemerer's voice wove a terrifying net of abstractions: the Deceased, the Memorial, Interment, Arrangement. To escape I said my list of names to myself—Vernon Brooks, Eric Ciraco, George N. Freitas, Maxine Cheng—each one a different, distinct shape on my tongue. Afterwards I couldn't remember what Mr. Kemerer looked like, only his voice, smooth and soothing. He said "Mm-hmm" at least every other sentence. "—Mrs. Hutchins, in this very difficult time, mm-hmm." Once a door opened behind me and there was a sudden stream of office sounds, clipped, cheerful—a telephone's buzz, the rapid clicking of a typewriter, a woman's voice, "—that drowning upstate?"—before it shut again. I looked at the leaded stained glass panel beyond Mr. Kemerer, backed by some unseen source of light so that its purple and deep-blue and gold design, carefully abstract, bloomed behind his head. Glass is transparent, Gort told me once, because it's actually in motion. Very slow, slow motion: over a period of a thousand years the bottom of a pane of glass will become just perceptibly thicker than the top.

"—cremation, mm-hmm?"

"No!" I said violently. Mr. Kemerer looked, for the first time, almost alarmed; then he recovered and we established ("Oh, mm-hmm, uh-huh") that Gort would be buried at Swan Point Cemetery with the rest of the Hutchinses. Shaking, I leaned back in my chair again. I had not realized how it would be, the decisions still to be made, the possibility of doing violence to the dead. Mr. Kemerer continued. I looked at the glowing stained glass behind his head. Brooks, Ciraco, Freitas, Cheng.

After a while, talking now about Effects, Mr. Kemerer handed me papers to sign, thick, stiff, pebbled sheets. He bit his fingernails, I saw; the skin around them was puffy and red. Effects? For a second I thought, His death will go on and on, the effects will never stop.

"—wallet, personal things, mm-hmm, watch, rings, things of that sort. There's a separate release form, then they'll be released to you. Mm-hmm."

I thought of someone sliding (yanking?) the wedding ring, his only jewelry, from his finger. I tried to remember what his hands looked like, the size of the knuckles, whether his fingers were warm or cool. I couldn't remember the last time I'd touched him, the exact last time: the night before he left? That morning? The blue of the stained-glass panel was like an ache. There was an equation to describe glass, the same kind of equation as for ocean waves.

"Pardon? I'm sorry, Mrs. Hutchins, what did you say?"

"Nothing," I murmured.

When I got up to go, Mr. Kemerer shook my hand. Libby, the red-haired girl, would take me up to the casket showroom on the third floor when I was ready. His palm was smooth and cool and powdery. In the morning they (They) would bring the Body here; I would not see it, or hold it. I could not remember the equation for glass.

▼

"Don't say 'passed away,'" Mrs. Muschlitz instructs us in Latin III, leaning forward slightly from the waist, her tone suggesting that this is advice to be remembered always. We're translating Lucretius; I'm sitting by the windows where winter sun falls hot through the glass onto my hand. "Don't say 'went to his reward' or 'found eternal rest.' Aim for a good plain style. Say, 'Died. He's dead.'"

▼

I told Lil and Susie first, because he was theirs. I waited until Officer Bassette called on Sunday morning, just before noon; then I called Lil at Clesta's, leaning against the kitchen wall by Susie's Cat House drawing, cupping the mouthpiece so no words would be lost—and asked her to come home. There must have been something in my voice, because she didn't argue, just said she'd borrow Doc's bike. I went into the living room and got Susie away from an old *Nature* special on "The World of Sharks" to wait with me on the front porch, scuffing the mail with one large bare foot and muttering, "*Why* do we have to wait out here? Why *do* we?" I felt so tired. I leaned against the wet clapboards. It had rained, on and off, all morning; now it had stopped. The spider web over the mailbox was dotted with beads of rain as round and distinct as tears. I couldn't see any sign of the spider.

When Lil came I took one hand each and held it, sweaty palm against my palm—comfort, a warning. The good, plain words came out curt, final: a door slammed shut. "Daddy's dead," I said. And then my courage, or my ruthlessness, failed, and I added, "It was an accident, up at the lake. He, he drowned."

I'd told them together so that they could comfort each other. But Susie, when she grasped what I'd said, threw her arms around my waist and pushed her face into my belly; Lil took her hand away and turned and looked out into the yard, which was wild and sad. Bees tangled in the rusty blossoms of the snowball bushes along the fence. The sound they made seemed so loud. I remembered my father complaining about his hearing aid—how it made everything the same, flattened the hills and raised the valleys so that every sound had the same weight, and he couldn't tell what was important anymore. Grief was like that. Susie shuddered silently against my stomach. It began to rain again.

Lil stood poised at the top of the steps as if part of her wanted to come to me, part to run down the steps and swing onto Doc's bike and pedal away. Who will she blame? I thought. Susie's face made a wet patch on my stomach through my T-shirt. I watched Lil sit down on the top step, slowly, awkwardly, as if it hurt. Will she blame me?

I went to her then, with Susie still twined around me, the two of us skidding a little on the mail, and crouched down and put my arm around Lil's thin, tense shoulders. She kept her back to me, but she let me hold her. The buckle of her sling felt cold under my fingers. Rain blew up onto the porch, onto the three of us hunched there, carrying the rich, sad smell of earth and cinders and rain-wet leaves. I leaned my forehead against Lil's sweat-streaked hair and my breath made a warm fog around my face. Part of me had known, all along, where he was.

FOUR

15

LIL

For two whole days after the funeral I stayed in bed. I was still at Clesta's, because Clesta was the Natural Object of my Affections, now. But there didn't seem to be anything to get up for. I didn't know what to do next. I didn't feel sad or angry or like bargaining, or any of the things Reverend Zinck had mentioned. All there was was this *blankness*. Like when you've forgotten and blown something off and you're scared, waiting to remember, because you know that whatever it is, you're screwed without it. Clesta came up every couple of hours with Red Zinger tea or a hot-water bottle or an ice-pack. I let her put her dry, shaky palm on my cheek and forehead, feeling for fever, because the look she'd had ever since Doc told her about my father left her face then, for a minute. I could see it made her feel better to be taking care of something. When she went out again I lay between the sheets with my clothes on and Bear and Bella Squirrel on either side of me, reading all my *Sweet Valley Highs* one after the other and listening to Nine Inch Nails on my Walkman. Rhoda sent me the tape from Boise; when she made it she put in parts of a record called *Teach Yourself Polish* every couple of cuts. I lay there practicing *Take me to the Hotel Bristol* and *Not too short around the ears, please* and tried not to think about anything.

▼

The service'd been at the cemetery. For some reason Mom didn't want to use the funeral home, the way they had for my Grandmother Eulalie, and they couldn't have it in a church because Dad never went to church, not even Protestant. Swan Point Cemetery, the North Burial Ground, where the Hutchinses always get buried. I'd been there when my grandmother died; but I was only six then, more than half my life ago. Everything was strange to me now, the way riding backwards in the limousine made the same old streets seem like ones I'd never been on before.

I stood beside my mother; Susie, on her other side, scuffed at cobwebs in the grass. We were all she had. Gramma Maude'd said she had to stay in Iowa with Grampa Gene, but really it was just that funerals are one of the things that set her off; and nobody could find my Uncle James. It was a weird day—the sky was low and heavy, as if it might rain, but it was wicked hot. The air smelled like Doc's shirts simmering in Fels Naphtha on the stove. A steamy gray boiled day. I was sweating in Rhoda's black leather jacket and the black skirt I'd borrowed from my mother, pulled in at the waist with Clesta's gold-link belt. I had to keep yanking the left shoulder of the jacket up over my sling buckle.

" 'In the midst of life we are in death.' Dear brethren, we who gather here today find an occasion—a window of opportunity—to try to grasp the reality of this fact and to find comfort—yes, comfort—in its promise."

Reverend Zinck's voice sounded a lot like Doc's Late Night Preacher, even though Reverend Zinck was from the Universal Life Church and Doc was a Baptist. Maybe they all sound like that—priests, ministers, rabbis, whatever—and I'd just forgotten because of staying home all those Sundays with my father. It was Clesta who'd found us Reverend Zinck. He had stiff, swirly white hair like cake frosting. My fingers touched the little X of purple ribbon he'd fastened to our chests before we got into the limo at the funeral home. "God doesn't ask our permission when he wants to take someone," he'd said through the straight-pins stuck between his teeth, "because we'd never give it." My father didn't believe in God; did God believe in him?

The coffin had so many flowers piled on it—white roses and pink and lavender gladioli and red carnations—that you could hardly see the wood. Floral tributes, they'd called them at the funeral home. He'd've hated them, those dead, tied-up flowers; he'd rather just have had the gone-to-seed dandelions and yellow buttercups growing in the grass around the oblong hole.

I could feel everybody looking at me. A bunch of strangers—people from Bethlehem Steel, my father's goofy boss, some butt-ugly woman named Grundy from the old people's home where my mother used to work (*she* never even knew my dad)—they were all free to gawk. Rhoda's jacket stuck to the back of my neck. Crabgrass scratched my bare ankles. So that I wouldn't cry, I checked out the gravestones all around us. The whole big square of crabgrass (I could see Clesta looking down through the veil of her hat, and I bet she was thinking, *ill-kempt*, like our family) was ours. A big marble block in the middle of it said HUTCHINS between two carved sheaves of wheat; on top of it a woman in a long robe stood looking down. One hand clutched a bouquet of flowers to her chest; the other was missing, broken off the outstretched arm. She was better than some of the stuff further up the hill, tall skinny things that looked like the Washington Monument. At the other end of the floral tributes, next to Clesta and Doc, Daniel stood trying to catch my eye. I could see his hands snatch at the lining of his pants pockets. I read the little gravestones set in the grass around us, like shoe boxes. Julius P., son of James and Harriet, 1822–1868. Fannie J., 1854–1883. Captain James Sebastian Hutchins, 1st Pennsylvania Volunteers. Susannah Schmidt, His Wife. The oldest was Anna Phoebe, April 9, 1791–January 4, 1864. The newest was my Grandmother Eulalie. It suddenly occurred to me that *I* could never be buried here—or Susie or my mother or Clesta—because it was Protestant.

Reverend Zinck finished praying and started talking about the Park of Life. Daniel caught my eye then. One hand came out of his pocket to scratch his head, and the fingers curved in the "O" that meant Medium-Sized Asshole. I hadn't spoken one word to him since we came home from the Observatory Friday night; he'd come up to my room with sad, doggy eyes after Doc told him about my father, but I'd just walked away. That night I'd forgotten *him*— But I couldn't think about that. I felt the way my breasts felt when I first started them, before they stuck out at all, just the nipples bright and puffy. So tender everything hurt, even my old cotton undershirt brushing across them. I felt that way *inside*. The lightest softest thought would hurt.

Mucoproteins, sodium chloride, sodium bicarbonate, lysozymes. Across the tarred path from our plot was a huge bronze deer with flaring antlers; I blinked at it, hard. Its sides and head had turned the color of Clorets, from the weather. A sign in the grass said "Elks Rest Lodge No. 14." There were a lot of little marble shoe boxes in rows under the elk, some with little American flags sticking up from them. A cardinal flew down and lit in one of the antlers. *That makes us both elks*, Daddy used to say,

175

when one of us said the same thing he did, or had the same idea at the same time.

Reverend Zinck said, "Some get more sunlit days in the Park of Life than others. For some of us the days are cut short, and though it's only midafternoon we are taken home—yes, home—to our heavenly Father. For others it's rainy and stormy—"

At that exact second it started to hail. Tiny pellets bouncing off the gravestones and the stone lady and the green shoulders of the elk, richocheting all over the place like Mr. Burson's movie about molecules last spring. They made a *tocking* sound like Clesta's clocks on speed. When I looked up they stung my face. It hurt; but it felt good at the same time. I kept my head back and shut my eyes. Reverend Zinck raised his voice and shifted to a poem, something I'd never heard, some weird stuff about compasses. Mom grabbed my good hand and her nails dug into my palm.

Then it was over. The hail stopped, just like that. Reverend Zinck said in a final-sounding voice, "Lean not on your own understanding but in all your ways acknowledge God, and He will direct your path," the same thing I'd already heard more than once from Doc, and I thought, *Bullshit*, and the mound of flowers began to sink down slowly into the ground. We all went up one by one and dropped a handful of damp dirt onto the battered roses and gladioli. Behind me Susie was sobbing out loud, an embarrassing gulpy noise like hiccups. I could hear the clatter, down through the flowers onto the wood, when I threw my handful in. A high hollow sound, as if there was just an empty wooden box. I turned away to follow Clesta's purple back—she was leaning hard on Doc and the heels of her strappy shoes kept sinking into the ground—across the grass.

It was then that I'd had the thought.

Maybe it isn't him.

▼

After lunch on the second day after the funeral—a toasted cheese sandwich and some kind of yellow custard that smelled like after-shave, Doc brought it up on a tray and I didn't even try to eat it—Daniel knocked on my door. I told him to go away; but he said softly, with his mouth against the doorjamb, "I've got something for you." When I opened the door, he was halfway down the stairs. I followed him into the empty kitchen. "Doc took Clesta to the doctor's," he said before I could ask. "They won't be back till five. It's in here." He pushed open the storeroom door.

The dirty glass skylight let in some watery light from the gray day outside. With my good arm I held the cast against my ribs and followed Daniel's white T-shirt. In the back corner all the trunks and boxes stood in shadow; the yards of shining cloth, the crystal vases and old shoes, lay where I'd left them a few days before. A whole family history written in *things*.

Daniel reached up and pulled the metal chain on a hanging light bulb, then knelt down in an empty space on the floor where the dust swirled into patterns. He pulled a screwdriver out of the back pocket of his jeans and started prying up the splintery floorboards. The coughdrop blister from his vaccination moved in and out under the edge of his sleeve as he worked. The boards made a noise like Susie's birds scolding. Daniel reached down into the hole and pulled out the yellow envelope.

Why had he gone to so much trouble to hide it? Maybe he knew I'd searched his room; but still. Well, it wasn't my problem. I put out my hand. Daniel hung onto the envelope and looked at me. In the yellow light his face was pale and his flat, no-color hair looked green, like moss.

"Give me a break, Lil. I thought you *wanted* to."

It was the same voice, the same eyes, that he'd used *before*. But I couldn't find mine anymore. "We had a deal," I said. That wasn't even true, not really.

"Lil. It wasn't that bad, what we did. Everybody does it."

"Just give me the envelope." No sermons, Mr. Honorable Moss-Head; not anymore.

"Everybody. My father." I could see his ribcage rise and fall under the white T-shirt. "Your mother."

That makes us both elks.

"What do you mean, my mother? You are really fucked, you know that? Just because your father screws everything that moves—"

"Lil. I saw her."

I almost put my hands over my ears, like a little kid. *Shut up; shut up.*

"At the restaurant. She was with some dude in a necktie. They were holding hands, and stuff."

My stomach kind of folded in on itself. So that was who the lipstick'd been for. And I bet that was who I'd almost decked in my living room—the guy who broke my arm. No wonder she didn't object when I said I was going to stay with Clesta. I wanted to slap Daniel right across his pale, round, earnest face. With the cast, I thought, I could break his nose, no problem. Then I got a grip on myself: it was *her* I hated.

Daniel just stood there looking at me, hanging onto the envelope as if he thought that that way he could hang onto me.

"Give it to me," I said. "It's mine. I earned it."

"Lil, that's not . . . It wasn't *like* that." *Bullshit. Bull. Shit.*

Daniel put out his hand as if he were about to console me. I could see he believed his own words, and I was really ripped. People who lie *to themselves* are just fucked. I took a step back, still holding onto the cast. "It was. It *was* like that!" I shouted, hating it that there were tears in my eyes, in my voice. Screw *strategy.* I could tell the truth now. "It *was* like that. And you knew it, too. That's why you kept that envelope—you knew I'd do anything to get it."

Daniel's face got that sealed-off look, like my father's did sometimes. He stuck out the envelope.

I stood holding it in my good hand—the thing I'd been looking for for so long—and just for a second I had this weird feeling of being trapped. A wish, almost, to give it back. I should've wanted Daniel to leave, so I could open it; but I didn't. As if he knew that, Daniel bent down and picked up a red satin shoe from the floor beside him. Red and gold sequins in a heart shape on the toe winked in the dim light. He turned it over in his hands and squatted where he was, looking up at me. His eyes were sad and doggy, the way they'd been on Sunday when he came up to my room, after Doc told him about Dad.

Rain clicked on the skylight over our heads like fingers tapping. Daniel kept on turning the red shoe over and looking up at me. The red-and-gold sequins flashed. I couldn't deal with it, that sadness, that softness. I turned my back and looked hard at the trunks and round leather boxes and jumbled net and satin. My fingers squeezed the yellow envelope tight.

"You didn't have to," Daniel said. "I would've given it to you anyway."

I heard the shoe hit the floor; then Daniel brushed past me. I heard him tap his way along the wooden railing. I heard the storeroom door click shut.

▼

15 April (Bitter Lake)

Up in old basket oak to watch sun down (6:14 pm). Saw raccoon approach my dinner. Long fingers cd manage waxed paper & half-opened tuna can. Turned to left, paused, turned to right—felt watched but cdn't find source. Body still, sides swelling in & out. Fear? or?

MADAM, I'M ADAM
A MAN, A PLAN, A CANAL: PANAMA!

21 June

Solstice. Virgo in western sky—headless angel falling

23 June

"I know well what I am fleeing from but not what I am in search of."
Montaigne? Soph English—Miss Small. Memorize! Memorize!

27 June

Found arrowhead, Heflinger's field. Knew before I looked: hand has memory? Heart-shaped (abt size of hare's heart), warm. F's eyes sharper—always found the most. Dropped them into my baseball mitt 1 by 1.

Eye = exposed part of brain. In octopus, eye = seat of memory.

DENNIS SINNED

5 July

New moon. "Last night I saw the new moon w/ the old moon in her arms." L @ 3: Daddy, look, the moon—like a toenail in the sky.

9 August

Article on tardigrades, Aug Natural History. Cryptobiosis = "hidden life." Under microscope—barrel-shaped, 8 legs, chubby teddybears. When drought or deep cold, they → cryptobiosis, stay as long as takes. ≈ people who have selves frozen after death? ≈ sinking to lake bottom when F made me try to swim, eyes ears nose all sealed.

11 August (Bitter Lake)

Barred owl (Stix varia) under basket oak. Dead 10-12 hrs(?)—stiffening in claws but intact. Abt 10"—prob a male.

In animals, no fear of death? Drowning kittens w/ F. Age 8(?) The mother crouched & hissed & spread legs into the 4 corners of her box. F 1/2 right—not her own death she feared.

"Fate, chance, kings, and something something." Miss Small. Fate = target that pulls arrow → it, the way metal draws lightning?

RATS LIVE ON NO EVIL STAR

30 September

Full moon. Blood-orange.
Here—catch! J naked in hall outside C's bedroom door, summer 1976. An
orange came towards me & my arm went up. Hand felt as big as the moon.
Orange slapped into it. Knew then I loved her.

18 April (Bitter Lake)

"Now I have leave to go of her goodness,
And she of mine, to use newfanglednesse"

F's boat caulked & repainted, copenhagen blue.

5 May

sparrow	*blackbird*
swallow	*mockingbird*
oriole	*grackle*
crow	*waxwing*
bluejay	*chickadee*
golden finch	*cardinal*
wren	*red-tailed hawk*

16 May (Bitter Lake)

3 bass, 1 sm pike. Golden Furnace Streamer lost, tied by F 1968.

June 1968:

Orange life-jacket (1 more failure)
Boat creaking
Pike's gills thudding
Loons
Sun → rainbows off sides of fish

Do I remember this? Or just (re)constructing?

Maybe I

▼

That was it. That was all there was. A bunch of nature notes, like something out of *Wild Kingdom*, and some stuff about Old Bob, and a lot of quotes from dead people. Not one thing about me, unless you counted a dumb remark I supposedly made when I was a baby.

Cheated—I felt cheated. I slapped the copybook closed. A little puff of dust came up. The cover was faded and stained and the corners looked chewed; there was a yellow splotch of bird shit on the black taped spine. In the white square that said "Name" my father had written "1994–95." *Shit.* It was an *old* journal—not one he'd left for me, just something he forgot.

I read it through again, just to make sure. The pages were brown around the edges like vanilla wafers. There was a big gap before the last two entries, and the whole rest of the copybook was blank. I was really ripped. All that stuff about Old Bob—he thought more about someone who'd been dead for twenty years than about his own daughter.

And then I knew, I knew for sure he wasn't dead. He never would've gone out without a life-jacket, the way I'd heard Clesta say to Doc; he never ever let *me* do that, and I could swim. And now I was sure I knew where he was. Not Africa or Chile but the same old place. I could go up to the lake and find him. Show him that I was faithful, unlike my mother; that I was good enough to be remembered.

I could hear Clesta calling me. I looked up. The rain must've stopped; the skylight was covered with little brown measles where raindrops had fallen on the dirty glass. I stood up and pulled the chain to turn off the light. My butt was sore from the splintery floorboards and my head ached. I stuffed the copybook back into the envelope.

At first I thought I'd go up to my room and put it with the Documents until later. I'll see what Daniel thinks, I thought; then I caught myself.

I had a better idea. I stuck the envelope under my cast and went back along the walkway, holding onto the rough board railing. In the kitchen I pawed through Doc's oddments drawer until I found a pencil and a sheet of stamps. Clesta's voice, still calling me, sounded from the living room. I tore off about ten stamps, ripping right through Richard Nixon's face. After I'd licked the stamps and slapped them onto the envelope, I shouted to Clesta that I'd be right there. I sealed the envelope and addressed it to my mother. Then I ran downstairs and out the door and shoved it in the mailbox at the end of the alley.

16

JUDITH

On the third day after the funeral I walked to Schoener Place so early that Thomas was still asleep, lying on his back on his usual stretch of wall with a brown glove over his eyes. From a distance it looked like a severed hand. I walked fast, it helped dissolve the stone in my stomach that was there every morning now when I woke up. How could grief feel so much like dread? When the worst had already happened? Somewhere Thomas had found a peeling blue-and-gray baby carriage; he slept with one arm through the spokes of its wheels. When I passed, a pair of leather boots, wedged upside-down at the foot of the carriage, bounced the rising sun off their soles.

"First thing is, get the balusters loose," Hop said. It was seven-thirty Friday morning; I hadn't been in the house three minutes. With Eli gone we had to start work earlier and stop later; Mrs. vande Zaag wanted to move in with her young niece before school started in September. "See how the toe's keyed inna this here slot? Pull it out, break the glue at the top"—he gave the wooden baluster a twist, and there was snap where it met the handrail—"like so. Okay?"

He took the freed baluster in both hands, swung it like a baseball bat, then held it out to me. Morning sun from the master bedroom angled into the hall. The dark wood shone with intricate turns and flutings.

"No machine did that," Hop said. "That's workmanship. Workmanship is everything. Am I right? There's only about a thousand bucks worth of materials in the average American house. A thousand bucks."

He came around the newel post and crouched down beside me. He showed me how to pry up the trim under the tread, go along the back with a hacksaw to cut through the nails that held it to the riser, then turn the whole tread over. Except for the dust, the other side looked like new wood. "Kinda like your fence boards," Hop said, and grinned. His morning breath smelled like bananas.

He stood up. A shaft of sun lit up the tufts of white-gold hair floating just above his ears, so that he looked like an aging cherub. "Now. You got your pry bar, your hacksaw, your hammer. Nippers?" He went into the master bedroom. The pliers shot around the corner and clattered at my feet. He called, "Just flip the treads that're bad. The others we'll sand. You decide." I heard the circular saw start up.

By the time I'd pulled all the sawed-off nailheads out of the tread Hop had pried up, my fingers felt as if they'd been on the other end of the pliers, and the skin at the base of my thumb was rubbed raw. I flipped the tread over and sat down on the stair below. With my shirt-tail I wiped the sweat off my face, running it under the metal nose-piece of my glasses.

We worked faster these days, the radio tuned to CBS news instead of Country and Western. When I'd come back to work on Wednesday, the day after the funeral, Hop had said, as he'd said on the phone Sunday night, "Judith, I'm real sorry"; after that he didn't mention Gort again. I was grateful for his reticence, his male absorption in the work at hand. Things were different for me now: what money meant; what work meant. Gort's insurance, unearthed by Mr. Archimbeault, would pay for the funeral and enough over to start a college fund for each of the girls; there was about five thousand dollars in Bethlehem Steel stock; and that was all.

What Hop and I meant to each other had changed, for both of us. He'd hired me because he'd had to, because he'd owed Paul a favor; now, he needed me. ("Can't trust the Irish," he said. "Am I right?") We were within a few weeks of finishing at Schoener Place, and he'd already signed me up for the next job, a geodesic dome somebody at the college wanted built out near Smoketown. Get yourself a pair of steel-toed shoes at Gertler's, he'd advised me, and watch out for ingrown toenails. Yesterday, watching me miter the black oak trim on the kitchen cabinets, he'd said, "You know, you'd make a good finish carpenter. You got the hands. There's a course over at Valley Tech, Armijo took it six or seven years ago. It pays more, finish carpentry." There was no more talk of being temporary, and it wasn't out of charity to a new widow, either. Hop worked me as hard as he worked himself; I could lose myself in it the way he did, the way men do. That was what Hop meant to me, now, a lifeline. Days, I had to think about what I was doing; nights, I came home too mercifully tired to think.

I heard Hop's workboots clump downstairs and then the kitchen radio came on loud. Someone had formed an Ollie-North-for-President Committee; the police were trapping boa constrictors in attics all over Philadelphia. I picked a stair that looked as if an animal had gnawed it. After I got the beautiful balusters off in one piece and leaned them against the wall by Hop's two, I attacked with the crowbar. By the time I'd gotten it free and turned it over, breathing hard, I'd forgotten everything else. The old pride swept me up: you'd have thought I'd turned the Tilghman Building over onto its fresh side.

The next tread was far enough up that I had to go and stand at the top of the staircase to get a purchase on it. I wedged the bar underneath the shoe-molding. "People get tired of your exotics," said the radio voice. "Rather have a cocker spaniel or a tabby-cat, so they drop 'em in a dumpster somewheres." I pushed down hard. There was a squawk. In one piece, the wooden molding shot up over my head and landed on the hall floor with a sound like gum popping.

Fly ball! I imagined Eli shouting. Suddenly I could see him on his knees under the roof windows, nailing baseboard and humming Dolly Parton out-of-tune, the little tail of dark-blond hair damp on the back of his neck. The first time I'd thought of him since Officer Bassette's teeth.

I didn't want to. I backed quickly down the stairs, my heavy leather apron flapping against my thighs, to pick up the molding. In the empty master bedroom the floor was strewn with tobacco-colored wrapping paper that said "La Mar Electrical La Mar" over and over, and insulation with the foil stripped off, fluffy pink cotton candy. I looked down at the trail dredged in the sawdust by Hop's workboots. It led straight to me.

▼

Everything was the same as always—the pale forest of arms and legs; the summer-evening sounds through the roof windows; the slanting, green-gold light. I sat down on the floor beside Mildred and crossed my legs like hers. The wad of bills Hop had handed me before he left made a comfortingly uncomfortable bulge in my jeans pocket. In the close, sun-warmed space Mildred's white shirt and white trousers, grimy around the edges, had that boiled-cabbage smell. On her head was a hat I hadn't seen before, made of black-and-yellow-checked cloth. The patchy rust-colored cat curled in the triangle of her legs.

I came up to see Mildred almost every evening now, to put off going home. I didn't care anymore about walking slowly through the house, admiring; but I didn't want to leave. Susie, who had developed an overnight maternal preoccupation with the previously repulsive Joey, usually had dinner at Lacey's. I had thought that once Eli and I stopped sleeping together, I'd go home to a house that no longer felt like someone else's, and I was right; but that was worse. The house, mine now, resounded with absence. I'd unzipped all the covers from the hammock cushions and washed them and dried them in the sun; I'd dusted for the first time in months, polishing the cedar slats of the park bench with an old linen hand towel; I'd watered the dracaena palm, which had folded up like an umbrella from neglect. It didn't matter what I did. The house terrorized me with absence.

In a tone of voice that suggested she was answering a question, Mildred said, "Take glass." Keeping one hand on Mustard, she held the wineglass I'd given her up to the light and squinted at it with her one eye. "Perfectly solid, but you can see right through it. Why, if you'd suggested such a thing before it was invented, people would've said you were crazy. Something that's there and not there, at the same time."

I pulled two granola bars and a banana out of my purse and put them on the floor between us. "Mildred," I said. "What'll you do when this place is done? When the owner moves in?"

She set down the wineglass. Her face was shadowed by the checked hat-brim, the eyepatch a spot of deeper blackness. Her hands tightened on the cat. "I do miss my yard. Charley Junior never let me go outside the trailer, for fear I'd yell for help. My garden was all outlined in white painted stones. Elephant ears, scarlet sage, snapdragons. The plumbago'll be coming into bloom about now."

I said, "Don't you ever think about going home?"

Mildred's eyepatch wagged when she frowned. She said sharply, "That feeling—that's what you got to veer off from. *Nostalgia.* In your heart, you know. Funny—there's a word for missing what's past but none for missing what hasn't happened yet. It's my *future* that I miss. Something to think forward to."

I hadn't told Mildred about Gort's death; somehow that had made her the only person I could really talk to. Even Lacey—there were things I couldn't talk about to Lacey now. She didn't approve of my relinquishing Lil to Clesta; she'd never have understood my getting involved with somebody like Eli; and the thought of Gort made her terribly afraid: what had happened to one husband could happen to others. The one thing Lacey never talked about, besides her childhood, was Gort's disappearances. Was it that, if Gort could leave, Paul could, too? It was Lacey's conviction that any good marriage entailed a man you had to manage. Maybe she and Paul were married; maybe not. In the seven years since she'd moved in next-door I hadn't succeeded in backing her into a sentence like *When I married Paul*. My stomach tilted when I looked too long at Paul's red-rimmed eyes, like a rabbit's, and thick, white skin; I preferred to believe, not. When I'd asked her once, years ago, why she was with him, she'd said matter-of-factly that she'd been having sex since she was eight and that she'd never felt safe until she met Paul.

Mildred was the only person besides Lacey that I'd ever really wanted to talk to. With Mildred I'd come to feel understood, which was odd, since we hardly ever had what you'd call a conversation. Now I felt cheated; we were out of sync, she'd gone somewhere I couldn't—was afraid to—follow.

Suddenly she said, "Come with me."

"What?"

"You come with me. We'll go on the road together. Buy a little silver trailer—those kind that look like beetles? Easy to maneuver. We'll go all over. Go to Utah." She put both hands on her head, one over the other, in a gesture of joy. It made me think of my mother coming up the hill in Dad's old felt hat swathed with bee veiling. Seeing its chance, the orange cat unfolded itself from Mildred's crossed legs, stretched, and padded back under the eaves.

"Mildred—I can't do that."

But for a second something in me leaped up at the thought, and Mildred must have seen that because she said, "Oh, *responsibilities*. See these brown spots?" She held out her hands. "I was younger than you, once. We used to wear glazed cotton dresses—cotton satin, we called it those wide skirts that stood out full, with crinolines. The boys'd glue mirrors on the tops of their dancing shoes."

Outside, the jingle of children's voices was gone, replaced by two dogs barking, a woman's voice calling thinly, *Don-nee, Don-nee.* Or maybe it was *Tommy.*

"Of course, there's those who think, What's a body anyhow, but housing for the part you can't see. Soul, or whatnot. Soul-house; bone-house."

Mildred lowered her hands, then raised them again, opening and closing the long fingers like fans. She looked at them thoughtfully. The last of the light shone red through the flesh around the bone. "We can't choose who we pity."

For an instant there, just a heartbeat, I'd seen the two of us on Route 78 heading west, the blue Dodge towing a humpbacked silver trailer. "I have to go," I said, and stood up. I nudged the granola bars toward her with my foot. "Listen, we'll be up on this floor on Thursday at the latest. Don't forget to eat."

I didn't think she heard me. She didn't say, Come back and I'll tell you the story of my eye. She didn't say anything at all.

▼

There was only one album of family pictures in our house. The photographs, which I'd never gotten around to fitting into the little black triangular corners, fell out whenever it opened. That night, after I'd tucked Susie in and read her the ritual story from the Green Fairy Book (often the same plots as her daytime reading, the *National Enquirer*) and heard her prayers, I went back downstairs. I sat down under the lamp in the dark living room with a glass of brandy on the floor beside me and the green padded album in my lap. Times when there was nothing I needed to do, no one who needed me—those were the dangerous times. That evening, for the first Friday in weeks, Lacey hadn't come over for Payday Dinner. I'd tried to put it down to late pregnancy (nine months of PMS), but in my heart, as Mildred would have said, I knew she was avoiding me.

Humid air filled the open window by my elbow. The bleat of an ambulance cut through the steady seesaw pulsing of the crickets. In the corner were all the wicker baskets of fruit that people had sent, as if Gort were going on an ocean voyage; their cellophane glittered and they filled the room with the sweetness of decaying pears. I hadn't said any word other than *accident* to anyone—not Clesta or my parents, and not the girls—and no one had said anything to me. It was the beginning of another Family Silence. But if I told them, Lil and Susie—if they knew it might have been suicide—his death would never end. That was why I let Lil stay at 110 Wesley Street; she was safer with Clesta, whose mind she couldn't read.

I shuffled the photographs and fanned them out on the bench beside me. Sifting through my hands, they made me into someone else, someone distant, like thinking of yourself in the third person. Pick a card. I closed my eyes and let my hand choose, as if I could read the future from the past.

▼

Egg (1982)

In another room, the baby cries. Shouting, the woman picks up an egg. The baby cries; the woman throws the egg. It breaks against the edge of the counter next to the man's clenched hand, slides down the white painted cabinet, pools on the floor. The yolk is bright yellow. They look at each other, appalled; then, at the same moment, they start to laugh. The man leaves the room and comes back carrying the Nikon.

CLICK! goes the camera.

Rose-colored Umbrella (1985)

Autumn is late this year. It's still warm enough for a barbecue, though dogwood and pin oak and maple leaves have been drifting down all afternoon, and the catalpa in the back corner of the yard is already bare. Gort sits in the wooden porch swing with his three-year-old daughter. He holds the hard little heels of Lil's bare feet one in each hand. On the steps Daniel sits pulling the petals off a yellow chrysanthemum. Gort sings,

> You're my little potato—
> You had wrinkles
> On the bottoms of your feet

Under the catalpa Judith piles handfuls of silverware into a blue bowl. The paper plates with their crust of baked beans she shuffles into a green plastic garbage bag held open by James. They wipe the wooden table with paper napkins and close the faded canvas umbrella for the season.

Before they turn to walk away, James puts the palm of his hand against the slope of her belly. He says, "Your eyes are a beautiful color in this light." He says, "Blue amber eyes." Silent, not knowing what to say, she watches the chickadees picking over leaves on the grass; an iridescent black fly lands on a coil of dog shit. Her main feeling is surprise: he must know that she doesn't want—has never wanted—anyone but his brother.

When she looks back from the porch, James is still standing by the dusty rose umbrella—like the folded wings of a huge moth—with the leaves glittering and falling all around him. He lifts the Nikon to his eye. Beside her, Gort rests his chin on their drowsy child's head. She can feel his love for Lil, he burns with it, as if he were an oven radiating love. CLICK!

> You're my sweet potato—
> You come
> From underground

▼

When I unclenched my hands the photographs stuck to my sweaty palms. I had to shake my wrists to make them let go. The noises of the city had quieted; the stop-and-start sound of the crickets had stopped for good. Remembering that afternoon with James made me think, for the second time that day, of Eli. I missed Eli—my body missed him—but it was Gort I longed for. Eli's absence made a gap for the old, familiar yearning to enter. *They are two so / As stiff twin compasses are two.* I'd thought I knew Gort, knew what he longed for, what he needed. I hadn't known him.

I remembered how he'd looked all this past winter. I thought of how he'd looked in June, the last time I'd seen him: his shoulders, in the blue-plaid flannel shirt I loved, hunched over his bowl of puffed wheat. Where was the man who'd photographed a broken egg, who sang songs to his daughter's feet? By the time he left, it was as if I'd been the one carrying something huge and heavy, so heavy I didn't know until I set it down that it was more than I could bear. The plain relief had been so great that I couldn't look beyond it. Not back, to what Gort and I had once had; not forward, to what would have to change if he ever came home. Stay in one world, I'd told myself, for the sake of the children; but really it had been for me.

Lacey was right to keep away. Grief, which I hadn't really felt in my life until now, ironed everything flat. My body felt the same as when I was afraid: trembly, yawning, stomach scooped out like going down in an elevator. Once the girls were born, I'd thought a lot about the precariousness of life, all the things that can happen; but I'd never really thought about death. I suppose I'd vaguely imagined it as a state, another plane of being. I hadn't understood that it was absence. Nothing. Blank. Nobody could follow me into that flat world. Not my mother, who'd called every day since the funeral she felt so guilty about not having attended. Not Lacey, who'd stood by the grave where I could see her blue chambray belly pushing out on the other side of Susie, and afterwards had come back to the house and fed me rice pudding and stayed with me until I fell asleep. Certainly not the Church I no longer (I discovered now) believed in. I was left in a place where no one could follow. Abandoned, *relict*—the word they used for widows on the oldest gravestones—relinquished, Latin for "left."

I picked up the photographs and laid them on the heavy black pages and closed the album. It had gotten cooler. I stretched my stiff, heavy arms over my head, licked the skin of brandy from the bottom of my glass. Then I locked up and went to bed. I lay there open-eyed in the dark listening for the whisper of plaster falling from the ceiling.

He used to talk about the ancient tribes who must have crossed from Asia on the ice sheet and slowly found their way down the coast. An era ended, and the ice sheet melted. The level of the ocean rose. The trail was lost.

▼

I woke from a sweaty doze, as if I had a fever, from a fever-dream of red fog and babies with their eyes on stalks, a horrible dream. I had the sense of pulling myself out of it, the way you do sometimes, when a small waking part of you throws a lifeline to the dreamer. I could feel a trembling tightness all over my body.

"Mommy." Susie spoke from beside the bed. "I couldn't *find* you."

I opened my eyes to darkness, undiluted by streetlights. The windowshade, its roller broken, was permanently drawn; the dark buzzed with pinprick points of lesser dark. I was in Lil's bed, where I'd been sleeping lately, the only place in the house where I could fall asleep. Whose dreams did I have there?

I lifted the covers and Susie climbed in.

"I dreamed that Death is white all over," she whispered. Her breathing was fast and shallow. "Death is a bone skeleton. With brown shoes." She arranged herself alongside my body with her head in the crook of my arm, the way she used to do when she was small and crawled into bed between Gort and me without really waking. The tightness eased a little.

"Me, too," I whispered back.

"What?"

"Me, too. I had a bad dream, too."

She pressed closer against me. Our bodies, in thin cotton nightgowns damp with sweat, stuck together. She had the smell of all sleeping children, dry and sweet, like switch-grass in September. Her large feet with their knuckly toes were hard and cold against my calves. Susie had stubby bones and dense, solid flesh—not like Lil, a wiry, ambitious baby with a new bruise every time I bathed her. Gort had had beautiful feet, narrow and fine-boned like his hands, the skin stretched smooth over the tendons down to the slender, tapering toes. Lil had his bones; Susie had mine.

Susie said, "Want me to scratch your back?"

"No. But thanks."

"A Scorpio's air— air-oh-genius zone is her back."

"Go to sleep now, Suze."

She scrunched around in the bed until her back was to me and the knob of her ponytail pressed into my armpit. The smell and feel of her comforted me. It didn't matter to her whether I loved her the right way, or some other way; my body spoke to hers in the only language that mattered.

"Rub your eyes," she murmured sleepily. "Then look. The dark is full of little tiny tadpoles. I'll tell you a story, so you can sleep."

"Okay."

"Once upon a time. A big bird came sliding down the sky. Big. A bald-headed eagle . . ." Her voice trailed off. I thought about moving my arm; but then she started up again. "The sky was all painted with flowers . . ." She stopped again.

I could feel our bodies growing heavier, loosening, sliding towards sleep. The dark room was warm and still and soundless.

Susie's body jerked. "A big, pinch-mouth bird. He . . . kept spiders in his pockets." She sighed a deep, shuddering sigh. "A big. Pinch-mouth. Bird."

She slept, her fingers locked under her cheek. I moved my face until it was against her hair. My eyes closed.

17

JUDITH

I hadn't thought of the knife for a couple of weeks, not since that morning at Clesta's when I'd tried to get Lil to come home; but it was the first thing that came to my mind when Lacey told me Lil was gone.

"Gone?" I said to Lacey. "What do you mean, gone?"

Lacey stood on the porch among the mail that was strewn all over, pleating and unpleating the ends of the red cotton bow slung under her chin. She looked pale. In the early morning light the freckles stood out all over her tanned face like cinnamon on toast. I had to think a second to remember when the baby was due—September ninth, the midwife had said. Three weeks.

"Gone, is what I mean. Your Aunt Christa and this skinny black guy came by. But you weren't—"

"Clesta," I said, "and Doc." As if that were the important thing, to get the names straight.

"Whoever. I came out to see if I could help. Since your *prowler*"— Lacey always referred to him in italics, to let me know she'd guessed who he was—"I try to keep an eye out. Shivery dick! Quarter of seven on a Monday morning, and you're just getting home? Where were you?" Her voice held all her saved-up hurt at the things I hadn't told her.

At sunrise I'd printed a note for Susie and walked down to the river and back, walking fast, trying to outpace my thoughts.

"Where did she go? Did they say?" But I thought, I can't; not now. I can't face this, whatever it is. I took a step backward, slid on some mail. The Sears August Lawn Sale; a pink envelope stamped COLLECTION NOTICE.

Lacey said, "They didn't know that's the whole point. They thought she might be here. Might've decided to come home."

Home. My foot shoved a stack of A&P circulars against the side of the house.

Lacey took a step toward me. Her face softened. "Judith? You okay?"

I couldn't, so I didn't; so I couldn't-didn't. I kept on pushing mail around and around with my foot, in widening, slithery circles, like a demented skater. TRUST US, said a large yellow ad made to look like a telegram. It was exactly a week since the funeral; Lil had only been out of the hospital twelve days. *Twelve days, one week, one day, twelve weeks, twelve one one twelve.* My mind was like my foot—a wooden, useless, tethered motion going nowhere. *The other foot doth obliquely run.* Suddenly I was laughing, no, it was more like something laughing me, laughter flowing over me and through me and lifting me up, dizzy and drowning. Lacey put her hands on my shoulders and pushed and pulled until the two of us were sitting on the top step. Then she shook me, hard. The laughing turned into sobbing and she pushed my head down onto her shoulder and let me cry.

When I lifted my head she pulled a ragged Kleenex out of the pocket of her smock and handed it to me. It was my turn now to understand without words. Without speaking, Lacey let me know that facts—all things I hadn't told her—didn't matter anymore. She forgave my silence; and I forgave her absence. We sat side-by-side in silence on the wooden step, looking out across our scrubby sunlit lawns like two women on an ocean liner facing out to sea. Then I rubbed my eyes and dried my chin.

The front door opened. Susie came out onto the porch and stood behind the screen door holding Lustyka by the ears, the way you'd hold a rabbit. Her grip pulled the skin around the cat's yellow eyes up and back in an expression of pained surprise. "*Run off*, was what Clesta said. I heard her."

Next-door Joey began to yell. Each separate howl started low and opened out, louder and higher, like a fire alarm.

"Fish testicles," Lacey sighed, and slowly straightened her back. We stood up.

"Listen, hon," Lacey said. "If there's anything I can do." What everyone says in these situations—only Lacey meant it. She really would do anything. Whatever happened to her when she was a child had somehow left her with this—this unboundedness, this ability to *enter*, to be where you were. I would never understand how she'd come to this tenderness, or how she hung onto it. She put her arm around my shoulders and hugged me; I could feel the hard ball of her belly against my side. Then she lumbered off across the two yards. With a hoarse cry Lustyka struggled free of Susie's grip, dropped to the porch floor, and vaulted through a hole in the lattice into the snowball bushes.

▼

I got the I-don't-know-what-I-want-from-you-
But-I-ain't-gettin'-it blues

Doc had the ironing board up in the middle of the living room and was pushing the iron up and down a khaki pants-leg and singing to himself. Clesta sat on the sofa with her mouth pinched together, unpicking stitches in the hem of something purple. I hadn't seen her since the funeral; she seemed to have gotten, not thinner, but smaller. I felt, standing next to her, as if I loomed. The television was tuned to *Days of Our Lives* without sound. It was noon: twenty-three hours since anyone had seen Lil.

I sat down on a blue petit-point footstool without being asked. "Clesta," I said. "I need to know what happened. Why did she"—I couldn't say the words *run away* for fear that would make it true—"why did she go off like that?"

Clesta, in a shaft of sunlight, bent closer over the purple cloth in her lap. Her scalp shone pink through the froth of fine, white hair, a dandelion gone to seed.

Doc spoke for her. "Don't anybody *know* why. Dinner came and went, parsnip-and-soybean loaf, child never showed up. Wasn't with Daniel—*he* was workin' evening shift at the restaurant."

I hadn't come here pinning my hopes on Doc. From his point of view Lil, and Gort too, had done the one unforgivable thing—they'd hurt Clesta. Only Lil could do it again, and that he was set to prevent. In his whole life he'd had two loves, Jesus and my Aunt Clesta, and I don't think even he could have said which order they came in. Love made him mean.

"She has brought trouble to Trouble Town. Don't nobody know what that girl is truly like. Ain't that so, C. H.?" He slid the pants into a wooden skirt-hanger and snapped its jaws shut. When he looked up, his black face was wet and shiny from the steam, drops of sweat rolling down into his fringe of beard. "She'll be okay. She is tough—no holes barred. Why, I used to say to her myself, I'd say, They get you under a streetlamp, they gonna throw you *back*."

He slapped the padded top of the ironing board. Under the sofa Chinky gave a perfunctory snarl.

Sun through the half-open drapes silvered the scum on Clesta's cup of cold tea and lit the dusty glass over a dozen photographs. None of me— she'd put them away somewhere after the wedding and never brought them out again. There were the girls and their cousins at various ages, usu- ally laughing ("Say 'sex'!" James would cry, and click the button). Lil's First Communion picture, in an orange-blossom wreath with a big gardenia in the center like a miner's headlamp. And Gort. I could feel the terrible crowdedness gathering in my chest. There were Gort and Lil fishing with their legs slung over the side of the old blue-painted boat; the sun shone on the top of their heads. Their eyes looked down, but I saw their thoughts streaming up, up, into the clean blue air. *Per aspera ad astra*, Mrs. Muschlitz used to admonish us. Set your sights on the stars. I thought of the two of them studying the night sky, pacing off the distance between constella- tions on maps cut from dark-blue paper, going together to the attic tele- scope, the roof, the Observatory on the mountain. Always going higher.

Doc sang, low-voiced,

> Don't you see my Jesus comin'?
> Don't you see Him in a cloud?

"She's only fif—fourteen," I said. Clesta looked worse now, pale and shivery and absent; but I had to make her see, get her to send Doc after Lil. It still hadn't occurred to me to go myself. I only knew how to be steady—*thy firmness draws my circle*—how to be the one who waited. I said, pleading, "We have to find her."

"We? You know where *we'd* ought to start searchin'?" Doc unrolled a dampened white shirt and flung it across the ironing board. "No, sir. She is okay. Police ain't heard a thing to the contrary."

When I'd gone to the station on Fogel Street, the sandy-haired cop at the desk had made me answer a lot of questions (height, weight, color of eyes and hair, tattoos or other distinguishing marks), then said "Not much we can do, lady. Ninety-nine percent of these kids come back in a day or so." What they *would* do sounded perfunctory a statewide APB ("probably won't do much good, though, these runaways tend to go out of state"), posters with no photograph. It wasn't enough, I told him. He'd shrugged, tapping his pencil on the dirty green blotter, eyes traveling over me (loose hair, new black jeans) with a look that had nothing to do with Missing Persons. "Usually, these kids, the parents know where they've likely gone to."

"I called up under a assumed name," Doc said to Clesta. "Asked about fourteen-year-old girls. They ain't a one been found, with or without long taffy hair."

I sat on the lumpy stool trying to think what words would be the right ones, the magic, moving ones that would persuade them. Clesta's buttonhook ate stitches one after another with little popping sounds. Now and then she consulted a black-strapped watch on her wrist, like an athlete timing herself. Above the sigh and thud of the iron, Doc sang to himself in a low voice that moved in and out of words. Otherwise, there was silence. The windows were closed against the sullen August afternoon; the clocks had been stilled, for a death.

> If I could I surely would
> Stand on the rock where Moses stood

I leaned forward with my elbows on my knees, to make Clesta look at me. I said, "Clesta—please. Somebody's got to go after her."

Doc said, "Wants somebody *else* to do somethin'. As usual."

Without looking up, Clesta murmured, "If you pick around, if you find the right stitch, the beginning stitch, the whole hem'll unravel all by itself."

"Clesta," I said.

"You have to keep picking. Pick and pick."

"Clesta. *Please*. Doc will go if you ask him."

Doc said, "*Two* somebody elses."

I shouted then. "For Christ's sake, Clesta! The girl has a broken *arm!* She's four*teen*."

The buttonhook stopped. Doc set down the iron and said, "Don't you raise your voice to your aunt, Judith Hutchins."

Clesta raised her head. She looked straight at me and said, "Don't you understand, Judith? You brought this on yourself. Brought it on us all. You *let* him—" Her voice was choked and terrible and sad. "Oh, my Gordon."

She leaned back and closed her eyes.

After sixteen years of silence she had spoken to me. I hunched, frozen, on my footstool; we stayed still where we were, the three of us, forgetting everything else for a moment, equal in our surprise.

Into the silence came the thud of the downstairs door. A clatter of feet—young feet, two-at-a-time feet—on the stairs. They came closer, paused on the landing by the kitchen, then slapped straight toward us. I could feel the blood in my face, the vein in my forehead pounding. I turned.

But it was Daniel in the doorway.

He said, "Aunt Clesta—" and then he saw me. His face went very red. He was wearing a green satin shirt that looked somehow familiar. Released, Doc unrolled another shirt and attacked, running the flat of his hand ahead of the iron.

Daniel said, in a peculiar twangy voice, all in one breath, "Well I gotta go see you at dinner bye Aunt Judith," and turned to go. On the back of his shirt the silver shamrock glittered. Then I remembered: Brannigan's, the last time I'd seen Eli.

In your heart, you know.

"Daniel," I said. "Do you know where Lil went?"

His face had gone from red to white. "No, ma'am." One foot, climbing the doorframe behind him, kicked at the painted wood.

"She didn't say anything to you before she left?"

"No, ma'am."

"She didn't tell you why she was leaving?"

Daniel hesitated in the doorway, hugging his green satin chest. His foot stopped. In the silence I could hear Doc's steam iron. I breathed in the smell of starch and clean cotton; I waited, my heart chugging like the iron, full of fear that he would say, Because of you. Because I told her about you.

He said, "No, ma'am."

I breathed out. His face said Yes; but his voice said No. A real mother would listen to the face, would keep on asking. I opened my mouth to speak; but I couldn't.

Behind me Clesta said to Doc, "It's time."

Doc said, "Almost. Almost."

She said hoarsely, "It's *time*." Her hands were wringing out the purple linen as if it were a washcloth. When Doc didn't look up, she raised the buttonhook in one hand and threw it at him.

His head snapped back. Without a word, he set the iron on its little stand and left the room. Daniel had disappeared: I could hear his feet clapping down the stairs.

I knelt beside Clesta. Under the sofa Chinky growled and clicked his jaws. Clesta's hands, shaking, smoothed the purple cloth over and over. I put my hand over one of hers; she flinched, but she let it stay. I could feel her trembling. She said, "The thing about pain. Is it. Never lets you forget you're in a body. Keeps dragging you—back." Her eyes, which had been looking straight at me for the second time in fifteen years, closed. Her voice faded to a whisper. "Old age is. Spinach."

She looked awful suddenly, gray and frail as tissue paper, like the Term C's, the patients with terminal cancer, at Clover View. It was too late now to ask what was wrong: too much had gone unsaid between us for too long. Or maybe I just lacked the courage. I knelt there with my hand on Clesta's and it seemed to me that I was passing on my mother's touch, her hand on my hair in the attic, in Iowa. It felt good, but not right, as if Clesta wasn't the one who should receive it.

Doc came back and crouched beside me on one knee. He smelled of Suave hair cream the way he always did—a buttery smell like movie popcorn. He set down a carved brass box on the carpet. Lifting back the lid, he took out a box of wooden matches and lit one. Then he took out a hypodermic and held the needle in the flame. I heard Clesta's breath draw in. After several seconds, Doc blew out the match, then lifted an ampule of colorless fluid from the brass box and filled the hypodermic. He pushed back one flowing lavender sleeve, pinched up the dry pleated skin, slid the needle in. "C. H.," he murmured. "Now, C. H." His thumb on the plunger shook; the knuckle was ash-colored.

After a few seconds Clesta sighed. She opened her eyes, blinking into the sunlight.

I got up and found the buttonhook where it had rolled, far short of its target, underneath the rosewood television cabinet. The metal rod in the shape of a question mark; the handle that was not plastic after all but yellowed ivory—I remembered then. Twenty years ago Clesta had given me a buttonhook from one of the mildew-embroidered trunks in the storeroom, given it with pleased authority, as if she thought girls still wore white kid buttoned boots.

I knelt and handed the buttonhook to Clesta. Her bony fingers closed around it. Shakily, she began pushing it at the purple cloth. She looked up at me. "Some days—" she whispered. "Some days you pick and pick, never come up with it."

"Time you left," Doc said to me. Not harshly—more in the tone of someone whose mind had moved on to other matters.

I turned, breaking a shaft of dusty sunlight, and crossed the room. I didn't need Doc to tell me that I was on my own—that Clesta was too far gone to part with him even if he'd been willing.

I went out, past the stilled tongues of the clocks, through the little hall, up the stairs to Lil's room.

With the shade pulled all the way down, the guest room was hot and dark. Lil's clothes hung in the closet; it looked as if she hadn't taken anything. No knife. If it had been there, it was gone. I stood holding a corner of her blue cotton blanket, feeling as immobilized as the Dutch girl in the painting over her bed. I knew, though she'd left no sign, that my daughter needed me, though I knew too that she did not want me. I could see what to do, but I couldn't do it. I was afraid.

On the landing Chinky caught up with me. His paws hit the bare wood steps in a three-cornered rhythm, kneeless back legs coming down at the same time. My feet fit themselves to the heavy rhythm—*I couldn't, so I didn't, so I couldn't-didn't*—my whole body felt heavy. We passed the living room, where Doc was still kneeling beside Clesta with his head close to hers. He was singing the song he'd sung at the ironing board, but soft now and yearning, like a lullaby. Neither of them noticed me. I went slowly down the stairs with my hand on the wide, shining banister, accompanied by the condemning click of Chinky's toenails.

▼

Mildred, I'd say, *How can I go after her*— No. First I'd ask Mildred to come home with me. There was Gurt's space in the attic, empty now; and Mildred and Susie would like each other, I had a feeling. First I'd invite her. Then I'd ask. *How can I go after Lil when I don't even know where she is?*

If—stood in a corner stiff. That's what I'd say to Charley Rust, when he'd start in with his I should've this, you should've that, if only.

You think she thinks he's still alive? That she's gone to bring him home?

Don't let go of what's yours, I'd tell him. Never mind should've should've is easy. My mother used to say, Everybody has an easy story to tell.

You think I should go and look for her.

I'd tell him, you haven't got time to spare. Mustard! Spit that out, you wretched animal.

But how would she get an idea like that?

I'd tell him: in your heart, you know.

But when I got to the top of the stairs, everything was changed.

The mannequins were gone—the clay-colored dummies with their fingertips like peeled almonds—except for one that stood, headless and armless, between the roof windows. The sun slanting in at its early evening angle made a halo of light where the head would have been. The scarred wooden worktable was gone. Instead, lengths of baseboard and shoe-molding, raw pink wood cut to size, lay across sawhorses, waiting. Propped against the sloping rafters were cut-up sections of wallboard, like the pieces to a huge jigsaw puzzle.

And the light—the spangled, floating green light—was gone. The sun bounced off silver insulation packed between the ribs of the four sloping walls to make a cold, colorless light that shivered through the room like tinsel.

I took a step, two steps, into the center of the room. My shoes sounded loud in the emptiness. From the corner of my eye I saw a flash of white shirt-front; but when I turned, it was only sunlight on a piece of drywall. The toolbox sat on the floor with its hasps up, its green metal lid open. I knelt down beside it and plucked a hammer out by its claw. Plaster dust clotted my throat.

There was nothing to show she'd ever been here. Nothing to show she'd ever even existed. I stood alone in the center of the big room, trying to remember the exact slope of her white-shirted back, the shiny knuckles, the thick striped hair with its crooked part—a list of Mildred. To steady myself I put out a hand to the eaves. The insulation was cool, almost cold; it did not resist me. If I'd wanted to, I could have punched through the foil deep into the wadded batting.

"Ten inches." Hop's voice sounded behind me. "R-22 mineral-wool blanket."

I twisted around, still kneeling.

"Didn't expect to find *you* here. This mean you're coming back to work?"

I hadn't expected to find him here, either, which was why I'd waited till well after five. Yet now that I saw him, I knew what I had to do, as clearly as if Mildred stood beside me murmuring in my ear.

"Because I need you back here. Am I right? Look at this, it's like dry-walling the inside of the pyramids." He waved a sunburned arm at the hip-roof rafters.

I sat back on my heels, still holding the hammer. "Hop—"

"Been out three days now, countin' week before last." Hop grasped fitfully at his new beard, which had come in rust-pink striped with white, like peonies.

"I need more time."

"How *much* more?"

"I don't know."

"Don't know? Look here, Judith. This's a business I'm running—it ain't on a drop-in basis. Am I right? You work for me, work." In the tinselly light, his face was hard, the skin not rosy but new-brick red, the furrows in his forehead no longer benign.

I kept hold of the hammer, feeling the tippy weight of it in my hand: the long, light wooden shaft; the blunt iron head. Through the open window by my head, cars ground over gravel driveways, lawn mowers coughed to a stop, screen doors clapped. Soon women's voices would begin reeling in the children one by one.

I said, "Two days?" I could hear Eli say, *When are you going to learn to demand things?* I cleared my throat. "Two days."

"That'd make it Friday, and then there's the weekend. So we're really talkin' Monday. *Monday*. Christ." He stopped, visibly getting hold of himself.

I looked around the room: everything glittered, everything was shining. I'd never heard Hop swear before. What was I doing, risking everything like this? I didn't, really didn't, know; but I was going to do it anyway. It crossed my mind that that was all courage was. I felt a terrifying exhilaration, like swinging out in the tire over Nonesuch Pond back home, the moment when it seemed the rope must let go of the maple branch and my whole body said yes to it.

I stood up; my bare knees, studded with plaster bits, stung. Squeezing the hammer, I said, "Two days, Hop. Please. There's something I've got to do."

He stood in the middle of all that shining space, unmoved. I could feel the vein down the center of my forehead ticking. My last day at Valley View flashed into my mind: old Mr. Yerkes's creamed chipped beef upside-down in his quavering lap. I took a deep dusty breath. "It's my daughter," I said. Hop was a family man. "She's run away. I have to find her."

Hop looked hard at me, rubbing a hand over his gaudy jaw. Finally he sighed. "Okay. Two days."

"Okay."

"Okay."

Plaster cracked like peppercorns under his heavy workboots as he turned away. At the top of the stairs he turned around again. "Almost forgot. I caught the poultry ghost."

The hammer slid out of my grip and bounced on the plywood floor. "What?"

"Yup." Hop was cheerful now, the spring restored to his voice, the roses to his forehead. "Won't hear more from that quarter."

I waited, standing very still, breathing in the vinegar-sharp smell of freshly cut wood.

"Kid down the block. Stopped by this morning, looking for a lost cat. We came up here, and there it was. I bet he camped out here once-twice at night. Came up that chestnut tree." He nodded toward the leaf-filled windows. "I laid down the law to him. He won't be back, him *or* his cat." He turned, paper wrappers snapping around his ankles, and crunched down my newly turned stairs.

"—sure you lock up," his voice floated back. There was the clatter of another set of stairs under the heavy boots; the thud of the heavy carved front door; then silence.

The sun had shifted; the light off the silver-covered walls was suddenly as benign and soft as moonlight.

I'd done it.

I stretched out my arms. Above my head, a fly buzzed, circling; it hit the insulation with little tapping sounds. I threw my head back, fixed my eyes on the point where the four shining walls met. Done it! Slowly at first, I began to turn around and around in the empty room. Twirling, like Lil when she was little, spinning dizzily across the living room to records Gort put on the phonograph—"Bolero," Scott Joplin, "The Skaters' Waltz"—until she staggered, drunk with motion, into his arms.

I turned faster, arms out, head up. The fly's buzzing filled the room like music. Mildred had escaped! She was out there somewhere, in her speeding silver trailer, looking for her future. Pure joy was what I felt, out of time, as if the last two weeks had never happened. Faster, around, around. The light came in waves, cold and clear as water; I kept turning. Faster, until my skull went hollow and the room blurred around me silversilversilver.

▼

By the time I got home, of course, the heavy feeling had come back. Mildred had escaped; I couldn't. Wouldn't. It was decided: I would be the one to go after Lil. But where? I knew that, wherever she'd gone, it had something to do with Gort. I thought of the places he'd gone to ground in over the years—the old Observatory, his college roommate's old summer place near Scranton, Bitter Lake, the woods west of town—and there were probably other places I never knew about. What had made Lil choose?

I'd read Susie to sleep and was in the kitchen putting the dishes away when I heard a furtive tapping at the front door. Not Lacey—she would have just called my name and walked in. I went barefoot through the dark living room. When I put on the porch light Eli stood there, blinking.

My heart jerked, thrusting up toward my windpipe. For a second we stood there, Eli in yellow light, me in shadow behind the screen door. He was shorter than I remembered. The sleeves of his white T-shirt were rolled up high; his bare arms shone.

Finally he said, "Hey, Jude."

"You can't come in," I said quickly. "Susie's—my daughter's upstairs." I wanted to stay in shadow; I was afraid of what my face would say to him.

He hesitated. A muscle twanged in one bare arm. I could see him think about insisting, forcing his way in, see him decide against it. He didn't want me that way.

His feet shuffled the mail on the porch floor. He touched the thick white web that covered the mailbox. "Not much of a housekeeper, huh?" He gave me a small, hopeful version of his shiny grin. "Listen, I ran into Hop down at The Sunny Side tonight. He said Lee ran away. Said you were gonna go look for her."

Thunder stuttered somewhere far off. I could smell rain coming, that earthy, earthworm smell. Next-door Lacey's stereo started up, the Beach Boys pleading, "Help Me, Rhonda."

"I talked to the police," I said. It rushed out, as if Eli's eyes fixed on my face pulled it out of me. "They won't do anything, they have to wait."

"The police? Get real, Jude. They aren't gonna bust their asses over one teenage girl." He fumbled in the pocket of his overalls for cigarettes, but came up empty. In the hard yellow light his eyes looked hard too, lines raying out from the corners like thin white scars in his sunburned skin. He looked his age. He said, "Jude. Let me help. I know some guys, tough guys, they're in on things all over the state. They owe me." When I didn't answer, he said, his voice getting louder, "Christ, Jude! You gotta take a risk, once in a while. Take a *stand*." Automatically I said, "Shhh." I thought about how it would be to just let go. Let Eli take over, take care of things—of me. My body leaned into the cold mesh of the screen.

"Come out here a minute," Eli said softly.

But some part of me hung onto my treacherous body, held my fingers back from the knob. I had to do this for myself. Eli wasn't part of this.

There was a noise upstairs, then Susie's voice, calling me. "You have to go," I whispered through the screen. "I can't—not now."

Not ever, was what I meant; but I saw him fasten on the *now*. "Will you call me?"

"Please, Eli. Go."

"Call me." He stood without moving, the almost-yellow eyes bright with the old *waiting* look. How he wanted me; even now, I basked in it, I wanted him to want me. From the top of the stairs Susie called, "Mom? Mom!"

"*Eli*," I whispered desperately.

"Call as soon as you get back. Call before, if you need me."

When he reached the end of the walk I turned out the light and went out onto the porch. Above the sound of Lacey's stereo playing "Wouldn't It Be Nice?" the thunder bowled closer. I watched Eli's familiar unfamiliar back in the white T-shirt and overalls until he turned the corner onto Heckewelder.

Susie pushed open the screen door. Her light-green cotton blanket was draped over her shoulders. In the dim light she looked like an enormous pale moth.

I tried for the upper hand right off. "What are you doing out of bed?"

"Sharks sleep with their eyes open," Susie said engagingly. "In the Gulf of Mexico. Who was that? Who were you talking to?"

"Nobody," I said, taking a step back, skidding on fourth-class mail. "Somebody from Jehovah's Witnesses. Come on, let's go inside."

"The Jehovah's Witnesses come in twos," Susie said suspiciously, "like Noah's ark. Who was it really?" Then she stopped. "Hey—hey, Mom. That's Lil!"

"What?" I looked around the porch. "Where?"

"It's from Lil. Jesus Christ! The yellow envelope, right there. The big one."

I looked down between our bare feet.

"See. See, she writes loopy."

Susie bent down and slid a manila envelope out from under some A&P Specials. I turned the porch light back on and tilted the envelope toward it. It was addressed to me. No return address, but the writing was Lil's. Slowly I straightened up. My heart was bumping. I paused, balancing the envelope on my palms. I felt the weight of it, familiar; the familiar square shape, the dull rounded corners through the yellow paper. And I knew it was one of Gort's notebooks.

"Aren't you gonna open it? How do they do that?"

"Do what?" I had a feeling of something coming, something still escapable, like a truck bearing down at high speed.

"Sharks. How do they sleep when their eyes are open?"

This was going to be hard, harder than I could have imagined; too hard. "No," I said out loud. My hands were shaking. The stiff paper crackled. "Susie, honey, get me a pen. Quick!"

I heard her bare feet slap the wooden floor, heard the squawk of the string drawer opening. She came back and stood behind the screen door. There was a crash of thunder. Lightning lit the porch from one end to the other.

"Aren't you gonna open it? Mom?"

"Quick," I said. "Quick!"

Susie pushed on the screen and stuck out a stub of pencil. I grabbed at it, dropped it, stooped to pick it up from the piles of mail. Still crouching, resting the envelope on one knee, I wrote across the front in large hasty letters, NOT AT THIS ADDRESS. My hand left a ribbon of sweat over the NOT.

Rising, I held tight to the envelope. I took it in both hands and shoved it hard into the mailbox. The spider web sagged, then snapped. It curled around the envelope and clung, shredding slowly, like bubblegum.

Susie believed in getting out of the way of trouble. I found her in the dark kitchen, standing in the bay window under the birdcage, fiddling with a piece of string.

I turned on the light over the sink. "Shall we feed Mary and Jim?" I said in a false, cheery voice. I got the sack from the cupboard and poured silky yellow seed into my palm and held it out. Susie shook her head.

The two birds hunched at the top of the cage, away from my hand. Jim's pale-blue wings opened and closed. For the first time, with Susie, I couldn't find any words—the way it had been for the last few months with Lil.

"There." I let the last seeds slide off my fingers into the little plastic cup. Susie's eyes, very green in the shadows, were still on my face.

"Susannah? What *is* it?"

Nothing; just those green, green eyes.

"Okay, then. Back to bed."

"Mole's balls!"

"Susannah! Go to bed."

Her blanket trailed a dirty pale-green triangle behind her across the kitchen floor. In the doorway she turned around. "Sister Alma Gertrude says, the truth always hurts."

She gathered her blanket together and slung it over one arm like a bride's train, then looked at me across the shadowed kitchen, giving me one last chance. Thunder crashed around us. Susie turned and swept out.

My hand was still inside the cage. I put my index finger under Jim's chin and nudged until he climbed on. The cold, leathery little feet curled around my finger and the claws bit down. Such easy sliding steps, I thought: from wanting the people you love to be all right, to telling yourself they're all right, to believing that they are. Believing your own lies. I rubbed my thumb over the blue metal band around one narrow leg. Every caged bird—every *reputable* bird, the man at Rumford's Pet Place had said—is banded right after it hatches. It wears the same band for life.

The truth always hurts. Truth. What would Mildred have said? That everybody's truth is different; that it doesn't exist at all, except as something you look for? That at some point, finally, you will have to risk everything? I thought of Eli standing under the porch light, the last sight of him, probably, that I would ever have. Until Eli, I had not known what it was to feel wanted, my own wanting had always been so strong; the truth was, I had not meant to go back. I hadn't wanted to return to longing.

And then, because I'd finally said this to myself, I knew what I had to do. I set Jim back on his wooden perch and hooked the cage door shut.

On the front porch I couldn't hear the sound of Lacey's stereo anymore. I pulled the sticky, smeared envelope out of the mailbox and went back inside and sat down on one end of the park bench. The first drops of rain tapped the window by my head. I put my thumb under the flap and tore it open. The journal was wedged in tight; I had to pull to get it out of the envelope. The black-and-white speckled cover was stained and limp, its edges caked with dried mud.

I snapped on the lamp.

FIVE

18

L I L

My face was wet from dew falling on it, as if my mother'd been sliding a washcloth over it while I slept, the way she used to when I was sick. I opened my eyes.

It wasn't all dark, because the roof of the old barn was mostly missing. Looking down from the hayloft I could make out the old wagon in the corner. Its shafts stuck up like the feelers of a giant praying mantis. When I breathed in, the whole place smelled like mold and rotting wood—the edges of the broken-down stalls'd crumbled like charcoal when I touched them—and rust. I'd been afraid to climb up the rickety ladder to the loft, but more afraid to lie down on the dirt floor below. There'd been mice, or maybe rats, splitting for the corners when I came inside at sunset. And there were snakes up here in the mountains—copperheads. So I'd crawled up, rung by rung, holding the flashlight in my bad hand and clutching the rungs with my good one, and tried not think about falling.

My third night on the road. All Monday night, the night I'd left, I'd just walked, keeping off to the side of the road so I wouldn't be noticeable, and cursing out my mother's burglar boyfriend—if I'd had two good arms, I could've been driving up to the lake in the Dodge. Near dawn I'd found a church that was open. The fluttery light from the votive candles in their little red and green and blue glass cups made me feel safe—the churchy smells of hot wax and incense and varnished wood—and I lay down in one of the back pews and slept all morning. Tuesday afternoon two girls in a red VW van picked me up; it had old mattresses spread out in the back, and we slept there that night, Lisa and Jen and me.

Outside, the wind was picking up. The barn creaked like a boat. A loose board knocked against a wall somewhere, and when I looked up through the rafters the stars seemed to flinch, as if they were snapping on and off in the dark-blue sky. The board floor of the loft was hard—there wasn't much straw. If only I'd brought a sleeping bag; but it would've been too much to carry, with one arm in a sling, plus my backpack. Anyway, I was warm enough in my sweatshirt and jeans. My arm hurt a little—I'd banged it heaving the cast over the top of the ladder—and I had cramps: my stupid period'd come early. But it could've been worse.

The scary part wasn't the bums in doorways or the guys yelling out the windows of their trucks or the hitchhiking, figuring out which to take and which to leave. The whole world was obsessed with sex—I saw that now. It was like there was a wall, and before, I was on one side of it, and now I was on the other. I gave truckers the finger when they roared past, cutting too close and hanging out their windows like puppies. Then yesterday, right before I met Lisa and Jen, one of them'd screeched to a stop up ahead of me; I saw his door open and I ran and lay down in the corn that was almost as tall as me. Lisa and Jen were seventeen and on their own. On the same side of the wall as me. They didn't ask any questions. This morning, before Jen turned west onto Route 80, I'd pulled my money doll out of my backpack; but they wouldn't take any, not even for gas. When I got out, Lisa'd given me some Tampax and a little sample-size bottle of lotion that said Intensive Care.

No, the scary part was when it was empty. Like now. When it was night and it was empty and there was nothing all around. What was it Dad used to say? *Alone, alone, all, all alone—alone on a wide, wide sea.* Maybe he'd felt like this all the time, even when he was with us. The way he sat, hunched to one side and elbows tucked in, as if he were inside a glass jar that sealed him off from everyone else.

A breeze came through the broken window at the other end of the loft; it carried the smell of apples rotting in the tall grass where I'd pissed at dusk, and the sound of crickets. Above my head a lightning bug winked on, then off. Its green light floated in the dark above the barn floor, blinking here, then there, like a code. When we were little, Daniel and I used to chase lightning bugs in the backyard after dinner. We'd catch them in our cupped hands and pull off the little jewels of light to wear on our fingers like solitaires, until they faded and went out. Cruel, Daddy called us, when he saw.

Daniel. I almost wished he were here; then I caught myself. I remembered how thrilled he'd been to tell me about my mother, all jittery with it, wanting to let me know that my Uncle James wasn't the only philanderer in the family. *That's it; we're both shit.* If only he hadn't told me—or anyway hadn't been so *glad*. It occurred to me that I'd used him, too; that maybe we were even. Then I thought, No. How could I forgive him? It'd be like saying that what my mother did was okay.

I could've decked that guy if I'd had some warning, even without the knife, even if he *was* six-and-a-half feet tall. The bigger you are, the slower.

I got a grip on myself. Daniel wasn't what mattered. My mother wasn't what mattered. What mattered was that I was going to find my father and—what was it Clesta always said?—bring him to account. Make him *see* me. I thought how he'd always gotten us to wait, hold off, hold back. When I found him things were going to be different. I wasn't going to let us lose each other, the way people do in families. The way Clesta lost my mother; the way my mother lost *him*. It wasn't true, what Clesta said—*The wind bloweth where it listeth*. I wouldn't let it be true.

▼

I'd thought of telling Clesta I was going. I went to her room the night I left, after I'd hidden my backpack and my double-thick Champion sweatshirt downstairs in the boot closet. She was in bed, in her nightgown the color of violets, watching *Double Chiller Theater*. On the screen a woman's head sat in a shallow pan with a lot of wires coming out of it, having a conversation with a man in a white lab coat.

"Do they do that now, do you think?" Clesta looked up at me.

"Do what?" I said.

"Head transplants." She patted the space beside her, and I slid in between the slippery rose-colored sheets and leaned back against the padded headboard. Under the bed Chinky muttered.

"I don't think so." I breathed in the mint smell of Bengay. It smelled *safe*. I realized I hadn't thought about how to tell Clesta I was leaving, or how to even bring the subject up.

"The eyes on that doctor person," Clesta said. "Like raisins in oatmeal. *He's* not to be trusted, that's certain."

217

"Clesta," I said; but the music swelled up loud to announce an excit-ing part, and she shushed me. The man in the white lab coat approached the head. Clesta's low, flat breasts rose and fell under the violet silk.

Fadeout. The head was replaced by a fast-talking ad for the Miracle Vinyl Repair Kit. AMAZing use it once and any hole rip or tear simply disap-pears NOW see how it works.

I started again. "My father—"

"I've been meaning to talk to you, Lilly," Clesta said. She sighed. In the changing light from the TV, she looked tired—more than tired, weary. The faint side-to-side quiver of her head was worse than usual. "Child. Sometimes people do things we can't understand. Not don't understand; can't. Some things can't be understood. They just have to be—accepted."

Oh, please. It was bullshit, what she was going to tell me next—I wasn't going to hear it. "I don't believe in that kind of faith. Church faith. You can only have faith in somebody. I know—"

Clesta's knuckles tapped my cast. "Child. Remember what I told you. People like your father, your grandfather—they don't see things the way we do. To them it's a terrible, terrible thing not to give what's asked of you. Not to make yourself give it. As if it weren't true that the wind bloweth where it listeth. As if you could go against your own nature."

Her eyes looked past me into the corner of the room, through the cor-ner, out into the night. The TV voice said, Pick up the phone and call right now SEE this miracle with your own eyes.

"I know he's—" all right, was what I started to say. But Clesta looked awful, dark shiny patches under her eyes, sad in some new way that scared me. I wanted her to know there was no reason to grieve; but I couldn't tell her I was going after him. It would be asking her to take care of me, to make me safe, when she needed taking care of herself.

Still looking somewhere far off, Clesta said in her quoting voice, "'The wind bloweth where it listeth, and thou hearest the sound thereof, but canst not tell whence it cometh.' I'm afraid for you, Lilly." She leaned forward and looked at me. "Faith is trusting that what happens happens for a reason, even if we can't see it. Maude never understood that. Ha!— it's been her main trouble all these years. 'To give our brutal wills some pause'—that's what faith is for. Now who was it said that?"

I believe in *myself*, I thought, that's who I have faith in. It was Thursday that Daniel'd given me the journal, before he left for Philadelphia; today was Monday. I'd waited too long already—no one was going to help me, not Clesta, for sure not my mother. Not anybody. It was up to me.

Clesta was looking at me with the same look my mother used to get when I was little, when I wished for something—a horse of my own, a big brother, a ride in the Goodyear Blimp—that she knew was impossible. I said quickly, "I understand, okay? It's all right. I understand."

I saw in her face that she didn't really believe me, but she was tired, so tired. Her eyelids quivered. She leaned back into the rose-colored pillows, and her eyes closed.

"Out!" said Doc, coming through the bedroom door. He hit a switch on the wall and the lamp on the night table went on. He was carrying the curlicued brass box. "Time C. H. went to sleep."

He skirted the foot of the bed, stopping to turn off the TV (two men in raincoats were loading the head into a van), and set the box down among the photographs on the night table. Clesta opened her eyes. She saw the box and smiled.

"Time you went, too," Doc said to me. "Now, get. Else C. H.'ll be mean as a tick, come morning."

I leaned on my good elbow to kiss Clesta goodnight. She smiled up at me and I wanted to hug her tight, tight; but she looked so fragile—her eyelids, the tissue-paper skin of her neck. I smoothed the silk sheet instead and pulled it up over her, tucking it in around her shoulders the way my mother used to do when I was little. Doc opened the brass box and took out a box of kitchen matches. He turned around and waved it at me with little *go away* motions. I looked around the room one last time: the rose and ivory and violet silk, the smell of mint and oranges and Yardley's Lavender, the photographs shining in the yellow light.

"Pleasant dreams, Lilly-Lil," Clesta whispered. I heard the snap of Doc's match and smelled the spicy smell of smoke. Clesta's eyes went past me to Doc's back; she smiled. I slid off the bed and left.

At two in the morning I split. I felt my way downstairs along the wide mahogany banister, pulled my backpack and sweatshirt out of the boot closet, opened the big wooden door and pushed Chinky's cold nose back inside and shut it behind me. I walked fast toward the shadows at the end of the alley.

▼

Above my head the stars were like little cold chips of metal. The barn rafters cut up the dark, roping off the stars into separate pieces of sky so that the constellations got lost. I couldn't find anything. It was scary to have the sky not make sense.

Don't skeeve now.

With my good hand I reached into my jeans pocket for the Documents. They were worn soft by now, the photograph felt like one of Clesta's tea napkins. They weren't much good in the dark. I felt for the ribbed bottom of my sweatshirt, wound it in and out through my fingers like the piece of blue blanket I used to sleep with. I'd lie in the buzzing dark, afraid to fall asleep, rubbing the thick wool between the V's of my fingers. Mommy would come and sit on the edge of the bed and whisper, *If you can't sleep, just rest.* Then she'd touch her mouth to my eyelids and I'd smell the waxy smell of her lipstick—

Bullshit. I didn't need her *or* Daniel. People who lied to themselves. I punched my backpack into a better pillow-shape, then pulled my father's fishing hat down over my face. At dusk I'd seen an owl dive from the rafters, a straight-down drop, then fly up with one claw clenched around something that wriggled. There'd been no sound at all. The inside of the hat smelled like coconut, from the old-fashioned hair oil he used. The camping stuff—the tent and the little stove and his sleeping bag—was gone from our garage. I'd gone back Friday morning to check. I couldn't believe I'd never noticed they were missing when I searched it the first time; he must've come back for them, in between. So then I knew for sure: he'd be on the bluff where we used to go. By tomorrow I'd find him. I'd make him come home. If I didn't believe that—if I didn't have faith—then I was like my mother. Unfaithful.

I turned on my side and listened to the blood in my ears. I started counting backwards from a thousand, slowly, by fives.

19

JUDITH

One misty, moisty morning
When cloudy was the weather
I chanced to meet an old man
Clothed all in leather

The old blue Dodge bucked and sputtered through streets that steamed from the night's rain. On damp, still mornings like this, my mother used to say it over and over, the rhyme that played now in my head. My thin cotton shirt, already wilting, was wet through under the arms. Misty; moisty. The car was like a huge boat that I had to row by myself. I shifted on the sticky vinyl seat and hauled the steering wheel from side to side.

In the garage there'd been a moment—repeated now at each red light—when my foot came down on the gas and the old car held its breath. Nobody'd driven it since Gort left in June—the windshield was coated with a thin layer of dust, like smoke. Relieved, ashamed, I'd thought gladly, *I can't go*; but then, as now, the old Dodge coughed grudgingly and began to move, carrying me with it.

I turned east onto Heckewelder. Ahead of me the gray sky showed a ridge of light at the horizon like the quick of a fingernail. Ten o'clock, and the morning rush hour was over, the streets fairly empty; a good thing, because the various things my feet and hands were supposed to do took all my concentration. Before he left, Gort had put in new Pantsaver floormats. The toes of my sneakers kept catching on the rubber ridges when I went for the clutch or the brake. Driving, I felt the way you do at the very end of pregnancy: the slowed-down, underwater movements; the hitch, like a dead spot, between giving your body the order to move, and moving. The motions required seemed to contradict each other—like rubbing your stomach and patting your head at the same time. I'd never understood why people were willing to do it.

I stopped for a light just in time. There was a sort of clap from under the hood, and I waited for the car to stall; but it didn't. In the bus shelter beside me, a boy about Susie's age was draped headfirst over the wooden bench, legs over its back, head down in front where your shins would normally be. His coffee-colored hair swept the damp pavement; his blue eyes looked straight up into mine. The driver behind me blew his horn. I felt for the gas pedal and we moved off down the street.

I'd left Susie with Doc, for the comfort of both, though neither saw it that way. Doc didn't want her, but I couldn't leave her with Lacey, who'd gone to Mercy at five that morning to have her baby, three weeks early. I'd promised to be with her—trained for it—and now I wouldn't. "Mole's bullshit!" Susie had shouted after the departing Dodge. I'd left her in the room that Lil always used, gazing bitterly at the painting of the white-capped girl with her buckets; but there she was in the rearview mirror, her stubby body stiff with anger, in the middle of the street. "Fish testicles!"

"Hey! *Lady*!"

I didn't realize how close the open manhole was until I heard the shout. Hastily I heaved the steering wheel to the left, but the old Dodge was a slowboat, a barge: the singers on the passenger side twanged against the manhole's iron railing, and the rear bumper knocked it so that it shuddered. My foot leaped off the clutch, and the car rattled, bucked, stopped dead. When I turned around, a head in a shiny yellow hat came up out of the hole, followed by an arm in a blue shirt. The owner stuck up his middle finger. I looked straight ahead and started the car, tightening my arch to keep my foot from wobbling on the gas pedal. It had been the same thing with the fencepost earlier: I'd seen it rushing closer in the rearview mirror as the car churned down the driveway, but nothing I did seemed to stop it.

I turned right onto Broad Street. On the low cement ledge in front of Irving Trust a long train of planter boxes had appeared. They stretched all the way from the corner to where the ledge ended, full of shiny green bushes starred with sly white flowers. The boxes filled every square inch of cement. Thomas was gone; they'd found a pleasant, gracious way to make him disappear.

I welcomed the rush of anger that came then. Pushing down on the gas, I drove past Lancaster, where I would have turned to cross the bridge to Schoener Place. After Luckenbach Avenue I nosed onto the turn-off for Route 47. We'd always avoided the interstate—too many crazy people, Gort said, too many people, period. Three cars in a row loomed up on my right and crowded in terrifyingly close to my front fender, then shot down the on-ramp. I banged on the brake. A blur of horns. Terrified, I made my foot push down on the gas pedal, the car heeling, the guardrail closing in. Then we straightened. The guardrail melted into one long streak of silver, and the road roared underneath me like the sound of falling. Warm, damp air poured into the car. I thought of Lacey alone in the bare white labor room with no one but the red-eyed Paul. I couldn't do this; but I would do it anyway. The way I'd done with Hop the day before. I put one hand down and felt for the envelope on the seat beside me. *Life is too short to do what you ought*, my mother had said, the only piece of advice I could remember her giving me since I'd turned thirteen, *do what you want*. I hadn't known what she meant, and I did not know now. Here I was; that was all. Slowly, clutching the steering wheel hard in my right hand, I rolled up the window. I drove north out of the city.

▼

After I had finished reading the journal the night before, I'd closed it and laid it on the bench beside me. A brown leaf like a starfish fell from the schefflera and lay across the scabby cardboard cover. I was trembling all over with anger. He'd done it on the solstice, like his father. All the time we'd been missing, waiting for him, he was already dead. He hadn't thought of me, or of his daughters—what it would do to them. For the whole rest of their lives.

This—*this!*—was closer to him than I had been in all the years. This arm's-length, abbreviated record with its clipped glimpses of love. The closest I would ever come, now.

I thought of the ancient ice-walkers, the great glaciers melting. *Now I have leave to go, of her goodness.* Had he thought I'd given him that?

▼

223

Catasaqua, Clementon, Neffs. Now and then another car loomed up desperately close in the rearview mirror, hung there for an endless minute, then passed me. I gripped the steering wheel in both hands and stayed well to the right. Just after Emerald, I crossed the Lehigh Gap.

Ashfield, Jim Thorpe, Nesquehoning.

As I drove, the weather changed. The blue sky was streaked with clouds as thin as scarves. By the time I got to Beaver Meadows it was a bright, blowy day, wind spiraling up off fields of corn and barley, small brown hawks riding the updrafts. In the ditches along the road, black-eyed susan and hawkweed and Queen Anne's lace whipped sideways as the car passed. Ahead, the macadam held shimmering pools of black that narrowed to nothing when I got close.

It was so long since the last time I'd made this trip—before Susie was born, I'd stopped going, and Gort had stopped asking—yet I seemed to know the way still. Not thinking, this turn or that, stop or keep on; just going by feel. I detoured around Hazleton (two-bit, too big, Gort always said) and crossed the Susquehanna River. By the side of the road two girls in cut-off jeans and halter tops squinted into the sun. Their thumbs were stuck out and one held up a sign made from a flattened-out grocery bag that said WE ARE FRENCH. Was it an invitation or a challenge? Driving on between fields dotted with yellow stargrass and wild mustard, I wondered who would pick them up, and whether they would survive the kindness of strangers.

Then it hit me that Lil must have hitchhiked along this road. She wouldn't think about the danger. Remembering the months she'd spent unrepentant—no, triumphant—in the body cast, I knew that much. The lake, I suddenly understood, was the worst place for her; and I thought, I could kill him for making her go there. Then I realized what I had said.

Nescopeak, Jonestown, Cambra.

What would I say to Lil when I found her? It made me angry all over again—the thought of her fierce, unyielding love; of what she would do to satisfy it. She would not want me there. My do it, she'd said at three, yanking the tiny shoelaces out of my hands; then, and all the years since. My do it.

At the intersection of Route 487, a yellow light swung in the wind. I slowed down and stopped. A small house, painted red, stood on the other side of the road; laundry on the line was white in the sun, sheets filling and emptying. I rolled down the window. The breeze carried the odor of grain, sun-warmed, and the sour familiar smell of cow dung. I could hear the sheets snap and telephone wires creak overhead. The light was still yellow. Then I remembered: the blinking ones don't turn red. I put the car in gear and drove.

My stomach hurt. The sun, in front of me now, looked like about two o'clock. I hadn't had breakfast, or dinner the night before. I remembered how Gort used to pack a white Styrofoam chest, bananas and cherry soda and tunafish sandwiches in waxed paper on the smoking ice.

▼

The statue in the center of town was probably William Penn—they always were, Gort said. Because it was easiest I took the first right after the little fenced-in triangle of rusty grass. Halfway down the block was a sign for the Blossom All-Nite Cafe. I angled the Dodge into an empty space in front of Adler's Hardware two doors away, singers twanging against the car on my right, and got out. Taped over the parking meter was a torn piece of paper that said in penciled letters BROKE. A black dog slouched past with a canvas hat in its mouth; an old man standing in front of the hardware store called after it in a low pleading voice.

Prying my damp jeans off the backs of my thighs, I looked around. As if I'd driven into a time-warp, the town (whose name I'd already forgotten) was like something out of my childhood. A Walgreen's drugstore with hygienically blank display windows; a small boarded-up movie theater; a cigar-and-newspaper store, with three or four teenage boys leaning against it in T-shirts with the sleeves cut off and the sides slit down to the waist. When they saw me looking, they flicked their cigarettes in my direction and made kissing sounds. Two men in painter's overalls were settling a ladder against the side of the hardware store. Its windows were hung with birdcages, toilet seats, knives and paintbrushes in descending sizes, black rubber doormats, Coleman lanterns, balls of twine. I looked into them as I passed, ignoring the T-shirted boys across the street. Behind me the old man called vainly after the dog, a word that sounded like "gutter, gutter."

I had to duck under the sagging American flag over the entrance to the Blossom Cafe. As the door closed behind me there was—not a pause, exactly, but a redirection of noise. The clatter of dishes, the snap of frying grease, the voices all seemed to shift and flow toward me. I fingered the hair coaxed into a fuzzy braid on the back of my neck, pushed my glasses up on my nose. Moving quickly down the narrow room, I sank onto a stool against the back wall. The old man beside me raised his newspaper and flapped it twice to show that he couldn't understand why, with all the empty places, I chose this one. *Wednesday, August 14*, his paper said.

4-YEAR-OLD GIRL ALIVE IN DETROIT
Mother's Love Saves Sole Crash Survivor

"You guys all coffee'd out?" the waitress asked a young woman holding a bald-headed baby in a ruffled yellow sunsuit. Catching my look, the woman swiveled protectively on her stool so that her back in its blue-checked blouse came between me and the baby.

Ceiling fans chugging overhead pushed the smell of bacon grease back and forth. Without the complicated, contradictory business of driving, my mind was too free; I could feel it shifting, trying to cast up terrors. *Reality check.* I studied the Specials, each on its own homemade cardboard sign taped to the wall behind the counter. *3 Eggs Any Way Any Time; Wednesday Wieners & Beans (app. sauce); Spilt Pea Soup; We Have Scrapple.* I swiveled on my too-small stool. In the booth nearest to me a young man with bushy dark hair sat talking to himself. He had a soft, rich voice like Mildred's, a voice that made you want to believe. What he said sounded as if it made sense, but didn't. "The body gets worse. *Pollution* gets worse. I believe they're open nine to five." He gestured and nodded to the watermelon-colored plastic partition opposite him.

"What'll it be?" The waitress, a kind-looking, walleyed woman, dealt out placemat, paper napkin, silverware. I had trouble deciding which eye to meet. The Special pushing eggs was right above the waitress's head, so I ordered that. Her sad, lined face looked sadder when she smiled.

The door at the front of the diner opened. Two girls about Lil's age came giggling in. The noise altered course and swam toward them for a moment. "Ekspecially, it's you," the black one said as they clattered into the last booth. A stand of magenta dyed hair curved over her forehead, like a cockatiel. "That's what he says to me."

"World *situation* gets worse," said the rich-voiced young man, and gave a quick little bugling cough. He made me think of Lil's baby talk—long, intricate, unintelligible remarks with the melodies of questions, orders, promises. How angry she'd get when Gort and I didn't understand. She'd squeeze her eyes shut and shout, until finally Gort folded her into his arms, laughing, and murmured into her ear a long nonsense string of his own.

At that moment I began to understand what lay ahead of me. *One world,* I said to myself. The cork-covered wall beside me was stuck all over with notices; I began to read them. Lost, one kitten; firewood split & stacked; babysitting eves. A large orange notice said *LOST 7/1/87 John Lowery,* and in smaller printing, *73 yrs gray eyes gray hair; Often Speaks in Whisper.* Underneath was a dim Xeroxed photograph that could have been anybody.

The waitress set down the plate of eggs, a glass of water, a cup of tea I hadn't ordered. "You look kinda pale," she said, and smiled her apologetic smile. "Tea's good for heat frustration."

I watched her go around the other end of the counter to deliver puffy soft pretzels and Cokes to the two girls. "Then he writes me this poem?" said the one with the hair. They took turns squeezing yellow worms of mustard over their pretzels. "It goes, I think about you all the time. I get in trouble at school thinkin' about you. I wish we could be naked like guppies."

The old man next to me slapped his newspaper into a small rectangle and stood up. He pulled a matchbook out of his pocket and wrote something on the cover with a ballpoint pen, then folded it, set it on the counter, and left. Still shielded by its mother's blue-checked back, the baby at the other end of the counter made soft little creaking sounds. I still did not understand, I saw that now. I had not really grasped that Gort had died; or how. These people here—this little space of time, this place—were the last I'd have before I knew. Knew, and couldn't un-know. Knew with my whole body what I already knew in my heart. I looked down at my plate. A smell like Borax steamed up from the yellow mass of potatoes and eggs. But if I closed my eyes I saw myself on the bluff above the lake, kneeling on the rocky ground, holding his too-light body in my arms. Counting up how much had been lost. All the things he had never been for us; all the things he would never, now, be. The bottom of my throat ached. *No word that means, a longing for the future.*

The girl with the hair said, "You don't let it touch your lips."

The man in the booth said, "A *person* gets worse."

Everything, everything would be changed. There would be the moment before; and the moment after. After, nothing would be as it was. When I leaned, no one would be there; when I turned toward the wall in my sleep, there would be only the wall.

"Will you look at this." The waitress, clearing the place next to me, unfolded the matchbook. "THANK YOU," she read, and snorted. "Every day, the same thing. That Wilmot, what a skinflint. Hon?" She looked closer at me, one eye on my left ear. "Around the end of the counter," she said. "Right inside the kitchen."

I made it to the tiny, windowless bathroom in time to throw up. Afterwards I stood with my stomach pressing the edge of the sink, looking at my blurred reflection in the empty metal towel dispenser. *serve Energy*, a torn sticker said. I turned on the faucet—only the cold tap worked—and cupped my hands and splashed cool water on my face. Then I scrubbed it dry with a thin white towel from a hook on the wall. I squatted over the toilet with my jeans bunched around my knees, not letting my buttocks touch the seat.

Out on the sidewalk, the warm afternoon was full of the sharp, urgent smell of fresh paint. The T-shirted boys were gone; the old man sat on his haunches in front of Goettner's Bakery, one arm around the black dog. I lifted my face up so the sun fell on it. In the distance a factory whistle sounded. It went on and on and did not stop.

▼

Back on the highway, for a while I felt better. It felt good to be moving; I almost forgot what the road was rushing me toward. After ten miles or so, a dark-blue pickup truck pulled out from a side road ahead of me.

It settled into a sane speed—it was a rickety-looking thing with both fenders dented—and I was happy to follow along behind. The back ledge was strung with heads on folded arms: three children and a dog. The children waved and made faces; the long jowls of the basset hound, hung with garlands of spit, glinted in the sun.

We started up into the mountains. The road curved around high out-croppings of rock; the trees got darker and steeper, evergreens punctuated by white birches and poplars whose flickering leaves were already turning yellow. The lowering sun picked out the mica in the road and made the dusty windshield glitter, melting them into one continuous shining path. Safe behind the dark-blue pickup, I flexed my stiff fingers on the steering wheel. After a few miles the children lost interest in me; the boys started to arm-wrestle and the little girl lifted the dog's ear and spoke into it. On the pickup's bumper a white sticker said "I Believe in MARRIAGE." The words "Marriage Encounter" appeared beneath a black-edged heart that ended in two linked black circles like handcuffs. Gort's view of marriage?

Now, *now* I understood—and it was Eli who'd shown me—how it might feel to have people *want* you so much. The fear they'd find out how small and flawed you really were; the knowledge that you'd fail them eventually; the loneliness of being cut off from yourself by all the people who needed you more than *you* did. I had not understood any of this, in all our sixteen years of marriage, or the years of love that went before. If I had understood, would Gort still be alive? After a point, Ms. Grundy said to me once, even innocence is a decision. A choice about how to live in the world. I had grounded Gort; but doing that had meant that neither of us could tell the truth. I had thought he would not speak to me; but neither could I speak to him.

Nordmont; Laport; Shunk.

The last real town before the lake was Dayville, a clutch of empty fac-tory buildings and mean little houses rising straight up from the narrow road. It was exactly as it had been the last time I saw it, as if eight years' decay wasn't enough to notice, added onto what was there already. I'd always dreaded Dayville; it seemed to me like the end of the world. In the driveway of a lone low ranch house at the outskirts of town, a child in a gray diaper watched us go by.

Abruptly the children in the blue pickup began waving again, hanging out over the back of the truck and grinning. The basset hound lifted its head; I could see the red leather collar slung around its throat. The pickup swung right, onto a narrow side road that cut between thick-growing pine and blue spruce. Then they were gone, the rosy, hectic children, the stolid dog. I was alone, as deeply and finally alone as I'd been the last time I'd seen Dayville.

▼

It's late in the day, late in the fall of 1987, that we go to Bitter Lake together for the last time.

We've been driving through rainy fog for six hours, seven, over narrow roads that run alongside dim November fields. Then trees, more and more of them—oak and hickory, paper birch, fir and pine and spruce—their colors muted as if under water. The inside of the car, newly shampooed for the trip, smells like Juicy Fruit. My jaw aches from yawning. I am two months pregnant.

By the time we get through Dayville, it is dusk. The sun, wherever it is, has set; the sky is as blank as the highway, they run together, broken only by the occasional greasy lights of an oncoming car.

"We'll have to stop." Gort flexes his fingers on the steering wheel. He hates fog: the closed-in feeling, the blankness where the headlights end, having to take on faith what's beyond.

I hide my gladness, flap the useless, inscrutable roadmap, peer with a concerned forehead through the windshield into the blankness. I hate the lake, or fear it; maybe both. The endless mutter of the water; the canvas tent struggling against the tent-pegs; the mildewed sleeping bags and sterno-tasting fish. But it isn't just those things, it's something else, something I can't name. It has to do with time. Is it possible for someone to be not in her right time, as in "not in her right mind"? At the lake it feels like that.

Each time we go, I think I'll say it is the last. But the lake is one place we can't refuse. Our grandfather, Gort's and mine, bought the land in the Twenties, hung onto it all through the Depression, the last lone remnant of Hutchins prosperity; Gort's father taught him to fish there. The lake is part of the family history, part of the family; the lake is the place Gort loves. The sign, its first letter unlit, says "alley of the Moon Motel" in one long tube of green light, so large we can see it from the road. We park between overgrown bushes spiked with red berries. Through a long uncurtained window I can see a man behind a counter looking out. He is large—not fat, but wide—in a faded flannel shirt, washed-out skin, hair that's nearly but not quite white.

Gort goes into the tiny office, talks to the wide-chested man, comes out. I crank the window down and the car fills with the smell of wet bark and kerosene. Gort touches my hair, frizzed up from the fog like Easter-basket grass. "Be right back." He walks away down the narrow cement strip with its row of identical green doors. The fog opens to take him in. He disappears.

I wait. Five minutes? Ten? Underneath the motel's name a white worm of light says "Eat—Rest." I have no watch. High on the wall behind the motionless motel keeper, the arrow-shaped hands of a black-framed clock point permanently at noon. Or midnight. I think of six-year-old Lil, left for the weekend with Clesta: the warm weight of her would steady me now.

It's absurd to be afraid. There's the motel sign's soupy light, the bright square window, the sweep of the motel keeper's eyes. But all of it exists just here, just now: a narrow band between blankness and blankness, like a moment without past or future. I am afraid. Afraid to get out of the car and follow Gort; afraid to stay.

▼

Lower now, the sun knifed between the trees as if it were blinking on and off. It would be dark in an hour, and Lil would be up there on the bluff all alone in the night. My foot came down hard on the gas. I passed the grassy gap in the pines where the Valley of the Moon Motel had stood. Light struck my face over and over. There were no other cars; no houses, no billboards, no signs. Just the road and the trees, the trees and the road. Alone with the light, I followed the curve of the metal fencing that shimmied along the sheer-drop side of the road. At about this spot Gort would point out, every time we made the trip, how beautiful the landscape was when there was nothing human in it.

But what spot was it, exactly? There was a dirt road that led to the lake. A side road, invisible, like the one the pickup had turned onto—easy to miss. It should have been about now. I looked at the little glass windows on the dashboard to see how many miles I'd come. Not 93,312;

it must be the other gauge. But 827 wasn't right, either; then I remembered that I hadn't set anything at zero when I started out. With one hand I felt for my purse, which I hadn't used in weeks, unbuckled the clasp, dumped the contents onto the seat beside me. Quickly I looked down. Among the leaves and insect bodies I'd forgotten about was a drawing of a shark in pea green crayon, wearing a nurse's cap. Susie must have put it in when I wasn't looking, a talisman, to keep me safe. I pushed it aside, looked up to check on the road, looked down again. There it was, the roadmap I'd stuffed in that morning.

The car swerved. I seized the steering wheel in both hands. Up ahead on the right I could see a clearing. I pulled over, bumping across the lumpy ground, to a low, grassy place. Between me and the black skeleton of an abandoned barn was a stretch of high grass starred with white horseweed, an old three-wheeled plow with ox-eyed daisies growing up through its ribs. Behind the barn the woods began again, dark, steep pines separated by fingers of orange light. When I shook open the map, my expired driver's license slid out onto the new floormat. I looked hard, starting from where the blue of water was, and moving left. But it was the same thing as always—a tangle of lines unraveling in all directions, blue ones like veins, thin red ones like fingernail lines of blood—it told me nothing.

My eyes ached; my head felt light. The pines on the other side of the road threw flat blue shadows across the hood of the Dodge. I'd forgotten how much earlier day ends in the mountains. What should I, what *could* I do? What would Mildred do? "What?" I said out loud to the empty car. There was no one. No one to follow, the way I'd followed Mildred to the house on Schoener Place that first day; the way, I saw now, I'd followed Lil as far as this clearing. I hated her then, my first-born daughter, who had sent me on this journey, who would not want me if I ever got there. I picked up Susie's nurse shark and held onto it, feeling hollow and light, sick with lightness, as if I would float up off the blue vinyl seat and out through the open window. I crossed my arms over the steering wheel and put my head down. I cried because I hated my daughter. I cried because I could only be what I was, because in order to live in one world I had first had to lie to myself. I cried because I could not read a map.

2 0

LIL

In the afternoon the dirt logging road stopped. I'd been on it for hours, scuffing through the dust with the hot wind like a lion's breath on the back of my neck and beetles snapping in the ditch alongside. I turned onto a trail covered with moldy leaves and pine needles and full of half-buried rocks. I kept on heading west northwest by my compass—at the end of summer the sun starts moving south, like the birds. Grown-together vines looped around my ankles and tripped me. My bare arm kept getting scraped by broken branches, but I couldn't do anything about that. I had to hold the cast in my good hand. I'd lost the sling just after sunrise—torn it off on the rusty barn door.

The trail got narrower and narrower, then stopped. Rocks and tree roots. I pushed uphill toward the water. I knew it was soon, maybe over the next rise, that all-of-a-sudden clear space that made your stomach drop. And it was.

From the bluff you felt you could walk right into the sky. The sun was low over the hill at the western end of the lake, but still warm after the woods. I stood there squinting into it. I felt dizzy and hollow, my stomach ached and my arm ached, but I didn't care. I was *here*.

At the edge of the bluff, right where we'd always pitched it—the tent.

I went closer. My heart started jerking slow and hard, like hiccups. The tent looked funny. It leaned to one side—the ropes were slack and the green canvas sagged. Slowly I untied the flap.

Inside, his sleeping bag was rolled up in one corner on top of the blue ground sheet, and his backpack stood next to it. At first, except that the ground sheet was wrinkled, everything looked tidy, the way he liked to leave things—the collapsible plastic net, folded on top of two cans of sterno; his orange life-jacket strapped into a neat bundle; the old green canvas tackle bag with the crescent wrench sticking out of one pocket.

Everything in its place, not jumbled around, even if you knew you were coming right back. It smelled funny, though—a nasty, *basement* smell. Then I noticed the water pooled in places on the ground sheet, and a little hardened pile of some kind of animal shit, and the way one of the sterno cans'd fallen over.

I thought, He must've stayed out all night, trolling. Strange that he'd forgotten the tackle bag; but he forgot things a lot lately. I touched the webbed strap of the sleeping bag and ran my hand over the slippery red nylon backpack. I didn't look inside—that would've been snooping. I knew where he had to be. No point going to the edge of the bluff to look for him; he'd be around the eastern leg of the lake, out of sight, in the place where the trees sort of leaned out over the water and the small-mouth ran big. The place we always went. I reached down with my good hand and pulled the ground sheet straight.

Four or five yards further along the bluff I found a bunch of rocks piled in a circle. The center was full of ashes melted down into black lumps. My father's firepit. I stood by a little bent-over spruce. From here I could see the far edge of the lake, the sun starting down behind the hill, dead birches sticking up out of the water. A pair of black-and-white loons made a noise like sliding down a harmonica. One of them arched its wings, then folded them back and dived.

Something made me stop there. No reason to keep going, I told myself. I mean, why look down on the beach for the boat, when I knew where he'd be? Why look down at the water at all?

There was a big oak I'd passed on the way up, almost at the edge of the woods, with these enormous thick roots that crawled out over the ground. The one my father'd climbed to watch the raccoon? It *could* be. I went back and sat down on the packing of needles and dead leaves where the trunk put out two big roots like an armchair. The bark was warm, alive but not breathing, and the moss in between the grooves felt hairy and plump, like Lustyka's paws. I slid my backpack off my good shoulder and unbuckled it. I took out the can of mace, the flashlight, the knife (this time I'd come prepared, not like that night with my mother's burglar boyfriend), and laid them on the ground. That was all—the food was gone, and I was wearing the clean underpants. Rhoda and I always talked about what we'd do if we had to split. Rhoda was always on the verge of running away; she fixed us up with mace and police whistles and taught me how to knee a man in the groin. First cross the street to make sure he's following you, she'd said; then after you knee him, yell *Fire*—people don't like to get involved with Help calls.

This time I was ready for anything. I breathed in the get-a-grip smell of the big pines, like cough lozenges. I stretched my legs straight out. The sweatshirt tied around my waist got lumped up under me, but I was too tired to undo it. My neck and arm and legs stung with scratches and bruises from the night before, and the night before that. I was hungry. There were mushrooms—I could've reached the little velvety caps from where I sat—but I knew better. There're about a million poisonous kinds. I was thirsty, too. But I didn't want to go down to the water. What if he came back by another way and I missed him? At least the ache in my arm took my mind off things. I leaned back against the trunk and rested my cast along the top of one thick root.

Now that I was holding still, the place was full of noises. Leaves shuffling over my head, bugs clicking and buzzing, a lot of rattling in the bushes close to the ground. I tried not to think what made the sounds. *Creatures*—Clesta's word. Porcupines; possums; raccoons, like the one my father'd watched. Black bears. Their sour breath on the back of my—

I picked up the knife and ran my thumb very lightly over the blade. A thin line of red sprang up.

Snakes. Snakes were the worst. *Reptiles may rely on deception.* Garter-snakes, milk snakes, racers, skinks. Copperheads! Oozing under the firethorn bushes, through the sumac, then—

I took my compass out of my sweatshirt pocket and laid it next to the can of mace. North was straight ahead to the lake. Up high somewhere I could hear the calls of blue jays, back and forth. I dug into my jeans pocket for the Documents and unfolded one. The witch in the hat. *Measure up, kitch window, lumberyard, J.* I didn't need to look at the words. The paper was scotch-taped together where I'd torn it—torn all the Documents—after I first read the journal. I rubbed my thumb along the smooth, shiny tape. He *could* be planning to stay out all night again, trolling, but I didn't think he would; he'd always said never to do that without a buddy.

Everything would be different, when he came. I'd make him see me.

We'd build a fire in the circle of rocks on the bluff, and the smoke would make our eyes water. He'd let me scale the fish—smallmouth, or maybe a muskie—running the knife tail to head, the cold scales like sequins flying up and sticking to my bare arms. Then he'd slit it and throw the dark, shiny lungs and liver down onto the beach for the birds. Peel away the shivery white ladder of backbone. Spread the body like a butterfly in the hot skillet. We'd feast. The Prodigal Son down on one knee in his blue-and-white tile on Clesta's fireplace, and then the joyful feast, the fatted calf. Fatted fish. *I have wronged you. Forgive me.* My father's eyes warm and shining behind his glasses.

The hot dogs at that place, the Rosebud Cafe or—what was it called?—that was the last time I'd eaten. Except for the apple, this morning at the Piggly Wiggly. I'd *had* to steal it. I was so hungry I felt faint, and I didn't know how long my money might have to last. The old guy's newspaper, the guy at the Rosebud counter yesterday afternoon, had said Tuesday—

147 FEARED DEAD IN DETROIT JET CRASH
"It Just Crumpled Like a Piece of Paper"

—so then Tuesday night was the barn, and this was Wednesday.

A mosquito fizzed in my ear. Looking up, I could see another one, and another, little light flecks against the dark-green leaves, like the first stars at night. Long shadows were crawling towards me, the light slipped between them in flashes, like pickerel in shallow water. The sun would've already started down behind the hill at the western end of the lake. It would be dark soon. I clicked the flashlight on, off, on. It had a new battery but it still wasn't right; the glass was cracked straight across. The shimmery circle of red light, like the iris of an eye, fell in two halves. I shone it on a cluster of white flowers growing at the bottom of my tree root where it splayed out into long dinosaur toes. I shone it on the trunk of the next tree, trying to pick out faces in the bark. There was always dark in the middle, splitting them in two.

My stomach miaowed some more. I thought of how he'd trained us not to ask for anything. How nothing we said seemed big enough to get his attention—seemed *worthy*. I remembered his eyes when he took his glasses off, what Clesta called Colorado eyes, gazing off into the distance, their blue bleached out from the light, the skin around them pinched from looking past you. My hand wavered. I snapped the flashlight off. Inside the cast my arm ached, a hard drumming ache, like somebody banging on the bones. The cast felt too tight, a trap, the way I'd been trapped in the body cast. I touched the cold plaster. If only I could take it *off*.

I'd have to tell him that I'd lost the hat. One of the fishing flies had snagged on something—a tree branch maybe—lifted the hat right off my head. I couldn't stop. I had to keep going. His dead father's hat. He wouldn't yell; but he'd be cold. I thought of Old Bob and the ladder and the lightning. *They don't see things the way we do.*

High up, an owl hooted—a barred owl, I could tell from its call. *Who cooks for you? Who cooks for you-all?* How old was I when he taught me that? I leaned back and closed my eyes. My hair, unbraided, caught in the rough bark. After the body cast, my mother'd made him stop bringing me here. We'd only come one more time after that; I couldn't've been more than nine. But I'd remembered the way. I'd remembered.

▼

Finally we come to the bluff. Pine and spruce and hemlock, stuck all over with snow, are like ghosts across the dark lake, but far-off and harmless. Safe, because I'm with him. We wait, letting our eyes get used to the dark, while my father sets up the telescope. We've picked a night with no clouds, windless, just before the new moon. A night when my mother's in Orient visiting Grumma Maude, because Daddy's not supposed to take me to Bitter Lake anymore. I cover my flashlight with red tissue paper. I spent so much time studying, these last few days, that the book opens by itself to the star chart for December.

First we look without the telescope. We look up through the darkness, our breath white above our faces; up into the bowl of stars. Like always, I feel dizzy and light. As if the sky were pulling on me like an enormous magnet, as if only the weight of my blue snowboots held me to the ground.

"There's Aries, the Ram." I point to its head turned back over one shoulder and bright Hamal at the corner of its mouth.

"And?" says my father. "Over there?"

"Perseus."

He tells me the story. How Perseus killed ugly old Medusa who had snakes for hair, whose eyes turned people to stone. How he held up his sword like a mirror, so that she looked into her own face, then cut off her head and saved Andromeda.

"Was that his daughter?" I ask.

"No." My father's laugh is a steamy trail of white. "No, Lilly."

He takes the telescope then. My eyes trace his outline against the sky. His dark-blue down jacket, almost the color of the night sky, makes a big bear shape. He stands inside it as if his body didn't touch the lining anywhere.

He lifts his head from the telescope. "It's the eye that makes the stars into constellations," he tells me. "They look as if they hung there motionless. But really they're spinning and scattering all the time. All the time, Lilly." His voice sounds strange. He squats down, one hand on the barrel of the telescope, and puts his arm around me. "You don't understand. But remember." His arm holds me tight, tight. "Remember, Lilly. It's only the eye."

▼

Cold. Goose pimples all along my bare arm. One arm hot; one cold. The broken one throbbed, this heavy, grinding pain. *Grind his bones to make my bread.* I put the back of my hand across my forehead, my cheek, like my mother used to do. My skin felt spongy and hot.

The owl called again—a hollow sound now, like the phone ringing in an empty house. A night sound. Maybe the same owl my father'd found—no, that one was dead. I was getting confused; it was because I was so hungry. I thought of the owl I'd seen dive to the barn floor, its too-big clawed feet reaching for the mouse. There was a kind of clicking in my throat, and I had to keep swallowing. My mouth tasted sour. My arm was aching worse than before—I could feel the muscles jump inside the cast, jump and twitch, like a fish when you're pulling the hook from its mouth. I held my father's paper, folded into a little square, in my palm. *Measure up, kitch window, lumberyard, J.*

I kept still and listened for the slap of water against the wooden boat, the scrape of its bottom over pebbles down on the beach. But there was nothing. Just the little broken sounds of the birds and the snap of the underbrush and my own breathing. The thought went across my mind before I could stop it: If I don't have him, who do I have? I felt a stab of fear; I pushed it down. He would come—he had to. I had to believe he would come.

Slowly, trying not to move the cast, I untied the sweatshirt from around my waist. I pulled it over my head and worked my good arm through one sleeve. I really had to piss; but what if I missed him? I couldn't see the sun from here, just pieces of sky, blank and blue, the light fading. On the ground the shadows ran together and lost their shape.

Every now and then my arm twitched, and the cast bumped the tree root with a sound like someone knocking. I clamped my teeth together to keep them from chattering. We'd cook the fish, the Fatted Fish, in the oval pan with the long wooden handle. Cold. Hot. My fingers found a piece of moss, peeled it off, held it. It warmed slowly in my hand. I wound it in and out through my fingers. My arm felt as if it were getting bigger and bigger, and there was this wire, like the wire Doc used to slice angel-food cake, tightening around the bones. *If you can't sleep, just rest.* Then she'd touch her cool lips to my eyelids—

My head went back hard against the oak tree. I shook the moss off my fingers. *Pain is spinach.* In my good hand I picked up an acorn and squeezed it hard, squeezed it so it bit into my palm. Made me not think about my arm, or about wanting my mother.

That was better.

Everything will be better, when he comes. The two of us. His back to me after he's climbed up onto the bluff. Home is the sailor, home from the sea. *Dad. Over here.*

The owl cried again, louder this time. I put the acorn into my other hand and picked up the knife and laid it across my knees.

Everything will be different—

My breath would only come in gulps, the air was too heavy. I could feel my heart inside my chest, feel the pain-wire squeezing my bones.

—when he—

I sat still, with my head up and my hand on the cold silver handle.

—comes.

21

JUDITH

It was getting cooler. I pulled down the sleeves of the cream-colored sweater my mother had knitted for me to take to college, and buttoned the remaining buttons. Then I walked on towards the bluff, over leaf mulch and pine needles, stepping through the stiff quills of the ferns, delicate as feathers until you got close. Overhead the huge pines creaked and groaned. The ground, the undergrowth, were alive with shadows that gathered and thickened as I waded through them, rising to my knees, my waist.

I stopped to pick a tick off my bare ankle, resting one hand on the cool, peeling trunk of a paper birch for balance. With my fingernail I flicked the shiny swollen head into a pin-cherry bush. A leaf drifted down onto the sleeve of my sweater, eaten away by insects so that it looked like hardened lace. I looked up. The birch was full of them, little skeleton leaves, brittle and brown: a death tree. They crackled like static in the light wind.

It had not been hard, after all, to find this place. "Simple," the little man in overalls had said when I'd stopped at Walp's Gas, two lone pumps in a corner of the mountain on the Silkworth Road. Hunching down, he rested one scornful elbow inside the open window. He snapped the fraying map and pointed. "Go back like so, till you hit the Loyalsock Road. A quarter-mile, and there's your turnoff. Simple." He leaned in closer and his eyes found the passenger seat, the small dried-out corpses of beetles and moths scattered over the sky blue vinyl. He jumped back. His thumb came up through a fold in the map next to Lake Wallenpaupack. Counting out bills into his oil-stained palm, I'd realized I hadn't paid for the eggs at the Blossom Cafe.

Up to my chest in shadows now. Birds made echoing, end-of-day sounds overhead, and somewhere an owl hooted. I climbed over a fallen swamp maple, snagging my sweater on its branches, and stepped out through the last trees onto the bluff.

There was the old unpleasant sensation—the land dropping away beneath my feet, my stomach dropping down fast, the sky filling the hole. The western sky was like a relief map—clouds heaped up in scattered, irregular shapes, with the canyons between them lighted from below by the sun, invisible now behind the hill. It mapped the terrain of dreams, of nightmares: the bright, unnatural orange and red and blue-violet; the clouds edged in pure painful light. In the east, a white moon was etched on the darkening sky, scratchy and faint like a child's drawing. West and east might have been two different skies.

I stood still, my arms pressed against my body, and looked at the two skies. Everything was silent: the woods; the water. I stood between silences, dizzy and light, free as air. It was simple, then—as the little man had said. I was free. Free to walk towards the sagging tent, the circle of stones, the water; free to turn and go back through the shadowed woods to the car. Freedom was just this—this terrible lightness, as if I had to hold myself down with my own arms, as if any second I might float away, drift out over the edge of the bluff into the space between the two skies.

"—you?"

I knew my daughter's voice; but still the first thing I felt was fear. I turned and scanned the shadows at the edge of the woods. A patch of white rose and began to move toward me. The ominous pink light fell on Lil's tangled hair, the stark white of her cast.

"You!"

Her voice quavered with disappointment, breaking the word in two. She walked stiff-legged across the stony ground. She was holding something pressed against her side, and her navy blue sweatshirt was slung across her chest.

I realized I'd been holding my breath. There had been that last fear: that I'd been wrong, that she wouldn't be here. I breathed out. Anger rushed through me, the anger that comes when you find your child safe. With the anger came the feeling: my daughter; *mine*. She was my daughter and no one else's—not Clesta's, not even Gort's, not anymore—and there was nothing either of us could do about it. It wasn't a matter of choice; but at that moment, I chose it. *Do what you want*, my mother had said; now at last I knew what she meant.

"Why are *you* here?" Her voice was scratchy and rough, the voice of someone who hadn't spoken in a long while. She was close enough now for me to see her face. Her eyes were dark-blue the way they used to get when she was sick, and the skin beneath them was stretched and shiny. There was a deep scratch across one cheek.

"I came to—take you—home." I had to push the words out one by one, as if my mouth were filled with mud.

"We don't need you."

I stood quite still. So that was it: she'd been expecting *him*.

"We don't want you."

"Lil. Your father—"

"We *don't want* you!" She was shouting and coughing at the same time. I could see her shaking. It had gotten cold: the light that looked like firelight on her angry face was as cold as lake water.

"Here. Put this on." I had one arm out of the raveling, cream-colored sweater. I wanted her to say, Mama. Just that. If only she would say that, then I could find the words to tell her what I had finally understood: that you couldn't stay in one world unless that world included everything. That if you shut anything out, you too would be divided.

I took a step toward her. She backed away. "No," she said violently. "I don't need it. Don't need anything"—she coughed—"from *you*."

I took another step. Lil moved sideways. My head ached and I could feel the vein beating in my forehead. My daughter's eyes were cold, her mouth clenched and ugly. We moved in a circle on the hard ground of the bluff. Slowly, needles crunching under our feet with a weirdly cheerful sound, we took sideways steps, one at a time. The empty sweater arm dangled down behind me like a tail. Now Lil's wild hair was pale against the trees; now her head was lit from behind by the fierce sky over the water. We kept circling. The wind blew long strings of hair across my face. Lil's nose was running; one untied shoelace flapped on the ground. She stumbled, but she kept moving.

"You let him go!"

No, I said—almost said; but I couldn't lie anymore.

"You let him go! You *sent* him."

I looked at my daughter's face, ugly and square with anger, and in her eyes the question I'd seen all those years ago, when she lay in the body cast: *Is this how the world is?* We were moving in a fragile dance that kept the distance between us always the same. My heart ached, but my tongue wouldn't move. I wanted to cross the space between us and grab hold of her, hold her until she understood that I wasn't the one who'd done this to her—that it had been done to both of us. But I was afraid.

I said, pleading, "Lil. We have to look—"

"He's coming. He'll be back before dark."

I tried again. "Lil. Where's the boat? Did you look down on the beach?"

"Before dark. He'll be—" She went into a spasm of coughing and stood still, finally, at the edge of the bluff with the red sky behind her. The white cast stuck out at an angle, and her good arm was pressed tight against her side, the hand down, clenched. My do it. But this she couldn't do, not by herself.

My throat knotted. I did not want to see her hope break, her body slump and sag. Before, I'd have lied, to save her that—to save us both that. But I couldn't—wouldn't—now. Lil had made us come here; I would have to make her see what we'd come here for.

I crouched beside the circle of blackened stones. My empty sweater sleeve trailed on the ground. Reaching out, I dug my fingers into the hardened ashes. I held up my hand. "Lil," I said desperately. "This fire hasn't been used in days. *Weeks.*"

Lil's stiff body rocked back and forth. I thought, My God—*she'll fall*. Shaking, I stretched out my arms.

She rushed at me, her arm raised. At the first silver flash I thought, crazily, of my mother's embroidery hoop. Then the knife came down. I heard the blade tear through the air beside my shoulder with a whistling sound.

The knife clattered onto the rocky ground. Lil squatted down beside me, dragging her good arm in the dark-blue sweatshirt across her face and coughing. She didn't look at me.

"Lil." So hard to speak. "We need to know what happened." The coughing turned into retching. On her knees now, she leaned over the circle of stones.

"We have to go and look. We have to." I put my hand under her elbow to help her up.

She jerked away. "I'm not a *gimp*."

Clumsily, separately, we stood up. Clumsily, separately, we walked to the edge of the bluff. I was more afraid than Lil was—more afraid than I'd ever been in my life—but I kept walking. I went first.

At the western end of the lake, between the calm spires of the firs, the red reflected sky spread through the water like blood. Below us, straight down in the shadow of the bluff, it was already twilight. Water lapped at the sides of the wooden boat that floated bottom-up between the rocks. It was a long triangle of faded blue, ghostly, almost white: a ghost boat come to graze in the reeds. It rode its own reflection in the water. Looking down, I saw our two white foggy faces. Beneath them, a blurred net of mirrored pine and spruce, the clean flat shadows of fish lodged in the branches. Beneath that—

My breastbone ached as if it had cracked down the middle. My mouth was suddenly full of a brackish, salty taste. I kept on swallowing. I felt light, insubstantial, wavery as air. I lifted my foot to step forward; but Lil grabbed my elbow. Her grip on me was so tight it hurt. She pulled me back, the way I'd come there to do for her. She kept on pulling me away from the edge, pulling us backwards, until at last she let go and sat down on the stony ground, suddenly, in a single motion.

Slowly, heavily—the air resisted me as if it were water—I knelt down beside Lil. I saw from her face that at last she understood. Her teeth were chattering and she kept turning her head from side to side like someone blind. With slow underwater movements I pulled off my sweater. Clumsily, with my free hand I spread it over her, wrapped the creamy-white wool over her shoulder and chest, tucked it under the cast. I tried to turn her face to me, but she jerked away. Then her head came down hard on my chest, bone against bone.

An owl gave its shuddery call. I opened my mouth to say something, I didn't know what; and warm liquid gushed out onto Lil's hair. That rusty, salt taste, standing on the bluff—I'd bitten my tongue. It was huge and sore and meaty. I couldn't speak.

The sound was low at first. Lil's body shook and heaved; I could feel her nails in my bare arm. The sound got louder. It emptied out of her, on and on, a wild grieving sound. The sound I would have made, if I could. She made it for me.

I held her, my daughter, who was broken. I knelt on the cold, rocky ground with my bare knees pressing into the pine needles, and her body lay heavily in my arms, across my legs, heaving, pouring out that wild sound. My shirt was soaked with her tears—my daughter, who never cried. I put my face in her hair, wet now with my own blood, and smelled the warm, dirty skin of her neck. I felt her all over with my hand, the way I had the first time I'd ever held her: her head, her shoulders, her elbows, her back.

At last she twisted a little on my lap. With her good arm she held me around my neck, her face still against my chest; the arm in the cast came clumsily half-around my waist. The weight of her warm, shuddering body held me down. I couldn't speak; but it didn't matter. I hung onto her while the blue dusk spread westward and the moon hardened into a round button of light. I hung on. I just hung on.

22

JUDITH

Lil huddled on the broad slippery seat beside me (I'd swept the things from my purse—the brittle leaves and lace-winged insects—onto the floor, where they were already beginning to crumble into dust), untying her hightops with her good hand. Her backpack lay between us with Uncle Bob's knife stowed carefully in the zipper pocket. I began to ease the car off the rocky verge. The yellow beams of the headlights sliced wildly through the trees, steadied, settled on the dirt road ahead. I shifted into neutral and pulled on the emergency brake, until I could gather my courage for the drive ahead. Over the drone of the motor I could hear Lil hiccuping, little bright chirps. She smelled sour, like yeast—Mildred's smell.

"Hungry?" I said. "There's some raisins in the glove compartment, I think."

Lil shook her head. The hightops dropped onto the floor. She slouched down in her corner of the seat with my sweater still draped across her shoulders, toes in dirty blue cotton socks gripping the dashboard. One hard, knobby knee appeared through a tear in her jeans. I forced my foot down on the gas, and we started.

It had been a long time since I'd driven at night. The moon, still climbing, was hidden somewhere behind the dark massed trees. Our headlights parted the dark for a little space, then stopped. All there was of the road was what they measured out—the rest was blackness, a flat drop off the edge of the earth. I remembered my father telling me, when he took me out on Sunder Creek Road in the pickup at Lil's age, to practice, that night was really safer than day. The lights of other cars announced them, he said; you couldn't ask fairer than that. Odd that *safer* isn't as safe as *safe*. I concentrated on the dull shine of the metal fencing as it snaked past on my right. My tongue felt thick and hot and I could still taste the faint salt taste of blood. From time to time Lil sniffed, hard. I knew better than to offer her a handkerchief. I didn't have one, anyway.

Birches sprang out skinny and white among the dark pines as the road curved and curved again, leading us down. It was miles, half an hour or more, before we met an oncoming car. Its lights splashed abruptly around a curve. Afterward the dark was darker. I slowed down and leaned into the windshield, trying to see as far along the guardrail as I could.

After another half-hour or so, with Lil still silent in her corner, we passed the skeleton barn where I'd stopped that afternoon. Lil's fingers, protruding from the cast, grabbed for the top of her backpack and she shivered—a private person now, separate, someone with secrets. For a second I felt sorry that I'd taken away her anger; it would have saved her, for a while.

We drove into Dayville. At the intersection of Route 414, just beyond where the Valley of the Moon Motel had stood, a Dairy Queen was still open, its lit-up sign urging, "Come as You Are, OR, Eat in Your Car!"

"Want to stop?" I asked Lil. She shook her head. In the triangle between her chest and her pushed-up knees her backpack rested like a shield, her good right arm tight across it. We left Dayville behind. Out of the mountains now, the three-lane road rolled out flat beneath our headlights, other cars appearing in the rearview mirror, swinging out to pass. Once, glancing sideways at Lil, her profile luminous for a second in the lights of a passing car, I thought of Gort looking up into the sky the day the skywriter wrote NOTHING across its blue blankness; and my heart clenched. I understood now that we would never know why. We would fit our Gorts together, Lil's and mine and Susie's, over and over, like the pieces of a puzzle, and still there'd be some missing.

After another long, silent half-hour a sign for Weintzburg loomed up ahead. I remembered the waitress in the Blossom Cafe and how I'd left without paying. "I'm going to stop," I told Lil. I heard her make some small, sudden movement; then, "No," she said—the first word she'd uttered since we'd left the lake. It came out a soft croak. I hesitated, lifting my foot off the gas so that the car slowed. Then I said firmly, "We have to, hon. I never paid for my lunch, I want to make it right." Lil didn't answer, but her feet came down off the dashboard and I could hear her feeling around on the floor for her hightops. I swung left off the highway.

▼

The kind-faced waitress was still on duty. She got up as we came in and stood behind the counter, and her face was anything but kind; her face said, *Stiffed.*

"Hi," I said quickly, "listen, I didn't, I forgot to pay this afternoon. I—we—stopped so we— It's good you're open all night—" Babbling, I sat down on the second stool—the place was empty except for us—and Lil swiveled onto the one next to me. Then I jumped up again so I could worm a wadded-up bill out of my jeans pocket. When she saw it was a ten, the waitress's face cleared. She tucked it into the breast pocket of her stained pink nylon uniform beneath a white patch that said "Pearlean," which I hadn't noticed that afternoon. With a shrug that was unexpectedly graceful, like a dancer's movement, she wiped away the past and gave me a clean slate.

"What'll it be?"

I ordered—not eggs this time, but a BLT, which seemed crisp and spare—and Lil, eyes on the watermelon-colored countertop, muttered, "Same." Pearlean gave her an odd look—one eye did, anyway, the other looked off past my left shoulder—and I thought probably crewcut bangs and matching eyebrows were rarely seen in Weintzburg; though what about the cockatiel girl that afternoon? But Lil looked truly disreputable, I saw now in the diner's unsparing light, with her dirty, scratched, tear-streaked face and scarred gray cast. Light poured out of sconces all around the walls, which I hadn't noticed that afternoon—bright pink plastic roses barely opening. The light they gave was the color of dawn. Blinking, I saw on the pie-sized clock behind Pearlean that it was only 9:55.

Pearlean shouted, "Sanjiv! Two BLT's, two Diets!" through a rectangular hole in the wall behind her; then she got a long cardboard tube out of the stainless steel refrigerator and picked up a cookie sheet and sat down companionably across from us, perched on her own invisible stool. Her too-black hair was drawn into a careful roll on either side of her broad, lined forehead; it seemed like a lonely person's hairdo. She whacked the tube against the edge of the counter, making Lil jump; a roll of pale, nude-looking dough emerged from the split cardboard.

"You two here for vacation?" she asked Lil. Lil shook her head, eyes on the menu which she'd kept open in front of her to ward off just such questions.

I watched Pearlean fold little triangles of dough like diapers and place them at intervals on the cookie sheet. Maybe it was the rosy light, but the diner felt somehow safe, comforting even; quiet the way your own house is quiet. No piped-in music; just the cook's thin, tuneless whistle and the bacon spitting in the pan, and once the silvery sound of glass breaking followed by a curt word in a language I didn't know. When our sandwiches came—Pearlean had added two diet Cokes, we must have looked like we needed the caffeine—I felt the push-pull of hunger and nausea; but the toasted bread was studded with sesame seeds, the lettuce tender and bright, the crisp, fluted bacon tasted like walnuts. I managed almost half.

"Don't you ever eat?" Pearlean said to Lil. She'd pulled her sandwich apart and sat tasting the edges of the golden bread. Without looking up— Lil considered eye contact a form of encouragement—she muttered something like "Hump." Pearlean got up and set the cookie sheet of little dough diapers in the pass-through. Then she began putting out white paper coffee filters, round ones like cupcake liners, on the counter in rows of four.

"Be a big rush, come 6:00 A.M.," she said when she saw me watching. "New girl's still slow. You see that piece on the news, about how decaf coffee's no good for you? Causes heart attacks."

"I *see* that; I *see* that," said Sanjiv, pulling the cookie sheet into the kitchen. His head, appearing briefly in the pass-through, wore a white boat-shaped hat that made him look like Nehru. Lil looked up, then down again. She'd given up on her sandwich. One dirty finger traced the figure for infinity over and over in the damp pink Formica of the countertop. If only she would talk, I thought. Her silence felt dangerous, and it was a minute before I understood why. Suicide was an option now.

"You two traveling on your own? I bet you have relatives in Luzerne County, right?" Pearlean said.

Abruptly Lil slid off her stool. "I have to pee," she said. Her back was toward me; as if she already knew where the john was, she was on her way around the counter before I could say anything. And what would I have said? She was fourteen years old—no, more: Gort's death had made her older than that, made her some age I couldn't even calculate—she didn't need anyone to take her to the bathroom.

Pearlean was watching me. She pushed some of the white paper cups in my direction, then handed me a can of Chase & Sanborn and a little long-handled red plastic cup. "Eight level per," she said.

Lil's stool was still squirming from the violence of her departure. I scooped coffee and poured it into the filters, breathing in the dark, loamy smell. It was this soon, then—the test? Let go, but don't let go. I thought of what Susie'd read to me about sharks sleeping with their eyes open— last night, it had only been last night. The fragrance of the coffee mingled with the teeth-edge smell of vinegar wafting from the kitchen, where Sanjiv whistled and banged pans; it made me think of dyeing Easter eggs when the girls were small.

"You got a good steady hand," Pearlean said. One eye looked after Lil. "She your only one?"

"No. My younger daughter—Susie, she's eight—she's at home."

"Sometimes I think I'm lucky to've had just the one. He's up at Allegheny Correctional sixteen months now. One and a half to go." She gave me her sad smile. "I'm divorced since 1986. What can you do. Right?" She waited for me to offer matching information. The word *relict* lurked behind my lips. I tried to smile back. Lil was taking too long. I stood up to go after her, then sat down again. I pictured the green ocean-bottom twilight, the sharks hanging wide-eyed in the watery gloom, asleep but still connected; and I understood that this test was the first of many.

Pearlean said, "That kind of thing happens to your kid, it's like a bomb drops inside of you. He had a good career goin', too—projectionist over across the way. When he finished the fight—he took out after this high school friend of his, some friend, I don't know what he did to Dudley but Dud cut him so bad he lost the use of his two little fingers." She held up her hand with the last two fingers folded under. "When Dud finishes the fight, he sits down on the stoop and cries, but for what? It's too late." Pearlean sighed, and her hands went back to the coffee. "You think you can keep people alive. You know? I been holdin' my breath for years."

Lil came through the kitchen doorway. She walked slowly around the end of the counter and stood next to me. My hand went up to touch her, an echo, like a tingle in my fingers, of some other motion. My mother in the attic in Orient, the pages of the *National Geographic* shining up from her lap. I made myself stay still. Lil's face was pale, but her eyes looked straight at me, not down at the floor or the smeared watermelon counter.

Pearlean said, "You two have far to go? I bet you got relatives in Hazle County."

Pretending she thought this was addressed solely to me (though Pearlean's hungry gaze was divided evenly between us), Lil crouched down to retrieve her backpack from the floor.

Pearlean said, "It's real unusual for folks to come through twice in one day."

I said, "We're on our way home now," and nothing more. Lil, setting her backpack on her stool, glanced at me with almost a smile. She pulled her painted Russian doll out of her backpack, opened it, and took out a cylinder of tightly rolled bills. She laid two of them, like short green cigarettes, on the counter between our two plates, then screwed the doll back together and pushed it down into her backpack.

"We have to go," she said to Pearlean, her first and last words to her. Trailing her backpack over one shoulder, she turned and started toward the door, then turned back to wait for me.

"Listen—thanks," I said to Pearlean, "thanks for everything." I slid off my stool and turned to follow Lil.

"Good talkin' to you," Pearlean said, only a little drily. "Safe journey." She tried one last time. "You finished your trip, huh?"

Lil pushed open the door. A cool breeze, smelling of cut grass and woodsmoke, like fall, curled toward us. I smiled at Pearlean over my shoulder.

"We're only just starting," I said.

▼

Lil threw her backpack into the backseat, as if she didn't need its protection anymore, and started pulling off her hightops. I turned the key in the ignition and switched on the lights, then sat there with the car idling. The sound seemed loud in the still night. "You didn't eat anything. Want to go back in?" I said to Lil. "Give it another try?"

She shook her head. "I want to go home."

Home. I backed slowly out of the space and started down the street. After the rosy light of the Blossom Cafe the night was dense and dark. I felt tired—*weary.* Once we left the streetlights and got onto the highway, I could barely see. Twenty miles an hour felt like the right speed for the amount of road measured out ahead of us. Then Lil reached over and fiddled with something beside the steering wheel, and our lights, dilating suddenly, leaped ahead. She pulled my sweater around her like a shawl and settled into her corner.

What was she thinking? I imagined her trying the word out. *Dead; dead.* Using different melodies. Thinking about writing to Rhoda, about telling the kids at school when it started in a few weeks. She'd practice in front of the bathroom mirror till then; later, remembering, she'd be ashamed.

Later. We would have lives after this, I promised Lil silently. After we'd begun to feel that the worst had happened and we had survived— after we'd found a way to survive surviving. Later we would learn to demand things. That, even more than his death, was what our lives would have to make room for. Later still, would we begin to understand the ways in which he had, after all, loved us?

We hit a frost heave and the car jumped. I braked lightly, then speeded up again. We'd be home by midnight. We would sleep, but not well; and when it began to get light I'd go to Clesta's and bring Susie home. The music of her angry voice—blessed, ordinary. In the afternoon we'd go to the hospital to see Lacey. I don't even know what it is, I thought, a boy or a girl.

Lil unsnapped the glove compartment. I heard the rattle of raisins. We passed Hazleton and made the turn onto Route 93, heading for the Lehigh Gap.

"Those are probably years old," I said. They'll make you sick."

"Raisins never spoil. You know that?" Lil's voice was slow and shaky, but clear. "Mr. Durson told us they found raisins in the ruins of Pompeii."

The moon was behind us now. I could see it from time to time in the rearview mirror, pale gold and large and firm against the night sky.

Lil said, "That waitress was a real nosey parker."

I rolled my window all the way down. The smell of skunk filled the car, rank and comfortingly familiar. Night air stirred along my bare arm, my neck, like fine silky fur.

I felt Lil's fingers on my mouth. Raisins. I sucked them in between my lips. They were cool and rubbery and slightly gritty when I bit down.

"Mama!" Lil said, more a shape than a sound, just before we bounced off the medial strip. I righted us and got a good grip on the wheel. We faced forward, traveling east, following the yellow track of the headlights into the dark.

ABOUT
THE
AUTHOR

Bruce Rosenberg

ANN HARLEMAN's collection, *Happiness*, won the 1993 University of Iowa Short Fiction Award. She has been a Guggenheim and Rockefeller fellow and received a PEN Syndicated Fiction Award in 1991. She is on the faculties of Brown University and the Rhode Island School of Design in Providence, Rhode Island, where she makes her home.